THIS STORY IS A LIE

THIS STORY IS A LIE

Tom Pollock

SOHO
TEEN

This book was originally published in the United Kingdom
under the title *White Rabbit, Red Wolf*.

Published in the United States by Soho Teen
an imprint of
Soho Press, Inc.
853 Broadway
New York, NY 10003

Library of Congress Cataloging-in-Publication Data

Pollock, Tom (Tom H.)
This story is a lie / Tom Pollock

ISBN 978-1-64129-032-6
eISBN 978-1-61695-912-8

1. Panic attacks—Fiction. 2. Genius—Fiction. 3. Missing
persons—Fiction. 4. Brothers and sisters—Fiction. 5. Twins—Fiction.
6. Secrets—Fiction. 7. Memory—Fiction. I. Title
PZ7.P76813 Thi 2018 [Fic]—dc23 2018004489

Interior design by Janine Agro, Soho Press, Inc.

Printed in the United States of America

10 9 8 7 6 5 4 3 2 1

For Jasper,
Welcome to the world.

THIS STORY IS A LIE

1:

ENCRYPT

NOW

Mum finds me in the larder. I crouch in the corner, flinching from the sudden light in the doorway. My mouth is full of blood and shards of porcelain.

I want to spit, but that'll show her the mess the splinters of the saltshaker have made of my gums. Jags of it are still digging in under my tongue and stabbing into my soft palate, but I can't swallow in case they stick in my throat. The salt rages in the cuts on my tongue. I try to smile at Mum while moving as few of the muscles in my face as possible. A drop of spit seeps through my lips and streaks red down my chin.

Mum exhales once, gathering herself, then bustles in through the doorway. She slaps a handful of paper towels over my mouth.

"Spit," she orders. I do. We look at the wadding in her palm. It's like a tiny battlefield, blood and bits of china bone—as if I've choked up the remnants of the fight that just took place in my head.

She pokes at the stuff with a finger. "What happened to counting?" she asks. I shrug. She tuts and sighs.

"Open," she tells me. I hesitate, then tilt my head back and gape.

"Aaaah. Oo I eed illings?"

She laughs, and I relax a little at the sound. Her hands, warm and confident, move my jaw to catch the light. Her laughter fades. "Oh, Petey," she murmurs. "Look what you did to yourself."

"Zit baa?"

"I've seen worse. You won't be heading to hospital, but still . . ."

She reaches into the pocket of her dressing gown for a pair of flimsy surgical gloves and pulls them on. Surgical gloves, I think queasily, in her dressing gown. At four in the morning. Wow, am I predictable.

She reaches into my mouth.

"Ready?"

I give her hand a squeeze.

"Three, two, one, and here we go." With a series of wince-inducing tugs, she pulls the remaining bits of china from my gums and drops them tinkling onto the larder floor. The base of the saltshaker is still gripped in my right hand. Its broken top rises in white crenelated jags above my fingers, a mirror to the teeth that crushed it.

I can still feel it giving way. The panic like a ratchet in my jaw, making it clench tighter and tighter around the porcelain, until the instant where I knew I'd pushed it too far and shrapnel exploded in my mouth.

When she's done, Mum pulls the gloves off, balls them, and sticks them on one of the empty shelves. She pulls a small pen and a black notebook from her other dressing gown pocket. I eye the thing resentfully, even though I know it's only her way—she's a scientist.

"Okay," she says. "Tell me."

"Tell you what?"

She gives me Look No. 4. If you have parents, then you'll know No. 4, the one that says, *At present, Sunshine, the shit you're in is only at ankle level, but push me any further, and you're going to need scuba gear.*

"This stuff may be inside your head, Peter William Blankman, but I'm going to have it out in the open," she says, palming the pen and picking up a tin opener from a shelf. "Even if I have to come and get it with this."

I snort and the shadow of the attack recedes a little further.

"I had an attack," I admit.

"I gathered. We talked about counting as a way to get you through it."

"I tried that."

"And?"

I look at the mess in my hand. "I was unsuccessful."

Another Look, longer and sterner, edging into No. 5, *Ve have vays of making you talk, Herr Blankman,* but all she says is, "Unsuccessful how?"

I probe the raw places under my lips with my tongue and wince.

"I ran out of numbers," I say.

Look No. 5 is replaced by outright disbelief.

"You ran out of numbers."

"I did."

"Peter, you're one of the best mathematicians your age in London, maybe the country."

"I don't know about the country." I do know about the country. If you don't think I check the rankings, you're out of your mind. "But—"

"You of all people ought to know that you can't run out of numbers. Just keep adding one, and presto! Another number appears. Like magic."

"I know, but—"

"Only, it's not magic," she says acidly. "Only maths."

She folds her arms. "If you managed to exhaust the limitless resource of positive integers, Peter, just think what you're doing to my patience."

Silence. I glance at the larder door and consider making a run for it.

"Petey," Mum says, and all the humour's gone from her voice. The shadows under her eyes are deep, and all of a sudden, I'm sharply aware of how big a deal today's going to be for her, and how every second we do this gnaws away a little more of her sleep.

"Why are you eating crockery? Talk to me."

I blow out my cheeks. "Okay . . ."

It was a tactical error, really, a screwup. I saw the attack coming a mile off; I should have been more prepared.

It was 3:29 in the morning and I was still awake. My eyes felt like pebbles in my skull, and the ceiling seemed to flex and warp before them like a cream-painted ocean.

Big day coming up, I thought. A big day that was due to start in three hours and thirty-one minutes, so it would've been a spectacular idea to close my eyes and get some sleep. Except, I couldn't, because I knew I had to get up in three hours and thirty-one minutes, and that fact was freaking me out.

Big day coming up, Petey. Huge, massive day, and so very, very public. One false move will ruin it, not just for you, but for the whole family, so you really, really ought to get some shut-eye.

I stared at the ceiling. I stared at the clock. Three hours and twenty-nine minutes. Conditions were perfect.

Peter, this is mission control. We are at DEFCON One. All green lights. You are go, repeat go, to have a screaming shit-fit.

It started the way it always does: the hollow ache in my stomach that I used to mistake for hunger, but that no food would ever satisfy.

Three hours and fifteen minutes. Three hours and four-teen minutes and fifty-three seconds, fifty-two seconds, fifty-one . . . That was eleven thousand six hundred and ninety seconds. I wouldn't be ready. Feel that? You feel sick. You can feel that nausea stretching in your stomach, and if you close your eyes, it will only get worse. You'll be a zombie tomorrow, and you need to be at your best. Because if you're a millimetre off your game, you'll have an attack *there*. Not here at home, where Mum and Bel can cover for you, but out there, in the world, where people can see, people with phones, filming it. And then it'll be on YouTube, your blood in the digital water. It'll drift and disseminate every-where, the stain of it. And everyone will *see* and *judge* and **know**.

I hesitate. Mum's pen hovers over her notebook.

"Usual physical symptoms?" she enquires.

"Tight chest," I confirm, ticking them off on my fingers. "Racing pulse. Dizziness."

"Hands?"

"Damp as Lance Armstrong's jockstrap."

Look No. 4 returns. "I can do without the colourful similes, Peter."

"Sorry." I close my eyes, remembering it. "So, I tried the three lines of defence, just like we talked about . . ."

One: get moving.

I scrambled out of bed and fled for the stairs. Motion is good; blood in the veins, blood in the muscles. It forces breath when breath is hard to come by.

Two: get talking.

I was a pressure cooker and my mouth was a release valve. Through gritted teeth I let the frantic stream of gibberish whirling around my head out into the world. Sometimes hearing the bullshit I'm thinking is enough to convince me it isn't true.

"You're going to have the biggest, most epic public meltdown in history. It'll go viral. Fuck viral, it'll go pandemic. They'll film kids reacting *to kids reacting* to watching you, and get hundreds of millions of hits. You'll change the lexicon. Meltdown will vanish from the dictionary and be replaced by "Petey," as in "doing a Petey." The next time a cheaply constructed uranium power sta-tion gets swept up in a tidal wave and the zirconium rods crack and gamma radiation floods out to blight the surrounding city with cancerous death, the nuclear Petey will be on every front page of every news site on the Internet!"

Okay, that sounded a little ridiculous. I started to feel a bit calmer.

"You will—literally—shit yourself in public."

I stumbled on the bottom step. That, on the other hand, sounded horribly plausible.

I ran into the kitchen and pushed myself up on the corner of the countertop like the world's clumsiest ballet dancer and cast frantically around the room for something I could use to get a grip. But all I saw were open shelves crammed with cereal and pasta boxes, pine-faced cupboards, the big silver fridge, and my hazy, monstrous reflection. The oven clock's green digits burned: 3:59 A.M.

Ten thousand, eight hundred, and sixty seconds.

Three: Get counting.

Distract yourself. Break the attack up into countable pieces, little chunks of temporal driftwood. Concentrate on keeping your head above water until you make it to the next one.

"One," I said. "Two." But my real, out-loud voice sounded weak and tinny next to the countdown inside my head.

Ten thousand, eight hundred, and forty seconds . . .

"Three . . . four . . ." I managed, but it wasn't working. A separate part of my brain had taken up the count while my panic continued, unimpeded and undistracted. I needed something else, some trickier puzzle to drag my attention off the hot, churning sensation in my lower abdomen.

"And that," I tell Mum, "is where I really screwed up."

"Oh?"

"I switched from counting whole numbers to their square roots."

She stares at me. "How many decimals?" she asks eventually.

"Six."

She winces.

• • •

"2.828427, 3, 3.162278, 3.316 . . ." I stumbled, syllables like marbles in my mouth, sweat clammy in my hands and between my shoulders. I tried again. "3.316 . . ."

But it was no good; I'd run out of numbers.

I looked around me in desperation, for something, anything else to fill the roaring whirlpool inside me. My eyes prickled and my heart lurched drunkenly behind my ribs. In the dim wash of streetlight, the kitchen seemed to be shrinking, the walls falling in towards one another. For a second I thought I could hear the beams creaking.

Sometimes when it gets really bad, I see and hear things that aren't really happening. Shit. How had this gotten so far away from me? I swallowed hard and reached for my last-gasp, in-case-of-emergency-break-glass, sanity-preservation technique.

Four: get eating.

I threw myself at the fridge and yanked out a Tupperware of last night's curry. The sticky brown mess was freezing to the touch as I dug my fingers in and started shovelling. I chewed frantically: a hopeless rear-guard action, knowing that I couldn't feed the hole inside me fast enough, hoping that the sheer weight of the food would push the panic rising out of my stomach back down again.

". . . and it just sort of escalated from there."

Mum frowns and scribbles. She's taken only the occasional note, flagging any details she thinks might be significant for later consideration.

"Okay," she says. "You ran out of numbers and you ate. Not ideal, but in the moment you do what you have to. Still"—she nods at the half saltshaker I'm still holding in my fist—"that doesn't seem to be the prime candidate for comfort eating."

Keeping her eyes on mine, she eases it out of my grip and replaces it with her hand. Her fingers squeeze mine. She pushes the larder door open and leads me from my hiding place.

The kitchen looks like a football crowd rioted in it. Cupboards hang open, drawers wrenched from their fittings and overturned on the floor. Cartons and pickle-smeared jars, bags and rinds, and fragments of dried pasta lie everywhere. Flour is scattered like a half-hearted English snowfall.

"I ran out of numbers," I murmur, shell-shocked. I don't even remember doing this. "And then . . ." And the shame, which has been licking its way up through me like a flame at paper, finally takes hold. "I ran out of food."

Mum clicks her tongue against the inside of her teeth. She closes her notebook, pockets it, crouches among the debris, and begins to put her house back in order.

"Mum," I say quietly, "let me."

"Go back to bed, Peter."

"Mum."

"You need to go back to bed."

"And you don't?" I practically wrestle a drawer from her hands. "You're the one collecting an award in seven hours. You have to give a speech." I can't think of anything more terrifying than giving a speech in public. And I spend a lot of time thinking about terrifying things.

She hesitates.

"Please, Mum. Leave me to do it. I think it'll help."

She can tell I'm serious. She kisses me on the forehead and rises. "All right, Peter, I love you, okay?"

"Okay, Mum."

"We'll work it out. We'll beat this."

I don't answer.

"Pete? We will. Together."

"I know we will, Mum."

She picks her way between the broken glass and the smears of spilled juice. As she leaves, she bends down and picks up a fallen picture, dusts it off, and puts it back on the fridge. It's a black-and-white shot of Franklin Roosevelt with the caption THE ONLY THING WE HAVE TO FEAR IS FEAR ITSELF. Mum finds the quote inspirational; me, not so much. Just sixteen days after those words left Roosevelt's mouth, the Nazis cut the ribbon on their first concentration camp at Dachau.

Uh, Mr. President? There are some German Jews here who'd like a word with you about your theory.

I shove the drawers back into place, slap the 32nd president of the United States facedown, and grab a broom.

I ran out of food. It was the truth—as far as it went—and Mum accepted it. I didn't tell her that while I shovelled curry into my mouth, I was looking away from the knives and scissors and sharp countertop corners; that when I'd bitten into the salt-cellar, it had felt not like an ending of something bad, but the beginning of something worse.

I keep having to break off to run to the loo to be sick. My belly may be able to hold up to four litres of compacted food, but it can't do so indefinitely. (Stomach acid in a lacerated mouth, by the way? Really hits the sweet spot in the Venn diagram of ugh and ow.) I feel like I've been turned inside out and am wearing my stomach lining like a soggy cardigan.

Autumn sunlight begins to stream through the kitchen windows. I'm rinsing the spilled milk off the fridge shelves when I hear a little click-click-click; it's coming from the phone handset, which is resting on the countertop. It hadn't been hung up properly. Mum must have been using it; she's the only human being I know who still uses landlines. Who could she have been talking to at 4:29 in the morning?

An empty tin can whirs, kicked across the tiles. I start, but then relax when I look round. It's Bel.

We're not identical, obviously, but the similarities are there—same skin, freckle-dusted in summer and winter alike; same dark brown eyes; Mum's sharp nose and sharper jaw-line; and . . . well, there are probably some features we got from Dad. There are differences aside from the obvious ones too—she's dyed her hair crimson, her cheeks dimple more deeply when she smiles. Oh, and I'm the only one with a four-by-two-centimetre dent above my left eye. As though a careless potter had left a thumbprint on me when I went into the kiln. An original flaw.

Only it isn't original, not even close.

My sister stomps into the kitchen, scratching sleepily at her head. She takes in the devastation, shrugs like it's no big deal, and drops to her knees on the floor. I rush to her side, and we work together, sorting and tidying, rebuilding and making right.

I don't ask Bel to stop. I don't feel guilty. I never have with her. We're quite the team.

I haven't shut off the tap properly. It drips into the sink with a sound like a bird tapping on a window.

RECURSION: 6 YEARS AGO

Rainwater dripped from the hem of my school uniform trousers where they dangled over the floor. I stared downwards and listened to the click-click-click of high heels striking polished concrete as they approached from up the corridor. Shouts and laughter carried from the playground outside.

Bel sat across from me, below a corkboard of school notices. She was folding a train ticket over and over until she had to pinch it hard to keep it shut. She looked up and winked.

"Don't worry about it, little bro. We'll be fine."

"Little?" I shot back. "You're eight minutes older than me."

She beamed at me, beatific. "And no matter what, I always will be."

After twelve strides, the clicking heels stopped and Mum stood between us, arms folded, her face set in a classic Look No. 7: *This had better be good—I was advancing the cause of science.*

She opened her mouth to speak just as the door next to Bel's chair opened and Mrs. Fenchurch, our brand-new and by-the-end-of-the-day-likely-to-be-ex headmistress emerged. Bel stood up respectfully and took a step towards the door, but Fenchurch waved her away like a wasp.

"No, Anabel, I wish to speak to your mother in private." She turned to Mum and stuck out a hand. "Mrs. Blankman."

Mum took the proffered hand and followed Mrs. Fenchurch inside. Bel and I exchanged an incredulous glance. Not only had Mum let this stranger touch her, but she also hadn't corrected her to *Dr.* Blankman. This really was serious.

"Mrs. Blankman," Mrs. Fenchurch said. "Thank you for coming. As I mentioned over the phone, here at Denborough College we have a zero-tolerance policy for this sort of thing. I'm afraid we have no alternative but to . . ." The rest was lost as she closed the door behind her. My stomach sprang up into my throat. No alternative but to what? Suspend? Expel? Bring back corporal punishment?

I stared at the door, desperate to know. Bel kept her eyes on mine, a weird smile on her face.

After a moment, the door handle began to turn smoothly counterclockwise. Without a sound, the door swung open, just a quarter of an inch. Something that had been jammed into the latch socket fell out and fluttered to the floor, where it squirmed slowly like a dying insect: a train ticket.

Voices bled through the crack.

". . . you not reconsider?" my mother was saying. "She's been here less than a week."

"I dread to think what she'd manage if we gave her a month, then!" Mrs. Fenchurch exclaimed. Mum sighed and I knew she'd just taken her glasses off to polish them. I also knew she was about to leave a long silence and . . . Yep, there it was, occupying the conversation without actually saying anything.

"She's . . ." Fenchurch was struggling. "She's highly disruptive."

"She's enthusiastic."

"She's a little demon."

"She's eleven. You're aware of Peter's condition. He relies on her. It's crucial that they not be separated."

"You know what she did?" Fenchurch demanded.

A pause, a flicker of paper. Mum consulting her notebook. "She pinned an older boy to the floor and inserted two live earthworms into his nostrils, one of which exited through his mouth via his lower-left sinus. As I understand, there was no permanent damage."

"But the boy hasn't stopped crying since!"

"I meant the worms were fine," Mum said calmly.

"Mrs. Blankman . . ."

"*Doctor* Blankman." Even I shivered as Mum issued the correction. "Mrs. Fenchurch, you are aware"—another turned page—"that immediately prior to the incident with the invertebrates, the boy in question—Benjamin Rigby—and his friends were attempting to intimidate Peter into giving up his rucksack."

Another silence. The kind that you can only squirm in.

"Rigby says he didn't touch Peter. Witnesses say he only said a few words, certainly not enough to justify your daughter's conduct. Even the words didn't amount to much."

"With my son," Mum observed drily, "it doesn't take much."

I flushed. I thought back to the playground, to the three boys, suddenly so tall and standing so close. And even though it was only my fifth day at the school, I could see, I mean properly *see*, my future, like a vision from a vengeful god, day after day, year after year. I could feel the bruises and hear their laughter and taste the blood running from my nose even before they'd laid a finger on me. It must have shown on my face because Rigby actually asked me, "What are you so scared of?"

He must have been delighted to have found so easy a mark.

No, it doesn't take much.

"Anabel can be very passionate," Mum went on. "Perhaps her reaction was excessive, but I'm sure someone with your disciplinary experience understands the value of putting down a marker."

"A marker?" Fenchurch sounded nonplussed.

"Peter is timid, Mrs. Fenchurch. That makes him a target and, if I may be blunt, junior school is a zoo. If he is to survive here, the other children need to know he has protection."

From her seat opposite me, Bel winked at me and mouthed "little bro" again. I flipped her a middle finger and she grinned.

"I'm sorry, Mrs.—Dr. Blankman." Fenchurch had regained some of her composure. "But I have an obligation to the boy's parents—"

Mum cut her off. "I've spoken to the Rigbys already."

"You have?"

"Yes."

"But . . . how did you . . . ?"

"Mr. Rigby works with a former colleague of mine, who put me in touch. They are willing to leave the disciplining of my daughter to me if I leave their son's to them. Which only leaves one question: are you willing to do the same?"

"Well . . . well . . . I suppose if . . . if . . ." Fenchurch sounded like she was drowning, trying to find a scrap of conversational driftwood to hold on to.

"Thank you. Will that be all, Mrs. Fenchurch? Only there's a neuron that requires my attention."

"Neuron?" Fenchurch said, sounding wrong-footed.

"A single brain cell," Mum clarified, her tone implying that said single cell was more interesting, and likely more intelligent, than the woman she was talking to.

Four seconds later the door swung open. Mum stood in the doorway, one black high heel placed very deliberately over Bel's ticket.

"Uh, Mum?"

"Tell me in the car, Peter."

No one spoke as we drove home. Any word could be the spark to light Mum's fuse. I was staring gloomily out the window when I felt something scratchy pressed into my palm. It was the train ticket. A series of apparently random letters had been scrawled on it in blue Biro.

I smiled. Bel didn't have my head for number codes, so we'd been messaging each other with Caesar shift ciphers. A Caesar shift is about the simplest code in the world—perfect for the Roman emperor, who was long on secrets but short on time.

To make one, you just write out the alphabet, A to Z, then pick a secret phrase, like—I dunno—O SHIT BRUTUS, and write it out underneath the first few letters of your alphabet, dropping any repeated letters. Then you follow it with the remainder of the alphabet, in order, so you get something like this:

ABCDEFGHIJKLMNOPQRSTUVWXYZ
OSHITBRUACDEFGJKLMNPQVWXYZ

Then you write your message, substituting every letter for the one below it, and—bam—your message is safe from the prying eyes of teachers, parents, and marauding Visigoths.

Unfortunately, because you only have to guess the keyword, codes this simple are even easier to break than my nerve. I studied the letters, tried a few combinations in my head, and stifled a laugh. "Demon," I mouthed. She smiled back. Like any secret shared, it was a hug, a way of saying I'm here.

Suddenly, Mum let out an exasperated breath and pulled the car over. For a heart-stopping moment, I thought she was going to tell us to get out, to never come home.

You'll have to go live with your father—he was her worst threat, the monster under the bed—*if you can find him.*

Instead, she sighed. "Don't do that again, Anabel," she said.

"I was only . . ."

"I know what you were doing. Don't. It's too big a risk. This time we got lucky, but not every meat-headed brat in that school will have a father whose job I can dangle in front of him."

"Yes, Mum."

"And, Bel?"

"Yes, Mum?"

The edge of Mum's mouth curled. "In case there is a next time—which I expressly forbid, you understand—don't use earthworms. They're lovely creatures and they don't deserve it. Use Coca-Cola; it'll hurt more."

"Yes, Mum," Bel said solemnly.

Mum nodded and pulled back out into the road.

I sat back, relieved and awed. A spitting rain flecked the window and I watched the wet, leaf-plastered streets slide past under the streetlights.

I wanted to be like my mum when I grew up.

NOW

YesWeCantor@live.com: I don't understand. A saltshaker?

KurtGode@gmail.com: Yep.

YesWeCantor@live.com: The *porcelain* thing?

KurtGode@gmail.com: The very same.

YesWeCantor@live.com: . . . did you *chew*?!

KurtGode@gmail.com: Hang on . . . It's kinda gory, hope you already had breakfast.

I tilt my webcam to get a shot of the eighties horror movie that is the inside of my mouth.

YesWeCantor@live.com: Daaaaamn Pete, that's gotta rate a 7 on the ballsuck at the very least.

KurtGode@gmail.com: Nope, only a 4.

YesWeCantor@live.com: *4* ?!?!?!?!?!?!?!?!?!?!??!?!

KurtGode@gmail.com: Leave some interrobangs for the rest of us, Ingrid.

YesWeCantor@live.com: 4? BS 4. How the hell do you get to 4?

KurtGode@gmail.com: Proximity, Duration, Damage. Mum helped me out of it, and the whole thing was over in under 20 mins. I ran the maths, it was a measly 4.

YesWeCantor@live.com: *Sigh* Always the same with you, Petey. Promising looker, no follow-through.

I brighten and type:

KurtGode@gmail.com: You think I'm a promising looker, Ingrid?
YesWeCantor@live.com: Only when it comes to sucking balls, Pete.

I snort. Ingrid gets me better than anyone, except for Bel. We bonded over our shared hobbies: rewatching Star Wars, mocking reality TV contestants, and staying up late into the night, reading online medical encyclopaedias, researching the tolerances of the human body for heat, cold, thirst, and velocity in order to understand precisely what and how we could survive—it's fetish porn for the anxiously inclined.

Ingrid's the only other person I've ever met who's (a) as into maths, and (b) as twitchy as I am, so it was inevitable that sooner or later we'd find a way to quantify our fear.

Enter the Ballsuck.

The Base-Adjustable Linear Logarithmic Scale for Unanticipated Crazy (BALLSUC) is calculated as follows:

BS (Balls Sucked) = Log_{10} (T) + Log_{10} (D) – Log_{10} (P)

Where T is the time the episode lasted, D is the monetary or sentimental value of anything or anyone you accidentally smashed or set fire to, and P is the proximity of people who can help.

(We have a pact that if the BALLSUC one day enters standard scientific use, we won't let them change the acronym. My surname's Blankman, and Ingrid's is Immar-Groenberg, so we could have gone for BIG BALLSUC, but we figured just plain BALLSUC was the classy choice.)

When your own special brand of crazy sucker punches you, BALLSUC measures how hard it is to get back up off the canvas. We based it on the Richter scale: violent shaking, aftershocks, wreckage. I think of the devastation in the kitchen; panic attacks are your own private earthquakes.

KurtGode@gmail.com: How's yours been, anyway?

There was a delay before she replied.

YesWeCantor@live.com: I had a 6.
KurtGode@gmail.com: Shit!
KurtGode@gmail.com: . . .
KurtGode@gmail.com: You okay?
YesWeCantor@live.com: Yeah.
KurtGode@gmail.com: What happened?
YesWeCantor@live.com: It clocked me when I left for school Friday. I suddenly couldn't remember if I'd washed my hands, so I went back to do them.
KurtGode@gmail.com: Ingrid . . .
YesWeCantor@live.com: I know, but sometimes we can't help it can we? I was 23 washes in when Dad dragged me out.
KurtGode@gmail.com: Christ . . . Want to meet up?
YesWeCantor@live.com: No, it's ok. You can't anyway, you've got your Mum's thing.
KurtGode@gmail.com: Exactly. Everybody wins.
YesWeCantor@live.com: Shush. It'll be amazing. The Natural History Museum, come on! How is that not awesome?!?!?!?!?!?!?!?
KurtGode@gmail.com: Just so you know, when the cops come around asking who's behind the great interrobang robbery, I'm sending them to you.
YesWeCantor@live.com: Funny. Go do your family thing Pete. I'll be fine.

I hesitate before I type.

KurtGode@gmail.com: Okay, but text me if you change your mind. I'll smash my way out with a diplodocus femur and come running.

YesWeCantor@live.com: Almost worth having another 6 to see that. You stay brave, ok?
KurtGode@gmail.com: I'll do my best.
YesWeCantor@live.com: 23-17-11-54, Peter William Blankman. I x
KurtGode@gmail.com: 23-17-11-54, Ingrid Immar-Groenberg. P x

I shut the laptop. Go do your family thing, Pete.

Your.

I've never met Ingrid's folks and she's determined to keep it that way. She says they find it tough to believe in any kind of broken you can't see on an X-ray.

"It could be worse," I mutter to myself. "I could have it like Ingrid."

I'm wrestling with the knot in my tie when Bel walks in wearing a dress (black, inevitably—she thinks black-and-white movies have one too many colours) and drops onto the bed.

"Hey, dickface," she says.

"Hey."

"Great, I was expecting a return insult. Now I just feel bad."

"Sorry, distracted. Trying not to strangle myself."

She snorts and leans forward. The knot magically comes apart at her fingertips.

"Gotta have the nails for it. Feeling better?"

"Yeah."

"You lying to me right now?"

"You can always tell."

"It's a twin thing. You don't have to come; she'll understand."

It's tempting. I'd be lying if I said it wasn't, but my stomach twists when I think about backing out. No, this is what you do. You're there for your family on big days. You clap and whoop and they see you do it. This is how you start to repay seventeen years of broken sleep and eroded patience.

This is what normal people do.

"I'm going."

"Okay," she says, lying back on the pillow. "You can chill anyway. No one's going to be looking at you. Hell, Uncle Peter could show up and do his Christmas party trick and no one would look at him, so stop worrying about it."

Uncle Peter's one of those not-actually-related uncles. His party trick involves a pink tutu, a turkey leg, and a rendition of "I Will Survive." There are probably bananas I share more DNA with than Uncle Peter.

"Whatever happens, you won't ruin it," Bel says, her head pillowed against her interlaced fingers. "Trust me."

I look down at her and the churn in my stomach calms a little. I do trust her.

"I always do," I say. "You're my axiom."

"You're a weird little kid."

"Weird, I'll take. But enough with the little. You're only eight minutes older."

"It was a race for the exit and I won. Margin of victory is irrelevant."

Mum's voice floats up the stairs, calling us.

I look to the posters on the wall for support. Ten centuries of epic mathematicians stare back: Cantor, Hilbert, Turing. *We're all squarely rooting for you, Pete,* they say. Maths humour, but you can't blame them. I gaze at Évariste Galois's pointy face. *I feel for you, Pete,* he says. *I felt the same way before I went into that duel in '32.*

That duel killed you, Évariste, I think back. *You got shot in the gut and died in screaming agony.*

Good point, he says. *Forget I said anything.*

Bel's hand finds mine.

"You ready?" she asks. "It's just a couple of hours and I'll be there the whole time. Just gotta find a way to be brave for that long."

There's a blue hardback notebook sitting on the corner of the desk. Its pages are curled and gummed together. I've not opened it in years, but there was a time . . .

Gotta find a way to be brave.

"Let's go," I say.

RECURSION: 5 YEARS AGO

Retreat! RETREAT!

As he skip-stumbled down the frost-speckled pavement, Agent P. W. Blankman (special citations for cunning, courage, and calculus) was acutely aware of four things:

The paralysing iciness of the October air in his lungs,

The thud of his trainers on the pavement,

The breeze tickling the hairs on his bare legs, and—above all—

The fact that if he relaxed the pressure of the hand he had pressed to his backside, his underpants would fall off.

He swore like the ex–Royal Marine commando he was. The underpants had sustained critical injuries, severed from the waistband almost all the way down to the thigh by an enemy blade, but if he could just get them back to the house, emergency surgery might spare them the fate of his trousers, their gallant comrades-in-legs. (He felt a brief pang of anxiety, wondering how he was going to explain the loss of those to Mum.)

Time to grieve for the fallen later, Agent Blankman thought grimly. He'd known when they'd volunteered how high the price of this mission could be, both in blood and—his stomach flipped over as he remembered pirating the operational funds from Mum's purse—honour. He tightened his grip on the bag in his other hand, the donuts inside bulging greasily against the paper. The objective had been achieved—that's what young Private Trousers would have cared about.

It was 6:04 on a Sunday morning, the streets were deserted,

and there were no lights in the windows when Agent Blankman pushed through the gate to his little front garden and made it to his door. He actually thought he'd got away with it until he realised he'd forgotten his keys.

And then Agent Blankman was gone, and all that was left in his place—shivering on the doorstep in my ruined under-wear, miserably chewing donuts until my fear of frostbitten testicles overcame my fear of my vengeful, disappointed mother—was me.

There was nothing for it. I rang the bell.

I held my breath as I heard the footsteps. Come on, come on, I know you sleep light. The door swung open and I exhaled explosively in relief.

"Morning, sis." I went for a winning grin, but with jam still caked around my mouth, I probably looked like a cannibal.

"Pete?" Bel rubbed at her eyes. Her hair was a halo of fire where she'd slept on it. "What are you . . . It's six in the . . . Where the hell are your *trousers*?"

I bustled in past her and shut the door as quietly as I could.

"Dog got them, big one, seemed very keen on them, figured it was best to let it have them. Got a newfound respect for our postman."

"You're lying."

"You can always tell."

She waited, but I didn't expand. All I could think about was how the blade felt slicing through the fabric. Some lies you tell, not to be believed, but because you can't bear what will happen if you tell the truth.

Her gaze travelled from my bare legs to the donut bag, and from there to the smeared sugar at my lips. Her posture soft-ened.

"Your attacks are getting worse," she said. "You're getting in food from outside so you can hide them. But, Pete . . ." I see her waking up, making the connections. She was there when I spent the last of my pocket money in the comics shop last week.

"Where did you get the money?"

I ignored the question. "Bel, please, I know Mum heard the door go, don't tell her about this, tell her it was a delivery but they had the wrong house. Tell her—"

"Tell me what, Peter?"

My gaze jerked up and my heart fell down. Mum was on the landing, calmly tying the knot on her robe.

All the predictable questions came. All those Bel had asked plus one more. The worst one: "Peter, did you steal from me?"

I fled, face burning, choking on tears and half-formed explanations, clomping up the stairs to my room and slamming the door.

I sat on the floor. Donuts spilled from my arms, rolling galaxy-like spirals of sugar across the carpet. I stared at them, hating them, hating my need for them, and hating the shame that had driven me to buy them in secret. Superheroes and mathematicians stared down from the walls in condemnation. Galois, in particular, sneered at me.

You broke, he whispered. *You coward.*

But they were my friends, and their displeasure was never going to last long. *Up*, they urged me. *To work. You can solve this. 'Tis but an equation. Rise, and bend it to your will.*

You can't blame them for talking like that; half of them died before 1900.

I went to my desk and opened the topmost of the hardback notebooks stacked there. On the pale red line at the very top of the page was written one word:

ARIA

Underneath, a string of equations unspooled down the page. Despair and hope warred inside me, and finally hope won, like it always did. I pulled up a chair, shivered as the chilly plastic hit my bare thighs, and got to work.

The fastest thing in the universe—light in a vacuum—travels

at 299,792,458 metres per second. That's a big number, but you still need to square it to get the energy released by a single kilo of uranium when it tears itself apart in the panic of nuclear fission. There were 64 such kilos in Little Boy, the atomic bomb that detonated in the air over Hiroshima one cloudy Monday in August 1945. Only 1.38 percent of that actually fissioned, but the blast still flattened concrete buildings, ignited a firestorm two miles across, and killed more than 66,000 men, women, and children instantly. And it all began with the decay of an atomic nucleus less than fourteen-thousandths of a millionth of a *millionth* of a metre across—a metre that's defined by the speed of light.

Maths governs everything in the world: light, gravity, rivers, moons, minds, money. And everything, everything's connected.

So, under the gazes of Burnell and Euler and Einstein, men and women who discovered the mathematics of quasars and mazes and space itself, I lost myself in the numbers trying to find the mathematics of me.

Trying to find a way to change those equations, a way to make myself brave.

NOW

The car brakes hard and lurches me awake.

In the front, Mum's swearing at a black Ford that pulled out in front of us without signalling. Donuts and knives and mushroom clouds go grainy and fade as I blink sleep out of my eyes.

What was I dreaming about? I've already forgotten.

I count under my breath, waiting for my stomach and pulse to settle.

I remember reading somewhere that the human body can survive (brief) forces of up to a hundred Gs in car crashes. What I just felt must have been less than 2 percent of that, but it was still enough to set all my internal alarm bells ringing. Ever hear that story "The Boy Who Cried Wolf"? Well, right now every nerve ending in my body is yelling:

WOLF! WOOOOOOOOOOOOOOOOOOOLF! WOLFIE WOLFIE WOLF WOLF! Is it a bird? Is it a plane? NO, IT'S A FUCKING WOLF!

"Well," Mum mutters. "We're here."

A heavy blanket of cloud lies over London, a pale sun showing through it like a lighthouse in heavy fog. The Natural History Museum rears in front of us, all cathedral-like spires and arches. In less than two hours, Mum will be receiving her award there, right under the blue whale skull.

Like I said, today's a big deal.

Bel looks across the seat at me.

"Leap of faith, Petey," she says.

I take a deep breath and hop down from the car. Bel shoves

her hands in her coat pockets and saunters off ahead, but Mum stops me with a touch on the arm.

"Anabel tells me you've been dreading today. She says you're scared you'll mess it up somehow. Is that why this morning happened?"

I stare at the pavement.

"Peter, you could never mess it up. Even if you wanted to. Today is because of you and your sister. My work, my life, I wouldn't have any of it without you, you know?"

She takes my face in her hands, tilts it up. Her face is glowing with pride, with love.

"I am so happy to have you here with me today."

Inside, light streams down from vast skylights and arched windows onto ash-coloured bones. At the end of the lazy sine wave of her spine, Hope the blue whale's massive skull gapes down at us. While I queue to pass through security, I count her bones (221), then the panes of glass in all the windows above us (368), and finally the paces between me and the door (55 and rising at an alarming rate). I can't help myself. Thank Christ I never started smoking.

Around us, the hall is being transformed. Barked instructions echo off the walls; wheels squeak over tiles and keys jingle on belts as black-clad technicians (8 of them) rig lights and drag flight cases into position.

"How are you doing?" Bel whispers.

"Swell, fabulous, invincible, magnificent, superlative, out—"

She sighs, cutting me off. "Look, worst comes to worst, you can step out." She points to a small black security camera wedged under the balcony like a roosting metal bat. "If you're that desperate to see people hooting and hollering for Mum, you can watch the tape."

A slick-looking man in a grey suit approaches us with a clipboard.

"Ah, Dr. Blankman," he greets Mum as he swoops. "And you must be Peter, and Anabel." He looks a little crestfallen when first Mum, then Bel ignore his proffered hand. "Delighted to meet you," he presses on. There are patches of white on his knuckles where he's gripping his clipboard. "Thank you for agreeing to come in early. If it's all right, I'll walk you through the process . . ."

He guides us around to the end of Hope's bony whip of a tail.

"Tables are being set up, as you can see—ah yes, thank you, Steven." He steps back as a techie wearing a black baseball cap rolls a big, round table past on its edge. There's a long, deep scratch in the black leather of his boot. The steel toe cap beneath glints.

"And the event proper should begin in forty-five minutes or so."

I'm starting to feel sick and I shiver inside my new suit. All of this; it's too big, too bright, too loud.

Wolf, the voice inside me whispers.

"Where are we sitting?" I ask.

"All the recipients and their families will be seated in this central area here," Captain Clipboard replies. "Brunch will take an hour and the presentation will follow immediately." He turns to Mum. "Dr. Blankman, please wait at your table until your name is announced, then head to the podium to collect—a handshake will of course suffice when he gives you the award, but he does like to go for the double kiss on the cheek, even though we keep telling him how French it plays on TV, so if you could indulge him . . ."

"I will decide," Mum says coolly, "who gets to kiss me, and how many times."

"Ah . . . indeed." Captain Clipboard's crest wilts a little further. "The PM's very much looking forward to your speech. The floor is, naturally, yours for as long as you wish, but we are trying to carve out a few extra minutes for his schedule today, so if you could, uh . . ."

"Yes?"

"Well, personally I always think brevity is the soul of wit. Don't you?"

Mum stares at him.

"Dr. Blankman?" Captain Clipboard presses.

"Yes?"

"You didn't say anything."

"I was being witty."

"Ah . . ." He looks again to his trusty clipboard, as though it could offer him somewhere to hide. "Er, well then, that's everything. The PM will be here in a half hour or so. He's looking forward to meeting you." Duty done, he retreats hastily.

Oh yeah, I meant to say: the Prime Minister's handing out the awards. He wants to look like he's big into British science and research. Like I said: BIG DEAL.

As we get closer to showtime, white-clothed tables sprout like mushrooms on the tiled floor, and white-jacketed waiters set each with silver cutlery so fancy the knife blades have little serrated edges and are even embossed with the museum logo, a black *nhm*. My mouth feels like a desert, so I take an orange juice from a table and sip. You know when that's not a good idea? When you've spent the morning chewing crockery and your mouth is full of tiny cuts. I gasp with the shock of it and put the glass of sunshine-coloured torture liquid back on the table. The black clothes of the technicians gradually give way to brighter colours, sharp suits, and elegant dresses. I count thirty-six people dressed like guests rather than crew. Captain Clipboard does the rounds with them as well. They smile and chat with him. None of them have Mum's wit, I guess.

I glance back to the central area where we'll be sitting, and the knot in my stomach tightens. I'm going to be surrounded by strangers. People I can't predict. I will be sitting with my back to them. A ruddy-faced man in a grey suit laughs with a black woman with braided hair in a green dress. Four more men and one woman show up. Their clothes look cheap and they're not drinking the Buck's Fizz. Security, I figure, for our nation's chinless leader.

I now see that single sheets of paper have been placed on the plates in the middle of our places. I sneak a closer look. They're TV waiver forms. Sweat prickles along the edge of my collar. I rub the back of my neck and look up. Above, on the landing of the great staircase, a TV camera perches like a predator ready to spring.

Wolf.

"Mum," I whisper. "Mum. Are they going to broadcast this?"

"He's the Prime Minister, Peter. It might make the news."

Shit. Don't freak out, don't freak out.

"The other people, sitting near us, do you know them?

Are any of them likely to make any sudden moves or loud noises? Do any of them go bump in the night? Will any of them trigger an attack? Mum looks at me, frowns, and scribbles something in her ever-present notebook.

"They're all colleagues, Peter, old friends of mine. It'll be fine."

Fine means okay, but it also means narrow, *close.*

An old colleague, laughing delightedly, touches Mum's shoulder. She shoots me a worried look—Are you all right?—but I wave her off and he leads her away to meet his starstruck friends.

"Get a grip," I mutter to myself, but I already have a grip on myself and it's tightening, squeezing the air out of me.

"Bel?" It comes out in a hoarse mumble, because I can barely breathe. "Bel?"

There's no air, my lungs are telling me. Nonsense, lungs, you big drama queens. This hall is 64 by 28 by 30. Even allowing for the internal walls, the staircase, and the arch in the ceiling, there are still more than fifty thousand cubic metres of the good stuff. More than I could breathe in a year even if this place were airtight. So you, Mr. and Mrs. Lung, have nothing to complain about.

I check my watch: it's 10:45 A.M. Still two and a half hours before I can get out of here and I'm already engaging my lungs in conversation.

Shit.

My hands are shaking and it takes me three goes to open my pillbox. I dry-swallow a lorazepam and it feels like a thornbush in my throat. I cast around for Bel, and I see her chatting amiably with the black woman in the green dress. She's smiling, but for the first time I can remember, her face doesn't reassure me.

"What?" she mouths at me, her forehead crinkled into an irritated line. "What's wrong?"

I spread my hands. Nothing. Nothing's wrong. That's the only sane, rational answer. Only there are too many people, or too few, or the tables aren't spaced out evenly enough, or the lights seem superfluous in a room with 368 panes of glass in the windows, or some other perfectly normal thing that today just screams, Wrong, wrong, wrong, wrong, *wrong*.

I can feel myself slipping, hear the familiar click of the talons as the prehistoric lizard advances down the hallways of my brain, prising my hands off the controls, wrapping its scaly claws around in their place. I'm fighting it, but I know it's inevitable.

Now the sweat's pouring in stinging sheets into my eyes and I blink it away. The red light on the camera above me blinks back. Did I imagine that? Are they filming already? There's still half an hour until showtime. A stagehand pulls a flight case across the room. The wheels growl over the tiles like a . . .

Wolf.

Black mites swarm in front of my eyes. People are talking to me, but I can't hear what they're saying. Now they're looking at me, faces confused, concerned, now blurring, because I'm moving fast, turning, spinning, almost losing my balance as I sprint for the door. 53 paces and counting, 52, 51 . . .

"Peter!"

Mum's voice, already a long way behind me. Movement is good; it forces breath, but not now, not today. I'm stumbling and wheezing and coughing but somehow still running. Wait, take a second; think. But my legs won't let me. I sprint down corridors lined with display cases of butterflies; inkblot eyes stare at me from their wings. Pins and needles race up and down my arms as I pump them. I can't feel my feet.

How did I get here? Which turns did I take? I look back. Identical dark stone corridors stretch behind me. Am I one turn of a corner from the hall, or twenty?

"Peter!" Mum's voice: though faint, she sounds furious and disappointed. I don't know how far I've run. Stop. Turn around. You're ruining everything.

I can't.

I blink sweat out of my eyes and see fossils, the grinning bones of a dinosaur. Desperately, I try to wrestle my thoughts back under control. There are twenty-three bones of the dinosaur skeleton; twenty three's a prime, primordial; these bones are the old lizard's primes, indestructible and irreducible.

I can't do it. I take off again down the hallway. The lights dim and the walls seem to fade until all I can see are the bones in the cabinets around me. My legs are screaming with the effort of running. It's as if there's something pushing back against me, like the darkness is solid. I'm no longer running through air, but earth. I'm buried and blind. I can't keep it up. My chest's going to burst. I stumble to a stop, coughing, and my legs fold up under me. Mr. and Mrs. Lung are backed up, full of dark, wet soil. I hear a whisper of welcome from the bones around me, my fellow buried things.

"Peter!" It's Mum, still faint, but still I hear an edge to her voice, a touch of hysteria, almost out of control. I've never heard Mum out of control before. "Peter!"

Oh god, I've really screwed up this time. I've embarrassed her, upstaged her moment in the sun.

Two: get talking.

"Sun. Son. Words. Fffuck!" My tongue and brain are numb, and the words won't come.

"Peter . . ."

And then,

"HELP!"

What? I spin around in the darkness. I want to run back, but I don't know which way *is* back.

"HELP ME!" She sounds as scared as I am. She needs—I shake my head disbelievingly—Mum needs my help?

"PETER!"

Pain. She sounds like she's in pain.

Three: get counting.

Count your steps. Turn around. Go to her. Go.

"One. One. One." I don't seem to know any other numbers.

"PETER!"

"One." I stammer it over and over, my legs still folded, useless under me. "One. One. One. One. One."

"Please!"

"One."

"PLEASE DON'T!"

"One."

"HELP ME!"

Four: get eating.

I jam my knuckles between my jaws and bite. Warm liquid spills into my mouth, and I spit it out reflexively. The fossils crowd around me, silently urging me on as I gnaw and chew, digging for my own irreducible, indestructible part. Pain shoots up through my wrist and into my chest and jolts my legs back to life. I'm running again, or at least shambling, spitting blood.

"Mum," I croak. "Mum!"

No answer. I can see the corridor around me again now. Dinosaur bones once more quiescent behind their copper nameplates.

"Mum?" I'm turning corners at random. I have no idea which way I came. I see light glinting off glass cases. Butterflies. I remember butterflies! I must almost be back at the hall.

"Mum?"

No answer. I calm a little, enough to feel the throb in my hand, and I cradle it. Maybe she didn't really come after me. Maybe I imagined her voice. Maybe she's still back in the hall. I check my watch. 10:58. I almost laugh. I've only been gone for a handful of minutes. The seething in my stomach settles and I wrap my hand up in my jacket; I know my way from here. If I hurry, I can make it back in time for the presentation. I'll clap and cheer and be the proud, normal son the way I ought—

Twenty strides ahead of me there's something on the floor.

It's black, blue, and red, some kind of fabric, billowed on the tiles. I can't quite make sense of the shape, although it fills me with the oddest sense of recognition. I slow, approaching cautiously. Nineteen strides. Eighteen. It's black in the middle, surrounded by blue patches edged with a thin rim of red. Seventeen, sixteen. At fifteen strides I see that no—it's not black. It's the blue of the fabric that surrounds it, dyed dark and glossy where something's soaked in. Fourteen steps, thirteen. The red is the dye, seeping beyond the rucked cloth. I know that shade. I look down and see it on my own hand where I bit into it.

Hand. I see a hand curled around a sodden mop of hair. And then the world snaps into focus and I recognise her.

Mum.

. . .

. . .

. . .

I come to on my knees beside her. I don't even remember crossing the last few steps. My head's empty. I throw my head back and I bay: "Bel! Bel! Help!"

I look down. My hands are immersed in bloody cloth.

Sometimes, when things get really bad, I see things that aren't there. Any second now, I'll snap out of it. I'll feel a hand on my shoulder and Mum will pull me into a hug.

There's so much blood. I'm surrounded by the smell of it. It's so thick it's almost a gel. I grope for her pulse and I can feel a flicker, like a butterfly pinned under her skin. I look down at her, helpless. She's bleeding and I don't know how to help. I don't know how to not make it worse. I claw the folds of her dress away from her mouth so she can breathe more easily. The human body needs two hundred millilitres of air a minute; I have to make sure she gets it. Her nose is red-black and crusted, split along both nostrils.

"Bel!" I yell, my throat almost tearing, but no one comes.

Blood. Have to stop the blood. You can lose a maximum of two litres of blood and survive it. I grapple with her dress. It's wet-heavy, hot, and clammy. "Be less than two," I urge the blood puddled around me. "Please be less than two." I hear footsteps. Shouting. I find the wettest part of the dress. Under my fingers I can feel the liquid pulsing out, thick as honey. The shouts get louder. I scrunch the fabric into a wad and press it against the wound. I pull my phone from my pocket, but there's no signal.

"Get away from her!" a gruff male voice shouts.

"She's my . . . she's my . . ." I gasp, but the words won't come. Blood is leaking around my fingers. Mum's eyelids are flickering and the butterfly flutter in her wrist is ebbing. Arms close around my waist, dragging me away, and I flail and screech like a baby.

"Mum! Mum! She's still bleeding! Let me *go!*"

Startled, the arms let go and I pitch forwards. I grope amongst the fabric, desperately trying to find the source of the blood again. Out the corner of my eye I glimpse the brown uniforms of security guards.

Any second now I'll wake up. Any second.

Please.

I hear the clack of high-heeled shoes. Bel?

"Let me through, you idiots. I'm a doctor!" a voice snaps. Dry, dark-skinned hands quest next to mine, find what they're looking for, seize my hand and place it. I feel the seep, seep, seep of the blood again. I look at her. It's the woman from the party, in the green dress and the high-piled braided black hair. Her face is tight with concentration.

"Press here," she tells me, "and whatever you do don't let up."

"She's my . . . mum," I gasp.

"I've called an ambulance," the woman says. "And this happened next to a room full of doctors. We'll keep her alive."

A room full of doctors. Of course. A lighter flame of relief flickers in my chest. They all work with Mum. Colleagues and old friends, that's what Mum said. They'll know what to do. The woman in green is already gently moving her. She slides an arm under Mum's hips and raises them gently off the floor. The wound I'm pressing with the heel of my hand is just below her belly button.

"Gravity's going to work for us," the doctor in green says.

"Bel." I cast about for my sister. "Have you seen her?"

"Bel?" she asks. "Anabel? Your sister? Where is she?" The doctor looks at me intently. "Wasn't she with you?"

"No. You're . . . you're a friend of Mum's?"

"That's right. My name is Rita."

"I . . . I ran." It's a confession.

"I saw," Rita says. "You're Peter, aren't you?" I nod. "You sprinted out of that room like you'd seen a ghost. A girl in a black dress followed you. Was that Anabel?"

I nod helplessly; I can't speak. Bel followed me? I hadn't seen her.

"Louise"—she winces as she uses Mum's first name—"was right behind the two of you. I would have been too if you were my kids."

I feel suddenly very sick, as if I've been punched low in the gut. She followed me. Whoever was waiting for her, I brought her to them. My fingers slip over each other as I try to maintain the pressure on the wound, and I patter frantically around to recover the spot.

A thud of boots. Green high-vis uniforms. Paramedics, four of them, with a stretcher. One of them crouches beside me.

With a pair of oversize scissors, he begins to cut away Mum's dress around my hand while another places a clear plastic mask attached to a red bottle over her face. I hear a rip behind me as a third paramedic opens a field dressing. The one with the scissors tries gently to lift my hand away, but I find myself resisting. What if the instant I take it away, the rest of her blood comes flooding out? He emits a small breath and just yanks my hand clear. The flap of soaking silk comes with it; underneath, the wound is the shape of an eye, as if someone had stuck in a knife and twisted it.

"You did good," he mutters to me as he presses a square of sticky bandage over the gash. Another of them smiles at me as he rubs disinfectant gel into my gnawed hand and winds a bandage around it. He looks vaguely familiar. My brain's flailing in confusion, trying to make connections where there shouldn't be any to make.

"Can we move her?" another voice asks from behind me.

"We're going to have to." Rita is authoritative. "Get the stretcher."

They lay the stretcher beside her and oh-so-gingerly inch her onto it. It seems to take years. Every tick of the second hand on my watch feels like a month.

"Anabel."

I look around sharply at the mention of my sister's name, expecting to see her finally here, but she isn't. Instead, it's Rita looking sternly at me.

"Peter, this is important. Where is Anabel?"

Clumsily, I fumble for my phone, but there's still no signal. My thumbs smear bloody prints over the glass.

"I don't know," I manage at last. "I don't know."

They've finally got Mum onto the stretcher. They count, "One, two, three, lift."

They settle her onto a fold-out trolley.

"You're sure?" Rita is tense, her face set into lines I can't read. "Think. Where might she go? You're her twin. No one knows her better than you. When did you last take your medication? Just recently? Good. Now, think."

I shake my head, dumb as a dog. I don't know. She should be here, with me, with Mum. Another awful possibility kicks me in the stomach. I think of the hallways I ran through. Is Bel lying in another one, bleeding out with no one to help her?

"What if she's hurt too?" I gasp.

"She's not," Rita assures me. "We've looked. She's not here."

"I don't . . . I don't . . ." But something's not right, something I can't place. When did you last take your medication?

How did she know?

Because she's Mum's colleague, you idiot. She's her friend. She called her by her first name. Of course she knows about your pills. She knows all about you.

But then, and the suspicion burrows like a worm into my head, why don't I know her? If she's close enough to Mum to discuss my pharmaceutical requirements, why has Mum never mentioned a Rita to me before?

Stupid, paranoid fucking brain. Concentrate, you useless shit. She's trying to help. She's telling you Bel's missing and all you can do is nitpick.

Mum and the paramedics are three-quarters of the way out of the door. One of them holds it open with his boot. It's a heavy boot, black leather. There's a long scratch over the toe, revealing the steel toe cap beneath. My stomach flips over.

"Wait . . ." I lurch forward just as Mum, her face half hidden beneath strings of sticky hair, vanishes through the door and it swings shut. "Wait . . ."

"Peter?" Rita's looking at me, concerned. "You can follow them, Peter. It's all right."

"Who are you?" I rasp, my throat thick with phlegm and tears.

"I told you," she says. "I'm a doctor; a friend. My name is—"

"I don't believe you." I cut her off. "If you're Mum's friend, why has she never mentioned you to me?" My mind's racing now and my words tumble over each other. "That guy had a scratch on his boot, same as the guy who put up our table. There were eight technicians, two teams of four. There are four paramedics when normally they only send two. And you talked to them like you know them. 'We're going to have to move her,' you said. *We.* Who are you? Who are all of you?"

I tail off, breathless. Shut up, Peter. Listen to yourself; you're wired up and paranoid. I stare at her, willing her to deny it so I can let go and trust her. I can't do this by myself. She'll explain, she will. She'll set me right. She'll help me.

Rita looks at me. Then she looks at her watch. She seems to make a decision.

"You can either believe we're your friends," she says, and her tone hasn't changed at all. "Or you can believe we're your enemies. In which case we have your mother, bleeding and helpless in our control, so either way, I think you should do what we say."

Everything inside me freezes. I stare at her. Her expression is blank, patient, waiting for me to make up my mind.

I spin back on my heel. Through the frosted glass, I can still just see them wheeling Mum away down the long adjoining hall. I want to fight them; the desire wells up in me so fierce it feels it will tear its way out of my chest and drag me after it, but there are too many of them and they're too big, and even if, in some hysterically unlikely universe I beat four fully grown men, then what? Too much time's been wasted already. Mum could die before another ambulance, a real ambulance, arrives. Her only hope is her captors.

Oh god, Bel, where are you?

I swallow down acid and say, "Tell me what to do."

Through the glass I see a blurry man-shape running towards us. It falters as it passes Mum's stretcher, then speeds up again and crashes through the door. I recognise the grey-suited man from the party, his tie now loose, his face flushed. When he sees me, something like relief flickers across his face, quickly replaced by puzzlement. He turns to Rita.

"Where's the girl?" he demands. He has an Irish-tinged, London accent.

Rita stays silent.

"You don't know?" he asks, incredulous. "How the fu—"

"Control yourself," Rita cuts him off coldly. His eyes flicker to me and then back to her. The girl, I think frantically. Does he mean Bel?

"She's gone? Did he take her?" he hisses. "How did this happen? How did he even get in?"

He, I think, my thoughts a welter. Who is *he*?

"I don't know," Rita admits.

"Covering the access points was your team's job," he says.

"And surveillance was yours, Seamus. You want to start throwing rocks?" Rita's voice is dangerously taut. Absurdly, I think, scuba gear time, sunshine.

"I'm not taking the rap for this."

"You are if I decide you are," Rita says, in a tone that brooks no argument. "Now, get back to your screens and give us a clear route out of here." She turns back to me and I watch him running back through the double glass doors.

"Walk in front of me," Rita orders me like she's got a gun to my head. But she doesn't need a gun; she's got my mum on a stretcher. "Stay no more than twenty inches ahead. Look at me." I meet her gaze. "You know how far twenty inches is?" I nod. "Good, then walk." She pauses, then adds, "Seems you've got decent instincts, so if you spot anything out of place, don't be shy about shouting."

She spins me around by the shoulder and shoves me at the door. My hands leave rust-coloured prints on the cold glass. Mum's blood's already drying, stiffening in the cracks and folds of my palms.

Behind me, I hear the tone of a mobile phone, Rita making a call. It only rings once.

"Home." It's faint, but I'm close enough that I can just hear the voice on the other end of the line.

"I have the rabbit," Rita says.

"And the wolf?"

I start violently.

Wolf.

The wolf who took my sister?

She hesitates and then, in a tone of voice I haven't heard from her until now, a tone I recognise better than any other: fear.

"In the wind."

RECURSION: 5 YEARS AGO

My toes curled over the edge of the wall with wet moss, cold and slippery as seaweed sliding between them. My school shoes—socks balled neatly up inside—were a pair of lonely quotation marks against the carpet of fallen leaves below me. The drop was less than three metres; it felt like the edge of a cliff.

Bel leaned against the wall eating an apple. She was always eating apples, not just the flesh, but the core, stalk, even the pips. I know what you're thinking: apple pips = cyanide = a quick and painful death, but I'd checked and she'd need more than three thousand of the things to get the median lethal dose. The trees that shielded us from sight of the school were on fire with autumn, and shreds of red-brown leaf were stuck to her hair and her school tights. This little clearing had always been ours, our place, our secret. No one else came here. Ahead of me the woods stretched up the hill into the distance. When we were younger, we'd played hide-and-seek in those woods. I thought longingly of all those hiding places now.

"C'mon," she said. "It's as easy as falling off a log."

"Falling off a *wall*," I insisted. I can be stubbornly literal, especially when I'm scared (which is a bit like a haddock saying "Especially when I'm wet," but still . . .)

Teach me—that's what I'd asked her, and this was her classroom. Fearlessness 101: basic principles of non-self-defecation. She'd already jumped six times to demonstrate, landing lightly and then rolling, throwing up a storm of leaves, laughing all the while, with no more protection than her school jumper. I had a bike helmet strapped to my skull and a pair of cushions nicked from the common room gaffer-taped to my belly and spine. I still couldn't make my feet leave the brick.

Bel sucked in a breath and expelled it in an overdramatic sigh.

"Come on, Pete."

"Seriously, you are the most impatient girl I know."

"A lot of girls you know have to teach their little brother to jump off walls, do they?"

"No, I think that's usually more of a dad job."

We were both silent for a second. I felt the queasy clench in my stomach I always got when I thought about Dad—like when you eat a prawn and suddenly remember a past savage bout of food poisoning.

"Do you . . ." I spoke hesitantly, probing the wound. "Do you ever wonder what that would be like?"

"What 'what' would be like?"

"If Mum started dating again?"

"Is . . . that what you want?"

"God no," I said hurriedly.

"You think it's likely?"

Another long silence.

"No," I said, finally. "Not after the last time."

"Yeah." We shared our relief. Better as we were, just the three of us. Safer.

"I'd like to see the man that could keep up with her," I put in. "He'd need like six PhDs to come close."

"Yeah." Bel grinned. "But you know what you don't need a PhD for? Jumping off a wall. Enough procrastinating, little bro. Get to it."

I looked down. My head swam. My stomach pitched. My arms windmilled. In fact, the only bits of me that didn't move were my feet. They stayed rooted to the brick. Bel sighed again.

"On the other hand . . ." Gripping the apple securely in her mouth, she jumped, caught the top of the wall and scrambled up. Straightening, she bit a chunk from the fruit and let it fall back into her palm. A white wound glistened in the acid-green skin.

"How about we do this your way?" she suggested, chewing thoughtfully. She held the apple out over the edge. "What happens if I let this go?"

"It falls."

"Thank you for that startling insight, Professor Einstein. How fast will it fall?"

I sighed. "It'll accelerate by nine point eight metres a second squared, then brake back to zero when it hits the ground. And by the way, it's pretty ironic you picking Einstein to demonstrate Newtonian mechanics when—"

"And how fast would you fall?" She cuts me off.

"Same," I said. "Gravity doesn't care how big you are; it drags you down all the same."

"How hard would you hit?"

I squinted down at the leaf-drifts.

"Fifteen kilonewtons," I mumbled reluctantly, "ish . . ."

"Which is . . . ?" she prompted, gesturing with the half-eaten apple. I didn't answer.

"Totally survivable," she said, finishing her own sentence. "Right? I mean, you *know* it is."

"I don't know if I know it, exactly."

"Come on, Petey, you know exactly how high a fall you can walk away from. You know all this kind of stuff." Another bite of the apple. "I bet you even looked up how many of these I could eat before I poisoned myself."

"I did not!"

"Uh-huh. Look, even if you hadn't just seen me do it a million times, think of the maths. Your precious numbers are giving you the green light, so what are you so scared of?"

What are you so scared of? For an instant I saw Ben Rigby's lips mouthing the words.

"Come on, Petey," I muttered. I tried to steel myself. I looked at her uncertainly, and she gave me a supernova of a smile and a thumbs-up. I inched around until I was facing the drop again. The trunks of the trees seemed to elongate away from me; the leaf-mould cushion seemed treacherously thin. I could hear the distant shouts and laughter of kids on the playground. Everything swirled and I felt like the world was tipping backwards around me. I screwed my eyes up and tried to bend my legs.

Three excruciating minutes later, I said, "I can't."

Bel sighed. "Why not?"

"Look, intellectually, I know I'd be fine. My brain trusts the numbers. It's just . . ."

"Yes?"

"I'm having a hard time convincing the muscles in my legs that need to do the actual jumping."

There was a soft flump below me. Bel's apple nestled in the leaves, the imprint of her teeth etched in the brilliant white flesh. She held out her hand towards me.

"These sceptical legs of yours," she said. "Do they trust me?"

I hesitated but then nodded. Of course they did. They'd shared a womb with her; she'd been there from the beginning. That's the deepest trust there is. Bel was my axiom.

"Then let them lead. If you can't trust yourself, trust me." She smirked. "After all, I'm kind of an expert. If there was a PhD in falling, I'd have it."

An alarm buzzed in her pocket.

"Shit," she said. "I've got to get back for science. You?"

"I've got a free."

"Then keep practising." She knocked gently on the helmet, hopped off the wall, landed perfectly just to rub it in, and sprinted off towards the school.

"Three, two, one, zero," I muttered. My feet stayed on the bricks.

"Three, two, one, zero . . ."

"Three, two, one—"

"Afternoon, Wankman."

I started and lurched forward, teetering. When I raised my head, there he was. Ben Rigby, flanked by Kamal Jackson and Brad Watkins, standing at the edge of the tree line. I went cold. There was no chance this was a coincidence; no one came here. They'd followed us, waited for Bel to leave.

And he was holding his knife.

His parents had given him one of those Swiss Army things with sixteen zillion functions that look like the contents of a cutlery drawer fused together in a nuclear blast. Right now, though, only the main blade was extended.

I'd thought a lot about that blade. I'd meditated extensively on every gleaming steel edge, because ever since he got it, Ben had been telling me he was going to cut my balls off.

Come on. All I had to do was take one step backwards and there'd be three metres of solid brick between them and me, but my muscles were like stone.

They started forwards, feet crunching the leaves. "Y'know something sad, Kamal?" Ben spoke like I wasn't even there. "Something really tragic. I think we might be the closest thing to friends Wankman's got."

Ben was a gifted bully. He had great instincts for it.

"Either that or all those donuts he had last week," Kamal replied. "I heard he stuffs his face when he's lonely."

I froze. I looked at the knife and felt a spasm of guilt. I had to get out of here. Fifteen kilonewtons, I told my legs. Move! Nothing.

"Is that true, Wankman? Were those donuts your mateless medicine?"

"I have friends." I'd meant it to sound defiant, but it came out as a whine. They weren't buying it. They'd seen me try to make friends. Too shy at first, then too eager, pressing in too hard, scaring people off.

"Really? Who?"

"Bel."

"Your sister?" Ben laughed delightedly. "I thought you couldn't get any more pathetic, but you're just the gift that keeps on giving, aren't you? You can name exactly one friend and she's related to you. But here's the thing, Wankman." He dipped his free hand into his pocket and pulled out his phone. "That's not what you said last week."

He thumbed the phone.

"My sister's a bitch. I hate her, she'll get what's coming to her."

It was tinny, distorted by the speaker, but it was still, unmistakably, my voice.

And then suddenly, I was back, lying prone in the alley behind the baker's at six in the morning last Sunday, the paving slabs freezing and grazing my arms, where Kamal and Brad held them down.

"Just say it." Ben was crouching beside me, holding his phone out. "Once for the record and we'll let you go. Otherwise . . ."

I remembered the tear-rip noise between my legs, the sudden feeling of cold air and colder metal pressing against the inside of my thigh. I remembered fighting not to wet myself.

My legs were trembling. If I didn't jump, I was going to fall. Bel was probably still in earshot. If I called out . . . But my eyes fell on the phone and the thought shrivelled up.

They were almost at the wall now. I looked down behind me. The other side was sheer. There was no way to climb down. It was jump or nothing.

If you can't trust yourself, trust me.

"THREE!" I yelled, so loud that they stopped, startled.

"What—?" Ben began, but I cut him off, continuing the shouted count.

"TWO . . ."

My legs bent under me, my weight tipping back.

"ONE . . ."

NOW

"Zero," Seamus's voice crackles out of Rita's phone, which sits on the dashboard. Over the last five minutes, his tone's gone from taut to outright panicky.

The ambulance is jinking through traffic ahead of us and we're in its slipstream, sliding through the briefly empty patches of road cleared by its sirens.

"I've checked the cameras over and over again, and there are zero entry vectors. There was no way to mount this attack, no way for anyone to get in or out without being seen."

"There's a bleeding woman in an ambulance ahead of me who disagrees with that assessment, Seamus," Rita says.

"I don't know what to tell you, Rita . . ."

"Then what is the point of you?" She reaches over the steering wheel and thumbs the device off.

There's a bleeding woman. I imagine Mum breathing, her chest rising and falling in time to it. Keep breathing, I tell myself as much as her, just keep bloody breathing. Think back . . .

Rita frog-marched me out of the museum through a series of back ways and staff exits, leaving her high heels abandoned next to the pool of blood on the floor. At one junction Mum's stretcher went right and I tried to follow, but Rita snapped, "Left."

"But . . ." I began, but tailed off when I saw her face, imagining one of her fake paramedics dragging a scalpel across the skin of Mum's throat. I turned left.

"It's just a shortcut," Rita said. "There are stairs they can't take the trolley up."

A pair of turns later, we were climbing a set of concrete steps, then descending another to a black door with a green fire exit sign. I reached for the metal release bar, but Rita said, "Wait."

She lifted her phone to her ear.

"Seamus, do you have eyes on the road? East exit."

Seamus's voice crackled over the line. "It's clear."

"That's what you said last time."

"Then either believe me or don't," Seamus said testily. "But then why bother asking?"

Rita swore at him and hung up.

"Okay," she said, pulling me round to face her. "Peter, through this door and exactly two hundred feet to the left is a black Ford Focus. It is unlocked. When I say go, you will run to it as fast as you can and get in. Pay attention, because this part is important. Your mother isn't leaving here without you. If you run anywhere other than my car, I will keep her lying bleeding in the ambulance until you come back, and she doesn't have a lot of time for you to waste. Do you understand?"

I swallowed back impotent fury. "Yes."

"Are you ready?"

"Yes."

"Then go."

I spun, threw myself at the door, and felt it give way. A blast of chilly air hit me and I sprinted left down the pavement. The city was a tunnel of blurred colours and noises, pavement grey, bus red, the drone of traffic. A black hatchback was parked by the curb over double red lines. Eighty-five strides, I thought, two hundred feet. I lurched at the passenger door and grappled with the handle, and it popped open. I scrambled inside.

A fraction of a second later, the driver's door opened and Rita slid in beside me. She must have been right on my shoulder, but I'd been so focused I hadn't even noticed. I glanced at her for signs of satisfaction at my obedience but saw none. She looked hunted; sweat was tracing chaotic pathways down her cheeks, and her shoulders were hunched up as if she were trying to protect her neck. Her eyes darted back and forth, peering through the windscreen. I followed suit, but all I could see were the buses, cars, and idling pedestrians of an ordinary Kensington morning.

"Okay," she said. She turned the ignition and the car rumbled to life. She put it in gear, then paused, absolutely still.

"What is it? What are we waiting—?" I started to say.

A siren droned up and down the scale, and a green-and-yellow-checked ambulance shot past, lights flaring.

Rita stamped on the accelerator and threw us in pursuit.

"What do I need to do?" I ask Rita. My brain's a welter. Impressions, images, car horns, brake lights, blood, blood, blood. I try to calm my breathing. I check my pulse and find to my astonishment it's actually slowing: eighty-eight beats a minute and falling. For a moment I can't make sense of it, then I catch a glimpse of the time glowing on the dashboard: 11:26 A.M.

Ah.

It's been forty minutes since I swallowed the tab of lorazepam. Right now, dear old Laura's busy rushing around my brain, shoving socks into the mouths of all the frantically chattering neurons, dampening the noise of the rioting crowd in my head. Even if she wasn't, you can only run at full, five-alarm panic for so long before your entire cerebro-synaptic complex collapses like an overweight asthmatic running a marathon. I'm hitting my upper limit. My eyeballs ache and my temples throb. I fight through the fog for the only question that matters.

"What do I have to do so you'll get Mum to a hospital?"

Rita barely glances at me.

"Shut up, sit tight, do as you're told, when you're told to do it."

"I've been doing that."

"And you'll notice in return that your mother is tearing through the streets of London in a big yellow van with flashing blue lights attached to the top of it. What does that normally signify?"

Normal? My mum was supposed to get an award today and got stabbed in the gut instead. I've been kidnapped by a doctor with the bedside manner of a serial killer, and I have no idea where my sister is, so no, I'm sorry. Normal didn't show up for work today. His replacement, Completely Batshit Insane, is here—can he take your order? He'd like to recommend the fucking veal!

Fighting to keep my voice neutral, I say, "We're heading northeast and the three closest hospitals to the Natural History Museum are all to the south and west. So I'm asking again: what do I need to do so that you'll get Mum help?"

Rita gives me a look, half amused, half impressed.

"You know that stuff, huh?"

"I'm a world-champion paranoiac. You think I go anywhere without knowing where the nearest operating theatre is?"

She smiles. Out the window, the columned sandstone bulk of Apsley House appears and vanishes in an instant as we plunge around Hyde Park Corner and into Green Park.

"We're taking her to a company facility." She hesitates before adding, "Employee benefits."

I stare at her.

"Are you telling me Mum's a . . ." I grope hopelessly for the right word. I feel a brief, needle-sharp pang: Bel, where are you? "A . . . whatever you are?" I manage finally.

"I told you Louise and I are colleagues," she says. "I never said doing what."

"But you threatened her. You said you'd let her bleed."

"I had to get you in the car." A hint of a shrug. "That was the fastest way to do it." She fumbles in the glove compartment and pulls out a box of tissues, a rattling can of travel sweets, and eventually a photograph. She hands it to me. It's old and dog-eared;

something black and gummy's streaked over the surface, but it still clearly shows three women standing in a field, smiling. Rita's on the right, a blonde woman I don't recognise stands on the left, and in the middle, a few years younger but pale, freckled, and unmistakeable: my mother.

I pinch the photo uncertainly between my finger and thumb. Rita glances at me out the corner of her eye.

"And being the world-champion paranoiac you are, you naturally think that's faked." She sighs, throws the car into a zigzag so violent I think my seat belt will cut me in half, then wrestles it back straight.

"What are you good at?" Rita asks. I don't answer. "Maths, right? You're supposed to be quite the human calculator. So, here's a question. What's one plus two?"

I stare at her blankly. I can feel cold creeping through me, numbing my lips and my fingertips. Locking my jaw is all that keeps my teeth from chattering.

She purses her lips thoughtfully. "Okay," she says, "let's try this: want to see what *I'm* good at?"

She winds down her window and digs under her seat. When her hand comes up, a ten pence piece glimmers in her palm.

"Heads or tails?" she asks, and then, perhaps guessing I'm not about to turn this conversation into a two-player game, answers for me. "Let's say heads."

She puts her hand out the window and flicks the coin up. My eyes track it through the sunroof as it glints and flickers, turning and turning and turning and . . .

BANG.

A shattering sound fills my ears. I smell hot metal and something like a freshly extinguished candle. The coin zips off its trajectory and out of sight. For a sickening second I think we've crashed, and I screw my eyes shut. My vertebrae bunch, bracing for flying shards of windscreen to slice my face off the front of my skull.

One second passes, two. My face still feels attached. The

motion of the car still pitches my stomach. I open my eyes, look down, and see the neat black pistol in Rita's grip. The stink of hot metal and chemicals fills my nostrils.

"Heads," she says, not bothering to look back. "You believe me?"

I do.

Outside on the pavement, heads have whipped around in the direction of the noise. But the car's already moved on and the gun's back inside it, pointed ever so casually, at me.

"What are you thinking?" she asks, perfectly calm, gaze flicking from the road towards me every now and then. "Describe what's going through your head right now."

The end of the pistol's like a black hole, sucking all the light out of the world.

Light . . . light . . . My mind races, trying to find some hope, some sum that will let it grip onto this moment and not leave me a slobbering catatonic wreck.

"Speak," she says. But I don't know what she wants me to say. Light.

"L-l-light," I stammer. I swallow and try again, trying to keep my teeth from chattering.

"Go on."

"A-add up the time it takes for the light to go from me to your retina, the electricity to shoot up your optic nerve and p-p-pinball around your brain and then head all the way b-b-back down your arm to your trigger finger, you get about a quarter of a second. You, me, and that gun have been alone t-t-together in this car for eight and a half minutes."

My nerve fails me.

"So?"

"So, you've had two thousand and forty separate chances to kill me, and you haven't taken any of them yet."

For a long second she just looks at me. Two dark pupils and the dark barrel of her gun. Then she mutters, "Jesus Christ, you really are a piece of work. How do you even know all that?"

How do I know how long it takes for a human being to make an irrevocable decision? I stare at her.

She tucks the gun away beside her seat. "You like counting, so let's count." She curls fingers out from the steering wheel, ticking off items:

"One: I could be an assassin. This could all be part of a convoluted plan to kill your mother. Only, as I just demonstrated, if I wanted either of you dead, you would be.

"Two: this is a kidnapping. I want Louise alive, except, why would I endanger my objective by giving her a gushing abdominal wound?

"Three: everything I told you is true. That photograph is real. Louise is not only my colleague but my very, very close friend, and I'm risking not only my glittering career but my elegant neck because I owe it to her to keep you safe. Now, *what's one plus two?*"

"Three," I reply, my mouth parched.

She nods. "Sometimes the obvious answer's the right one."

Her phone buzzes and jiggles over the dash, spitting out the trumpets from "Mambo No. 5." She thumbs Answer, cutting Lou Bega off in midflow.

"This is Rita," she says. "I'm on speakerphone."

"Understood, Rita. This is Henry Black. Report."

"I have both Louise and the Rabbit. We're six minutes out."

There is a brief, startled pause.

"You're bringing the Rabbit into 57?"

"Affirmative."

57? I think. What's 57? Why am I the "Rabbit"?

"Rita." The man on the other end of the line sounds appalled. "You can't . . ."

"I can and I am."

"Rita . . ."

"He's Louise's son, Henry. If this was your daughter, would you want me to leave her out in the cold?"

There's a shocked silence coming from the phone. I get

the feeling Rita's crossed a line. She hangs up. We're on the Embankment now and the traffic's thinned. She yanks us up onto the north side of Blackfriars Bridge with, frankly, unnecessary force.

"Who was that?" I ask at last.

"My boss," she says tightly, "for as long as I continue to be employed."

For the rest of the journey neither of us speaks. All I can think about is what's going on in the back of that sealed steel box rolling ahead of us. Have Rita's fake-real paramedics stabilised her? Or are they even now scrambling around with paddles and syringes, trying to save her life?

Don't be dead, Mum. Just don't be dead.

Eventually, we turn onto a residential street in Hackney, brick terraces on both sides, the one on the left bandaged up in scaffolding. The ambulance pulls in and cuts its sirens, and we park up behind it. I don't want the door to open; it feels as if whatever has happened inside won't be real until I see it. Rita seems to read my mind.

"They'd have called if they lost her," she assures me. "She's still with us."

I try to grip onto that reassurance, but it's slippery. A terrible loneliness surges through me: a premonition of loss. The handles on the back of the ambulance turn, and my pulse quickens. Where are you, Bel? We need each other right now. We need to face this together. I grasp empty air with my right hand as if I could feel hers.

The door to Schrödinger's ambulance swings open and a ramp unfolds. They're pushing Mum out onto the pavement on her gurney. Fussed over by her green-coated minders, she vanishes under the scaffolding. In between the struts, I see tired-looking brick and dirty windows with pea-green paint peeling from their frames. The nearest door has a pair of splotchy brass numerals screwed to the bricks beside it, wonky in a way that makes my teeth ache: 57.

As we approach the door, Rita arrests me with a hand on the shoulder.

"I am out on a limb for you, you understand?" she says.

"How can I?" I ask hoarsely. "You haven't told me anything."

She snorts, but I see a flicker of a smile on her lips.

"Yeah, you should get used to that. World-champion paranoiac, huh?"

I nod, wide-eyed.

"Good. Don't let me down."

RECURSION: 3 YEARS AGO

"Sir?"

Dr. Arthurson's head swung towards the sound of my voice. Eyes like soaped-over windows screwed up to peer at me.

"Peter?" He was all but blind, but he had a killer memory for voices.

"Yes, sir." The space between my shoulder blades itched. Dr. A might not have been able to see, but at least half the class were staring a hole in my back. I gulped air. "I'm struggling with this bit of the problem, and I was wondering if you could give me a clue."

"Oh, well, of course." He patted the desk in front of him and I slid the sheet of paper I'd been working on under his waiting fingers. For the main part of his lessons, he typed onto a laptop that got projected onto the board while a text-recogniser spoke into his earbud. But for marking, he held it right up in front of his nose.

I pointed to a random line on the page and said, "It's this bit here," before I leaned into his ear and muttered,

"I'm pretty sure this is right, but the last time I was the first to find the answer in this class, we had chemistry next lesson and someone "accidentally" spilled a blister agent down the back of my trousers. Guess what our next lesson is now—double chemistry! So please play along. Act like I've made some really basic mistake and give me something else to work on, please? I'd stare out the window, but the view of the sixth-form block air vents isn't going to move me to poetry, you know?"

In the reflection of the glass clock face, I could see Ben Rigby.

He saw me see him and mimed a wank with his right hand. Kamal snorted.

"Ho ho ho!" Dr. Arthurson burst out, like a corduroy-clad Santa Claus. "Oh my, you have made an elementary error, haven't you?" Dr. A had what I guessed was a fifty-four-inch chest, and his fake laugh shook the light fittings. He tabbed off the projector so only I could see his screen and typed:

I was quite the actor in my university days you know!!

"Uh-huh," I said.

I played Falstaff!!!

"That . . . makes sense?" I hazarded.

Try the problem at the top of page 297. Your secret is safe with me!!!!!

I had a horrible feeling that if he'd had a working eye, he'd have winked.

"Um, thanks, sir. I'll give that a try. Sorry."

Behind me, Rigby fake-coughed, "Dumbass." A couple of people laughed and I sat back down, feeling like a spy after a close shave at a dead-drop. The sweat cooled on the back of my neck as I flicked to page 297.

Find the maximum, always holding . . . Huh, calculus.

I made a couple of false starts, then realised that this one was going to need a Lagrange multiplier. I snapped the cap off my pen and was just getting down to it when I noticed something odd.

The rest of the class were working on a problem on page 86, but the occupant of the desk immediately to my right had her textbook open much further in than that. It was the fat bank of white pages pinned under her left hand that had fish-hooked my attention.

I leaned back into a fake yawn and stretch so I could see her properly. It was the new girl—Imogen? Ingrid? I knew it started with an I. She'd joined the class at . . . some point. She hadn't been here at the start of the year; I knew that. She had an erratic thatch of blonde hair and wore fingerless gloves even though the classroom radiators were set one notch below "active volcano crater." I looked at the thickness of the paper under her hand, then back at my book to make sure.

She was. She was on page 297 too.

The silence in the room was suddenly more intense. I felt myself flush hot. I tried to go back to the Lagrange but kept stealing glances at the girl. She was all business, scribbling away, pinning her fringe out of her eyes with one gloved hand.

Could I talk to her after class? I wondered. What could I say? *"Hey, you know before, when I sounded like an idiot? I was pretending! Wanna get together after class so we can swap notes on differential calculus?"*

Not the single worst chat-up line of all time, but definitely in the top five. I had a half hour left to work on it.

I went back to the sums, but I couldn't concentrate. I was full of curiosity, fizzing with it, like sherbet in the blood.

I looked to my right again. She'd stopped writing and was running her pencil over her work, checking it over and over. She was frowning. She tucked her hair back behind her right ear, but it was too short and came loose again. She tucked it back, again and again like a tic.

Did she need a hint? Did she even know about Lagrange multipliers? She looked anxious, desperate even, and suddenly the most important thing in my world was whether this girl knew how to solve constrained optimisation problems. She was a fellow agent, embedded deep behind enemy lines. She needed help, and I had to get it to her. But how, without giving us both away? I spied out the others in the class, hunched over their desks, quiet and dangerous like mines drifting in dark water.

I checked the index of my textbook and found the page for Lagrange multipliers: 441. I spun my pen around in my hand, hesitated, and then tapped it against my desk: four taps, then a pause, then another four taps, then another pause, then a final solitary strike that to my nervous ears filled the classroom like a thunderclap.

I looked across at her. Nothing. Of course nothing—because

neither of us really were spies, so neither of us attended a secret training school in a big English country house where we learned the dark arts of clandestine pencil-tapping. I mean, think about it, Pete. She'd have had to be telepathic to . . .

She was looking right at me.

She had that same frown on her face. Not an unhappy frown, now I saw it full on. She looked interested, in a "this isn't as straightforward as I thought" kind of way.

Not taking her eyes off me, she flicked towards the back of her textbook. Now I was holding my breath. She stopped at what looked from here like page 441 and studied the page for a second. An "Oh duuuuh" expression swept over her face, followed immediately by a look of intense irritation. Then she started scribbling on her notepad fast—I mean really fast, like I wouldn't have been surprised to see smoke rising from the paper. She tapped three numbers into her calculator and held it up so I could see the display:

322.

She raised her eyebrows and slightly opened her hands: Well?

I started, flailed, and almost impaled my thumb on my own compass. I wasn't even halfway through the sum yet. I churned through the calculation as fast as I could. After what felt like a hundred years, flustered and embarrassed and unutterably relieved, I held up my calculator: 322.

Her lip quirked at the corner.

I felt my face heat up and I smiled back at her. I had a feeling we were on the same wavelength and it was fantastic. I luxuriated in it.

She tapped on her calculator keys for a second and then held it up again.

579,005,009

What the fuck?

She leaned back in her chair, arms folded: Go on, then, work it out.

I sat there and racked my brain: 579,005,009. What was that?

Was it prime? It wasn't a Fibonacci. It wasn't—I thought with a brief flash of sadness—her phone number. I started to sweat. She was still watching me, still smiling expectantly. I mean, seriously, what? Its square root was something in the twenty-four thousands. Its natural log would be . . . twenty . . . something? But none of that meant anything that . . .

My eye fell back onto the textbook. I flicked to page 579: it was the last page in the book, the acknowledgments. The fifth word was *thanks*; the ninth, *friend*.

I glowed. I flicked back to the calculus problem, typed into my calculator, and held it up.

297,018,002

She checked the page, found the words—No problem—and smiled. It felt good to see her smile, so I sent her another, only one word this time.

345,009—*New?*

104,006—*Correct.*

181,007,005—*Working out?*

Her smile turned a little shy, and she nodded in my direction.

276,008,009—*Positive signs.*

I stifled a delighted laugh. HQ, this is Agent Blankman—contact established with Agent Blonde Calculating Machine.

We talked like that, secretly and silently, for the rest of the lesson, and I had sherbet blood the whole time. The brief delay while she deciphered each snippet filled me with eager anticipation. It was the first time in my life waiting had been fun rather than frightening.

Even another fit of coughing from Rigby—"Mateless freak"—didn't ruin it, because it wasn't true anymore.

She rolled her eyes, glanced back at him, and tapped out:

112,003,190

I looked: page 112 had a couple of test papers with those "Pretend you're a zookeeper/café owner/football coach . . ." problems on it. 003,190 made "monkey sausage." I glanced back at Rigby and smirked. I knew what she meant.

The bell went and I felt a sharp kick of disappointment. I'd totally lost track of the time, and I never lose track of time. I fell in beside her desk, trying to be nonchalant.

Now or never. I remembered the pressure of cushions gaffer-taped to my chest, my feet leaving brick. My brain went utterly blank and I reached for the first thing I could think of.

"Want to meet up later? We could swap tips for differential calculus."

Damn, meant to work on that.

She looked at me oddly, then shrugged it off. She had a great face. Warm brown eyes, neat little nose. She looked a bit like Ada Lovelace.

"Lunch?" she said. It had the ring of a counteroffer.

"Lunch would be phenomenal." Nonchalance, as it turned out, was not my strong suit.

She grinned hugely; apparently it wasn't her strong suit, either.

"Twenty-three, seventeen, eleven, fifty-four," she said.

"What?"

"Look it up," she said. "Page one." She tucked her hair out of her eyes one more time, shouldered her bag, and walked out.

So I looked it up: page 1, words 23, 17, 11, and 54—Don't let me down.

NOW

The cold makes it feel like there's frost creeping through my blood vessels. I stand on the doorstep and shiver while Rita rings the doorbell. Through the lace curtain on the front room window I see a TV flickering and an armchair facing it. A slight figure struggles out of the chair and moves out of sight. A second later the door opens as far as a brass chain allows, and a wizened face peers through the gap.

"Oh, hello, dear," she says with the sunny gratitude of an old lady who doesn't get visitors as often as she'd like.

Rita's smile is tight. "Good morning, Mrs. Greave. May we come in?"

"Of course, dear."

She slips the chain and stands aside for us, and I follow Rita over the threshold.

I look around the hallway, feeling wrong-footed. I don't know what I expected from the ominous-sounding 57, but it definitely wasn't pink-and-cream-striped wallpaper and a gilt-framed portrait of a terrier in a tartan waistcoat.

"Make yourselves at home, won't you?" Mrs. Greave says. She looks at me and a muscle in her cheek twitches. "That him?"

"What do you think?" Rita says.

Mrs. Greave makes a hissing sound in the back of her throat, like a disgruntled cat.

"Only got the word from Henry you were bringing a house-guest when you were coming up the path," she says. "Thought you were compromised, nearly gave the boys the nod."

Rita blinks and she breathes out hard. "Well, I'm glad you held off."

"Didn't feel like redecorating."

The crack in Rita's composure makes me ask, "W-what boys?"

"Snipers," she replies briskly, "in the attic of the house opposite, with orders to shoot any strangers who try to get in. Standard security measure when things get a bit hairy, which, you might have noticed, they have today."

I stare at her. "You just gun people down in the street in broad daylight?"

"And risk getting filmed on some local kid's phone? Oh no, dear." Mrs. Greave has one hand on the still-open door. "No, we invite them in, and then the boys drop them on the doormat, when they're standing, oh . . . just about where you are now." She gives a fractional nod towards a window under the eaves across the road. Something gleams under the open sash and my neck seizes with the premonition of impact. Then the door swings shut and I'm still standing here, heart hammering but still beating.

That's 0 for 2 on having your skull exploded by a high-velocity bullet, Petey. Good work, keep it up.

Mrs. Greave gives me a sugary smile. "Make yourselves at home," she says, and shuffles back into the front room, closing the door behind her, muting the voices bickering from the TV.

Rita moves swiftly, producing a big bunch of keys from under the hallstand. Little fragments of dried blood flake off her bare feet and dust the carpet. She stops by the stairs, beside an open walk-in cupboard about the same size and shape as the larder I stood in seven hours and a lifetime ago, when the worst of my problems was an uncontrollable urge to chew pottery. I glance inside: shelves of fly killer, peeling old phone directories, face-down picture frames, dusty birthday cards—one of those places where meaning goes to die.

Rita pulls the door shut. There's a brass keyhole just under the handle. She selects a key from her bunch, inserts it, and turns it clockwise. She gives the door a good shove with her shoulder. It swings inwards and the doorframe goes with it, but only to about forty degrees. I gasp. Where a moment ago there were shelves of tat, the cobwebbed bricks of the terrace's cavity wall are now visible. Rita looks down, and I follow her gaze. The closet floor's dropped away too, and now a staircase coils up out of the darkness to meet us like a black iron snake.

I look at the angle the door cuts across the space and the width of the wall cavity, and whistle softly.

"The closet collapses and slides into the cavity when you push the door. What, is it on rails or something?"

Rita doesn't answer. I run a hand over the inside of the doorframe. There's nothing out of the ordinary visible; no electrics, no flattening of the wood grain where it's been drilled and filled. You could take this whole house apart with a sledgehammer and you'd never find it.

"Who . . . what are you people?" I feel dizzy and out of breath.

"In a hurry," Rita says shortly, her expression fixed.

We descend, my uncomfortable formal shoes clanking on the metal. The mechanism slides back silently above us. She leads me down into the dark.

The staircase ends in a brick arched tunnel. Halogen bulbs on the ceiling yield a mortuary glare. Rita sets off down it on her stained feet, and I hustle along after her.

"This tunnel leads back under the road, doesn't it?" I ask. She ignores me. "That house, number 57, it's just the entrance. Our destination isn't even on the same street."

Still no reply. There's something physical, something stifling about the quiet down here. The tunnel turns corner after corner. It's a maze, I realise. You need to know the path. Left, right, right, left again. I pull a pen from my pocket and scratch notes on the bandage on my hand to keep track. Every five metres an identical light; every brick the same. It would be so easy to lose yourself. I imagine being alone down here, stumbling around in circles until I starved or ate myself, watched by the unsympathetic lenses of the little black cameras set into the ceiling.

Maze, I think. There's a theorem about mazes. I remember Dr. A laughing as he told me: *Learn this and you'll never be lost in one.* I grasp hungrily after the shreds of memory, but I'm too wrung out, and they elude me.

Side tunnels lead off every ten metres or so, some on the left, some on the right. Faint, chill draughts kiss my cheek as I pass them. Routes to the outside?

"Jesus," I mutter. "Random doorways."

Rita still doesn't reply, but the rhythm of her footsteps falters.

"That's right, isn't it?" I press. No response. Nervous energy lifts the hairs on my neck like static. Come on, I implore silently. Give me something.

"You don't want to leave a pattern, you can't let anyone see you visiting the same house over and over again, so you've got ways in all over the neighbourhood."

Still no answer, but a muscle tightens under the skin of her cheek. She's like a rusted tap, I think. You grip and turn as hard as you can and it feels like she's giving a little, but that might just be your hand slipping.

"Are all the other entrances at the 57th house on their roads, too?" I ask. "Is that why you call this place that?"

She barks a short, flat laugh—finally—the first drop.

"Why on earth would we do that? The house numbers are random too. As you said, it's all about patterns. There will always be patterns, unfortunately. It's our job to obscure them, make sure they're as complicated and confusing as possible."

"You create static around the signal?" I ask. But she's fallen silent again.

Left, left, right, left again. The sheer, methodical paranoia of this place takes my breath away. But terrifying as it is, I feel a weird kind of kinship with it. This place was built by very clever, very determined people who were very sure they were very under threat.

Possibilities flicker through my head, each one only deepening the chill I feel.

Terrorists, religious cult, organised crime . . .

And they called Mum a colleague.

We turn one last corner and the tunnel ends at a big metal door with a camera lens set into it. Rita leans into the lens and lets it take some sort of scan of her eye. There's a deep clunk and the door bevels slowly outward. The door's thick, like "built to survive a nuclear apocalypse" thick. Somewhere in my motor cortex, the lizard slams a scaly foot on the brakes and I. Just. Stop.

I can't make myself take another step. I glance at the sequence of blue Biro Ls and Rs scrawled on my bandaged hand. *Walk*, I urge my legs, but they've gone on strike. They know that there is still a way back, but not if I let that half-ton hunk of steel close behind me.

I ask one final time.

"What is this place? Who are you people?" Rita turns to look at me. "I . . . I won't, I can't, take another step, until you tell me what's waiting behind that door."

Her gaze seems to weigh me for a second, then she says, "We're 57."

"You're named after an address that isn't even really your address?"

"You're named after an uncle who isn't even really your uncle."

I feel jiujitsued. That scrap of knowledge, so casually tossed off, seems to hint at limitless libraries, volumes filled with information not just about my famous neuroscientist mother, but about me.

"How do you—"

"By being halfway competent at my work." She cuts me off, rolling her eyes towards the brick ceiling as if praying for patience. "Fine," she mutters.

"In 1994 as part of his commitment to 'open government'"—her lip curls as though the words have curdled in her mouth—"the then Prime Minister John Major officially acknowledged the existence of the Secret Intelligence Service, probably better known to you as MI6."

"So?"

"So, on the same day, 57 was given the primary responsibility for the clandestine pursuit of Britain's interests. We're the knife in the nation's pocket now."

"So . . . the first thing this 'open government' did after officially revealing a spy agency was replace it with another hidden one?"

"Sure," she says impatiently. "You either have a secret service or you don't. But if you do, it should be fucking well secret."

Somewhere behind us water drips. I stare at her, Rubik's Cubing the idea in my head until it makes some kind of sense. "My mother's a *spy*?"

"No, your mother's a scientist. She just works for spies."

A thought occurs to me then, an appalling thought, and it must be amateur hour in the paranoia centres of my prefrontal cortex, because it didn't occur to me earlier. A fresh rain of warm sweat stipples my shoulders.

"How . . . how can you show me all this and then let me walk away?"

I've been drawn into a secret, and only those sworn to secrecy will ever know I'm here. I look at the curving brick walls and think, *Crypt*. I'm being encrypted.

"I'm never leaving here, am I?"

She stares at me solemnly, and for a second I think, *Shit, I'm dead,* but then she laughs, sudden and shocking in this tomb-like place.

"Don't be such an arse! Of course you can leave. You're a good kid. You're the son of my best friend and I probably saved your life today, and if that's not enough"—she half shrugs—"I can rely on the twin facts that you're the boy who's afraid of everything and I am tremendously scary."

I'd like to contradict her, but when you're nailed, you're nailed.

"Now"—she jerks her thumb at the massive door—"behind me is your mother, some answers, and a cup of tea that I will honestly kill you if you keep me from any longer. Behind you"—she nods down the tunnel—"is a man with a knife. Decide."

Well, when you put it like that . . . I take a step towards her, so hesitant I almost lose my balance. She puts an arm around me, steadies me. I take a deep breath, and enter 57.

Beyond the door is a short brick hallway, then another set of doors, glass this time, and then a square chamber, yet more bare brick. Judging by the three sets of elevator doors on the far side, it was once just a lift lobby, but now it's rammed with trestle tables, computers, half-unpacked cardboard boxes, and bustling people; all the gangly paraphernalia of an organisation that's had a growth spurt but not filled out into it yet. Men and women, twenty-five, no, twenty-six of them, push past one another in the narrow spaces between the desks and type away at the makeshift workstations.

The dominant sound of the "knife in the nation's pocket" is the click of fingers on keys, but the odd snatch of conversation is audible: someone says "him," someone says "wolf," and "cipher" and "lost" and "attack." There are numbers I can't make sense of. It all seems random to me, but I know it isn't.

It's just static around the signal, I think.

Randomness is surprisingly hard to fake. Now—right now—imagine tossing a coin a hundred times. If you're like most people, you'll have imagined close to fifty heads and fifty tails, and you won't have a run of more than three or four of either in a row. Toss the coins for real, though, and those runs will happen, almost with certainty. True randomness is indifferent to our petty human expectations of it, and today's events don't have any of its telltale traits.

Everything that's happened—the blood, the panic, the

apparent chaos—it isn't random. There is a pattern. I just have to see it under the gore, hear it under the screaming, and when I do, I won't merely cope; I'll find the rancid sack of animal shit that did this.

Come on, Petey, patterns are the one thing in this Gödel-forsaken world you're actually good at.

Rita coughs and a couple of heads pop up over monitors, and the voices fall silent. "Frankie," she calls across the room, "have we found the girl?"

The woman she's talking to hasn't noticed us yet. She's late thirties maybe, bottle-blonde hair, grey Gap hoodie, and frayed jeans. She's bending over a monitor and doesn't look up.

"Not yet," she replies. Her brow furrows in irritation. "We've tried a few times. Got the boys in the kitchen trying to find a way to cook up a message she'll respond to—if she's listening, but if we wanted someone who could break ciphers on the fly, then frankly we . . . lost . . ."

She tails off. Her face takes on the wondering expression of someone whose brain has just caught up with their ears. She runs a hand back over her ponytail and looks up at us.

"The wrong twin," she murmurs. She hurries over to us, banging into a trestle table in her haste, her hands half raised.

"Thank god," she says. "Ca—"

"Rita," Rita interrupts her. "Outdoor names only, Frankie, while we have a houseguest."

She steps aside so Frankie can get a good look at me and drops her hands. With a start I recognise her—she was the third figure in the photo Rita showed me.

"This is the Rabbit?" she asks. She sounds alarmed.

"You can't tell?"

"You brought him here?"

"His mother's having her abdomen sliced open upstairs for the second time in an hour. Where else could I take him?"

"But we're not prepared for—"

"Look at him, Frankie," Rita says patiently.

Frankie squints at me and some of the doubt ebbs from her voice. "He does seem to be taking this remarkably calmly."

Rita nods. "I suspect we have some mixture of shock, exhaustion, and benzodiazepines to thank for that."

"Benzodiazepines?"

"His file says lorazepam. We have an hour. Two at the outside."

"File? I have a file?" I ask, bewildered. They don't answer. That's becoming a theme—spies, go figure. I have another go anyway. "What file? An hour until what?"

Frankie turns to face me. She's smiling, but pale as if she's had a nasty shock and is trying not to show it, like an arachnophobe who's been given a pet tarantula for Christmas by a new best friend she really wants to impress.

"Until your medication wears off and you can have some more," she says. "We know you sometimes have a tricky time adjusting to stress."

I blink, so stunned by the magnitude of that understatement that I almost—but not quite—miss the fact that that was definitely not the true answer to my question.

"I'm so sorry this is happening to you," she presses on. "Louise is very dear to all of us here. We're doing everything we can for her."

"Th-thank you."

"My name's Frankie," she tells me, her smile sympathetic and confiding. "It's okay . . ." Her hand moves to my cheek and I shiver as I feel it against my skin. "You're safe now, your mother too. Anabel's still out there, but we'll have her safe as soon as we can. We just have a few questions about what happened."

"Frankie," Rita says, "have you got the museum footage?"

"What little there is. Why?"

"It might jog Peter's memory."

"Are you kidding? He's not ready for that—he's still in shock. His lips are blue."

"So he'll feel it less," Rita replies firmly. "Better now than later. We're running out of time."

Frankie stares at her, eyes wary, and starts to shake her head. "Rit—"

"*I want to.*" My voice is small, but its firmness surprises even me. They both turn to look at me.

"Please, if I can help, I want to. I want to find who did this."

There's a silence. Frankie's jaw goes tight, but she pulls around a monitor so we can all see it. She opens a folder and double-clicks a file. A black-and-white video plays silently. With a lurch I recognise the exhibit-lined corridor where I found Mum. It's empty. In the bottom right corner of the screen, a clock ticks off minutes, seconds, tenths, and finally hundredths of seconds, racing headlong, almost too fast to see.

My chest and throat freeze up. Now it comes to it, I actually don't know if I can watch this. Frankie, eyeing me warily, starts to narrate.

"We have footage all the way up until ten fifty-two, when you . . . well, here you come."

A figure runs through the shot from the left: skinny, pale arms pumping, lips moving, though there's no one to talk to. I squeeze my bandaged hand until the pain flares.

The camera clock ticks off eight more seconds, and then another figure enters the hallway.

"Mum," I whisper. She has her heels in one hand, her skirt bunched in the other, and she's running, but she doesn't exit the shot like I did.

She stops dead in the middle, and the expression on her face . . . it's horror and recognition and desolation and despair. It's the look of confronting your worst fear and knowing it's finally come for you, and that you aren't ready, and you never could be.

She takes one hesitant step forward, then starts to stumble back, her mouth stretched in a cry for help, a name, my name. She turns to run and then the screen goes black.

I jerk around to Frankie, tears in my eyes.

"Turn it back on!"

"It is on," she replies. "Something was interfering with the signal—look at the clock."

I look back at the screen. The playback clock's still perfectly clear, and still running, five seconds of darkness, six. I lift my hands towards the screen, as though I could tear away the blackness hiding my mother like a shroud.

Then something weird happens. The clock freezes; for two complete thuds of my heart, it reads 10:58:17:00, and then, like a stumbling runner regaining her footing, it charges onwards. Three seconds later it stalls again, just long enough for me to heave a shuddering breath in and out again: 10:58:20:00. Then it runs on, time spilling on and on into the darkness. My eyes ache from staring at the screen's not-quite-black glow.

"Keep watching," Rita says.

The clock halts once more: 10:59:13:00 for two full seconds.

Then the picture flashes back.

"Mum," I breathe, though from the camera's vantage she's barely recognisable. It's just the wreckage of her, tangled limbs and bloody cloth, and I'm on my knees beside her, my hands stained dark as they patter desperately over her body. I look down at those stains on my hands now and feel the same wordless panic fill my throat.

"Freeze it," Rita orders.

Frankie hits a button and the black-and-white me stops moving.

"We have no footage of the attack itself," Frankie says. "But you were the first person on the scene afterwards. Did you see anything the attacker might have left behind? Anything at all could be a clue. Look at the screen, remind yourself."

I shake my head, useless tears stinging my eyes.

"Anything at all, anything that could help us find them?"

No, except.

"Peter?"

"The clock," I whisper, and my voice is hoarse. "During the blackout, it stops three times. The frequency . . ."

"We've already looked at it. It's irregular," Frankie says. She frowns. "There's no pattern."

"It's not irregular," I insist, "not completely. The pauses come precisely on the turn of the second. Look." With numb fingers I take the mouse from Frankie and drag the cursor on the video back to the point where the clock first stopped.

"The first one on ten-fifty-eight and seventeen seconds *exactly*, the second at ten-fifty-eight and twenty seconds *exactly*." I dragged the cursor forward, and then again. "And the last burst at ten-fifty-nine and thirteen seconds *exactly*. What are the odds of that happening by accident?" They look at me blankly, so I answer the question for them. "Exactly one in a million. It's not random. Those numbers mean something. Seventeen, twenty, and thirteen."

Now I've said it, the pattern seems small and absurd. I expect Frankie to dismiss it, but to my surprise, she looks thoughtful.

"I'll compare it to footage of the lab break-in," she says to Rita.

"What lab break-in?"

Frankie's already pulled the screen back around and is hammering at the keys as she answers.

"At four o'clock this morning, your mother's lab at Imperial was broken into. The cameras went down there as well. A virus was uploaded that wiped every file on the drives."

"You think the two are connected?" I say. The fog in my head is starting to clear.

"Hell of a coincidence if they aren't."

"S-s-so . . . this is about Mum's work?" I ask shakily.

Rita raised her eyebrows. "She's a strategic research scientist; it's not going to be about her cooking."

"But . . . but then . . ."

I remember her saying they'd tried to contact Bel multiple times. I remember what she said in her status report when she picked up her phone. *I have the Rabbit.* And I know the Rabbit is me. Her first question as she walked through the door was, *Have we found the girl?* She could only mean Bel.

I'm risking not only my glittering career but my elegant neck, Rita had said, *because I owe it to her to keep you safe.*

Even now, the question's hard to formulate, I guess because it involves looking past my hardwired assumption that everything must naturally be about me, and that assumption has hitherto obscured the fact that everything I've seen and heard today has been *unusually, suspiciously,* about me . . .

. . . me and my still-missing sister.

"If this is all about Mum's work," I ask quietly, "then why the obsessive focus on her kids?"

For a second Frankie looks startled, then recovers. Get counting. I look over my shoulder, past Rita. Fifteen steps from the door. A door nine inches thick. Eight hundred and fifty paces back to the exit to the street through a lock I can't operate. I check my watch: ninety-three minutes since my life as I knew it ended. I don't want to ask my next question, but there's nowhere to escape from it.

"Whoever's behind this, they don't want just Mum, her work, her colleagues; they want Bel, and they want me. Why?"

"Because of who he is."

He, I think, remembering Seamus's shaken face at the museum. She's gone. Did *he* take her? How did *he* get in?

"You already know who did this."

"We have our suspicions. But we didn't want to prejudice your memory of the crime."

I wait. There's no point asking the question, the question that's hanging in the air around us like gas vented from a drain.

Frankie glances to Rita, as if for permission. Rita nods. Frankie exhales and says:

"Dr. Ernest Blankman."

There's a cold knot at the base of my skull. Kidnapping.

Kidnapping. How did I not see this coming? Come on, Pete, patterns are the one thing you're good at. It takes me three tries to open my mouth, because my tongue's fused to the roof of it.

"Dad?"

RECURSION: 3 YEARS AGO

It was the bad kind of laughter, and it was coming from just outside the girls' bathroom.

Ordinarily, I would have put as much distance between me and it as possible, turned on my heel, and headed back down the hall. Today I set a collision course right for the clutch of uniformed bodies at its source. I couldn't have told you why. Maybe because it was just one of those days, the golden days, the brave days, the oh-too-rare days when anything seemed possible.

My trainers squeaked on the lino. I kept my gaze on them and my hands on the straps of my rucksack. I tallied the day's accomplishments.

Talk to new girl: *check.*

Arrange lunch date with new girl: *check.*

Don't chicken out and actually go to lunch hall for date with new girl: incredibly, astonishingly, *check.*

Wait, and wait, and wait some more, back pressed against the lunch hall wall, enduring the stares of the kids in line for fish and chips and aerated cardboard sponge, until the bell for the end of lunch goes and she still hasn't shown: *Check, check, bloody check.*

I veered left a little as I passed the laughing huddle, and even though they were whispering, I could hear them.

"I know, right, she's a total freak!"

"Should we tell a teacher or something?" One of them sounded worried.

"Please, this is just too entertaining."

"Ugh—what is he looking at?"

"He" was me. A tilt of the girl's head and a lilt in her voice accused me like the finger of a Witchfinder General. Additional laughter. My throat caught and my face heated up, but I was past them, and in seven or eight more seconds I'd be out of earshot. Then I heard a new voice carry through the open door of the bathroom. It was familiar; I'd heard it for the first time earlier that day asking me if I wanted to get lunch. But it wasn't speaking now.

It was crying.

I stopped dead, one foot out in front of me like a toy soldier whose clockwork's run down.

I tried to turn around but couldn't. A nasty little voice in the back of my head whispered: *Girls' bathroom*, and then *attention*, and finally *target*.

On any other day I would have fled. Fear sat in my heart like a clot. I was already counting the steps to the exit (22) and calculating the time before I could raid my locker for my emergency Hobnob stash and cram them into my face in a blizzard of gnashing teeth and flying oats (210 seconds—I'm not athletic). But like I said, today wasn't an ordinary day. Today was a brave day.

My shoulders went up and I turned on my heel. I recognised three of them: Bianca Edwards, Stephanie Grover, and Tamsin Chow, looking at me like I was a giant, walking, white-headed zit, ready to burst. Behind them was the door to the girls' bathroom, and beyond that . . .

Sometimes being brave is just working out which thing you're more afraid of.

Eyes fixed firmly on my feet, I marched past them. Toy soldier; simple mechanics, left-right-left; the frantic ticking of my heart like clockwork. You can do this.

"Oy!" Bianca shouted. "Where do you think you're . . . ?"

She never finished. I crossed the threshold. I was in the girls' bathroom.

Oh Christ.

To my left, a row of stalls. In front of me, a row of sinks and mirrors, and between me and them, a little semicircle of girls' black polyester-jacketed backs. One of them muttered something and there was more laughter. Another had a phone in her hand. Was she filming? The key in my clockwork heart gave another twist.

"Uh . . ." Had that syllable seriously come out of my mouth? "Excuse me?"

Exactly one of the girls turned around at my meek intervention, the girl with the phone. It was Tanya Berkeley, her neat black fringe like a lacquer photo frame around her face.

"Oh my god, get out!" she shrieked.

Suddenly I felt manic, high and getting rapidly higher like an untethered balloon. My mouth was out of control, my jaw chattering, up and down in a nutcracker jabber, but I couldn't find any words. Tanya was looking me right in the eyes. I watched as her expression changed from outraged to . . . frightened?

"YOU GET OUT!" I finally found my voice.

And then—unbelievably—the sea was parting. They were getting out.

They were fleeing from me.

As they pressed themselves against the walls to pass me, I saw my own fear reflected in them, multiplied a hundredfold. Their eyes fixed on my face as if they couldn't tear them away. I felt the heat rise in my cheeks and forehead. No mistake; they were terrified.

As the crowd cleared, I saw a thatch of blonde hair, shoulders hunched over the sink. The sound of fleeing footsteps gave way to the rush of running water and the hissing rasp of a scrubbing brush. She was moving her arms very fast and hard. Water was flicking out past both sides of her; some of it was red.

"Uh . . . excuse me," I said, suddenly realising that I had no plan.

No answer.

"Ingrid?" I hazarded.

"Get out." She didn't turn around.

"Are you sure? You don't seem . . ." I groped for a word, but all I could come up with in the moment was, ". . . comfortable."

"Well, shit." She sounded like she was gritting her teeth. "Arthurson was right—you really are a genius."

I stepped up to her shoulder. In the mirror, her face was puffy with crying, and little beads of bloody water flecked her forehead. Her fingerless gloves were balled up next to the taps. Under the foaming waterfall in the sink, the back of her left hand was a mess of red raw skin, and still she sanded it with the scrubbing brush.

"Fuck," she muttered under her breath. "Look, I'm sorry I stood you up, okay? I'm having a bit of a moment. Could you just leave me the fuck alone?"

"Is there anything I can do?" I had no idea where to start. "Anything I can get?"

"Out. You can get out."

"Sure . . ." On fire with shame and humiliation, I turned to go. Whatever she needed I didn't have it. "Only . . ." I hesitated, teetering on the back of one heel. Oh screw it.

"Twenty-three, seventeen, eleven, fifty-four."

She didn't stop scrubbing, but she did switch hands.

"What?"

"'Don't let me down,' you said." My hands were balled into fists. My cheeks were burning. "And I . . . I kinda feel like I would be . . . if I left."

She looked back over her shoulder at me. Her hands continued on autopilot. I saw the twitch in her cheek every time the bristles scraped over the raw skin.

"We met less than an hour and a half ago," she said.

"So?"

"So why do you care?"

"I . . . I just . . ."

I just do, I was about to say. But I was suddenly starkly aware of how vulnerable she was, standing in front of that sink, with the back of her hand hanging off, and if I wanted to stand with her, the least I owed her was to be honest, no matter how loserly I sounded.

"You called me your friend," I said. The rush of the taps sounded very loud in the pause that followed. "And I know that I'm not, not yet. But . . . I'd like to be."

She didn't reply, but her shoulders relaxed slightly, which I took to be a good sign, and then started to heave as she began to sob, which I took as a bad one. I stepped back to her side.

"What is it?" I asked quietly. "What are you afraid of?"

She threw me a startled look, her eyes distended by tears.

"What's going through your head?" I pressed. "Right now?"

Get talking, I thought.

She was breathing in sharp, shallow little gasps.

"Right now? I'm thinking I heard four kids sneezing on the way in here. And there were two absent from my class when they took the register. There's a bug going around, one bad enough to keep you at home, and if I don't wash my hands really, really thoroughly, then I'll miss a bit. And if I miss a bit, I could get sick and it'll be my fault. And if I get sick, I can't come to school, and I have to come to school. I really, really can't be at home during the day. So I really, really have to make sure I clean under my fucking *nails*."

The last word was a barely audible snot-choked growl. Her hands were speeding up again. Instinctively, I reached out to them, but there was nowhere to touch that wasn't bloody.

My fault, she'd said. Something inside me clenched.

"Four point five seconds," I said.

"What?"

"You're completely covering your hand every four and a half seconds."

"What?"

"Four and a half seconds, times two hands is nine seconds."

My voice was getting louder, speeding up. "You've been in here for forty minutes; that's two thousand four hundred seconds: enough time for two hundred and sixty-six complete washes. Your hands are clean . . ."

Her face was tense with misery. I knew that look. She was looking at the bars of a cage closing on her.

"Trust me," I urged her. "If you can't trust yourself, just now, just for this moment, trust me."

Nothing. Just the rush and splash of her hands in the sink. Then they started to slow, and slowed further, until at last the scrubbing brush plinked off the porcelain as she dropped it. I reached across, my heart hammering wildly in my chest, and turned off the tap.

She dipped into her pocket, pulled out a tiny bottle of iodine and a cotton wool pad, and dabbed at the grazes on her hands. Small, efficient, practiced motions. She didn't even wince, but she was trembling, a high-frequency vibration running through her; her own personal earthquake.

She grabbed her gloves, swabbed the sink clean of her blood with a paper towel, and without a word, turned and walked quickly out of the bathroom.

The sun was painfully bright when I pushed through the fire-escape door. I knew all the ways in and out of that school, which ones were alarmed and which weren't; my little rabbit runs. The bell had gone seven minutes earlier, but I needed to talk to Bel and I knew where she'd be. I put my head down against the October wind, and made for the school wall.

"Where the hell were you?" Bel demanded when I reached our secret spot under the oaks. "I was scared sick something had happened to you." A furrow of crushed red-brown leaves was squelched into the mud where she'd been pacing. The knuckles of her right hand were puffy, and she'd even managed to crack some of the bark off the nearest tree.

It's Bel's one fear: something happening to me.

"Something did," I said. I was still out of breath from it.

"What?"

"I made a friend."

It was another week before a paper aeroplane came sailing through the classroom window at registration. Written on it was a page number and a sequence of word references; it was signed off:

23-17-11-54

I x

I met her on the back steps of the changing rooms as she'd asked. It was one of a hundred out-of-sight places in a school as old as ours. It was cold and grey, but the rain was as light as sea spray. Her gloves were back on, and she was staring fixedly out across the city.

"My dad," she said. They were the first words out of her mouth, no hello, no nothing, just picking our last conversation up where it had left off. "I'm afraid of my dad."

"Yeah," I said, sitting down next to her. "I know how that feels."

NOW

"How much do you actually know about your father?"

The ventilator hisses and beeps, carrying the woman attached to it from breath to breath, from heartbeat to heartbeat, stepping-stones over a pit I don't want to think about.

My gaze follows the plastic tube to the mask fitted over Mum's face, her eyelashes still thick with that morning's mascara where they press to her cheek; the lank skeins of her hair spread over the pillow; the wires and pipes that sprout from her, carrying air and water and plasma in, urine and data out. It's hard to see where she ends and the machines begin. With every breath, there's a hitch as the ventilator resets: a split second when it feels like the machine has stopped, like all time has stopped—

*A CCTV clock freezes for two full heartbeats—10:58:17:00—*and then it beeps and hisses again, returning her to the same suspended animation. Nothing's decided, everything's still poised: a poker hand waiting for the final card to turn, an equation with an unbound variable.

"Peter?" Frankie says. Her tone suggests she's been saying my name for a while.

"Sorry?"

"I asked, how much do you actually know about your father?"

"Know?" I have no memories; only impressions, glimpses from dreams and imaginings; a faceless man in a dusty black suit with meaty, thick-palmed hands.

"Almost nothing."

"Louise didn't tell you anything about him?"

I barely hear her. Frankie had gotten a call to say Mum was stable but unconscious. She told me they didn't know when she'd wake up. Her fractional hesitation before saying "when" made me feel like I was teetering on the edge of a cliff.

We rode in a lift up to this small room, an office repurposed to a surgery. I can see the grooves in the lino where the desk was dragged out. They'd anointed my hands with alcohol gel and wrapped me in green sterile cloth as if this were some kind of sacrificial ceremony. We put on green surgical masks and then they'd brought me here to face my work.

"You sprinted out of that room like you'd seen a ghost. Louise was right behind you."

I led her to this. I'm the reason. I'm the bait. I'm the rabbit, the rabbit who ran, and she followed; the boy who cried . . . Jesus, Peter, get a grip, just shut up, shut up, shut—

"Up," I say aloud.

"Up?" Rita says. She's standing next to me, her plastic-gloved hands folded in front of her. Frankie's on my other side. And suddenly Rita seems so neutral, all her acidity drained. It would be easy to talk to her, as easy as talking to myself.

"It was something Mum used to say about her marriage, she said most relationships have ups and downs, but hers and Dad's had only ups. They met up, hooked up, got her knocked up, then split up. It was one massive fuck-up."

Rita's eyes crinkle above her surgical mask.

"Yes," she says. "She said that to me too."

"Did you ever think it was strange, Peter," Frankie asks from my left, "that there were no photos of him in your house?"

The pressure of their almost-touch on my shoulders is making it hard to think.

"No."

"No? Your mum kept a photo of Franklin Roosevelt in the kitchen, but none of the father of her children anywhere?"

I flinch. Another scrap of knowledge, casually tossed off. I picture Mum's rueful smile every time Bel or I asked about our father. Look No. 66, a complicated one—*I don't want to talk about it. It was a long time ago. It was no big deal.* I remember the tremble in her fingers, her hands betraying the lie.

"He scared her." I look down at her and my throat tightens. Christ, she's just so still. "And now I know why."

From the corner of my eye I see a look pass between them. Rita says, "He scares us too."

I look up sharply.

"Your father's a thug, Peter, but that's not all he is. Louise met him at Cambridge in the mid-nineties, soon after they got their doctorates. I'm not sure I can believe it, but their classmates say he was even as brilliant as her."

"Dad's . . . a scientist?" I don't know why I'm surprised, it's not like an IQ anywhere sub-160 would have been good enough for Mum.

"A neurobiologist, like Louise." Rita steeples her fingers. "Peter, your mother's work for the past seventeen years, work that has . . . seismic economic and strategic implications, was work your parents began *together.* They argued fiercely over which direction it should take and their relationship frayed under the strain. Then, on the twenty-fourth of February 1998, exactly one month after you and your sister were born, he disappeared."

Her gloved hands mime a puff of magician's smoke.

"Went to his lab and didn't come home, vanished into thin air, never to be heard from again, completely off grid and out of sight." She looked up at Frankie and nodded fractionally. "Until last night."

"Last night?"

Frankie clears her throat and takes up the tale.

"Well . . . three-fifty-three this morning, actually. A virus was uploaded remotely to your mother's server at Imperial; it erased everything. We called Louise, but there was nothing she could do."

My mind flashes back to the larder this morning, my mother

wearily pulling shards of pottery from my gums. The handset lying on the table. That's why she was awake.

"And then," Frankie continues, "at ten-fifty-seven at the Natural History Museum—"

Blood-soaked blue silk. A knife flashing under the museum lights.

"Are you sure?" I ask quietly. "Are you sure it's him?"

"Without footage, we can't be certain," she admits. "But by all accounts, he was a vicious bastard. Not just violent, but egomaniacal, and for all his intellect, petty. Erasing your mother's work, and then gutting her right at the moment of her greatest professional triumph? It fits our profile of him." She shakes her head in disgust and mutters, almost to herself, "No recent photos, either; four hundred thousand CCTV cameras in this city, and we might as well be blind."

Dad. Ernest Blankman. Neither name feels like it fits. The idea of him appalls me, it always has. I've always been able to name my fears; I've made a science out of analysing them. All except one. All except him.

"He had to have heard she'd made a breakthrough." Rita lays out the case like a deck of cards. "One that had eluded him. If, as we suspect, he's spent the last decade and a half pursuing the same research, that would have enraged him. So, he decided to put her out of the picture, freeing him up to pursue the work himself. That's why Frankie and I get to hunt him in office hours."

"Office hours?" I don't follow. Rita grimaces behind her mask.

"Loyalty and payback are all very well, Peter, but they're personal motives, not institutional ones, and our firm usually wouldn't indulge them. A scientist as brilliant as Louise Blankman, though?" There's an awed note in her voice. "One with no institutional ties, no link to his country, no leverage. Nothing to stop him from selling their research to the highest bidder? That's got the top floor shitting itself, and with good reason."

"What research? What was Mum working on?"

Rita doesn't answer.

Frankie gives a half-embarrassed shrug.

"Sorry, Peter. We're spies. You have to expect us to have a few secrets."

I don't know where to look, so I stare at the human wreckage my father turned my mother into. Rita's and Frankie's faces are turned to mine, only their eyes visible behind their masks, and close enough that I can feel their breath through the fabric.

Christ, it's so hard to think, but there's something not quite . . .

"Erased her data," I mutter.

"Sorry?"

I look up at Rita. "You said Mum was close to concluding whatever she was researching? And Dad was researching it too. She'd had a breakthrough. He hadn't. So why would he wipe her data? Wouldn't he want to steal it?"

They exchange a look, a combination of admiration and chagrin, like this is something they were hoping I wouldn't pick up on.

"You're right," Frankie concedes reluctantly. "The virus erased Louise's research, but Ernest wouldn't have done that if he didn't already have access to it."

"How would he have gotten access?"

"Well, we aren't sure, but . . ."

"Yes?"

Her eyes are all sympathy. "Anabel."

I flinch like a prey animal. It feels like they've accused *me*.

"We don't believe it was malicious," Rita rushes to assure me. "It wasn't her fault. It could just as easily have been you. A stranger runs into you on the street one day. You can't explain why, but you have an affinity with him. It starts slowly, but over time you see more of each other. You don't tell anyone; normally you're such a close-knit family, but it feels good to have something no one else knows about. One night, over pizza maybe, or Chinese food, or something else greasy and fun your mum doesn't let you have, he tells you who he is. He lets you know his side of the story. Turns out your mother might have . . . exaggerated a few things. He doesn't need to ask you not to tell your family; you know they'd go spare if they knew you were seeing him. But he's so much fun, so much more chilled out than your uptight mum, and he listens to your problems too, in a way that makes them seem smaller, more manageable. It's impossible to reconcile him with the ogre you've been told about. So you don't.

"It's months before he even asks you about your mother's work, and months more before he first asks you for something from her lab. Something small, some scrap of research that was really his anyway, that he'd left behind when he left. And you don't want to disappoint him, and he somehow manages to ask you on a day when she's pissed you off. And when you get right down to it, you realise you're angry with her, because you're starting to love this man, really love him, and you could have had this years ago if only she'd told you the truth. So you do it. You steal for him, just to stick it to her . . ." Rita shrugs. "It's a recognised technique. He could have everything Louise ever worked on out of Anabel in less than a year."

She falls silent. Both she and Frankie watch me, tensed, as if I might puke or punch them or put a Pete-shaped hole in the wall. And in a horrible instant, I realise why.

"That's why you're so worried about Bel."

"Yes."

"Because she's seen him, spoken to him, knows what he looks like, maybe she's even been to his house."

"Yes." Her voice is dreadfully even.

"And he's been staying, what did you call it? 'Off grid.'" I think of the museum hallway, how the camera footage cut out, just before the attacker showed his face.

Loyalty and payback may be personal motives, but tying up loose ends is just good business.

Fuck fuck *fuck*. Again, I think of the blank museum footage, the way the clock stopped at seventeen, twenty, and thirteen seconds past the minute: 17, 20, 13. I turn the numbers over in my mind, over and over. I want to help. Help Mum, help Bel; be of some goddamn use to somebody. I work out the positions of letters in the alphabet and come up with QTM. Meaningless. I want to scream with frustration.

I'm cold and I hug myself; my bandaged hand throbs under my arm. Frankie puts a consoling hand on my shoulder, and it feels quite natural to turn to face her.

"We have to find Anabel before he does. You're her brother; no one knows her better. Is there anywhere she'd go? We've got people watching your house, but is there anywhere else? A place she'd go if she was scared?"

That kindness, that warmth that Frankie seems to emit; it feels like the heat from a steaming bath after hours battling against a shrieking November wind, and I can feel myself swooning into it.

My eyes fill with tears and for a second Mum's hospital bed blurs into two: I see Bel's prone form next to Mum's, wheezing with the same dreadful monotony. My dusty-suited, faceless father hovers between them, his hands vivid and bruised and bloodstained.

Fuck you, I think. *I will protect her from you.* All I have to do is speak.

Red brick and falling leaves flash through my head. I was scared sick . . . If Bel went anywhere, she'd have gone there. I part my lips to tell them . . .

But . . .

Something Rita said niggles me, like a thorn in the soft flesh of my brain.

"*You're starting to love this man, really love him.*"

But I wouldn't. I couldn't, and neither could Bel; it would be an unthinkable betrayal. However pissed off she was at Mum, whatever he told her, Bel would never help Dad. She'd never give him anything but a black eye if she had the opportunity. Their story doesn't make sense.

But why would they lie?

"*We're spies. You have to expect us to have a few secrets.*"

Oh god, I don't know, I don't know. Maybe they are telling the truth. Once again I'm stumbling around in the dark.

My mind flits back again to the blacked-out museum footage. Those pauses at 17, 20, and 13 seconds exactly past the minute. Dead on the second—the one microsecond in a thousand where the digits read 00, three times in a row.

Randomness is hard to fake, but that clock wasn't even trying. *17-20-13.*

Randomness is hard to fake. *17-20-13.*

Static around the signal.

There is a pattern. There is, there is, there is.

17-20—Come on, Pete. I catch myself before I say it aloud.

"Peter." Rita takes a half step towards me. "Are you all right?"

I try to smile, to reassure them. I look from one set of green polyester-framed eyes to another. Their masked faces suddenly look cold. They stand one on either side, comrades, eager to keep my family safe from my murderous father, when what this really is, is . . . an interrogation.

They're interrogating me about Bel. They've asked me thirteen questions about her since I got here.

There will always be patterns, Peter . . . It's our job to obscure them.

Randomness is hard to fake.

"Peter?" Frankie asks me again. "Tell us. Where would Bel go if worst came to worst?"

"*If worst comes to worst.*" Bel said those exact words to me earlier, at the museum. I remember her, nodding at the CCTV cameras.

The cameras. The pauses. *17, 20, 13.* Could the message be from Bel? I remember sitting in the back of Mum's Volvo, swapping Caesar shift ciphers with Bel on long, sick-making car journeys.

To break a Caesar shift, you only need to know the key word, and I always knew Bel well enough to guess. But what if it's not a word? What if it's a number? What number would she use?

Rita's staring at me intently. I still haven't spoken. Everything has a number. Everything's connected. Mum's respirator beeps and resets. She was attacked by Dad. Dad disappeared one month after Bel's and my . . .

Bel's and my birthday: 24-01-98

Desperately, I try to think. My fingers twitch for a pen, but I can't show any sign I'm trying to work it out. I try to visualise the code in my head: 24, 1, 9 and 8, and after that every other number from 1 to 26, with the alphabet right beneath it.

24 1 9 8 2 3 4 5 6 7 10 11 12 13 14 15 16 17 18 19 20 21 22 23 25 26
A B C D E F G H I J K L M N O P Q R S T U V W X Y Z

17-20-13

R-U-N

My mouth runs dry. *If worst comes to worst.* In my mind I see my sister in the dinosaur hall, talking and laughing with Rita. Was Bel sounding her out, working out who she was?

"I . . . I . . ." I look from one green-masked face to the other and back to Mum and make a decision.

"There's nowhere," I lie. "Bel doesn't get scared."

Frankie stares at me for a second. She peers into my eyes, as though she'll find what she wants printed on my retinas. She doesn't believe me. I begin to turn, to obey my sister, to run. I see their surgical gloved fingers twitch towards me, and I lash out, slapping and punching. Frankie fends me off with practised ease. Her hand strays close to my mouth, and I try to bite it.

Rita says, "We're out of time."

Something black is pulled tight across my head, cutting out the light. I struggle and spit and gag on acid. Hands are gripping my wrists; my ankles are lifted off the floor.

"I don't get it," I hear Frankie say, her voice muffled by the fabric. "I really don't."

A searing electric pain sparks into my side. I jerk and convulse. "Iiiiii reaallllllly dooooooooooooooooooon—"

The world is drowned in nothingness.

RECURSION: 2 YEARS, 9 MONTHS AGO

Ingrid's brow furrowed. You could almost see her rearranging the ideas in her head, like repacking a suitcase, trying to make room for what I'd just told her. I waited anxiously, shifting my weight from foot to foot.

"I don't get it," she said, "I really don't."

Which was hardly surprising. I was explaining myself badly, talking too fast because I was nervous, because the only girl I'd ever thought about *like that* was looking up at me, lying sideways across the bed where most of my thinking about her *like that* had been done, her blonde head nestled against my Nightcrawler duvet cover. I wished I'd had a chance to change the sheets; I wished I'd at least had a chance to empty the *thinking like that* tissues out of the bin under the desk. I really, really hoped she didn't want to throw anything away.

Four hours earlier I'd seen her walking towards the school gate with stiff, reluctant steps, gripping the straps of her rucksack like an escape parachute. It had seemed like the most natural thing in the world to ask: "Hey, do you want to come round tonight, like . . . for dinner or something?" After all, if she didn't have a family who understood, maybe she could share mine.

Only, that night my family wasn't in an understanding mood.

Bel had picked up a two-week suspension for . . . something involving frogs. I didn't know the details, because the minute she'd come through the door Mum totally lost it, dragging Bel into the kitchen and shrieking like a steam whistle about her "responsibilities." Ingrid lined four peas up on the upper right quadrant of her plate in a prearranged distress signal, but the way her fingers twitched towards her gloves already had me on my feet. I abandoned my chicken Kiev to slowly bleed out its garlic butter on the porcelain, and I pulled Agent Blonde Calculating Machine away from the crossfire.

The only place in the house out of shouting range turned out to be my room: top floor under the eaves. I kicked yesterday's pants under the bed while she pretended not to notice. (They got caught on my toes. It took three goes. She pretended very well.)

And so to my collection of X-Men posters ("What, no Jean Grey?" "The idea of telepathy always freaked me out." "Oh . . . okay."), and my Legends of Maths posters ("What, no Newton?" "Newton was a dick." "I am so glad you said that, Peter. I'm not sure we could have stayed friends otherwise."), and then—inevitably—to the blue hardback notebooks stacked on the corner of the desk. Their very neatness screamed their significance in a room that was otherwise a bomb site ("Study in entropy, Pete? Or just a slob?" "Who can say, Ingrid? Who can say?").

"Peter," she'd asked, turning the pages and tucking a stray lock of that metamorphic blonde hair behind her ear, "what does 'ARIA' stand for?"

I stared at her, dumbstruck. Her casual question had flipped my five-year private obsession into the air like a ten pence piece.

Heads: she looks at you like you're crazy.

Tails: she says it might actually work.

Yeah, the voice inside me bit back, *like the odds are that evenly split.*

I started to mumble something evasive and nonspecific, but then I thought: *She's your friend, Pete, your friend, and she's basically a maths ninja . . . She might even be able to help.*

I swallowed hard and decided to go for it.

"You have obsessive-compulsive disorder, right?" I asked her. She knew I knew, but in the six months we'd known each other, she'd never come out and said it. She looked at me warily and nodded.

"They give you pills for that?"

The muscles in her jaw tightened. For a second I worried I'd pushed too hard, but then she said, "Ana."

Her lip quirked ruefully as she said it. It was short for Anafranil. I'd been on Ana too for a while.

"Laura for me." I pulled a foil-covered blister of lorazepam out of my pocket.

"And how's Laura?" she asked, mollified. It was a familiar kind of trade. You show me your biochemical crutch and I'll show you mine.

"Like a sandbag to the temple, but when I need her, better than the alternative. How's Ana?"

"She messes with your head." She smiled sourly. "But sometimes she takes the edge off. What's your point?"

"My point is that thoughts are chemistry." I tossed the lorazepam onto the bed beside her. "And chemistry is physics—electrons swapping around—and physics, at least where it counts, is mathematics.

It doesn't matter *what* we're made of—carbon and hydrogen, protons and electrons—so are bananas, so are bloody oil wells. What matters is *how much* of it there is, and *how* it's arranged. What matters is the pattern, and patterns are the stuff of maths."

I sucked in a breath and held it for a second in a silent prayer—*please don't tell me I'm crazy*—then let it go.

"There's an equation that's you, Ingrid, and an equation that's me. I'm going to find it, and I'm going to prove it."

She watched me for the longest time.

Please.

"Okay," she said. "Where do we start?"

We. My grin made my face ache. I opened the notebook, flicked to the second page, and passed it to her.

"Here." On the page were scrawled some simple sums.

$0 + 1 = 1$

$1 + 1 = 2$
$2 + 1 = 3$
$3 + 2 = 5$
$5 + 3 = 8 \ldots$

And below it, the general formula for the series:

$$n = (n - 1) + (n - 2)$$

Ingrid frowned.

"The Fibonacci sequence?"

"Yup, every term the sum of the two before it. It's the simplest recursive formula I know."

"So?"

"So"—we were getting to it now, and my heart felt like an old-fashioned alarm clock ringing in my chest—"think about it. What are you, Ingrid?"

"A . . . girl?"

"No."

"No? I really am, Pete, but if you're looking for me to prove it to you, wow, you are heading in the wrong direction."

"I—I—I . . ." Great. Not only was I severely tongue-tied, but the way she rolled over, blew the hair off her forehead, and smirked at me made my blood abandon my brain for a dramatic surge southwards. I breathed out hard.

"I mean," I said, speaking slowly so as not to stammer, "what makes you different than anyone else?"

She frowned, stretched out her arms, and propped her chin on steepled fingers.

"Okay," she said, "I'll play." She thought for a moment. "My memories, I guess," she said. "They're the only thing I have that no one else does."

"Exactly!" I resisted the urge to air-punch. "And what are memories? They're experiences that changed you, and then you remember them and they change you again; the sound of your mother's heartbeat, the first time you eat a strawberry, the first time you step on a Lego and fall down swearing . . ." I groped for more examples.

"The first time you have sex?" Ingrid offered.

I flushed. "You did that just to see what colour I went, didn't you?"

"Or maybe I got tired of waiting for you to find a mathematically perfect way to ask me out."

I blushed harder. "The point is, your memories drive your choices, pushing you into your next experience, which becomes your next memory: a self-extending set, always adding itself to its endlessly recurring past, always the sum of those before it, just like . . ."

But she didn't need me to lead her there. Her eyes were already on the formula, her mouth open in a little O.

"So, if the essence of us is memory, and the essence of memory is recursion, then what if recursion is the essence of *us*?"

"A-R-I-A." I drew the letters in the air as I said them. "Autonomous Recursive Intuition Algorithms. Songs that sing and hear themselves. I just need to listen hard enough to work out the notes."

I became aware of my voice, desperate, filling the room. I shoved my hands into my pockets, suddenly shy.

"And then I'll know," I said.

"Know what?"

"What I'm so afraid of."

She looked at me for a long time, her brown eyes wide.

No, don't say it, don't . . .

"Pete, it's impossible."

I felt myself shrink. No.

"I mean, it's a lovely idea, but even if you're right, the complexity of the calculation, the number of variables, it's . . . it's unrealistic."

"It's science."

"Sounds more like science fiction."

"Doesn't everything?" I pleaded. "We live in a world where we can drag hundred-tonne trains along at hundreds of miles an hour by harnessing the motion of electrons that are *ten million* times too small to see. We can blast people into space and calculate their return trajectory precisely enough to get them back not crushed, not asphyxiated, and not fried to a crisp. We can steal memories from rats by giving them a chemical *while* they're remembering them. You think ARIA's impossible, Ingrid?" I held her gaze. "With all the insane things that happen in the world every day, how could you possibly know?"

I crashed down beside her on the bed, suddenly very tired, and closed my eyes. I thought about all the times I'd hugged myself on that Nightcrawler duvet, unable to stop shaking; all the times I'd shoved myself full of food and waited waited waited to vomit it up, my stomach an overripe fruit ready to burst; the plastic taste of all the capsules of Laura I'd ever swallowed, and the way it slowed my thoughts like a muddy river bottom; all the times I'd seen people chatting, heard them laughing, and held myself back, stood away, scared of having an attack around them, scared of their judgment, their contempt, until my world had shrunk and shrunk until it was basically just me, Mum, and Bel . . .

. . . and now Ingrid.

"Undeniable, mathematical proof of who we are." Ingrid almost sounded like she wanted it more than I did.

Please, I thought, just let me have this. Please believe with me.

I felt a hand, the palm clad in scratchy wool, creep into mine.

"Pete," she said quietly. I didn't open my eyes.

"Yeah?"

"If . . . if you ever were looking for a mathematically perfect way to ask me out, you know, for real . . ."

I took the shallowest breath I could and held it so she wouldn't notice.

"I think you just found it."

NOW

I vomit into darkness.

My stomach muscles buck, and bile burns up my throat. The vomit spatters into a fabric barrier close to my face, flecking me. I . . . where . . . what?

I can't see, I can't breathe. I gulp for oxygen and suck fabric and chunks of acid puke back into my mouth. I want to scream, but I can't let it out.

I can't move. Christ, help me, I can't move. Something vicious bites into my wrists as I struggle. I huff sick, astringent like glue fumes, and blow the cloth as far from my face as I can. But there's not enough air. Not enough. Not . . . enough.

Where am I?

"Shit." The voice is female, hard and familiar. And then I remember. Rita. 57. I'm stretched out on my back, swaying in time to footsteps. I think I'm being carried on some sort of stretcher.

"He's having some kind of seizure. He's going to suffocate."

Fingers snare the fabric, peel it up above my mouth.

Fresh air chills my vomit-caked chin, and I suck it down greedily; one frantic breath, two, and then finally I scream.

Why? I want to ask. Why? But my jaw muscles don't work anymore. And going around and around in my head, over and over and over, are numbers:

172013172013172013172013172013172013172013172013
RUNRUNRUNRUNRUNRUNRUNRUN

A door slams open near my head. The swaying stops. Cold

metal is pressed against my wrists and my bindings are cut free. I'm carried by my wrists and ankles. Rough hands shove me, making me gasp, pressing me to a bed. A blistering cold frame.

"He tried to bite me. Secure him."

Four hiss-zipping noises. My wrists are held again. Help me. Help me.

17-20-13. My legs try to move, but my ankles are bound too.

Oh god oh god oh god oh god. Breathe, just focus on breathing; a respirator beeping, in and out, in and out, every two point five seconds. Mum.

They have Mum.

I remember Rita telling me, *Sometimes the obvious answer's the right one*, and then, only a handful of minutes later, on patterns, *It's our job to obscure them, to make sure they're as complex and confusing as possible.*

I trusted her. I trusted her when she as good as told me she was lying to me.

They have Mum, but she's alive. She survived, Pete. You can too.

My breathing calms just enough that I can make out voices.

"Get the damn machine in here."

Stricken as I am, I can hear the shock in the silence that follows.

"Do tell me," Rita adds acidly, "if you have a better idea."

Another second's hesitation. Then the squeak of rubber soles on a concrete floor as Frankie leaves the room. The door slams.

Nothing. Silence and panting breath and blindness. A suspended moment. The door bangs open again and I jump. Shoes on concrete, different shoes. The whir of runners as something heavy is wheeled in.

"I'll prep him." Rita's voice, solid and expressionless as rock.

Air burns in my retch-raw throat. I twitch and jerk at every sound.

A scrape of metal on concrete. The click-clack of scissors below my chin and my chest is exposed to the air. Goosebumps pucker on my skin. Something sticky is pressed down hard on my chest. Fingers, startlingly warm, creep up under my hood and press more sticky pads to my temples. I want to struggle, but I can't. A high-frequency jolt shakes my skeleton, and I scream with the shock of it.

"Dose one," Rita says.

"Dose wha—"

FUCKFUCKFUCKFUCKFUCKFUCKFUCKFUCKFUCK

I can't think. Everything seizes up. White noise. Searing, sickening pain. Black ink blooms in front of my eyes.

"Dose two."

Whirring pain, like a drill boring into my temple, spitting fragments of skull, a red spiral of brain curling round the bit. I can feel myself dying.

"Hold."

My lips peel back from my teeth with a horrid, adhesive sensation, and I start to keen.

"Dose three."

A sound like a whip crack inside my head, and I'm sagging, plastic ties buried in the flesh of my wrists. I can feel bruises blooming along my spine where I must have slammed back through the thin pad onto the bed frame, but I don't remember doing that. I must have blacked out.

"Okay, let's try him." Rita's voice is muzzy in my ears.

My head lolls back. I am spent, the same exhaustion I feel at the end of a full-on five-alarm panic attack. It's almost a relief. My endocrine system has left it all out on the field.

Shreds of light creep in at the bottom of my hood. The fabric is being rolled up over my face. Fingertips check my pulse. The light dazzles me and, through watering eyes, I see a hand retracting from the side of my neck, a hand with white fingers but a black palm.

No, not a black palm, a gloved one.

The hands are clad in fingerless gloves.

She's standing over me. Her face is tense, her blonde hair

scraped back behind her head. Her eyes lock onto mine. Seven long seconds pass.

"I . . . In . . . Ingrid? No! NO! Don't you d-d-dare f-f-f-fucking hurt-t-t-t her . . ."

The syllables come out like Morse code, but then I tail off, because she's not zip-tied to a bed. Ingrid doesn't look like a prisoner.

"Wh-wh-why? What? W-wh-what are you . . . What are you d-d-d . . . ?"

"What are you d-d-d . . . ?"

I hear another voice echoing my words, flat and emotionless as a speaking clock. I see Ingrid's lips moving in perfect time, matching mine, dot for dot, dash for dash.

I fall silent. My throat is full of broken glass.

"How are you doing that?"

And even though I'm only thinking the question, it's *Ingrid* who voices it, in that flat, sterile voice. I watch the piercing in her lip bob as she shapes the words.

Her eyes flicker up over my head, and only then do I remember Rita's still behind me.

"I'm tuned in," Ingrid says.

Tuned in? I think. Tuned in to what? What the fuck, Ingrid?

"My name's not Ingrid, Pete," she says. "It's Ana."

She's looking at me, scrutinising my face, her eyes flickering back and forth as though she's reading.

"Peter," Rita asks, still behind me, "where's your sister?"

But I can't take my eyes off Ingrid's face.

Why is she doing this? Ingrid, no, I think. Please, we're friends.

"We are friends, Pete," she confirms. "You're my best friend and I'm sorry I had to lie to you." Now her voice throbs with sincerity. "I'll explain everything, I promise, but you have to tell us where Bel is."

Shit. She is. She actually is. She's actually reading my mind. How? Ingrid? Please get me out of here. Help me. Help Mum. She gave you chicken Kiev. Ingrid. Ingrid. Christ!

She looks up at Rita and shakes her head.

"You pushed him too hard. He's confused. I can't get him to focus on the question long enough to pick up an answer."

Rita leans in close, studying me. I feel her breath washing over my neck. It smells of pepper.

"Maybe I'll dose him again," she ponders.

"No!" For a second I think Ingrid's voicing my thoughts again, but she's halfway towards Rita, hand extended in protest. "No, there's no need, just let me . . . just let me talk to him."

My head feels like soft clay. Through my blurred vision, Ingrid's blonde hair gives her a halo.

This can't be happening. This is impossible.

"With all the insane things that happen every day"—the familiar brown eyes are calm—"how can you possibly know that? Come on, Pete, you're a mathematician, a scientist. This is the scientific method; adjust your theory to fit the evidence. I'm here. I'm evidence. So adjust."

I grit my teeth. Then how? Explain it to me. How are you reading my mind?

"Do you know how many distinct sounds there are in English?"

I do not.

"Forty-four. Do you know how many muscles are involved in your facial expressions? Forty-three. Add in micro-gestures and your body is more than capable of broadcasting every thought in your head without you speaking, Petey—especially yours—and I'm . . . I'm just particularly well calibrated to receive them. Well, *reflect* them, really."

Reflect. A memory wells up through the exhausted mess of my brain. Mum, years ago, hands bridged over her potato waffles, trying to explain something she'd been looking into at work.

"M-m-mirror?" is all I manage to get out, but Ingrid understands—of course she does.

"That's right, Petey." She nods. "Mirror neurons. The same

thing that lets you intuit when your sister is having a bad day, or when your mum needs a drink. Everyone has them. I just have more—two hundred percent more. I'm a mirror. What you feel, I feel. What you think, I think."

Suddenly, absurdly, all I can think of is the sticky tissues in the bin under my desk and me thinking of the tissues then and me thinking about me thinking about the tissues now. And then I remember a maths textbook open on the acknowledgments and how proud, how outstandingly *elated* I was to have a friend who got me, who was so on my wavelength that it seemed—and I want to laugh and scream and claw my face off—it seemed like she could read my mind.

No Jean Grey?

The idea of telepathy always freaked me out.

My face is hot and tears of humiliation spill down my cheeks.

"Yeah," she says, and there's a catch at the back of her throat, as if she wants to cry too. "Sorry."

I turn my head away and the suction pads on my temple pull at burned skin.

"T-t-t-tort . . ." I begin

"This isn't torture, Peter," Rita almost tuts.

It fucking feels like it is.

Ingrid looks as stricken as I feel. "I know it hurts," she says. "And I'm sorry. I know it hurts so much. But we have to. You were panicking and we can't communicate with you when you panic. Your pulse was at 220; you were spiralling. We needed to shock you to interrupt that, to the point where I could read you. Do you understand? I'm sorry, but it was the only way. We have to find Bel."

Every word throbs with sincerity. Or maybe that's imagined. I look up at her with eyes that feel heavy, and think one word.

Why?

Ingrid swallows hard before she answers. Her eyes flick to Rita behind me. "You know why."

And I do know: a faceless man in a dusty black suit with meaty, thick-palmed hands; that expression of horrified recognition on Mum's face in the museum CCTV footage.

Wolf.

My dad, I'm afraid of my dad.

"I know, Petey, I am too."

I look down. Red-raw bracelets encircle my wrists where I've pulled against the zip ties. My jaw feels loose and a long string of drool descends from my bottom lip like a spider on a web.

Watch, listen, think. Look at what they've done to me. *We had to.* Could they be telling the truth? Could I still trust Ingrid? Hope kindles in my chest. Could she still be my friend?

As that thought crosses my mind, I swear I see Ingrid flinch. For the barest fraction of a second, her mask slips and I see her as I saw her at school, reflected in the girls' bathroom mirror. Scared and vulnerable and scraped raw.

No. She's not my friend. These people are not my friends. They've exposed themselves with zip ties and hoods and the fucking car battery they have wired up to my skull. When Bel told me to run, she didn't mean from Dad; she meant from *them.*

Rita comes to stand by Ingrid's side.

"Peter," she says, "tell us where Anabel is. Where would she go if she got scared?"

Bel. They want Bel. In my mind I see red bricks and red leaves. I hear my sister's voice: I was scared sick something had happened to you.

"Yes!" Ingrid starts forward. "Yes! There, where's that, Peter? Where is that place you meet her?"

Shit! Frantically I shove the thoughts out of my mind. I think of elephants and hula hoops and the taste of salt and vinegar and clods of earth and . . . I need a distraction . . .

Get counting.

1, 1.414214, 1.732050, 2, 2.236068 . . . There's an acid taste in my mouth. Even as I start, I know I can't count forever. I can feel the knowledge of our secret place battering at the walls of my mind as hard as the panic ever did. 2.449 . . .

"I had something for a second," Ingrid's telling Rita. "But I didn't catch it. Now he's doing square roots."

Rita's silence indicates she doesn't follow.

"Of the integers," Ingrid goes on, "to six decimal places."

"We don't have time for this," Rita mutters. She walks behind me again, raising her voice, as if she's speaking for a recording. "I'm going to dose him again."

"Peter, stop," Ingrid begs me. "Stop this. You can't keep it up."

2.828427, 3 . . .

"Please"—and there are tears in her eyes—"if you don't stop, we'll have to shock you again, and again until you can't resist anymore. Until you can't even *count* anymore."

3.162278. I'm snarling, even in my head. I won't give Bel up to her. 3.3166 . . .

"Petey," Ingrid whispers.

"Dose four."

From behind me, Rita's voice is like a morgue drawer slamming shut.

The world goes white. I clench my teeth so hard I hear them cracking, feel them splintering. The numbers in my head flake into ash. I can't see or hear. I spit and gibber and try to scream but manage only a low moan. I dig my fingers hard into the trolley below the bed frame, and a paper-thin curl of plywood comes away in my palm. For a single, blissful second, my mind goes blank, but then red blots into it like blood into a bandage. I try to push it back, but I can't. I'm exhausted. Red. Red leaves. Red bricks. I grasp after numbers to banish the image, but I can't think of any. The woods behind the northwest corner of school. My school. The place where Bel and I meet when things get bad.

And as I think it, I know Ingrid's seeing it. I listen, waiting for her to tell Rita.

I wait.

I wait some more.

I open my eyes. Ingrid's gripping her arms, her knuckles

white. She's shivering. Her mascara's running in little black rivers down her face. Rita seems unperturbed by her distress.

You feel it, I feel it. Her words rise like smoke from my burned brain. *You're my best friend.*

What if that wasn't a lie?

Her hands inch towards the backs of her gloves. Her eyes flicker across my face. She looks panicky; she could be faking it, but I don't think so. I can feel her, poised, uncertain, guiltily looking over my shoulder at Rita, and then at me and back up again. She goes to speak, hesitates, and swallows.

I grit my teeth. My eyes seek hers, and she can't tear them away. ARIA, I think. A proof of who we are. I think of battered maths textbooks and page number codes. This is a ten on the Ballsuck, I think, but we can get through it. She shakes her head minutely, pleading with me to stop, but I don't. I think of interrobangs. I think of the feel of her hand in mine and the warmth of her body lying next to mine on my Night-crawler duvet. I think of kissing her. I think of a bloodied scrubbing brush bouncing into the sink. I think of how much I love her.

If you can't trust yourself, trust me, I think.

Beads of sweat have appeared on her forehead. They crawl down her face like condensation on cold glass. Rita doesn't speak, but I can feel her behind me, watching, expecting.

Ingrid, I think.

"Ana," she whispers, her lips barely moving. "My name is Ana, Ana Black."

Ingrid.

She looks at Rita, opens her mouth, hesitates. I can see her wavering.

"B-boyfrien . . ." I blurt out, just as her lips start to move. My voice is slurred, but, minus a few consonants, I manage to shape the words. Ingrid looks at me in astonishment.

"What?" Rita demands.

"Bel'sss with her boyfrien . . ."

Rita comes into view behind Ingrid's shoulder. She looks up at a camera in the corner and then back at me.

"We don't have any record of a boyfriend. Louise—"

"Mum doesn't know," I interrupt. "Bel never tol' her, 'caus' he's so much older . . ." Feeling is beginning to return to my jaw. I look straight at Ingrid. She stares back at me.

"He's twenty-three," I said. "And she's only seventeen. They've been together eleven months."

23-17-11 . . .

"Where does he live?" Rita presses me.

I let my head sag, shake it slowly, as if I'm trying to clear the fog.

"I only remember a house number," I mumble. Ingrid's looking at me stricken, but I don't look away. "Fifty-four."

Rita stands patiently, waiting for Ingrid's verdict. Ingrid swallows hard, and when she speaks, her voice is tear-hoarse but calm.

"He's telling the truth."

Rita leans in, peels back one of my eyelids, and holds my gaze for a moment while she considers it.

"We'll check it out."

RECURSION: 2 YEARS, 9 MONTHS AGO

"I'm telling the truth," Dr. Arthurson insisted.

I stared at the equations on the screen until my eyes watered and all the X, ∫, and ∑ symbols curved and ran together like ripples in a pond.

"I don't see it."

"It's right."

"I'm not saying I don't believe you, Dr. A. I'm not calling you a liar. I'm just saying I don't understand *why*."

Dr. Arthurson's eyebrows knitted as he frowned. He had truly monumental eyebrows, grey, bushy, caterpillaresque. At that moment those brows were unified into a single hairy stripe.

"You remind me of bloody Gödel," he muttered. "Scrawny, twitchy, prodigious. They called him *Mr. Why* when he was a kid, and look what happened to him." He waggled his eyebrows ominously.

"What did happen to him?" I asked.

The eyebrows rose in astonishment.

"You mean you don't know?"

"I barely know anything about him."

"You never studied Gödel? What happened to your nerdish compulsion to cram the Wikipedia entry of every famous mathematician in history into your head?"

The brows continued their dizzying ascent of Mount Arthurson. When they reached his hairline, it was like two lost mountain sheep finally reuniting with their flock.

"I haven't got to him yet," I protested. "There's more than

twenty-five hundred years of mathematical history and less than sixteen years of me. Somebody had to lose out to eating and sleeping."

"Well, you should look Gödel up. It's a good story," Dr. A muttered. "And by good, I mean horrifying." He gestured to the screen that was only a hazy rectangle of brightness to his failing eyes. "Is the why of this really so important to you?"

"Yes."

Dr. A nodded glumly and glanced at the clock. Ten to six. He'd offered to take me through a few more advanced theorems on Wednesdays after school. Rain crackled against the window from an ink-swilled sky. It was getting dark, but I hadn't bothered to switch on the lights. I'd pulled my chair up next to his, and we huddled around the glow of his laptop like it was a fire in the wilderness.

"I blew off an evening with Dean for this," he grumbled. "He was going to cook. He always does three courses, and he makes these little chocolate truffle things to have with coffee afterwards."

"Fancy," I said.

Dr. A smirked. "It's still early days; he likes to show off for me."

"Give it six months and it'll be all takeaway fried chicken and loud farts on the sofa, huh?"

"I wouldn't turn my nose up at fried chicken right now."

This was punctuated by a sound that I took for thunder, but that turned out to be Dr. A's cavernous stomach rumbling. It was time to go.

"Come on," I said. "Let's call it a night. You and Chef can still get most of an evening together."

"You sure?" he asked, teasing the bud from his ear. "We can look at this again tomorrow. Don't worry, I'll get you there."

"I know you will. You're the best maths teacher in the country."

He beamed at me, but it couldn't be far short of the truth. There were fewer than a hundred blind teachers in the UK.

One hundred out of more than six hundred *thousand*. To make head of maths at a fancy school like mine, Dr. A had to be hot shit.

I stood and slipped my notebook into my bag, took his arm, and guided him towards the door. Not that he needed help; he taught in this classroom nearly every day, but I liked doing it and he let me.

"So you broke up with George, huh?"

"Rather the other way round."

"Oh, I'm sorry, Dr. A. What happened?"

The atmosphere went chilly and straightaway I felt I'd stepped on a conversational land mine. I did this sometimes, deprived of practice, when I tried to make friends. I pushed them too far in my eagerness to be liked, interrogating them in an attempt to show interest, turning over earth they wanted left undisturbed.

We walked together towards the exit, the only sound the tapping of Dr. A's cane on the lino.

My phone buzzed in my pocket.

Going to be late. Something's come up at office. The rats are turning somersaults. Explain later. Be there by 6.30. Mum X

I sighed.

"What is it?" Dr. A asked.

"Mum's going to be late. And Bel's still suspended . . ."

I left it hanging, but he understood: I was going nowhere. I'd never discussed my embarrassing dependency on my sister to Dr. A, and he never questioned it. He was good like that.

"I—" He hesitated. "Look, I completely understand if you don't want to talk about it, but how's it going, being here without her?"

"Fine," I lied.

"Given what you've told me," he went on, "I imagine things

must be a little tense at home right now, with Bel and your mother, I mean."

I didn't reply.

He looked awkward. "Listen, Peter." He reached into his jacket and held out a piece of folded paper. "I want you to take this."

I unfolded the A4 page. In huge, bold black marker letters was written *419 GABRIEL STREET SW19 7HE.*

"Just in case," he mumbled. "In case you ever need somewhere to go. Aboveboard, of course. Make sure your mother's okay with it. But if things ever get too . . . well. Just in case."

"I . . ." But I couldn't finish the sentence. I hurriedly folded the note and put it in my pocket. I felt it there, a promise of refuge, fragile and precious.

"Thank you," I managed finally.

"I keep a spare key under the fourth brick from the front of the flower bed. If I'm not there, just let yourself in."

"Thank you," I said again. I couldn't think of anything else to say. "Thank you."

We waited and chatted at reception until Dean arrived to collect him. He was friendly and handsome in a "just walked out of a moisturizer advert" kind of way. I was happy to see the little dusting of cocoa powder on his sleeve.

"Mum late again?" Sal, the receptionist, enquired sympathetically.

"Acrobatic rats," I explained. She nodded sagely.

"Want me to phone the library and let Julie know you're coming?"

"Ta."

With Dr. A's offer in my hoodie pocket, I all but bounced into the library and high-fived Julie, the librarian. Julie was awesome. Auburn-haired and hyper, she was roughly the shape of an old-fashioned egg timer and buzzed at pretty much the same frequency when she was in a good mood, which she always seemed to be.

"Hey, Petey," she said. "What'll it be tonight? Meteorology? Phenomenology? Herpetology? I've just got a book in on the chemical make-ups of the deadliest venoms in the animal kingdom. I know how you like a grisly demise on a Wednesday."

A grisly demise. *You remind me of bloody Gödel, and look what happened to him.*

"How about a biography?" I said.

I slouched down into a ketchup-red bean bag and cracked open the hardback Julie had handed me, promisingly entitled, *Unprovable: The Madness and Mastery of Kurt Gödel.* There was a black-and-white picture on the inside cover: a stick-insect of a man in a jacket and tie, dark eyes staring out from behind bottle-top spectacles.

I sat there for a long time. That gaze held me like a tractor beam. The eyes were deeply shadowed but more than that: his stare made me feel I was complicit in some terrible secret.

Scrawny, twitchy, prodigious, I heard Dr. A saying. *You remind me of Gödel.*

"Yeah," I muttered under my breath. "Me too."

Normally, when I read up on a mathematician, I like to take my time. I imagine myself in the warm sun of ancient Greece, or under the smog of industrial revolution Hamburg. I savour the sting of their early setbacks, the out-of-touch old men who laughed at their theories, relishing their coming triumph. And when it comes to their big moment, I read and reread the relevant passage, committing it to memory, then close my eyes and live it; that incandescent moment when they scratch out the final line in their proof and realise they've done it. They've proven that there are multiple infinities, or that space and time were one.

Not today.

Anxiety crabbing at my belly, I flicked through the pages until I landed on the one word I was looking for: death.

Gödel died in January 1978 at the age of seventy-one. It wasn't a sickness of the body that killed him, rather a sickness of the mind. He suffered from paranoid delusions and was convinced that someone was trying to poison him. He trusted only his wife, Adele, to prepare his food, and when she was herself hospitalised in late 1977, he starved himself to death.

"Holy shit," I murmured under my breath.

A doctor who attended him in his final weeks said later in an interview: "We tried to persuade him to eat, but he refused. We told him—no one's trying to poison you, but he wouldn't believe us. He kept saying over and over that there was no way to be sure."

When Gödel died, he weighed just sixty-five pounds.

He trusted only his wife . . . I thought, closing the book, aware of the sweat cooling between my shoulders. She was his axiom. And when he lost her, all his proofs and theorems, his understanding, the life he'd built on her came crashing down, demolishing him on the way.

Something else on that page snared my attention: He suffered from paranoid delusions . . .

You remind me of Gödel.

That's what Dr. A had told me.

A chill crept from the base of my neck up to my hairline like spider's feet. I flicked back to Gödel's photograph. He looked haunted, as if he harboured a dreadful secret. But what was it? What was so shattering that it drove him to starve himself?

I tried to imagine how it must have felt; the hunger pangs, the dizziness, his hand at a standstill halfway from plate to mouth, his jaw locked tetanus-tight in refusal. What could have brought him to that?

I flicked to the index. The largest number of page references appeared under the heading of something called *Incompleteness Theorems, pp. 8, 36, 141–146, 210.* I skipped to page 141. In bold black letters it said:

THIS STATEMENT IS A LIE.

"Huh," I muttered. "The liar's paradox." It can't be true without being false, and it can't be false without being true. Pretty much the most decrepit cliché in all of philosophy. It had always struck me as a pointless linguistic trap. Besides, the "truth" is a woolly concept at the best of times.

On the page below it was another, similar sentence.

THIS STATEMENT IS *UNPROVABLE*.

I felt a queasy rumble in my belly. I saw the point, of course. That second sentence really *was* unprovable, because proving it true would prove it false and that's a one-way express ticket back to paradox land.

It's just a word game, I told myself. Just a clever trap based on the fuzzy language we use to talk about coffee and kittens and nuclear wars. You'd never get away with anything that imprecise in maths.

But Gödel was a mathematician, and I had a horrible feeling I knew where this was going.

After all, if you could find an equation that declared itself unprovable, I thought, then you really would be in trouble; basically you'd have broken maths.

I remembered the haunted look in Gödel's eyes and my fingers trembled as I turned the page.

Shit.

Equations sprawled down the page. All this time, I've been at this school and this book's been sitting here in the library, waiting to shatter my universe.

I read it five, six, seven times, hoping against hope to find some mistake, some error that could have been missed by the hundreds of readers whose greasy thumbs had stained these yellow pages before mine.

There wasn't one.

I reached the last line of the chapter and there it was, the coup de grace.

$$F \vdash G_F \leftrightarrow \neg Prov_F(\ulcorner G_F \urcorner)$$

The unprovable theorem.

That was it. Maths wasn't complete. It couldn't justify itself, and there was nothing outside of it more fundamental or certain that could do the job.

Shit.

Shit shit shit shit shit.

Suddenly I could feel the congealed mess of my lunch high in my chest. I wanted to vomit. I gripped the book so hard I could hear my knuckles crack.

I stared at it.

An unprovable theorem. An unanswerable question. A problem that I and a thousand others like me and a billion, billion supercomputers could work at until the sun burned out and never get close to solving.

And if there's one, a nasty voice asked from the back of my brain, *how can you be sure there aren't more?*

I sagged into the beanbag.

ARIA was dead.

The whole project had depended on two basic assumptions: first, that my panic attacks were, at root, a mathematical problem, and second—an assumption so basic I hadn't even known I'd made it (and aren't those always the ones to fuck you up?)—that any mathematical problem could actually be *solved* with maths.

Gödel had blown a hole in the second assumption big enough to steam an aircraft carrier through. Any equation could be a hideous, insoluble, life-swallowing trap in disguise.

All the screwed-down hope, the plans I'd shared with Ingrid, echoed hollowly through the corridors of my mind:

"There's an equation that's me. I'm going to find it. And I'm going to prove it."

I'd dreamed I would define, perfectly, the theorem of my fear. And then I'd know, I'd know if it was ever going to stop.

The book fell from nerveless fingers and I didn't hear it hit the floor.

But ARIA might not be like that, a voice inside me protested. *There might still be an answer. There might still be a proof.* But the voice was weak. My dream was fracturing and however I tried to cup my hands, I couldn't catch the pieces. I pictured myself, hunched over my desk, gnawed on by age and doubt, calculating for year after year, never knowing if I was getting closer to an answer.

I looked down at the floor. The book had fallen open again and the starved eyes of Gödel stared up at me.

. . . there was no way to be sure.

THIS STATEMENT IS A LIE.

A lie that demolished certainty in everything.

I fled the library, Julie's face and voice blurred by tears as she called after me. I ran down the hallways randomly, purely for somewhere to run. The rain besieged the windows, hundreds of drops per second, too many to count.

The hall clock bit off seconds: 6:47 P.M. and still no sign of Mum. I pulled my phone from my pocket and dialled Bel, but she didn't answer. I tried to call Ingrid, but I couldn't make myself press the button. I remembered her eyes when I'd explained ARIA to her, the hope that had lit up in them, and I couldn't, I just couldn't kill it.

I slumped against the lockers and slid to the floor, tears pouring hot down my cheeks. I felt utterly alone.

But I wasn't.

It took me a long time to register the footsteps. "What the fuck," said Ben Rigby, rain dripping from his hair as he unslung his football bag from his shoulder and stepped forward from his gaggle of friends, "are you still doing here?"

NOW

"One . . . One . . ."

Test one. The memory of the electricity coursing through my temples shatters my concentration. My eyes water, their lids heavy. Sleep. I need to sleep. Tendrils of exhaustion wrap around my limbs, pulling me down into the dark.

I reach inside my ruined shirt. My fingers find the scaly mess of a burn, still sticky with electrode glue. I grab the edge of a bit of skin and pull.

The pain dispels the fog, and I inhale sharply through my teeth. I blink my eyes clear and go back to staring at the door.

"One . . . t-t-t . . . One."

I sigh. I've been staring at this door for what feels like forever and I've got to know it pretty well. It's made of metal, covered in flaking blue paint, and draped in twisted ropes of shadow from the cobwebs covering the one bare lightbulb. It doesn't seem to have a lock, but sadly it doesn't have a handle on this side, either. It does, however, boast a ring of neat little rivets running around the edge. I'm hungry, exhausted, confused, and frightened, but it would all be a little bit better if I could only count those rivets.

"One, one . . . one . . . Shit."

It's not going well. Also, I don't seem to be able to stop drooling, and my right hand is currently wedged between my arse and the paint can I'm now sitting on because it was shaking so hard it was distracting. (There are tins of government-issue magnolia eggshell everywhere. I guess they don't have any actual prison cells here in spy HQ and they've thrown me into the maintenance cupboard.)

Worst of all, I can't count past one. I can't even rebuild myself beyond that, before the panic knocks the bricks over.

Ingrid's warning echoes in my head: *We'll shock you until you can't resist any more, until you can't even* count *anymore.*

But I keep trying because, if I can count the rivets, then I can estimate the size of the door. If I can estimate the size of the door, I can guess the volume of this closet. If I can estimate the volume, then I could convince myself there's more air in this crushingly tiny space than there is in your average mass-produced coffin. And if I can do that, then maybe I could stifle the urge to vomit up scream after hysterical scream currently caged behind my teeth and do something useful.

Like plan.

I peel more skin off my burn, wince, wipe what I really hope isn't the pus of incipient infection off my hand, drool some more, and stare at the door.

"One," I say firmly.

Along with the paint cans, my cell does have one amenity that most coffins don't: a vent in the wall high above me, covered by a metal grille. Agent Blankman (bitten by a radioactive plot device as a child) might have climbed up there, levered it out with his . . . teeth or something, and gambled on the ten thousand to one chance it led to freedom and not the furnace of a central heating plant.

He probably would have made it too; that kind of shit happens in spy stories.

But Agent Blankman's gone. It's just me now, and the only way I'm getting out of here is with help. I just have to be ready for it when it comes.

I stare at the door. The door stares back.

"One . . . one . . ."

As I seem to have some time on my hands, I compose a eulogy. *Agent P. W. Blankman spent years under astonishingly convincing cover as a snivelling coward, but was in truth the bravest officer in the unit. He met his final fate today, bleeding out on the floor of a dingy interrogation chamber, the backbone he so skillfully pretended not to have impaled on the blade of a treacherous double agent—*

The latch clunks. The hinges creak. The door opens, and there she stands in silhouette, her blonde hair like embers and shadow. I take a deep breath.

"Agent Blonde Calculating Machine"—and for a second Agent Blankman's ghost animates my lips—"what a pleasant surprise."

She crosses the space to me in two short steps (hey, *two*, there you go!) and unseen hands close the door behind her. She takes me by the chin with one hand. Her gloves are damp, as if she's pulled them on over wet skin. The tang of iodine stabs into my nostrils.

Her familiar brown eyes flicker across my face.

"You aren't surprised to see me, Peter."

"Aren't I? Well, I guess you'd know."

"*Age*"—her voice is flat with accusation—"*House number, duration of relationship*. It's not much of a description, but sooner or later . . ." She tails off, apparently too angry to carry on, so I pick it up for her.

"Sooner or later," I say, "the people you work for will realise that no boy who matches that description has ever been near my sister's pants, and then they'll know."

"Yes."

"That you lied—to them, for me."

"So what was this, a fucking *trap*?" She hisses, her eyes wide and so close I can almost count the tiny capillaries.

I hold her gaze.

You lied to them, for me. It's been the other way around ever since I met you, Ana, and indignation's not going to get you where you want to go. Feel free to read that out of my fucking mind if you want.

"This is my family, Peter." She's almost pleading. "He's my dad."

For a moment I don't follow, and then—

My dad, I'm afraid of my dad. They were among the first words she ever said to me.

Ana, she called herself, Ana Black. And from earlier in this endless day, Rita in the car on the phone to her boss, a man called Henry Black, saying, "*If this was your daughter, would you want me to leave her out in the cold?*"

"You're the boss's daughter?"

A tight nod.

"So why did you cover for me? You knew what I was hiding. Why not tell them?"

She glares at me fiercely, but whatever she's looking for she doesn't find it, because now she's looking at the paint, at the cobwebs, anywhere but at my face. Her hands move towards the hems of her gloves. When she finally speaks, it's not an answer.

"They're already getting suspicious. The search parameters are too vague to be a total bust, but none of the matches look promising." She flaps a hardback notebook at me.

"LeClare sent me down to see if you'd be any more forthcoming when we'd fed you."

She nods over her shoulder to a store-bought ham-and-cheese sandwich and a bottle of water on a tray by the door; they must have shoved that in behind her when she came in. My stomach yawns ravenously—it's been a long time since breakfast, which I threw up anyway—and I lunge for them.

"LeClare?" I mumble around a mouthful of plasticky bread.

"Carolyn LeClare, the deputy director. She would have told you an outdoor name." She waves a hand vaguely. "Sandra, Pamela, Jessica . . ."

"Rita?" I spray crumbs incredulously. "Rita's the fucking *deputy director?*"

"She's Daddy's right-hand gal," she says, her voice taut, "and by the look she gave me when she told to me to grill you 'about this mysterious boyfriend' . . . I don't think she believes a word of it."

"So why not read her mind?" I ask. I can't believe I just said that so matter-of-factly, but I'm so punch-drunk from the rest of the day's surprises I no longer feel shock. "That's what you do, isn't it?"

"I can't read minds, Peter." She eyes me sullenly. "I can only read yours."

For a moment, the only sound is the dripping pipe.

"I'm a mirror, but only a cloudy one. I feel people's desires, passions, emotions. But I have to know a subject *incredibly* well for those feelings to coalesce into thoughts. You—"

She hesitates, bites a phrase back, literally, her teeth are so deep in her lip I'm surprised there's no blood. Then she adds:

"You don't know how lucky you are. To have someone who knows you that well."

"I thought I knew you pretty well."

Her face is cobwebbed in shadow, but I see tears glimmering in the corners of her eyes.

"I wish."

In rooms above us fingers are hammering keys, and computer power on a scale I can't even imagine is churning and chuntering and eroding the little time we have. I have to get out of this plywood-shelved tomb. I have to find Bel. I have to do it now . . .

And yet.

There are forty-three muscles involved in human facial expression and every one of hers is telling me to take this slowly.

My heart thuds in the base of my throat.

"Then tell me," I say.

"Tell you what?"

"Everything: what happened to you, how you got here."

She stares at me.

"You want me to know the real you?" I push. "Then tell me about her. Start at the beginning."

She looks at me warily, but I've seen that expression once

before: it's mixed with hope. This was how she looked when I told her about ARIA.

"I don't know the beginning," she says slowly, reluctantly, but at least she's talking. "The beginning was before I was born. But as far as I can piece together, an all-staff email went out saying 'Volunteers needed, expecting children.' The sales pitch? A chance to dramatically increase the emotional intelligence of a child, to the point of creating a fully functional empath."

She drops an ironic half curtsy.

"Let me guess," I say. "That wasn't an opportunity the head of an intelligence agency could afford to pass up?"

"Correlation versus causation, Peter," she tuts. "I'm surprised at you. You think I'm the way I am because Daddy's the boss? Daddy's the boss, because of *me*. This is a spy house. Its world is stitched from double crosses. It *exists* to find the pressure points it can use to bend and break people. And it's all so uncertain, so riddled with doubt and second-guessing: 'Do they know we know they know?' and all that dreary, anxious bullshit. And then along comes little Ana, able to spot a lie at a hundred paces, able to feel the dearest, darkest, most deeply buried desire of your target, simply by being in the same room . . ."

She tails off, stares past my shoulder. I don't think she even sees me anymore, just her memories, reshaping her mind as they recur.

"I am this company's greatest asset, and pretty much from the day I could first talk, Daddy worked me."

She starts chewing her cheek, fit to put a hole in it, the same remorseless rhythm with which she washes her hands.

"It is impossible to explain what that was like."

"Try me."

She stiffens, braces her feet like she's waiting to get punched.

"I spent two days," she snaps, "watching terrorists in Seoul, and I became so obsessed with a reunified Korea I was willing to firebomb an elementary school for it. Then they flew me out to Venezuela, and for a week I was sick with lust for a Caracas rent-boy—oh, and I was *twelve* . . ." Her gaze rakes over me and my skin crawls. "Then they nailed that guy too and the love vanished, just like that. Only to be replaced by a long weekend on another target in Poland, feeling only his burning, insane hatred for Jews, because it turns out that when you work as an empath for a spy agency, the people they want you to empathise with aren't very *nice*."

Her voice stays low, to keep it from the guard outside. She sounds murderous.

"I felt like a matchstick in a hurricane. Their need and rage and hate filled me up, shoving me in a million different directions. I begged my dad for a break, for some time alone, and finally he relented, but it was too late. When I got back to my room and closed the door, I felt . . . nothing. The mirror was empty.

"I tried to reach, to gather up some sense of who I was, of what I wanted when I was just me, but it was like grasping at fog."

Her breath patters quickly against my eyelids and I can feel her fear.

"And then they put me on you. For three years, they put me onto you. And you burned so bright, brighter than anyone I'd ever seen. You were a lighthouse in the fog. I got home at night, and your panic and your love for your family, your passion for numbers were still there, in me, and, all right, most of it was fear, but at least it was *something* and it was like . . ." She tails off, then shrugs.

"And then when I saw you splayed out like that, in front of me downstairs, I just . . . I couldn't, I couldn't undo you like that. It would have been like undoing myself."

"So you lied."

"So I lied."

"23-17-11-54."

She tucks her chin into her chest, her gaze on the floor, and laughs silently, the tears running down her cheeks.

"The whole thing was a fucking botch anyway," she sniffs. "I should have had days to prep, to work you over, but the top floor's just so freaked out right now—I've never seen anything like it. I mean, I'd never met your mum before they put me onto you, but I'd heard of her. She's a big deal in-house, and you'd expect a shit storm when any one of us are targeted, but even so . . . to have less than an hour to crack you . . . and you were panicking, so I was panicking too and . . . fuck," she breathes. "What am I going to do?"

Daddy worked me. I think quickly while her eyes are fixed at the floor. Don't make her feel cornered. If she feels cornered, she'll play safe, go back to what she knows, i.e. her family. It's what I'd do.

You have to give her a choice.

"Way I see it," I say carefully, "you have three options."

"One." I uncurl an index finger. "You go to Rita—LeClare, whatever her name is—right now and you tell her you made a mistake. You read me wrong. I conned you. You tell her what she needs to know. That's your way back in."

Please don't want back in.

She stands there, head bowed, and says nothing.

"Two." Another finger. "Tell them the truth. You wobbled a little, but you're back inside now."

Except you aren't, are you?

Still no response.

"Three." My third finger uncurls. "You and I leave, right now."

Still no response . . .

. . . and then:

"How?" It's barely audible, but relief floods through me.

"What?"

"How do we leave? Jack's standing right outside the door."

"Well then, *you* leave now, take him with you, lose him, double back, and—are there loos on this floor?"

"Right down the hall."

"Good, meet me in the loos. Knock five times on the first stall."

She looks at me like I'm an idiot.

"But how will you get out of this closet?"

I tear a side from the cardboard pack the sandwich came in. I fold it in half, then in half again, and again. With every fold, the pressure pushing back on my fingers squares. Exponential origami.

I get up and knock on the door, sliding the empty sandwich tray towards it with my foot. The handle turns and I stand aside meekly.

"Trust me," I whisper to her as she passes. "I learned from the best."

Eleven minutes later, Ingrid's dragging me down abandoned basement corridors at breakneck pace, past a shuttered-up canteen ("we put the pies in spies!"), back out into the maze, and, after only a handful of turns, into an ancient cargo lift. The lift clatters and creaks as it ascends in a way that screams, ESCAPED PRISONER! GET YOUR ESCAPED PRISONER RIGHT HERE! But Ingrid doesn't seem worried.

"There's one thing you haven't told me," I say. She has her back to me. I watch her rock with the motion of the lift. "Why? Why did they put you on me for three years?"

She seems surprised at the question.

"Pete, your mum's the most strategically important mind since Turing—think about it."

For a moment I'm baffled, but then I remember Rita's voice.

"*A scientist as brilliant as Louise Blankman . . . selling their research to the highest bidder.*"

"Insurance." As soon as I've said it, it's obvious. "You weren't watching me; you were watching Mum, making sure she stayed on the right side, except . . ." I fall silent.

Except why snuggle up to me instead of going to her directly? Because, Pete, *she's* a savvy operator embedded deep in the secret world; she'd be wise to that sort of thing. I, on the other hand, was falling over myself to make a friend, any friend. I was the easy mark, her entry vector.

The lift creaks to a halt. It spits us out into what looks like a young family's garage. A rotting plastic tricycle lies embalmed in cobwebs in one corner. A brown streak on the concrete catches my eye. It's too red to be rust. With a jolt, I realise this must be where they brought Mum in. Ingrid lifts the door and the honeyed sunlight of an autumn evening floods in. Cool air washes over me and I inhale deeply. It's only been *four hours since* I last tasted it. It feels like years.

The light's broken up into slats and slabs by a mess of scaffolding over the exit. Ingrid peers through it.

"This should give us cover," she murmurs. I come to her shoulder and peer out at the innocent-looking terrace. I imagine the sharpshooters behind its dormer windows.

"Isn't it a security risk having the scaffolding up?"

"It is, but then so would having the whole false front of the agency's secret HQ sliding off because of subsidence. Thank god for crappy foundation work and soft London clay."

"Thank god indeed."

Ingrid hesitates only once, at the corner by a heavily graffitied postbox. She looks back, her fringe shading her eyes. I recognise that stance, the same half hunch she makes over a sink when she's washing her hands, hand over hand until the sink runs red.

I think of the missions she's been on, all the slaps on the back from her proud dad.

Repetition builds meaning; repeat enough times and that meaning becomes a cage, a cage whose bars you can rattle and shriek at, and never move.

"*This is my family.*"

I'm asking her to give it up. And I know how that feels.

In my head I hear the regular mechanical breaths of Mum's ventilator. I feel the electrode burn on my chest, and the nauseating anxiety of leaving her here, with these people—people she thought were colleagues and friends, people prepared to hunt and torture her children.

She can't have known what they'd do to me.

Ingrid pulls her phone from her pocket and drops it through a sewer grill.

"They can track it."

"Come on," I urge, pulling her arm.

"Where are we going?"

"Well, since every gun that Britain's secret intelligence service can call on is out hunting for my sister, I figure we should warn her. Why? You wanna go for some ice cream instead?"

17-20-13, I think. You're on, sis.

We start to run.

RECURSION: 2 YEARS, 9 MONTHS AGO

I started to run.

Up until that point, I'd just been walking, fast and stiff-backed, squeezing the acid back down my throat like toothpaste down a tube, trying to pretend I wasn't afraid. But now I broke, my feet hammering on the concrete floor. Behind me, the rhythm of their footsteps shifted to match mine like an echo, an auditory shadow dogging me.

I fled from the maths block to the old wing, through wood-panelled hallways and past portraits of old head teachers. I knew every inch of the school, every disused maintenance hatch and old service stairway.

I guess I only had myself to blame for the place I wound up.

The door reared up in front of me. I kicked it, and a chain I knew was barely more than rust gave way. Rain hammered down on my face and shoulders, plastering my hair to my scalp as I emerged into the night. Under me the floor turned to slippery tile, and sloped sharply down. I skidded and threw out my arms for balance, grabbing onto a redbrick chimney stack.

Barren trees, black and blasted, reached into the storm-swept sky, and I was level with the tops of them. I could barely see where the roof ended and the drop began.

Behind me, the footsteps faltered. For a blessed instant, I thought they wouldn't follow, but then the tiles behind me clinked.

Ben Rigby stood on the roof with me. I didn't turn, but I knew it was him.

"What are you so afraid of, Blankman?" he called over the wind.

I didn't know. I didn't know and perhaps I'd never know. Gödel's black-and-white photo, dark, starving eyes staring out from behind thick spectacles, blurred into Mum's picture of Roosevelt smirking at me from the fridge.

The only thing we have to fear is fear itself.

I could feel the panic mounting in the back of my throat, eternal and nauseating. I was afraid of being afraid of being afraid of being afraid of being afraid of being afraid of being afraid of being afraid . . .

"Wh . . . wh . . . wh . . ." I began, but I couldn't even finish.

"What?" Rigby snapped, and I heard his patience snap with it.

"What do you *want*?" I whined.

He thought about it for a long time, and then said, "I want you to jump."

I looked around then and our eyes met. And I saw something change in his face, or maybe it had been like that this whole time and I was only just now seeing it. He was as scared as I was. Perhaps he was afraid of the fall, the treacherous rain-slick slate. But mostly I think he was scared of his friends, of losing face, letting this opportunity slip away in front of them: me, up here, alone with him, with no staff and no parents to hold him back.

Sometimes kids need someone to hate. He'd chosen me.

"Jump!" he said, louder this time. I shook my head, but without much conviction. I looked out at the boiling weight of the storm.

I eased my weight forward a little and my feet slid closer to the edge, my fingers still clinging to the chimney.

"Jump!" he barked. I started and scrabbled, slipped, caught myself. He smiled at me, his teeth nightmarish in the rainy half-light.

Bel. I imagined her springing from behind a gargoyle, slamming his face into the slates, grinding them up into powder, and making him snort them. I imagined her taking my hand and guiding me back inside.

But Bel wasn't there.

"I'll do you a deal, Peter," Rigby said, leaning casually against the doorframe, ignoring the assault of the rain. "If you jump, if just once you show some guts, you'll never hear from me again. Otherwise I will be on you. Every day. It will never stop."

My feet slid a little farther towards the edge, until the toes of my shoes slipped over it. *If just once you show some guts.* Fighting it was so hard and giving into it suddenly seemed so easy.

It will never stop. Ever. I pictured myself at university, at work, at home, gnawing my knuckles and counting and crying; eyeing up the potential of every sharp object; afraid afraid afraid. Forever.

Maybe it will get better, I tried to tell myself. But *maybe* wasn't anywhere close to enough. ARIA was dead. Gödel had killed it, and without it there was no way to be sure.

"JUMP!" Rigby screamed at me, and I almost did, a jolt shooting up my spine. He laughed. I was shivering, freezing rain running down my collar like electrical currents.

I looked out at the storm.

"Jump," Rigby ordered in a flat, deadly voice.

My teeth chattered so hard I could barely whisper the words: "Bel, where are you?"

And there she was, standing next to me, her warm hand curling into my freezing palm.

"*It's okay,*" she whispered to me. "*Do you trust me?*"

"You're my axiom," I told her.

"*Then look down.*"

I looked and I could have laughed. The wall where we'd practised our leaps of faith was a dizzying distance below, carving off churned playing field mud from unyielding playground concrete.

"*Do the maths,*" Bel whispered. "*How fast would you fall?*"

"I'd accelerate at nine point eight metres a second squared," I said. "It looks about twenty-five metres down."

"*So how hard would you hit?*"

"About a hundred and sixty thousand newtons, give or take."

"*Survivable?*"

"It's a toss-up," I said. "Feetfirst, maybe. Skull-first, not a chance. Depends how I fall."

"*Ah.*" Bel smiled, a secret smile that only I could see. The knowing smile of someone with a PhD in falling. "*What do you want to do, Petey?*"

I didn't know. I was one with the weather, so delicate and chaotic a system that every raindrop that struck me seemed to change my mind. I kept flickering: yes/no, on/off, true/false, heads/tails.

I felt drunk, violent, unpredictable, random.

I dug a coin out of my sodden pocket. It glimmered in my bloodless palm. "Heads, I do it," I whispered.

"*Okay,*" Bel whispered, and gave my hand a reassuring squeeze. I squeezed back, but my fingers curled around empty air. I was alone again.

I flicked the coin. Caught it. Turned it. Looked.

If Bel had really been there, maybe I could have held out, but she wasn't.

And without her, I was incomplete.

It takes a quarter of a second—

I jumped.

I pitched forward, over the edge. I was tumbling, spinning, end over end, my knees by my ears.

Heads or tails, heads or tails, heads or tails . . .

Heads. The ground surged up. *Heads,* I thought. *Heads.* I tried desperately to wrestle my legs behind me, angling my head downward, to make sure.

Heads heads heads . . .

A tree branch blurred for a second at the corner of my vision. There was a savage pain on my forehead. I saw an instant's brilliant daylight, and then—

NOW

"Nothing." Ingrid looks around glumly. "There's nothing. There's no one here."

I turn in a slow circle, taking in the school's crumbling terra-cotta facade, its black drainpipes and whitewashed window ledges, the three-metre-high brick wall running around its grounds, hemming it in; Bel's classroom for Fearlessness 101. Behind me, a curtain of trees, their branches on fire with autumn, seal out prying eyes. It's just as it was the last time I was here.

I run a reassuring thumb through the rough-scarred dent in my forehead and squint up through the canopy, as if I could identify the branch that made it. There's so much of my life—mine and Bel's—in this quiet bubble behind the school that I marvel that anyone could describe it as nothing. But I guess it all depends on what you're looking for. To me, this place matters, but to Ingrid, it's all noise and no signal.

I trudge through shin-deep red leaves. They break up the ground beneath like static.

"You're sure this is the place?" she asks me.

"You know I am."

"Then . . . I don't know, Pete. Maybe you don't know her as well as you think."

A part of me hopes that's true, that Bel's taken her own advice—*17-20-13*—and run and run and is warm and safe, far away. I like that part and I wish it was the whole of me, but it isn't, because another deeper, realer part is whispering, *My axiom my axiom my axiom,* over and over in breath after panicked breath, while the world pitches on its axis at the thought that she could be gone.

"Peter." Ingrid sounds worried and I follow her gaze up. The light's draining rapidly from the sky. "If she isn't here, then we shouldn't be, either."

I nod dumbly, but instead of heading back out through the trees, I trudge towards the school, kicking up puffs of leaves like a ten-year-old. Couldn't we wait? I want to ask. We've only been here five minutes. But Bel's had five hours to get here if she's coming.

If we leave, I don't know how I'll ever find her again.

My right toe kicks something hard. Something that skips and rolls and comes to rest against the wall. I freeze.

"Peter?" Ingrid says from behind me. "What is it?"

An apple. A Granny Smith apple, brilliant green against the red. It nestles in the leaf mould at the bottom of the wall. A concave wound of purest white stands out starkly where sharp teeth have taken a bite out of it.

"Peter?" Ingrid asks again.

I stay frozen, sweat pricking my neck. *Stop. Go. Red. Green* . . .

White. For a dreadful instant, my brain is blank and then, thank Gauss, I begin to think.

Enzymes in fruit don't mess around. The chemicals in apple juice will oxidise flesh exposed to the air fast. If Bel's teeth met in that apple much more than about six minutes ago, its flesh wouldn't be white; it would be toffee brown.

Six minutes. We've been here five. And we didn't see anyone leave.

"Peter?"

"*Maybe you don't know her as well as you think.*" Maybe, but my heart's beating faster with relief and fear, because I bloody bet I do.

In which case . . .

A chasm opens up in my stomach as I think it. We did get away awfully easily, didn't we?

For a world-champion paranoiac, Pete, you're really slipping.

I turn back towards Ingrid but peer past her, to the thicket of trees that shield the clearing. Deep in the shadows, something glints.

I exhale once, to steady myself.

"It's nothing," I say.

Keep it cool, Pete, not too loud, not too showy, make it just clear enough to carry. To my ear, my voice is cracked, my fear spilling out of it.

"She's not here." I stick my hands in my pockets and set off towards the tree line. "Let's just go."

"DON'T MOVE! DON'T FUCKING MOVE!"

I'm expecting them, but my heart still shrinks to a tiny point as they run at me: four figures in dark jackets and jeans with black guns levelled at my head.

"TURN AROUND AND GET ON YOUR KNEES! PUT YOUR HANDS ON YOUR HEAD! TURN AROUND NOW!"

I'm a skinny unarmed kid, but they're screaming at me like I'm juggling grenades. My spine locks up at the violence in their voices. I turn and sink to my knees, interlacing my fingers on my scalp. Despite the cool of the evening, my hair is soaked in sweat.

The apple sits blithely in my eye line, nestled against the wall. I will a wind to pick up, to blow the fallen leaves over it, but it just sits there, screamingly green for all to see.

Something hard presses into the back of my skull.

"Peter Blankman." It's a male voice, Irish-tinged. Familiarity tantalises me for a moment; then I have it: Seamus, from the museum. "If you even think about turning to face me, I will blow your head clean off your shoulders and all the way to Ballymena. Clear?"

"Yes," I croak.

"If you try to run: Ballymena. If you lie: Ballymena. In fact, any attempt by you to do anything I don't like will result in an all-expenses-paid trip to County Antrim you will find difficult to enjoy. Clear?"

Out of the corner of my eye, I see Ingrid. Did she know? In that half a heartbeat I try to read her like she reads me. She's corpse white, her eyes flicker from me to the apple and my breath stalls, but her lips stay pursed shut.

"Are we CLEAR?" Seamus bellows at me.

"Y-y-yes."

"Good. Now, so that we can all go home, tell me. Where the fuck is your sister?"

I start to shake. A hot, wet stain spreads down the side of my trousers, sticking the fabric to my thigh. My jaw's trembling. Good, it'll make the lie harder to spot.

"I—I—I don't know. She must have gone."

"Jack!" Seamus calls to someone else. "Can he be right? I thought we were certain she wouldn't leave him behind. What does her psych profile say?"

"Her psych profile says that the only thing that knows her better than her psych profile is him."

This voice is familiar too. My memory offers up a flash of paramedic green. "*You did good.*" The museum again. This must be the same team—makes sense. It's a secret agency; there can't be that many of them. With every new person that you let in, you take on a little extra risk of blowing the whole game. My heart is beating wildly and I grasp frantically for details. Details are control.

Seamus spits, and a foamy gob of saliva hits the leaves to my right.

"Check the woods."

Behind me I hear the crash and rustle as they enter the trees. A couple of moments later two of the agents—a bald man in a leather jacket and a woman with a pixie haircut—jog past me to the wall. The man treads the apple into the mud with one heavy boot, but doesn't look at it. I try not to breathe too hard.

Neither of them look at me, either, which is just as well, because I suspect right now my tear-twisted, frantic face would be pretty useless for poker. The man slips through the green metal gate and vanishes into the dark. When he reappears, I can just about make him out, flitting from window to window in the empty school like a ghost.

"No sign, Seamus," he says when he returns exactly six minutes later. (I know it exactly because counting is all that's keeping my head from exploding without the intervention of Mr. Ballistic Travel Agent behind me.)

"Shit," Seamus says, and sighs. "All right, secure the Rabbit. We'll have to take Henry's temperature on what to do with him when we get back."

My arms are wrenched back behind me and with a hiss-zip, plastic bites into my already raw wrists. I roll my eyes right and see Ingrid on her knees in the leaf mould too.

I look at the apple. I look at her. My own words snake treacherously back into my thoughts:

"Option two: tell them the truth. You had a wobble, but now you're back on the right side."

Her lips are trembling, like there's a current running through her, but her eyes are blank. She knows what I know and I am sickeningly aware of how tempting it must be right now for her to tell them, to win back the favour of her family.

Her lips stay shut.

The pressure on my skull eases. I hear leaves crunching behind me, Seamus backing off one, two, three steps. The click of a phone unlocking. The other three agents stand in a loose huddle near Ingrid. One of them tucks his gun inside his jacket and pulls out a pack of cigarettes. Weapon gone, he is at once utterly forgettable. I doubt I'd recognise his bland white face and brown hair on the street if I saw him again. That anonymity is probably what he gets paid for. He strikes a match and lights the smoke.

Come on, I think desperately, because even half buried in muddy leaf mould, that apple is still staring right at me. Get on with it, get us out of here, you can collect your lung cancer vouchers on the way back.

He drops the match and I watch it fall next to his feet.

Dropping a still-smouldering match onto dry leaves. Jesus. Okay, whatever this guy gets paid for it's not his smarts.

I stare at the match where it falls. It doesn't start a forest fire, mercifully, but I keep staring anyway.

I keep staring because right there, where the match fell, right in front of the agent's scuffed black boots, the static of the red leaves suddenly gives way to the *signal* of curly red hair.

"Rita, this is Seamus," Seamus mutters into his phone behind me. "It's a bust. No sign of Red Wolf."

Wolf.

There is a tornado of leaves.

It happens so fast I forget to breathe. She surges up from the ground, breaching the leaf litter like a dolphin out of water, corkscrewing as she rises. Pixie-Cut Woman's the first to react, but she seems to forget about her gun halfway through raising it, clutching her hand instead to the bright red liquid suddenly spraying from her throat. Something gleams in her fist, something that glides smoothly through the same perfect Archimedes spiral to slash through the neck of the bald man, who's desperately trying to find an angle that won't shoot his dying comrade.

The smoker, who I guess won't die from cancer after all, doesn't even get his hand back inside his jacket. His body falls beside the others. Three dead in under two seconds. Three dead with geometric precision.

Three dead, I think, shock and acid fear in my throat, but there are *four.*

And I'm twisting, struggling halfway to my feet, my bound hands unbalancing me, and Seamus's phone is only just hitting the ground. He's levelling his gun at Bel, not looking at me, the skin of his face stretched taut with shock and incoherent rage. I shove myself across the empty ground towards him; now he's four paces away, three . . .

I launch myself at him. In the split second before the air blurs, I see how thickset he is, how strong. I feel a trap door open in my gut. I only weigh fifty-seven kilos. The back of my brain does mass-velocity calculations, and even as he rushes up at me, I know it's not enough. He'll shoot me, then shoot my sister. The face of our soon-to-be-killer fills my vision.

I collide with his gun arm. It barely moves. A crooked elbow drives the wind from me and I flop down into the leaves. He looks down at me in surprise,

And his face . . .

"*. . . If you even think about turning to face me, I will blow your head clean off your shoulders . . .*"

His eyes meet mine, and he hesitates. His expression alters, bloody rage ebbing to white, abject terror; and it's like looking in a mirror, like looking at my own face, the face of a man who knows he's going to die.

Why didn't you want to look me in the face, Seamus? I guess now I'll never know.

I stare at the dark eye of his gun. I wait for the bang, the blow, the bullet. I wait for the pain and the sudden stop. I wait and I wait and I wait.

BANG.

I'm deafened, air screaming into my ears at unbearable velocity. The face before me jerks backwards, red erupting behind it.

BANG.

A second explosion, from behind the right temple. Leaden, I turn slowly, my eyes tracking the invisible path of those bullets to their source.

Her hair's bunched up behind her head, her arms locked as they hold the gun. Then she's sprinting towards me.

"Bel—" I begin, but she runs past me. She levels the gun at the human mess in the leaves and fires twice more into his chest. I watch dumbly as she crouches beside Seamus, lays down her gun, and takes his instead. With a click, she slides the black clip from the handle. Nine bulletheads glint there. She slams it back in. Her movements are smooth, direct, efficient.

She stands, and for a moment she is just Bel, my sister who I haven't seen for five hours and a lifetime, who I thought I'd never see again. I throw myself forwards and press myself against her. Cold metal slides against my wrist and my hands spring free. I cling to her, barely conscious of how my arms shake. Bel pulls me in tight. She whispers in my ear, her tone soothing, but her words not.

"Petey, Petey, there's no time . . ."

It's only then that I feel the nightmarish slickness of her clothes, her skin. I step back. She's painted in blood.

Red Wolf.

"Come on!"

She tries to pull me away, but I drag myself free of her. Ingrid's staggering towards us, her hands still zip-tied behind her back.

I go to help her and Bel doesn't argue. I grab Ingrid's arm and we sprint towards the woods. The second we make the trees, Bel stops us. She holds my gaze. The horrified numbness ebbs a little; as always I can't help but feel calmer when I look at her.

"You're okay," she tells me.

My jaw finally loosens. I look behind us. The agents still lie there, obstinately real, obstinately dead.

"H-h-how . . . W-w-where . . ." I manage finally. "How did you learn to do that?"

"Same way you learned differential calculus," she said. "Same way anyone learns anything. I studied and then, when I had the theory down, I practised." A tiny shrug. "It's all I've ever really wanted to do."

She raises a silver-handled knife and tosses it to me. I begin sawing at Ingrid's cuffs. It's only when the plastic frays and springs apart that I take a good look at what I'm holding. It's not a combat knife or a kitchen knife. It's a table knife, an expensive one with wicked sharp little serrations. The black design stamped on its blade is bloody but clearly visible: *nhm.*

The Natural History Museum.

"Bel."

The way I say it makes her look up at me. Brown eyes, a red-rimmed, eye-shaped wound my desperate hands couldn't staunch. The knife feels so ordinary in my hot little hand.

"It was you? You stabbed Mum?"

She nods, her face puzzled. "Of course it was," she says. "Who else did you think it was?"

"They . . ." I blink stupidly at Ingrid, fighting to think. "They told me it was Dad."

"Dad? What has Dad got to do with all this?"

Nothing. I realise, and suddenly, it's obvious. He was never here. He's the monster under the bed, the nightmare our mother always threatened us with. And 57 knew that. Of course they did. They used it to try to scare me into giving you up.

I think back to the museum, to all the pointed references to "him" they must have meant me to overhear, then the way Rita had gently herded me at Mum's bedside:

"A vicious bastard . . . egomaniacal . . . petty. It fits our profile."

Yeah, mine too, and they knew that. They were working me from the beginning.

Dad's never been anywhere near this. It was *you*, Bel. You are what they're afraid of. You're the wolf.

I drop back a step, as though I'll see her better: my axiom. I thought I knew her; I built all my understanding on her, and now I can feel it all falling down.

Like Gödel, and look what happened to him.

"Petey." She reaches for me. I jerk back from her hand and I can see in her face how much that hurts. She looks confused, betrayed, and even now in the midst of everything I can't bear to be the cause of that pain.

"But you know me," she pleads. "You've always known me. You were there at the beginning."

She doesn't say it. She doesn't have to.

You've always known I was a killer.

I feel like I'm choking on a sharp rock.

"But . . . Mum? B-but why?"

Her expression turns flat.

"She made me mad."

Beyond the wood, engines growl.

"Shit," she mutters. "I didn't think they'd be on us that fast."

She grabs my wrist and plunges us into the cover of a tangled coppice. Ingrid stumbles groggily after us.

Bel presses a finger to her lips. We crouch in the musty, wooded dark, listening past our own too-loud breath. The engines grow louder and then stop. Doors slam, barked orders in the distance.

Bel flicks the safety off her gun, seems to consider giving it to me, then thank Gauss, thinks better of it. Instead she swings it almost idly past me and—oh shit oh shit oh shit oh shit—aims it at Ingrid's forehead.

She knows, I realise then. Somehow, she knows about Ingrid.

"Bel"—I just about strangle my voice to a whisper—"yes, she was one of them, but she got me out. She saw the apple. She could have given you away and she didn't. She's with us now."

Bel barely seems to hear me. Her eyes are locked on Ingrid with the same dreadful concentration as when she killed Seamus. The tendons in her arm are as taut as cello strings; a single twitch in one of them could signal the curl of her trigger finger.

Ingrid darts a beseeching look at me, and then speaks.

"He's telling the truth. I can help. I want to help. I can tell you how they'll come for you."

The gun doesn't move, but neither does the trigger finger. The rustle and crack of advancing boots draw nearer.

"Two teams on the road by the front of the school," Ingrid continues, her whisper tight but controlled. "But only one team—four agents—coming in through the woods."

"Four people?" I say. Bel looks at me sharply. "Four people isn't nearly enough to cover the whole of the woods. They'll leave a gap. Is that why they're making so much noise? So we run the other way?"

Ingrid nods, very carefully.

"But why leave a gap at all? Why not just send another team?"

"They did," Bel says drily, and jerks her chin back towards the four corpses glistening bloodily in the clearing.

The shouts are so close now I can place them. They're coming from directly behind Ingrid's head. There's a snap off to the right, and I don't know if it's a twig breaking or a pistol cocking. Bel jerks her gun towards the sound, snorts, and finally lowers the damn thing. A breath I didn't even know I was holding rushes out of me.

"You get my message, Pete?"

Her tone is so casual. She tried to kill our mother, but she looks and sounds exactly the same as she always did.

"The Caesar shift in the camera clock? Our birthday as the key? Yeah, but barely; it was pretty obscure."

"It was the best I could do. By the time I realised the place was crawling with their people, the cameras were the only thing I could still access. Still, it was good advice, little bro, and it's time to follow it. Don't argue." She cuts me off as I open my mouth. "I'm your big sister. I know best."

"God, Bel, you're only eight minutes older." My response is automatic. I'm too punch-drunk for anything else.

"It was a race for the exit, and I won." Her eyes track the motion of something behind the trees. "Don't let that happen this time."

"Bel—"

But then she's off like a hare, plunging out of cover. Through the mesh of branches, I see her racing between the trees, careless of the noise as she crashes through the foliage.

"What the hell is she doing?" Ingrid demands. "Why's she heading for the school? The gap in the cordon is the other way!"

Fear for my sister tightens around my heart.

"She's leaving a trail, leading them away from us," I say. Seventeen seconds later, I hear boot steps, and through the leaves I spy black-clad figures sprint headlong past our little hiding place, guns ready, breaths heaving. *Red Wolf,* I think, and I hold that last image of her in my mind: that blood-streaked incarnation. They may be hunting her, but there's nothing about her that is prey.

"Come on," I whisper to Ingrid, and slip out of the back of the coppice. "Before they have time to cover back."

"Where are we going?" she asks.

I barely hear her. Bel, you're my sister, I love you and I know you and you tried to kill our mother; something had to have driven you to that. I have to retrace your steps, go where you went; see what you saw. I have to know *why.*

"We're going to find answers," I tell Ingrid.

Three dead in a heartbeat. A perfect Archimedes spiral.

I studied . . . I practised.

I pull Ingrid, unprotesting, behind me. Bel and I used to play hide-and-seek in these woods and I know all the secret places. It's almost dark. Soon we will be invisible.

You got my message, Pete. It was good advice. Time to follow it.

In my mind's eye, I see the static flaring out of the dusk, like a semaphore spelling that message out.

Run.

Run, Rabbit.

Run.

2:
INVERT

RECURSION: 2 YEARS, 6 MONTHS AGO

The fire raged, white and spectral against the night.

Even on the crest of the hill opposite, we felt the heat on our faces. We gawked and jostled amongst a crowd from the nearby village. A woman in a lavender dressing gown and wellies was jiggling a baby on her hip, but its crying only emphasised how silent everyone else was.

Firefighters scurried below, their shadows stretched and distorted like vast stick insects on the grass, but there was nothing they could do. Because this fire was fuelled by propane; the flames had caught at a mere 400 degrees but now they were up to speed and burning at a metal-chewing 1,800. The Kent Fire and Rescue Service would have needed a Sahara Desert's worth of dry powder to extinguish them and they didn't have it. There was no strategy but to let the relay station burn.

The next day, when the whole steel-and-concrete complex was blackened slag, churned up by spring rain, an investigation would begin. The report would conclude that while the damage made it hard to be certain, the evidence was consistent with a leak in the station's main condensate pump; the same as had caused the fire at the terminal in Augsberg, Pennsylvania, a year previously, and at Berry Hill, Australia, two years before that. All three facilities were owned and maintained by the same contractor and no one would be particularly surprised.

At least this time, unlike Berry Hill—I'd seen the pictures of the aftermath of that disaster, and those faces would erupt, peeled and screaming, into my dreams for weeks afterward—no one was hurt. The fire caught at one in the morning, the station's mechanism was fully automated, and a frantic search for the two security guards on duty had turned them up at a pub lock-in down the road in Durmsley, where they'd been drinking off the worst of the shakes at *almost* being caught in the explosion.

This time, they'd got lucky.

Bel turned to me, flames reflected in the tears in her eyes.

"I'm sorry, Pete," she said.

"It's okay, Bel," I told her. I hugged myself despite the heat coming off the fire, and wished there was a way to get the smell of gasoline out of my clothes. I put my hand to my forehead. My fingers came away red, blood from where I'd scratched my scab off earlier that night. I fretted about leaving DNA, but that's what the fire was for, and anyway, it was too late now.

"It'll always be okay."

NOW

"And in the shock to end all shocks, I find myself . . . in a cupboard."

"What?" Ingrid whispers.

"Nothing," I whisper back. The whispering is partly because of the need for secrecy, but mostly because of the cramped space. The proximity of our mouths to each other's ears means anything above a whisper would likely split our eardrums open.

It's not just our faces that are close together. All manner of Ingrid's bits are pressed against all manner of my bits in a way that is making me *extremely* conscious of the evolutionary biological purpose of said bits, which I guess would be exciting if we were stuck in this boiler closet for recreational reasons (my fourth cupboard in the last thirty-six hours, by the way, because you *know* how I like to keep count). Except these aren't recreational reasons; they're hiding-for-our-fucking-lives reasons, and I'm concerned that the blood flow to my . . . *particular* bits won't recognise the difference, especially since it's been exactly nineteen hours and forty-three minutes since we were struggling out of our ripped, bloody clothes, and Ingrid looked at me and smiled and . . .

An alarming trouser-wards shift in circulation warns me: *Don't. Think about. That.*

Think about how we got here instead. Think about what we need to do. After all, this plan has a lot of moving parts, a lot of wheels and cogs, big, toothy cogs you could very much get caught in and chewed up by, so focus, Petey.

Focus.

• • •

Last night: we were just about to break the tree line when I dragged Ingrid back. She lost her balance and sprawled onto the leaves.

"Pete, what the hell?"

"Wait a minute," I panted. Peering between tree trunks, I could see the road. It was deserted under the orange glow of the streetlights, the semis on the other side as neat and quiet as dollhouses. "They left a gap in their cordon."

"I know. That's what we're heading for."

"But wouldn't they *expect* us to do that? I mean, if they catch Bel and we're not with her, wouldn't they immediately assume this was our escape route?"

Frankie's words from earlier in that endless day bobbed to the surface of my mind like mines on water. *Four hundred thousand CCTV cameras in this city* . . . We had to assume 57 had access to them all. I imagined their lines of sight spread out across the whole of London, an invisible net to snare us. There was no way we could avoid all of them. Two bloodied, exhausted teenagers stumbling around the streets of South London with nowhere to go and no place to hide; 57 would be on us in a heartbeat.

"You have a better idea?" Ingrid asked. "We can't stay here."

I looked back towards the familiar edifice of the school, bulked against the night, and though I could almost hear my past self laughing hysterically at the idea, school was as close to friendly territory as I could think of right now.

"You know what? Maybe we can."

It was a nervy retreat. Making it to the edge of the woods had taken less than three minutes; retracing those steps took nearly forty-five, wary as we were of every loose stone and dry twig.

Night seemed to teeter eternally on the edge of dusk, then fell full and sudden. The wood became a dense nest of overlapping shadows. We listened to the small sounds of it, the rustle of animals, the inquisitive peeps of birds. Two heart-seizing cracks that might have been gunshots echoed in the distance, then another two, then one farther off, and a vague hubbub of shouting before the firefight moved on. I comforted myself with the memory of Bel's grin, its vicious confidence. She'd be okay. She had to be. I checked my watch: it was 8:20 P.M.

"Come on," I said when the sound died down. "Inside, before they come back."

The school had alarms, but the 57 agents had broken in to look for Bel, so they must have disabled them. There were cameras, but I'd been dodging them for years. We were careful to close doors behind us and kept our ears pricked for footsteps in case the agents decided to make another sweep, but the minutes ticked by, and no one came. With luck, they'd followed our trail to the edge of the woods and assumed we'd run for it.

First stop was the school shop storeroom. Our skins and clothes were covered in a stinking laminate of blood and terror sweat in a style that could best be described as "postapocalyptic abattoir worker" and that was unlikely to pass unnoticed on the street tomorrow. We smuggled stolen uniforms, scarves, and anoraks to the boys' changing room.

Without a word, Ingrid began to struggle out of her clothes. It took a second and a half (bloody shirt slapping to the floor) for me to realise what was happening, and another three-quarters (bra unclipped and hanging dangerously from her shoulders, back arched like a swimmer ready to dive) for me to twig that this was an invitation. I blushed hard, hesitated, babbled three gibberish syllables, and then turned my back, just catching a glimpse of her exasperated expression as I fought not to lose my balance and impale myself on my own erection.

I was ridiculously, unaccountably horny. My sex drive had kicked up about eleven gears, which, given I'm a seventeen-year-old boy, put it at escape velocity. I'd read about libidos spiking in the wake of a big adrenaline hit, but I'd never experienced it before. It's really weird: your brain chemistry shouting contradictory instructions at you like a war-movie drill sergeant.

Private Blankman! ATTENTION! Run! Hide! Run again! Good! Now you're no longer in immediate physical danger, father as many off-spring as possible in the next sixty seconds, in case the threat comes back! AT THE DOUBLE, YOU MISERABLE MAGGOT!

I stood with my back to the showers, hearing the water run, my face on fire, feeling like I'd just fluffed the biggest opportunity of my likely-to-be-foreshortened life. So why did I hold back? If Ingrid had asked, I would have tried to rationalise, said our relationship was already as complicated as the Riemann Hypothesis and didn't need to be any more so. But she didn't need to ask. She knew the ridiculously predictable truth: I was scared.

Scrubbed and dressed, we crept through the corridors and the ivy-covered cloisters, their unfamiliar emptiness making them feel cavernous. Next stop was the kitchens for dinner (panic yawned in my gut at the sight of the huge cellophane-covered tubs of ham and coleslaw in the fridge, but the need for secrecy held me back and I took only a little from the top of each). Then came the computer lab, where we liberated a boxy laptop whose IP address couldn't be linked to either of us.

The adrenaline that had coursed through our bodies for so much of the day drained from us, leaving us shivering and exhausted, but there was still work to do. Eventually, when we had everything we needed, we bedded down in the staff common room on cushions dragged off sofas and traded jokes about the headmistress's portrait on the wall. For a moment, it was as if time had stopped. There was no past and no future; only the bubble of present, and I really could have believed my best friend and I were just sneaking around school after hours for a laugh. But then Ingrid stretched and turned over, and the only sound was the ticking of the mantelpiece clock. I lay awake, counting the seconds that my murderous, hunted sister was having to survive out there in the dark.

After eight hundred and sixteen of them, I gave up on trying to sleep and went to the window. The night was calm and moonlit, a breeze carving parabolas in the grass. Even after showering, I could still feel the slipperiness of the bloody knife under my palm. The fresh blood belonged to the agents Bel killed in front of me, but underneath, dried into the grooves of the engraved letters on the blade, was my mother's. *Mum.* Blood throbbed in my temples, and with every thud, I heard the beep of Mum's breathing machine.

Bel. It was you. You stabbed Mum.

And Bel's shrug as she said, *She made me mad.*

You and the whole world, sis, because nothing makes sense now.

What if I never saw her again?

What if Mum *died?*

I felt alone then. Truly alone. Like I'd fallen down a well and worn my throat hoarse from shouting for help that wouldn't come. When I turned back towards our makeshift bed, Ingrid's eyes were open, watching me. She didn't need to say anything. Ingrid was my best friend. She knew what I was thinking, knew me better than anyone, but that didn't mean she could make it better.

Please, please don't be dead, Mum.

Don't make Bel your killer.

Don't be dead.

At 5 A.M. I woke with Ingrid's hand over my mouth.

"Cleaners have just arrived," she whispered in my ear. I could hear the faint whir of a vacuum down the hall. We rose quickly and silently, reset the cushions, and slipped into this boiler closet, where, for the last eleven and a half hours, we've been sweating and waiting. I've prayed to all the gods I can think of that the school's central heating wouldn't need maintenance today, all the while listening to the shouts, laughter, and swearing of the school day playing out around us like a radio play.

I check my watch over Ingrid's shoulder.

"Ready?" I mutter to Ingrid. "We're going to have to time this *just* right."

"Yep, I . . . Wait, Pete, listen."

I freeze, thinking she's heard footsteps, or worse, the creaking of the cupboard's hinges, but then I catch it—the rattle of raindrops against the windows in the corridor outside. I can't see Ingrid's face, but I know her grin matches mine as we pull our anorak hoods up.

"Finally," she whispers, "some good luck."

An instant later the end-of-day bell goes, clanging like a fire alarm.

"Now," I mutter.

Ingrid fumbles for the doorknob behind me, and we spill out into the corridor about a fifth of a second before it floods with chatting, laughing, uniformed figures. We separate, as we'd discussed, catching each other in the corners of our eyes without looking directly at one another, letting the pressure wave of schoolkids carry us down the steps and out into the rain. I hunch my shoulders and duck my head against the downpour, smiling as I see others around me do the same.

A security camera peers down from atop the main gate, but all it will see is a tide of undifferentiated blue-grey-clad students, the same as it sees every day at 4:30 P.M., the same as every traffic and CCTV camera on every street for the next five blocks will see:

Noise around the signal.

A little knot in my chest loosens; this might actually work.

We meet up about a half mile from the school gates. The rain has doubled, falling in freezing, drenching sheets, but Ingrid and I eschew the buses that throw gull wings of water from the gutter as they growl down the road. It takes fifty-five sock-squelching minutes to walk to Streatham.

"Just so you know," I tell Ingrid, blowing rain off my top lip and squaring up to the front door of 162 Rye Hill like an opponent in a wrestling match, "if this goes horribly wrong, if there's an alarm we can't shut off, or a dog we can't calm down, or if Anita Vadi's dad is some kind of psycho mad scientist and has the welcome mat wired up to fry intruders with sixty thousand volts, I'm blaming you."

She gives me a long, level look.

"Me?" she says evenly. "This was *your* idea."

"Yeah, but I was relying on *you*, as the professional spy in this partnership, to come up with something better."

"What can I tell you, Pete?" She shrugs. "Sometimes an idea can be the best on offer and *still* suck enormous elephant balls."

The idea, which so manifestly sucked, was born last night between dinner and lights-out, when, randomly trying door handles, I found the school office unlocked and pulled Ingrid in behind me.

"Those mad leet hacking skillz you're always on about?" I asked as I flicked on the computer and brought up a password screen. "They just talk, or do you reckon you can break into this?"

"Bit of an odd time to fix your physics grades, isn't it?" she asked, arching an eyebrow.

"My physics grade is stellar, as you well know,"

She peered over my shoulder. "Try 'Wuffles2012.'"

I frowned, but typed. The log-in box changed to an egg timer.

"Holy shit, you really do have mad leet skillz."

She held up her right hand. A yellow Post-it was stuck to the index finger with a password scrawled on it in tiny writing.

"The madness," she said drily. "The leetness."

I flushed and hammered in the password. I clicked through a few of the folders on the desktop until I found the school roll. I scrolled down through the names, reading the notes next to them.

My heart seized a little as I went through the *R*s: fear muscle memory, even though I knew *Rigby* wouldn't be there. Goading me off the roof of the senior block was pretty well Ben's last act at Denborough College before his family moved up to Edinburgh. Rumour was, his mum was in a psych ward up there. I remembered the shudder that had passed through my body when I'd heard: of relief, but also of pity. *If my mum was locked up in an asylum,* I'd thought, *maybe I'd be a bullying prick too.*

"This one," I said at last. "Anita Vadi. Know her?"

"Tall girl, year below, good in jujitsu, and I've got the bruises to prove it. Why?"

"Her parents have pulled her and her little sister out of school for this whole week to go to a family wedding. We're going to need somewhere to crash where your former colleagues won't think to look. What do you reckon the odds are the Vadi house is empty?"

"Peter, that's criminal. I'm impressed."

I glowed. Even though she'd been a cuckoo in my life the whole time I'd known her—Ingrid's approval still mattered to me. I was startled by just how much.

Thank the gods of stochastic weather patterns for the rain. Only three people pass by on the street, and none of them brave the deluge long enough to enquire after the two schoolkids loitering under the porch of the handsome redbrick house.

"I'll keep watch," Ingrid says. "You knock in the bottom right pane in the door."

"Shouldn't it be the other way round?" I counter.

"Why?"

"You could pick the lock or something."

"That's burglars you're thinking of. I'm a spy."

"So your skill set's more 'get other people to do incriminating things against their better judgment'?"

"Bingo."

When I reach inside for the latch, no alarm sounds, and there is no dog, but a tiny ginger guard cat does come bounding up the hall and rolls ferociously over to have its tummy rubbed.

"Cats are such sluts," Ingrid observes disapprovingly. She's always been a dog person. The post piled up against the door is a good sign, but Ingrid still insists on checking upstairs to confirm that the house is empty.

When she comes down again, I've set up at the kitchen table. But the first thing I did was pull off my belt, thread it through the fridge door handles, and tie it shut. Ingrid cocks an eyebrow at it.

"A reminder to myself," I say. "An extra couple of seconds to think. I don't want to leave any signs we were here, and Hurricane Pete's trail of devastation through Grandma's special quiche would definitely give the game away."

Ingrid nods. We all have our tics; she knows that better than anyone. Her hands are bare and the scars on the back of them are pink where she's been scrubbing them. I thought I heard the water run. She pulls up a chair and flicks on our contraband laptop.

"What are you doing?" I ask.

"It's more what *you're* doing."

She spins the laptop towards me.

"The Police National Computer? What the fuck, Ingrid?"

"We need to get our report card." This earns her a blank look. She sighs. "My old firm is long on influence but short on bodies, and if we really *have* lost them, they'll have dragged in the local bobbies to lend a hand in the search."

She nods at the laptop.

"The PNC's based on UNIX servers and the infrastructure's embarrassingly old. You might even be able to use that back door that hit the dark web in August. I wouldn't be surprised if they haven't closed it yet."

Casting a wary look at her, I start to type. "This'd go faster if you did it," I grumble. "You're better at this than I am."

"But then how would you learn, young padawan?"

She watches over my shoulder and smiles as the log-in box gives way to a loading icon. She sits, spins the laptop back to face her, and hammers some keys, and her smile stretches to a grin.

"Congratulations, Pete," she says. "Not just the Met, but every police force in the country has been alerted to arrest you on sight."

She scrolls down a bit more.

"Aaaand me too. Although nobody had *better* recognise me from that; that's a *terrible* picture. I look like a middle-aged accountant after a disappointing orgasm."

"Let me see."

"Not a chance." She shoves me playfully back into my seat and keeps tapping.

"Bloody hell," she mutters. "They've even put Interpol on notice. You pulled off a world-class vanishing act, White Rabbit. They think we might even have left the country."

The relief in her voice is audible, but I can't share in it, not yet.

"Bel?" I ask.

More keystrokes. Her smile falls.

"No mention of her."

I shove myself away from the desk, filled up suddenly with disappointment and dread. Before I know what I'm doing, I'm tugging at the belt on the fridge door, a gaping vacuum yawning in my belly. I have to feed the maw.

Before I can get the belt undone, a scarred hand's on mine, warm, gently pulling me away.

"It doesn't mean they have her," Ingrid says softly. I can feel her breath on my ear. "It doesn't mean she's caught. It just means they haven't told the police."

"Why?" I demand, staring at the black-and-white-tiled floor. I'm suddenly stubborn and childish. "Why wouldn't they tell them?"

There's a catch in Ingrid's voice when she answers, and I know she's thinking of the bodies fallen among the leaves.

"Who on earth would you send to arrest her?"

I slowly relax my death grip on the belt. I let Ingrid lead me back to the table, and my gaze falls on the laptop.

"We're on the police network right now?" I ask.

"Yep."

"Can we pull old case files?"

"Top left." She indicates an icon. I click on it and a search form pops up, and I start to fill it out. Looking over my shoulder, Ingrid asks, "What are you looking for?"

A slow frost creeps up the skin of my back as I answer. Sometimes hearing the crazy shit I'm thinking aloud is enough to convince me it isn't true.

But not this time.

"Unsolved murders, from March two years ago."

Ingrid looks at me sharply. "Unsolved *murders*? Why?"

In my mind's eye, I see a tornado of autumn leaves, a perfect Archimedes spiral, three bodies falling, three lives taken with geometric precision.

"She said she practised." My throat is parched.

Ingrid doesn't question me again. I hit Return, and the form disappears, replaced by a string of results.

Ingrid peers at the screen and whistles quietly.

"Is there anything specific you're looking for? A place, a . . . technique?"

I shake my head. "We need it all. From everywhere. Shootings, stabbings, strangulation, the works."

I keep my voice flat, my language blunt, even though every word feels like an electric shock in my mouth. Euphemisms would be worse, though. I have to be scientific, precise. It's the only way I can keep going. Reflected in the screen, Ingrid's expression is starkly horrified.

"Investigating a crime is searching for a pattern," I tell her. "It's cryptography. It's maths. Each body is another data point, and Bel knows that and she'll have done all she can to keep them from being connected. She'll have tried to make them look random . . ."

"But random's hard to fake," Ingrid finishes for me. She's very pale.

"That's what I'm hoping."

Very gently, Ingrid pushes the laptop aside and comes to sit on the edge of the table, right in front of me.

"Pete," she says quietly. "How do you know all this?"

"I shared a womb with her," I reply, trying to sound flippant. But she's looking at me and I know she's reading the truth from my face, and I make no attempt to hide it. I feel the memories pushing up through the soil of my mind like zombies.

I know this is how Bel operates, because I taught her.

RECURSION: 2 YEARS, 6 MONTHS AGO

"Who is he?" I asked.

Bel's voice was wrung out from crying. Her makeup had run and sweat plastered her hair to her forehead. She sounded empty as she said, "I don't know."

It was such a beautiful night. Summer had come early, and the vice of the day's heat had slackened blissfully into evening. The trees cast long blue shadows over the lawn, just visible in the last of the light. I was finally off crutches, still limping but improving. I felt free.

It seems callous now, but even with Bel's warning ringing around my skull, I still felt joyful to be led by her hand, barefoot over the grass.

That joy only faltered a little when we slipped through the gap in the fence and out onto the railway tracks. Never in a million years would I have crossed the tracks by myself. The thought of a train surging suddenly out of darkness—glaring headlights and momentum and shattering force—would have frozen me solid. But I wasn't by myself; I was with my sister, and with her I was invincible. We picked our way between the sleepers, scrambled down the verge, and belly-crawled under the ivy-covered loose chain link on the other side into the alleyway between the tracks and the estate. I took in nine sheets of discarded newspaper, six rusting drink cans, and a roll of carpet left so long it was growing mould. So far, so familiar.

Only there was *something* new. Sticking stiffly out of the end of the carpet, laces dangling from a trainer, white skin stretched between bones and muscle where the scummy jean leg had ridden up over the ankle, was a human foot.

I don't remember feeling any shock when I saw it, just a sense of inevitability. Almost a kind of relief: *It's finally happened.* The worst had come. I grasped the ankle, feeling for a pulse. I didn't find one.

"Tell me," I said.

"I—I . . ." Bel stumbled as she started to speak, as though her lips were numb. "I was coming back from the gig. I think he was in the same carriage with me on the tube, but I'm not sure. He must have followed me off at the station—"

I interrupted her.

"Just you, or did others get off there as well?"

She frowned.

"Others."

"How many?"

"F-five or six."

"Was it five, or was it six?"

"I don't know."

"Think."

"Five."

"Okay, go on."

She faltered and then picked up the story.

"They went up the road and I came under the underpass to here. I had my headphones on. I didn't know he was behind me until he grabbed my wrist. I tried to pull away, but he wouldn't let go. He said he wanted my phone, my purse. He said I was pretty and I should smile, like, hey, he was mugging me, but he was doing me a favour giving me the *attention*, you know?"

She went quiet for a second, and then:

"He had a knife."

A knife. I felt a spark of hope. The part of me that was still trying to piece this together in a way that left our life intact latched onto that word.

"It was self-defence," I said. "We can go to the police, we can tell them that . . ."

But Bel was already shaking her head.

"No, Petey," she said gently, willing me to understand. She showed me her hands; her palms were pristine. No defensive wounds. Her face was unblemished in the streetlight.

"You were afraid for your life," I protested. She looked at the floor, and her tone hardened.

"I wasn't afraid. I was angry. All I could think about was how tight his hand was on my wrist and how fucking certain he was, how . . . entitled, how he just knew, he just *knew* I was going to submit. And then I found myself thinking about Dad, and how Mum's eyes look when she talks about him, all puffy and exhausted and . . ." She tailed off, but I knew what she meant.

"Bruised," I said. She nodded.

"And I wondered if Dad had ever held Mum's wrist like that. And then I hit him. I hit him fast and hard, and I kept hitting him."

She wasn't looking at me anymore. She was staring back through the chain link towards our house.

"So he tried to use his knife, and I took it."

Her voice cracked then, and fear flooded into it. An answering fear rose in my chest. And a welter of emotions came with it: shock—I'd never heard Bel scared before—and a pinprick of white-hot fury at the man who had reduced her to this.

"I'm sorry," she whispered.

In an instant, I glimpsed our future: capital-E Empty spaces in the house and at school where she ought to have been, long drives into the middle of nowhere to a squat grey building of razor wire and concrete, Bel behind scratched Perspex, puffy faced and slurring, telling us she's *fine* and me knowing she is lying because she won't tell me the truth if she thinks it's going to hurt me.

"It's okay," I told her. What else could I say? "It'll be okay."

She looked at me, her eyes wide and very white in the darkness.

"How?" she asked, and I needed an answer. Later, when it was too late, I'd wonder if I should have felt doubt, or guilt for the slowly stiffening corpse in its carpet sarcophagus, but at the time I just . . . didn't. All I felt was a piercing, urgent clarity in the cool night air. My big sister needed me. After fifteen years of having my back, *she* needed *me*. I couldn't let her down.

Bel hugged herself. She was trembling and I knew that in a better light I'd see her lips were blue; I knew exactly how that felt. She was my inverse, my opposite, but in a way that made her the same—a mirror image. Bel was scared, and so was I, but the difference was *I was used to it*. She might have a PhD in falling, but I was the one who'd made my home in the dirt.

I tried to think. I dragged my hands through my hair and down my face, and they came away bloody. Shit, I'd pulled the scab off my forehead.

A train rocketed past, briefly deafening, light sneaking through ivy leaves, the vacuum in its wake tugging at our clothes. When insight came, it came so naturally. Pain surged in my brow, but it only made me feel more clear-headed. Without even thinking about it, I walled myself off from my emotions with numbers, as I'd done so many times before.

Get counting.

5 passengers exited the train with Bel, any one of whom might plausibly have been the last to see this man alive. 3 CCTV cameras between here and the station, but crucially, 0 since the overpass, which was the last juncture where he could have changed course. 6 windows in the estate that overlooked this spot, but all a long way off, and I doubted anyone behind them could have seen anything in the dark. Very few people used this trash-strewn alleyway and then pretty much only as a shortcut to and from the station. I checked my watch: 10:26 p.m. 94 minutes until the last train, and about 7 hours after that until daylight.

Bel stared at me as I hustled around the alleyway, gathering up newspaper and cardboard and laying it on top of the carpet, weighting it down with chunks of brick.

"Come on," I said when it was as covered as I could make it. I took her hand; it was very cold. *Get her through this. You have to get her through this.* You *have to.*

"W-we're just going to leave him?" she asked uncertainly.

"We can't move him until the trains stop; there's too big a risk someone might walk through." I checked my watch again. "That gives us . . . eighty-nine minutes to look."

"Look for what?" she asked. She sounded lost and I wished I had time to stop and explain it to her, but we were already under the fence and I was hobbling hurriedly on my bad leg. The pain and the effort were making it hard to speak. Now it was me leading *her* by the hand, back across the moonlit grass, back home.

There's only one way to make sure you aren't found, and that's to make sure no one's looking. If that man, whoever he was, was reported missing, they'd be searching for him. If he turned up *dead,* they'd be searching for his killer. We couldn't let that happen.

We needed a fire, a fucking hot one; we needed it somewhere a fire could reasonably be expected to burn, and we had less than an hour and a half to find it.

I threw up as many proxies and IP masks as I knew how. I'd always had a vague interest in hacking, but I'd only started investing serious time in it since I'd met Ingrid (I know, I know, "teenage boy's renewed fascination in common interest with pretty girl shocker"). Shields duly up, I flew into research. I was bathed in sweat inside my T-shirt, and my fingers kept slipping off the keys as they typed, my right hand marking them with minuscule flecks of blood from my forehead.

I started by looking for the temperature at which human teeth, the hardest, most mineralised part of the body, would burn. That gave me 900 degrees Celsius. Then I searched for fuels that would burn that hot at full blast. Whoever the patron saint of arson and perverting the course of justice was, she must have been watching over us, because methane topped the list: ordinary domestic gas. An idea formed, the beginnings of a feverish plan: an industrial accident. But could we do it without hurting anyone?

Another search found a company—Methinor PLC—which had a history of their facilities going up in flames (there are a truly terrifying number of those still merrily doing business), and a third turned up Methinor's closest installation to us—a relay and sampling station outside Durmsley, Kent. According to Google Maps, it was only a two-hour drive away and—I actually punched the air when I read this—

Fully. Fucking. *Automated.*

I glanced at the clock in the corner of the screen: 10:59 P.M. One hour to go. Bel fretted and fidgeted on the bed, rolling her eyes over the posters, from maths genius to mutant and back again. I kept my head down and worked.

More digging gave me Alterax Protection Solutions, the UK security contractor that listed Methinor as one of its testimonials. A couple more clicks turned up someone's dissertation from the marketing module of their MBA, the appendix to which contained the pitch Alterax had used to win Methinor over, including a slide on how the proposed placement of security cameras could cut down on personnel costs. Even better, as part of their deal with the Australian government after their last disaster, Methinor had made the blueprints for their facilities available on a database on a closed industry website, so engineers from other companies could point out safety concerns.

For a few precious seconds, I sat staring at the pieces of the plan I'd concocted, scarcely believing our luck. Surely this bomb-in-waiting should be better protected? But then, I realised, there was no *reason* for it to be. It was in the middle of nowhere, supplied nowhere strategic, and held nothing valuable. There was no obvious motive to sabotage it, and hence no motive to spend the money to secure it.

I blinked. Suddenly, more clearly than ever, I saw the network of little assumptions and compromises and accommodations that our society was built on. They were necessary fictions that made everything else work, like the square root of minus one— the so-called "imaginary" number that mathematicians had dubbed i—an impossible number that made bridges stay up and aircraft fly.

All those little compromises and mutual understandings were bones in a skeleton; society was stretched over them like a skin. Bel and I were outside that skin now, hostile foreign bodies probing it for weaknesses. The mind-set felt familiar, and I realised: it was just like checking a proof, combing the logic for the single, fatal, unwarranted leap.

By the time Bel put a hand on my shoulder and murmured, "It's time," I had what I needed.

I stood and was startled to find myself unsteady. My hands shook and droplets of sweat dotted the keyboard.

"You got the cling film?" I asked.

"Yes."

The body was just as we'd left it. We dragged the coverings off it. A beetle picked its way over a patch of bloodless skin showing at the ankle. I swatted it away. The flesh under my hand felt like refrigerated meat. The night was darker now, quieter, and we worked swiftly and silently, the washing-up gloves squeaking on our fingers as we wound the cellophane wrap around and around the rolled-up carpet until it looked like a vast spliff. Just before we sealed up the part that covered the head, I gestured for Bel to stop. I felt a sudden urge to peel back the carpet, to look at this man's face, but I didn't. Partly, I didn't want to see what she'd done to him—I imagined a sagging tear in his throat, drooling black where the blood had fled it, echoing his mouth—but it was more than that. If anyone ever came around flashing a picture of him, I didn't want to recognise it. I didn't want so much as a flicker in the muscles of my face to betray us.

"Done?" I asked when we were finished.

Bel nodded. I risked a little light from my phone screen to check for rips, but the plastic was intact.

"Bring the car around," I said.

Mum was away at a conference until Monday, and if we were careful, there would be no telltale stray hairs or threads in the back of her Prius to indict her children for murder.

The body was locked solid and the carpet made it more manageable, but I still almost dropped it twice as I struggled under my end of it with my ungainly limping waddle. (The corpse was already an "it" in my mind, not a "him." Never a "him"; I couldn't have done this if it was a "him.")

Bel slid in behind the wheel. Mum felt driving was an *Important Life Skill*™, and that it was her job and "not the bloody government's" to know when her children were ready to learn. She'd been letting us practise since we turned fifteen.

We passed the drive south in silence, city lights giving way to the near total darkness of country roads. I kept thinking: *This is how it happens.* This is how you become one of those faces you see on the news: square-on and sullen-eyed in the harsh light of the police camera. You can't rely on not being "that kind of person." No one *is* that kind of person. One moment, one violent, drunken stranger rearing in front of you, one loss of self-control is all it takes.

I looked across at Bel's pinched face in the wash from the oncoming headlights. I thought of my daily fight for control of myself, and how often I lost. How long had it taken her to kill this man? Five seconds? Ten? I counted them out in my head:

One Mississippi, two Mississippi, three Mississippi, four Mississippi, five Mississippi, six Mississippi, seven Mississippi, eight Mississippi, nine Mississippi, ten Mississippi.

That's it. That's how long it takes you to fuck up your life.

We pulled up well short of the relay station. Bel slipped out to scout, the printout of the blueprints with my hand-scrawled guesses of where the cameras would be clutched in her hand. Even then I was impressed by how silently she moved. In her wake, the darkness pressed in. I kept waiting for blue flare of police lights to rupture it. I was so tensed for the scream of sirens that if they *had* come, I might have broken my back with the jolt.

I thought of the body in the boot, imagined it moving, struggling inside the shrink-wrapped carpet, pushing at it like an insect inside a vast chrysalis, suffocating, choking. I fought to swallow against a gummed-shut throat. Could we have got it wrong? Could he still be alive? No. I'd felt the chill of his pulseless ankle, and I'd felt his stiffness as we carried him. There's a reason they call it deadweight.

Who was he? Did he have a family? Kids? I besieged myself with questions, abetted by the quiet and the dark. It dawned on me then that I could never know the answers. Any attempt I made to research him would draw a thread between us that could be followed back to me, and from me to Bel.

Still, I couldn't help picturing his kid, a little girl maybe, tossing and turning under her duvet, unable to sleep because she didn't know where her dad was.

Bel melted out of the dark.

"Two security guards, you said?" she whispered.

"I think so."

"They're both in the hut on the far side; steam on the windows says they're having a cuppa."

I exhaled hard, once. "Then let's go."

Inside the relay station, it took me seven minutes to find the condensate pump, and for every one of them I was heart-stoppingly terrified the blueprints were wrong.

"No," I told Bel. The bulging plastic-wrapped cocoon squeaked as she dragged it over the floor. "Not that close. Shield it behind that piping."

"Why?"

"There'll be a blast," I said. "A shock wave."

I thought of Hiroshima. *66 kilos, 1.38 percent, 18 atmospheres, 2 miles, 66,000 people dead.* There was maths for everything.

"We need it to burn. The last thing we want is for identifiable body parts to be distributed all over South Kent."

And I heard how matter of fact I was, and I felt sick, and I looked at Bel and forced the nausea back down my throat.

Get through this. Get her *through this.*

My fingers hesitated over the pump's release valve, but it only took one look at Bel's face to stiffen my resolve. I twisted it and heard the hiss. We fled, chased by the echoing trickle of petrol from the open can Bel was trailing behind her. Out the door and up the hill, Bel at a run, me at a stumbling, hobbling skip, lungs burning, flailing with my arms and my head for extra speed. From the slope, I could see the security shed on the other side of the compound. A lance of torchlight stabbed the darkness. It was closing, but still far enough away.

"Now," I whispered.

A tiny arrowhead of flame illuminated Bel's fingertips. The glow caught her face, enraptured by the fire.

"Quick!"

She didn't respond. The torchlight drew nearer and suddenly, sickeningly, I wondered if I'd worked the blast radius out wrong. I had an image of a dumpy, bleary-eyed security guard; hot shrapnel tearing through his cheek, his brain. The torchlight advanced and above the beam, a cigarette glowed.

"BEL!" I yelled.

The flame fell, became a bright streak racing away ahead of us, and I slammed my hands over my ears for the bang.

NOW

"Eat, Etep, Peat. *Peter!*"

Two syllables. A name. *My* name. Sound is the first thing to come back. Then light. Everything's out of focus. A cream-and-yellow blob hovers in front of me, making concerned noises. I blink, my eyelashes like flies' feet on my cheeks, and water . . . *tears* clear from my eyes.

The blob resolves into Ingrid, her face pinched and even paler than usual.

She saw it all.

I swallow stale tears. I squint into the shaft of sunlight from the kitchen window. The weather's cleared. How long have I been sitting here, hunched over the table, fingers gouging my thighs? A long string of drool connects parched lips to a spot of wetness on my groin. I try to spit it away, but I can't dislodge it. I try to stand, but my muscles are like rubber and they don't answer . . .

I must have had an attack, an avalanche of memories that overwhelmed me before I even knew it was coming. No time to count, no time to speak, no time to fight. I feel the frantic trip of my heart begin to slow. Ingrid's lips move and it takes me three of its exhausted beats to make out what she's saying.

"*Jesus, Pete.*"

And I know. She saw everything.

"B . . . but . . ." It takes me a couple of tries as it dawns on me. "You already *knew,* you had to know . . ."

"Pete." Ingrid's eyes are huge. "I had no idea."

"But . . ." I run my hand through the air over my face, a

clown's mime, applying makeup. "With your *thing*. You must have read it off me before now."

"It happened two years ago," Ingrid says. "I'd only known you for a handful of months before that. I told you, I had to get to know you *incredibly well* before I could read you that fully. I mean, I could sense something was wrong, but you didn't talk and I had a rapport to build. I didn't want to push you too hard too early."

"But . . ." My brain seems stuck on that word. "But *since* then . . ."

"Peter." Her brown eyes are troubled. "I honestly don't think you've thought about it since then."

I sag back in my chair like a defeated boxer. Can that really be true? I have to grip the chair arms to push myself to my feet.

So, this is what it feels like to suppress a memory.

No fanfare, no ostentatious gap in my past, just a total absence of attention. *ARIA*, I think. Christ, what a thing: a creature of self-extending memory, and not just self-extending, but self-*selecting*. Able to take up a scalpel and excise any part of itself it deems too shameful, too dangerous.

I feel like a drain's opened up in my stomach.

What else have I forgotten? What else have I *done*?

"Do you need to rest?"

I shake my head.

"I really think you should . . ."

"*No.*" I bite my lip and taste metal on my tongue. "I need to get working. I need to, to fix . . ."

I don't even finish the thought it's so inadequate.

Ingrid doesn't look convinced, but she turns the laptop around to face me anyway.

"Okay, then. The data pull's complete. Do what you have to do."

I begin by flicking through files, page after page of the faces and fates of strangers: *bludgeoned, stabbed, strangled.* It forms a gory nursery rhyme in my head, twisting itself around rhymes I learnt as a kid. *Bludgeoned, stabbed, strangled, divorced, beheaded, survived!*

Alongside these top three all-stars of the cause-of-death world, there were other, more exotic ways to snuff it. A middle-aged man in pyjamas was found locked in an eighteenth-century tea chest with a hole bored into the side, his skin cherry pink from carbon monoxide poisoning. There were close-ups of the splinters under his fingernails. The coroner speculated that the assailant (still unknown) had drilled through the box, backed their car exhaust up to the hole, and (*Jesus*) turned the key while the victim clawed and hammered at his impromptu coffin. Then there was the body of a young girl, hands, head, and feet missing, dismembered at the joints, each piece individually shrink-wrapped and shoved into an industrial butcher's freezer in Hammersmith alongside the pork legs and the beef ribs. Her right calf and her left forearm were still missing. The investigator was resigned to them having been bought, and in all likelihood served by one of the butcher's high-end restaurant clientele. And then there was one where . . .

Concentrate, Pete, I berate myself. *Don't get lost in the details. Stick to the stuff that matters.*

"I didn't think there would be so many," I say.

"Official unsolved murders are relatively rare," Ingrid replies. She's flicking through a Jilly Cooper novel she found on a shelf in the front room. "But I pulled in the accidentals, the suicides, and the unexplained ones too. Figured if your sis is as good as you say, she might have disguised her work."

"What a comforting thought." I open up a blank spreadsheet and start to fill it in.

Each row is a death, neatly encapsulated inside the flickering tramlines. In the columns I put any characteristic I can find in the reports that I can link to a number: victim's age, height, weight, income, hours between death and discovery, minutes it took them to die, number of plausible suspects, size of immediate family . . .

I'm encoding, translating these drily bureaucratised stories of death into a language I can work with. In a sense I'm *encrypting*. All translation is encryption, after all. There's no such thing as plaintext; there are only codes you understand and codes you don't.

I work until my eyes feel like marbles in my head and dusk cloaks the world beyond the windows. At some point Ingrid taps me on the shoulder and takes over, taking the laptop to the basement, where neighbours won't see the light from the screen. I go upstairs but can't bring myself to get into any of the beds. I feel like I'd be stealing: a fairy-tale demon thieving nights of rest from innocents simply by lying in their beds.

I curl up on the sofa in the darkened front room, starting each time headlights sweep through the gauze curtains, in case this is the time they stop and I hear footsteps on the gravel and a key in the lock or, worse, a boot hammering through the door.

To take my mind off it, I study the bookshelves in the near dark and recognise the covers of a bunch of Terry Pratchett books I have at home. On the mantelpiece an Indian family smiles at me from a photo: a husband, a wife, and two daughters. I recognise the older one—Anita: a face glimpsed in school corridors and assemblies and on the cork noticeboard in reports about the jiujitsu team. I never thought of her as someone who read Pratchett. I never thought of her as anyone in particular at all.

An ankle, I think, *pale as death, a body lying stiff under my fingers, shrouded in a mould-specked carpet and covered in sterile plastic.* He was someone in particular too.

I close my eyes and see all those faces from the files. Their expressions have the blankness of the morgue. They were *all* someone in particular.

I practised.

Christ, Bel, what have you been doing?

It's still dark when Ingrid wakes me. I stumble down to the basement, wiping grit from my eyes. My clothes feel crusted onto me and my teeth are too big inside my mouth; my healing gums taste septic. The cellar is bare concrete, relieved only by six dusty wine bottles in one corner. The laptop sits in the middle of the floor. I drop myself cross-legged in front of it and get back to work.

Ingrid's come a long way while I slept. Running regressions, finding coefficients, looking for patterns—any thread in the data we can pull on. I pick up where she left off, charting time of death against hair colour, minutes of travel to hospital against sexuality.

Before long, the whole thing looks like one those Buzzfeed memes: *These seventeen charts about the graphic slaughter of innocents will blow your mind!* Or perhaps: *He came at her with a meat cleaver—you'll never guess what happens next!*

Well, on second thought, you probably will.

I work. I find nothing. I keep working. I keep finding nothing.

"Random's hard to fake," I whisper to myself like a mantra.

Hours pass and Ingrid relieves me. I sleep fitfully and tag her out again. I lose all track of time; my world is one endless twilight, eyeballs aching in the light of the screen.

On the second night, I'm stumbling back up the cellar stairs when the bare bulb above my head starts strobing—*on-off-on-off-light-dark-light-dark*—creating and obliterating my shadow on the concrete steps. I hear a hitched gasp and it's Ingrid, flicking the switch over and over, tears of frustration flowing down her cheeks.

"Hey," I say softly. "What is it?"

"I just . . . they might, someone might see it. A little glow. A little tiny one, sneaking through a window . . ."

"Okay, so just leave it off."

"I know, I just . . ." *Dark-light-dark-light-dark.* "I . . ."

God, Ingrid, look where I've led you to.

"Do you miss it?" I ask. "57?"

"I was born into the company, Pete. I never had a choice."

"I know, but they're still your friends, your family."

She shakes her head. "You don't understand. I'm saying, *I* never had a choice, but that wasn't true for most of them."

"So?"

"We're spies, Peter." Her lips whiten as she smiles tightly. "We lie and betray and seduce others into lies and betrayal, twelve hours a day, fifty-two weeks a year, for *hilariously* inadequate government pay. Do I miss them? The question you ought to be asking is: who looks at that job description and thinks, 'Yeah, that's me'?"

I snort a stifled laugh and then she does too. The strobing slows—*light-dark-light*—and comes to a rest . . . *dark.* She exhales into the gloom.

"You okay?" I ask.

"Yeah, that was no big deal."

"You lying to me right now?"

"Very much so, yeah."

"You don't need to do that."

"I know."

In the amber wash from the streetlight outside, I see her set her jaw.

"I can feel myself shrinking," she says at last. "Every time I flick the switch, or soap my hands or whatever, I feel like a little more of me disappears."

She snorts again and shakes her head.

"Ignore me. I'm just tired."

"Then go back to sleep," I tell her. "I'll carry on, do a double."

"Pete . . ."

"It's okay, I want to. I'm kind of on a roll anyway."

This is a lie. I'm nowhere. I couldn't be more nowhere if I was standing naked and rolled in salt in the middle of the Atacama Desert at midday with no water and a busted compass. But the light's off, so she can't tell, can she?

"You sure?"

"Yeah, she's my twin sister. Give me a little more time with her."

• • •

Maybe it's just fatigue—I've had a total of four hours and thirteen minutes of sleep over two nights (the answer to the question "But hey, who's counting?" is *always* "Me") and the screen is blotting in front of my eyes like a Van Gogh painting. But every now and then I get a flicker.

I've never been a savant, one of those lucky bastards who can get the numbers to speak to them, someone for whom 3 *feels* like 729, or who sees all primes as blue. I *worked* to make myself a mathematician. I had no innate talent for it; I sweated at it because the clean, hard-edged answers it yielded were all that eased the fear that squeezed my heart.

And now, as I scan the numbers, I sense . . . *something*. Not a pattern exactly; more like a shape where the pattern *isn't*. Like the image on the inside of your eyelids after looking at the sun.

Excitement flickers in the back of my throat like a pilot light.

Finally, the numbers are talking to me.

But no, I realise, that's not quite right. It's not the numbers. It's *Bel*. I feel like I can almost see the Red Wolf they named her for, bloody-furred, bounding behind the black digits on the screen as though they were barren trees on a snowfield. There is something of Bel in these equations, something familiar that—even though I'm reading about decapitations and hangings—I can't help but be comforted by. The numbers are just a language, but it's my sister doing the talking, and I'm soothed by the cadence of her voice.

But . . . I still can't quite out make out what she's saying. The pattern's too obscure. I think of ARIA—all those hours I spent trying to uncover my own pattern, while all the while Bel was labouring just as hard in rivers and graveyards and rainy alleyways to cover hers up.

She is my inverse, my opposite, my counterpart. Without her, I'm incomplete.

I miss you so much, Bel.

"Random's hard to fake," I whisper again as I scroll back, hunting for that flicker of familiarity, that glimpse. I follow the wolf deeper and deeper into the wood.

"How's it going?" Ingrid asks—I don't know how much later. She's a silhouette at the top of the stairs, her hair a dandelion haze, framed in the doorway by the dawn.

"I think I have something."

She stumps down the stairs. I indicate a scatter chart on the screen. The points look as random as fly specks on a windscreen.

"What is it?"

"Bodies, all male, plotted by the dates they were found. There was no sign of foul play, but there was basically no sign of *anything*. In each case the coroner noted that the body was so badly decayed that it was impossible to establish the cause of death."

"So?"

"So, the reason it took so long to find the bodies is that no one was *looking*. None of these men were ever reported missing. They all lived alone and were either jobless or self-employed. No search, no manhunt. Their rotting corpses were stumbled over by members of the public."

"Okay." Ingrid seems nonplussed. She indicates the mess of specks on the screen. "But there's no pattern there. It's just noise."

"Ah, but noise is the key, right?" I can hear the excitement bleeding into my voice, and I try to dampen it. "I mean the *key* to this whole thing."

Ingrid looks at me like I'm deranged, but I point at the screen.

"There is noise here—a random element—the time it took for some stranger to *just happen* across the body in the river or forest or bedsit or park or wherever they were found."

You've come a long way, Bel, from the girl who couldn't

work simple number codes if you're using statistical noise to cover up multiple murders.

On second thought, I probably shouldn't be so proud of you for that.

"If you filter out that noise," I say, "using the estimated time since death in the coroner's reports to work out the *dates* they died, and then adjust further for the margin of error . . ."

I hit another button. The data points arrange themselves in a neat flat line, evenly spaced over time.

"*Whoa*," Ingrid breathes.

"One kill every nine weeks, regular as clockwork. Except *here*, and *here*"—I point to breaks in the line—"where I'm guessing the body hasn't shown up yet."

"Fine." Ingrid eases herself down against the wall with an *aah* noise. "So *someone's* offing loners. What makes you think it's her?"

"Just a hunch," I reply. I can hardly say *These kills just feel like my sister*, can I? "Can you see if there's any more info in that police database on each of those victims?"

It takes her exactly seven minutes to find the connection.

"They've all been arrested for assault. Looks like . . ." She frowns. "Looks like there was enough evidence to make a case for all of them, but they never went to trial—*huh*. Their victims wouldn't press charges. Every one of them refused to testify."

"And who were they?" I ask, even though I'm sure I know the answer. I see Mum's exhausted eyes. I hear the tremor in her voice as she says, *It was no big deal*.

"Their wives. Not one of them pressed charges, but it looks like all of them separated later."

The last wisps of doubt vanish from my mind like fog in a high wind.

"That's her. That's Bel."

I slide down the wall next to Ingrid, feeling winded. There are thirteen dead.

Sis, that puts you in the top five most lethal British serial killers in history.

"I can't believe it," Ingrid says. "I mean, I'm trying but . . . I couldn't believe it back at school, even when I saw it with my own eyes. Craig, Andy, Seamus, those guys were professionals and she was just . . . so *fast*." She shakes her head. "I can't believe it."

"I can. Easily."

She looks at me, aghast. *"Why?"*

"Because they were only professionals, because to them it was a job, but to Bel? Do you have any idea how much *time* we had as kids, with Dad gone and Mum at the lab all day? School for seven hours, sleep for another seven—that's still ten hours a day, every day, that she could dedicate to *this*." I pinch the bridge of my nose against sudden vertigo. "They say it takes ten thousand hours of study to master a skill. If Bel got interested in killing people around the same time I got interested in maths, she'd been done by the time she was *ten*. By now she's a master four times over."

It's all in the numbers, Ingrid. I don't have to tell you that. We're silent for a long time.

"Pete," Ingrid says at last.

"Yeah?"

"Going from hunting down domestic abusers to shivving her own mother, that's quite the change-up."

"Yeah."

"Why do you think she did it?"

"I have no idea," I reply. "But I think I know where to look."

Under the roll of death, I add another name: Louise Blankman. Forty-two years old. I think of her lying in the makeshift hospital ward in 57 Headquarters. Is she still there, balanced between life and death like a coin on its edge? I hit Return and another tiny black cross appears on the plot. Suddenly, all those marks look like gravestones, a whole snowbound cemetery seen from a distance, and I have to look away for a moment.

Please, please don't be dead, Mum.

"You okay, Pete?" Ingrid asks.

"Yeah." I exhale hard and turn back to the screen. I uncurl my fist—my nails have left three little half-moons in my palm—and with a spread finger and thumb I indicate the gap between Bel's last kill and her attack on Mum.

"Whatever changed Bel's behaviour, it happened *here*," I say. "In these eighteen weeks, and her pattern indicates she attacked one more person during that time. The cops haven't found him yet . . ."

"So we have to." Ingrid's way ahead of me. She pulls the laptop over and her fingers fly over the keys. "I'll pull every record for a domestic violence arrest without charge for the past five years."

"What are we looking for?" I ask.

"Anything that jumps out."

There are a crushing number of them. I remember Bel telling me that two women a week are murdered by their partners in the UK. When I first heard that statistic I couldn't believe it, but reading through page after page of this . . .

"It is true," Ingrid says shortly. "And it's the worst thing in the world."

I stare at her. "You mean you . . . ?"

"Not me, personally," she says tersely. "But around a quarter of women get beat up on by their husbands and boyfriends at some point in their lives and I've spent seventeen years sponging up different people's emotions, so do the maths, Pete. You always do.

"I mean, people do some awful shit to each other, I get that, but still . . ." She sighs and closes her eyes. "Feeling your nose and your ribs break and your eyes swell shut under the fists of the man who's supposed to love you more than anyone else, then having to share a bed with him the same night because he fathered your kids and they still worship him. The threshold of every room feels like a trip wire in case he's in it. Every left-out coffee cup, every unconsidered word feels like a trap in case it sets him off. *Domestic* violence," she spits. "It makes it sound so fucking mundane, but that's your *home.* That's your *life,* your *family.* That's supposed to be your safe place. Where can you go if that becomes a threat?"

I swallow hard, feeling sick and guilty. I'm spying on these women, peering through keyholes at the most intimate details of their lives, secrets they never meant for me to see. I look up and Ingrid's watching me. Recognition is writ large in her face. *Welcome to my world.* I guess this must be how she feels all the time.

Reluctantly, I keep reading, but nothing jumps out at me. I speed up, wanting to get it over with. Name after name flickers by: *James Smith, Robert Okowonga, Daniel Martinez, Jack Anderson, Dominic Rigby . . .*

Wait.

Dominic Rigby.

That's Ben's dad's name. I met him once when the school dragged him and Mum in to supervise a grudging and pointless hatchet-burying ceremony between Ben and Bel and me in Mrs. Fenchurch's office. The truce lasted precisely until we crossed the threshold back into the school hallway.

I open up the report. On the eighteenth of November two years ago, officers were called to Rigby's house in Camberwell at 10:45 in the evening by a neighbour who heard screaming and banging from the first floor. Upon arrival, the police found Rachel Rigby with bruising to her face and arms and—*Jesus*—a broken collarbone. There are photos in the file. I try not to look, but I can't help but catch one out of the corner of my eye: a close-up of a wrist with yellow-purple-black bruises banding it like manacles.

The report said Dominic Rigby admitted manhandling his wife, but claimed he had been attempting to restrain her when she "had some kind of fit." He claimed she had a history of mental instability, which they'd been trying to manage "inside

the family." Mrs. Rigby was unresponsive to questioning that
night, but the following day corroborated her husband's assessment, considered the matter private, and did not wish to press
charges.

"Ingrid," I say. My throat's tight with anticipation and dread.
"Find out everything you can about Dominic Jacob Rigby."

"On it," she says, no longer questioning. She doesn't need to;
she's seen every thought flicker through my head. She takes the
laptop back. A few minutes later she whistles.

"What?"

"Well, I know why there's a gap in your sister's little corpse
collection."

"Why?"

"Because Dominic Rigby's still alive. Just."

I don't speak. I curl my toes inside my shoes and wait for her
to tell me the rest.

"He was dumped outside Edinburgh Royal Infirmary with a
broken femur, a depressed skull, a dislocated shoulder, a frac-
tured cheek and eye socket, severe concussion, and four broken
ribs, one of which punctured his lung. Burns on his chest and
back." She blanches. "It looks like she pulled a knife. He's still
alive, going in and out of consciousness. This is—Pete, this is
fucking *brutal*. None of Bel's other victims suffered this level of
punishment; they didn't even go down as homicides. I mean,
she really went to town on this guy, like she didn't care who
knew."

"When?"

Tell me the number, Ingrid. It's the only thing I need to
clinch it.

"Nine weeks ago yesterday."

"Let's go."

RECURSION: 2 YEARS, 6 MONTHS AGO

I had my headphones on, so I didn't hear Bel the first ten times she knocked.

"How was the gig?" I asked when her face appeared around the door.

"Intense," she replied. Her hair was plastered to her cheeks with sweat. "I'm still breathless."

"Looks it." I nodded towards her hand where it gripped the door. Four purple bruises swelled, one around each of her knuckles. "Someone get a little handsy in the pit, did they?"

She laughed. I smiled and briefly pitied the guy.

"Well, I don't know, sis," I said. "You know what these Death Plague Rabbit Grenade fans are like when it comes to mosh etiquette."

She stuck her tongue out at me and came in.

"Nice try," she said.

"Okay, what were they called, then?"

"Neutron Funeral."

"Damn. So close."

"Death Plague Rabbit Grenade's not bad, though," she said. "If I ever start a band, I might use that."

"Well, I look forward to telling some obscure Subreddit earnestly that I thought your early work was better."

She dropped herself onto the corner of my bed, shaking her head in theatrical despair.

"Wrong again, Pete. That's hipsters, not metalheads."

"Curses—0 for 2. So you won't grow enormous beards and wail into mikes about inflammation of your genitals?"

"Chin rings, I think, rather than beards. And strictly no definite articles. I won't rule out the genital thing, though. Talking about dicks is good for business."

"Fiery dicks?"

"Extra points for those."

"You sellout!" I accused her. "Although you're right: a beard wouldn't suit you."

"You're only saying that 'cause you can't grow one."

"Guilty," I admitted, and laughed, and she laughed too, and I heard it. That tension, stretched like a cheese wire across her throat.

"Thanks for letting me go, though, Pete. Seriously, I appreciate it. Mum would flip if she knew . . ."

She didn't finish the sentence, and she didn't need to. *If she knew I'd left you alone.* I felt my thumb go towards my forehead and pulled it back. Bel caught the gesture anyway. She tilted my head and examined the wound above my eye.

"That's healing up nicely." I caught the guilt in her voice. I touched the scab; it still felt fragile, like one too-rough touch could tear it away.

Mum had been called away to a last-minute conference. I'd overheard her instructions to Bel: *Watch out for any signs of depression or stress.*

Given that such signs included overeating, undereating, sleeping too much, sleeping too little, and general symptoms of anxiety—Mum had basically told her to look for one specific strand of dried grass in a haystack. A fact Bel understood well enough to sack the whole thing off for the night and skid around a beer-slicked dance floor to a band I'd never heard of.

Which was the only thing that was weird.

"Bel, seriously. I know we take the piss and all, but I have never heard of Neutron Funeral. You haven't been holding out on me in the riffing department, have you? You know how much I like guitars that sound like buildings falling down."

She blushed deeply. "I'd never heard of them before yesterday, either," she confessed. "I went to meet someone."

"*Someone*, as in a *boy*?"

She blushed even deeper, although she didn't smile.

"Yeah, well," she mumbled, "like I said, thanks."

"No problem." I shrugged. "You don't have to watch me all the time, you know. As Frankenstein said to his monster, one of us should have a life."

"Sure, it's just . . ." She got up again and started pacing round the room, nearly head-butting Richard Feynman in the process. She was so damn twitchy, and it was putting me on edge. When you're that close to somebody, their every little tic feels like an electric shock.

"It's just what?"

She hesitated, then came out with it.

"She blames me."

"Who?"

"Mum."

"For what?" For a moment I didn't get it, and then, "For me? For *this*?" I pointed at my forehead. "That's ridiculous." I felt a little needle of anxiety. My sister's been saving my arse all our lives. More than anything, more than scorpions or Ben Rigby or drowning in open water, What I fear is her getting sick of it.

"No, Pete." She hugs herself. "No, it isn't. I should have been there."

"I told her it was an accident."

"She is apparently unconvinced."

"Anyway, you were suspended at the time, remember?" My voice rose in alarm. "If you'd turned up on school property, they'd have booted you out for good, and how would that have helped?"

"Yeah, but . . . I promised her, and I promised *you*, that that wouldn't happen. That I'd be careful, but I fucked up."

She bit the edge of her cuticle, tearing it until beads of blood appeared. Bel was normally so cool. I'd never seen her like this before. It was freaking me out.

"You want to tell me how?" I hazarded. It wasn't like Bel to be ashamed of her suspension, but maybe there was something she needed to get off her chest.

"Sure." She nodded. "Sure," she repeated. "Okay." She ducked her head and pressed her palms together between her knees as she sat.

"It was biology. We were in the lab."

"Ferris?" I asked, needling her along. I had no idea where she was going with this, but at least she was talking.

"Yep."

"Ugh."

Bel had Dr. Ferris for biology, a bullet I had mercifully dodged by squeaking into the higher set. He had a beard I swore he washed in the leftover chip fat from the canteen and he scratched his backside, but far more important than any of that, he was, without mitigation or restraint, an arsehole.

"We were doing the frog lesson."

I groaned and fell back theatrically on the bed. This at least won a grin from Bel, but it vanished almost as soon as it appeared, like a brief glimpse of sun on a stormy day. Our school, being private, had the freedom to deviate from the national curriculum, and Dr. Ferris, the charmer, exploited this latitude to make his students cut up live frogs.

"Honestly," I said. "You guys are really lucky he can fit that valuable lesson in between leech therapy and groping skulls to find their owners' character flaws."

"I know, right?" Bel said. "So anyway, we were in the science lab and the place stank of ammonia. I was feeling light-headed and I near as dammit puked into the white enamel basin in front of me.

"Then Ferris brought the frogs out. One each, no sharing. I looked down at mine, and I was shocked by how small it was—splayed out on its back. Its belly was a pale yellowy white, like candle tallow. It had been injected with some kind of paralytic. And if you really looked, you could see its tiny belly rising and falling with its breath.

"Ferris told us to be careful we didn't puncture any vital organs. 'We don't want them to die on us before we're good and ready.' He actually *said* that. All around me, the others were busy digging in, cutting the skin open—folding it back, exposing the ribs, mopping away the blood.

"But I . . . I just . . . stopped."

She paused to wipe a bead of sweat from her forehead.

"I had the scalpel in my hand, but I couldn't do it. It wasn't that I thought it was too gross or anything, just too . . . sad.

"So I put up my hand. Ferris thinks I'm trouble." A brief bark of laughter. "I guess he's right, and he ignored me. So I came out from behind my bench and started walking towards him, slowly, one hand still raised, the other holding the scalpel. I remember that background burble you always get in class was gone, and I didn't know when it had stopped.

"'What is it, Miss Blankman?' he said finally, and he kind of leaned on the *Miss*, and I swear to god he rolled his eyes.

"'Sir,' I said. I mean, I was polite as *fuck*. 'They can't feel anything, can they, sir?'

"He snapped at me. Said they were anaesthetized, of course they couldn't feel anything. So I asked him how he knew. I mean, you read about people going under in surgery and not being able to move or speak, and when they come round, they say they felt everything."

"Anaesthesia awareness," I interjected. Paralysed, but conscious, under the knife. It was my eighth-biggest fear in one hell of a crowded field. "Happens in 0.13 percent of cases."

"Right," Bel said. "But no one ever asks the poor frog after surgery if they could feel the knife going in. There is no *after* for them. So I asked Ferris, 'How do you *know* they can't feel anything?' And as much as I hate that greasy prick, I wasn't out to embarrass him. I really *wanted* him to have an answer, because there were two dozen frogs in that lab with their sternal skin folded back, and I didn't want them to be in pain.

"He just stared at me for the longest moment, and I could feel my ears and the back of my neck heating up. And he just said, and I remember his exact words, he said, 'Get out, then, little girl, if it bothers you. Stand in the corridor and let the rest of us get on with some real science.'

"And then I . . . sort of lost it.

"I could have walked out. I know I could have. I know I *should* have. Maybe then I wouldn't have been suspended and you wouldn't have . . ." She sighed, and shook her head. "All those dominoes, right? But I didn't want to. And I knew, I just *knew* he wouldn't have talked like that to any of the *boys* in the class. And what good would it have done? Two dozen frogs would get slowly sliced up anyway, and what if they could feel every motion of the knife inside them? I still had my scalpel, so I did the only thing I could think of."

Her jaw locked and I couldn't tell if it was a smile or a grimace.

"I cut their throats."

At this point, I felt I had to clarify. "The . . . frogs?"

She winced. "All of them. It was chaos, blood everywhere, the wood slippery with it. Jessica Henley and Tim Russov screaming, and I couldn't help thinking they weren't so squeamish when *they* were holding the knives. Ferris came after me, but I knew how to slip between the other students. I'm good at that. And I made sure. I put all two dozen frogs out of their misery. Quick, sure cuts. Most painless way to the exit, short of nitrogen asphyxiation."

I didn't ask how she knew that.

"My heart was slamming in my chest like a machine gun bucking," she went on. "And I felt fierce and free and happy, and then it was over. Ferris was dragging me off to see Fenchurch. I only realised halfway there I was still holding the blade, which wouldn't have looked good, so I dropped it in the bin as I passed. It was easy, slippery with all the frog blood, and it didn't make a sound as it slid down the inside of the bag. Three hours later I was on a two-week suspension."

She took a long, shuddering breath. I looked up at Faraday, staring huffily down from his poster as if to say, *In my day we didn't see anything wrong with electrocuting frogs.*

It took me a few seconds to realise Bel wasn't done. She was staring at me silently, rubbing her hands together, squeezing her bruised knuckles. There was something else, something she was desperate to tell me but couldn't. The frog story had been a run-up, but she'd skidded to a halt before the sandpit. She was willing me to guess.

Bel, I thought helplessly, *if I was a supercomputer capable of a trillion guesses a second, it would still take me until the sun burned out before I could brute-force the code of your mind.*

Code. If she couldn't bring herself to tell me out loud, maybe she could write it down. If she couldn't say it in plaintext, maybe she could do it in code.

I took a scrap of paper from the bedside table and scratched out a quick Caesar shift cipher. Like any secret shared, it was a hug, a reassurance, a hand extended: a way of saying *I'm here.* I made the key *I love you sis—ILOVEYUS* and encoded my message:

You can talk to me. Whatever it is.

She stared at the note for a long time before scrawling her reply. When she handed it back to me, her eyes were full. She went to the window. I unfolded the message. It took me twelve seconds to decrypt. I knew what it would say after the fourth letter:

A-C-A-D—

I-K-I-L—

I killed someone.

NOW

Man, I hate hospitals.

Don't get me wrong—I'm very glad they exist. The men and women who work in them set bones, measure and inject life-saving drugs, and perform emergency surgery on vital organs for nowhere near enough money and on barely any sleep; that's heroic.

On the other hand, the men and women who work in them set bones, measure and inject life-saving drugs, and perform emergency surgery on vital organs for nowhere near enough money and on barely any sleep; HOW IS THAT NOT TERRIFYING?

Besides, hospitals are by their nature, flypaper for sick people. I'm always conscious of the possibility you could—in the worst free upgrade in history—show up with a broken collarbone and leave with Marburg haemorrhagic fever. It's like *Congratulations! You're our five millionth customer! Now bleed from the eyes until dead.*

We've driven through the night. Mercifully, the Vadis left their car garaged and the keys in the bowl on the sideboard (I really, really hope we get a chance to put it back). The police report on Dominic Rigby's injuries strongly implied that every minute we delayed was another minute he might take the opportunity to die in.

As the doors whir shut behind us, the eye-scouring light and the fragrance (antiseptic, urine-soaked fabric and politely restrained desperation) tell me before I even see a sign that we're in A&E—Accident and Emergency. Tonight seventeen casualties perch on the moulded plastic chairs, and several have a distinct "3 A.M. Saturday" flavour, including a whip of a man with dried blood covering his bald head like glaze on a donut, and what appears to be fragments of a Newcastle Brown Ale bottle still embedded in glittering constellations in his scalp. The walking wounded aren't the ones I'm worried about, though—head injuries aren't generally known to be infectious. It's the others, the ones clutching their stomachs, the ones with unfocussed eyes and greasy sheens on their foreheads, that scare me. I recall from somewhere that the world-record distance for a projectile vomit is 3.62 metres and I try to maintain an invisible bubble of that radius around me. Flinching whenever someone breaks my impromptu quarantine zone, I pick my way towards the desk.

"Intensive care, please," I ask. The hard-eyed, grey-haired woman in blue scrubs behind it glances at me.

"Ye don' look like ye need it," she says in a Glasgow accent you could paint the Forth Bridge with. "Jes' take a number and we'll get ta ye as soon as we can."

"No, I'm not hurt," I explain. "I'm here to visit someone."

She stares at me. "It's three A.M. You gonnae watch whoever it is ye've come to see sleep? Who are ye here to see, anyway?"

"Dominic Rigby."

Her snappishness vanishes.

"Oh Christ, follow me."

She leads us down the antiseptic hallways and flags down a tiny Asian woman in blue scrubs.

"Here ta' see Rigby," she tells her.

"Are ye his son? Are ye Ben?" The new nurse's accent is, if possible, even thicker than her colleague's.

I swallow hard.

"Yes," I say.

The change is immediate. This is a woman who works intensive care. She spends her days tending gunshot wounds and draining the fluid from the lungs of kids drowning from cystic fibrosis. She must be hard-core, is what I'm saying, but on hearing my lie she pales.

"*Holy . . .*" she mutters. "Thank god. We've been trying to get hold of you for weeks, but the hospital where your mother's staying says she's too fragile to talk to us, and the boarding school the police had listed for you had never heard of you. Some admin cock-up, but it meant we had no idea where you'd been."

She tails off, as if expecting me to speak, but she hasn't asked me a question, so I don't. I feel as though I'm barefoot and this conversation is a dark room with a floor full of thumbtacks.

"He's only had one other visitor," she starts up, "before he started regaining consciousness—tall black lass, Sandra . . . Brooks, I think?"

I force about a third of a smile; it's all I can manage.

"Uh, she's a, a family friend."

She nods. "I was just doing rounds, and I actually think your father's awake. He'll be so happy to see you. He's been saying your name in his sleep."

She disinfects her hands with alcohol gel, indicates that we follow suit, and leads us through a pair of double swing doors.

"*Sandra?*" Ingrid whispers as she falls in beside me.

"Ten to one on that was LeClare," I agree. "She was here ahead of us, so she's found the same pattern. We need to be very, *very* careful from here on."

"No shit."

The nurse leads us into a low-lit corridor with cubicle-like rooms off it. We pass rank upon rank of metal beds, filled with people unobtrusively dying. I know, I know, we're *all* dying. Men in this country live to 79 on average. That means every minute that passes, we creep around one-forty-two-millionth of the way closer our deaths. There's a tiny clock built into every cell of brain and blood vessel, just ticking down. The fact remains, though, as I look around me, these people's clocks are ticking down *fast*.

The sharp-white smell of the antiseptic floor cleaner teases a memory from my brain.

I'm lying flat on my back. Bel's fingers trace the pulpy crater of blood and bone in my forehead and follow the saline line into my arm. I can still feel the heat of her fury, crossing the years like a supernova of a distant star.

We pause at the last cubicle on the left. Gesturing for us to wait, the nurse slips inside, then reemerges.

"He is awake, but I don't know how long he'll stay that way." Her face is sympathetic, but her tone's all business. I guess nurses, more than anyone, have to strictly ration the number of fucks they give. "He's very, very weak. I've told him you're here. Be gentle and quick, okay?"

We nod and she steps out of the way as we slip inside.

The cubicle is dimly lit by the bedside lamp, and only the edges of his injuries are visible, gleaming wetly before they bleed away into shadow and gauze, that milky-sweet smell of open burns and ointment. But it's his *shape* that most appalls . . . I can't help but stare at the sprawl of him, distended with swellings and bandages. When he sees us, his head strains back against the pillows, desperate to get away but unable to make his crippled body follow.

His eyes are stretched wide, clear in the wash from the night-light. He looks terrified.

But he doesn't look *surprised.*

"Ingrid?" I say quietly. "Is he surprised Ben's not here?"

"No."

She sounds puzzled, but I'm not. Ben's absence from his ailing father's bedside starts to make sense in a terrible new way. Dominic Rigby knew his son was never going to walk through this door.

The boarding school the police had listed for you had never heard of you.

"Shit," I mutter. "Ben's dead."

On the bed, Dominic Rigby looks at me like I'm the one who put those burns on his chest. It takes me a second to recognise the mangled sound that comes out of his swollen jaw as speech. I lean in closer to hear him.

"*Fuck you,*" he wheezes with a snakelike rattle. I can hear the wretched effort in every syllable. "*And your whole fucking family.*"

I eye him levelly, even though the ward is pitching darkly around me. Silently, I count. See, Petey? You've already made it to three seconds. You can do this, no problem.

"You know who I am." He doesn't answer, but that's okay. It wasn't a question. "Who did this to you?"

"*You know.*"

"Mr. Rigby, tell me what happened."

One eye rolls towards me, but he doesn't answer. I can feel the fear coming off him and it's not hard, not hard at all, to intuit what he's afraid of.

"I'm not her, Mr. Rigby," I say, keeping my tone as even and polite as I can. "But she is my sister. Look at me. See the family resemblance, and ask yourself. How hard would it be for me to convince her to come back here?"

He takes a sharp breath and then releases it in a slow hiss. Reluctantly, he starts to speak.

"*She came to the house. I was working. I opened the door. She was just . . . just . . . a girl.*" Shreds of disbelief still cling to his voice. "*She jabbed me with something, and I blacked out.*"

"Go on," I say. He's not looking at me anymore, and I remember how Rita and Frankie interrogated me, side by side like a comrade. I drop myself into the visitor's chair, close but out of his line of sight.

"You woke up, where? The basement?"

His eye bevels towards me balefully, but he doesn't contradict me.

"Pete," Ingrid asks uneasily, "how did you know that?"

"Soundproof," I reply shortly, my throat dry. I keep my eyes on Rigby.

"What was it like?"

"*Cold. I was cold, naked.*"

"You were on the floor?"

"Hanging. Wrists tied over my head, burning. My toes only just scraped the floor. My legs and back were agony. She kept pacing, around and around me for . . . felt like hours. Pain got worse and worse and worse. It became . . . I thought I was going to pass out. I begged her to cut me down, to let me go. Kept asking her 'Why?' No answer."

"Did she say anything the whole time?"

"Only the last time I asked her 'Why?'"

"What was her answer?"

"Two words: 'Remember Rachel' and then she . . ."

His voice just stops.

"Mr. Rigby?" I prompt him.

"She . . ."

I see his lips contort, the steel wire beneath them glints, but no sound comes out. His face goes purple with the effort. After a solid minute he falls back to wheezing. I look at the limp, helpless fear on his face. Mutely, he tugs aside the sheet and peels up the hem of his hospital gown. A puckered, tightly stitched slash zigzags up his abdomen like a seam of black lightning ripping through a storm cloud.

"The fat was white," he murmurs. *"I saw it just before the blood came out."*

There's fear etched in every line of him, in the way he's twisted on the bed, his jaw clamped in refusal. I get up, pull the sheet back up to his chin, and crouch beside his head.

I look into his eyes and see them widen. I can see the horror in him as I feel it growing in me. It's like looking into a mirror, fear feeding off fear, like an infection. Every part of me is cold now, frozen by disbelief. Bel did this? The bandage across his face falls in a way that suggests his nose isn't all there anymore. A voice shrieks in my head. *Bel did this?* The slashes across his chest and stomach, across the tendons in his heels so he couldn't run. *Bel did this Bel did this Bel did this.* My voice shrieks in my head.

Did I ever know her at all?

The hatred in Dominic Rigby's eyes is absolute: a thin layer of ice over a bottomless lake of fear. I count fifteen capillaries on the white of his eyeball.

"Mr. Rigby, when she said 'Remember Rachel,' did you know what she meant by that?"

He closes his eyes, exhausted. He nods.

"I told her, she didn't understand, that I loved Rachel, I always loved her. I only wanted to protect her."

I blink, and for a split second I see the police report, the pictures of a bruised face so strikingly familiar. Ben always did look like his mum.

"Protect her from what, Mr. Rigby? Tell me from the beginning."

For eleven seconds, he doesn't move a muscle.

"Protect her from what?" I repeat.

"Your bitch mother," he snarls.

His vehemence shocks me, and I feel my veneer of calm crack.

"It started in April, the year before last. Ben . . ." Again his voice hits that wall, but this time he manages to push through. *"He went out to some club, some rock band, Neutron Funeral."*

I freeze.

"You're sure that was the name of the band?"

"You'd be sure too if your son never came home from their show."

I hold myself perfectly still. In my mind's eye, I see an ankle, white as bone protruding from a roll of carpet. All those excuses I made for not looking inside it. Had I guessed even then? Did I know?

"We called the police. They said they would investigate, but they never called us back. We called again and again; days went by, then weeks. We made posters and put them up all over London, but the next day, they'd all been torn down, even the ones near our house. All the links to the website we made were broken. We thought we were going mad."

One red-cracked eye fixes suddenly on me.

"Do you know what that's like? To doubt your eyes, your senses, everything you know about the most important thing in your life?"

Yes, Mr. Rigby, I know.

"We kept calling the police. We kept going to the station in person, but nobody would see us. In the end, I said if they didn't give me something in three days, I'd be going to the papers. I gave them three days." He sounds so betrayed. *"I still thought they were on our side.*

"On day two, your mother came to the house.

"My boss, Warren Jordan, was with her. He was sweating, kept rubbing his hands dry on his jacket. They didn't sit. Didn't even look at the tea we made them. He never said a word. It was her that did the talking."

He pauses for long enough that I feel I have to prompt him.

"Mr. Rigby? What did my mother say?"

His voice goes flat as he recited from memory. He remembers every word.

"'Your son is dead. His body will never be found. Any attempt to investigate his death will fail. Tell the media and they will ignore you, and you will be punished. You will not be able to work. You won't qualify for welfare. You will lose this house. You will not be able to turn to your families for shelter or food; if you do, the same will happen to them. You will be toxic to everything and everyone in your lives.

"'Do what is best for your family, grieve in secret, and move on. Leave your jobs; means will be made available. You both have more than thirty years to live. Don't waste them.'

"She didn't even look at us. Just read the whole thing out of another one of those black notebooks."

I feel a chill, but I *can* hear Mum saying it, steeling herself to be that cold, that clinical. Still, something in that sentence catches me, like a burr. I don't interrupt him. His voice is starting to crackle. Strands of spittle web his lips. I'm scared if he stops he won't start again.

"Rachel started screaming at her, right in her face, but she didn't bat an eyelid; she just stood and walked out, my boss trailing after her like a fucking spaniel.

"That night Rachel cried herself to sleep. She kept saying over and over, she can't do this to us and get away with it. She clung to my arm and made me say it with her, and I did. Even when she fell asleep she was still saying it. 'She can't, she can't.'"

"And I went into the back garden and buried Ben's pocket knife under the big pear tree, because I knew she could."

"So you decided to take my mother's offer," I surmise. "And when your wife couldn't accept that, you hit her to shut her up."

Dominic Rigby writhed on the bed. For a moment I could see him hanging by his wrists from a basement lintel.

"You have no idea what it was like," he protested. *"I found emails she'd sent to journalists. I tried to talk to her. I swear I tried everything, but she just wouldn't listen; she was hysterical, out of control. I was just trying . . . I was just trying to make her understand."*

With your fists? I want to say. But like a good little interrogator, I keep my mouth shut.

"And then Warren came into my office at work," he went on. *"He was so pale. He said he'd been given a message: If I didn't find some way to shut Rachel up, they were going to kill her.*

"I lay awake for the next three nights, trying to find a way to tell her, and knowing she wouldn't listen. I threw up everything I ate. Then I found the number for a name I didn't recognise in her phone. When I googled it, it was some hack at the Guardian. *I called Warren and agreed to for her to be sectioned."*

"So she isn't really sick?" I feel a jolt in my stomach.

Dominic Rigby's mouth opens in a shape that might be a scream or laughter, but there's no sound to tell us which.

"She wanted to fight," he murmurs. Spittle gleams on his jaw where the wire stops his mouth from closing. *"She wanted to fight, but I couldn't let her. I couldn't. They would have killed her. Like they did my boy."*

His voice drops to a whisper.

"I was there. When they came for her. I lied to her. I told her it would all be all right."

His eyes close. He's so still that for a moment I'm worried

we've killed him, but then I see the steady rise and fall of his chest.

"Come on, Pete," Ingrid says. "We should go."

It's only then I notice the way she's avoiding looking at his face. I guess she doesn't want to empathise with this man, and I don't blame her, but we don't have what we came for, not quite.

"Mr. Rigby," I say carefully. "You said my mother read her speech from 'another one of those black notebooks.' What did you mean, *another* one?"

"Your sister had one too. Kept reading it as she paced around me. Like she was psyching herself up."

It's like someone's let all the air out of my lungs. I turn to Ingrid.

"Let's go."

In the doorway, she mutters in my ear. "Something's not right. Even if they wanted to put the arm on him, 57 wouldn't have sent your mum. She's a research scientist. She has no field experience."

"They didn't. She went on her own account."

She shoots me a startled look, but it's obvious enough that she shouldn't need to read it from my face.

Mum didn't conceal Ben's death for 57; she concealed it *from* them. And that meant she had to know that Bel was behind Ben's disappearance. Had we been less careful than I thought? Or had she simply seen one of the Rigbys' posters and put two and two together? But for what kind of mother does 2 plus 2 equal "my daughter's committed murder"?

The IC nurse is loitering outside, checking off items on a clipboard.

"How was he?" she asks.

"Fine, he's sleeping now." I try to smile, but I seem to have forgotten how to coordinate the component muscles, and my expression caves in like a matchstick house.

The nurse nods sympathetically. Her face is a kind of small kindness dispensary. "It's . . . well, it's good he saw you."

As we walk out, past the ranks of beds, Ingrid falls in beside me and, as ever, says what I'm thinking.

"Terrible way to spend your final hours, in this place, alone."

"Yes," I say.

She nods thoughtfully and says, "It's exactly as I would have him."

RECURSION: 2 YEARS, 8 MONTHS AGO

You could argue I should have picked up on the warning signs, but the point at which I really *knew* I'd screwed up was when the ceiling caught fire.

I'd left the window open to get rid of the smoke, but it had been dead calm all day; the clouds hung like vast anchored ships in the sky, and you'd have to be a *witch* to foresee the gust of wind that blew the end of the curtain into the metal bin, a bin in which the remnants of the first two ARIA notebooks were merrily burning.

The flames raced up the drapery like a candlewick and feasted on the ceiling paint, which, joy-oh-joy, was flammable too, bubbling and spitting and blackening merrily.

At this point, somewhat belatedly, I panicked and tried to make a run for it. I know, I know, delayed panic isn't like me, but it's tough to shit yourself in a timely fashion when you're as thoroughly drunk as I was.

Something else that's tough when you're drunk? Running. Especially when one leg's in a cast.

I face-planted *hard*, scraping my face over the carpet.

"Ow, fuck," I muttered, clutching at the small ember of a friction burn glowing on my nose for a good four seconds, until I felt heat on my back and remembered that the inferno of possible *future* burns raging only eight feet above me were probably more of a concern.

I flailed and struggled, but I didn't seem to be able to get up.

The door banged open and a pair of fluffy monsters appeared on the carpet at my eye level. *Only,* I thought, *in the nightmarish imaginings of a slipper company executive could those things count as bunnies.* I was briefly aware of the crackle of flames before they were drowned out by the fire extinguisher's roar. Flame-retardant foam drifted from above like grey snow, kissing my scraped-raw nose.

The demon bunnies squelched past me on the now-sodden carpet, and I rolled over to see Mum perched on my bed. She was wearing Look No. 101: *I don't have to put up with this kind of shit from lab rats.*

I struggled to get up.

"Don't get up," Mum said.

I stopped struggling.

She peered at me solemnly from over the top of her reading glasses. The lines around her eyes contracted into tight little webs of suspicion, and then Look No. 101 gave way to an expression I'd never seen before, and one I really, *really* didn't want to see again.

"Peter William Blankman," she fairly hissed. "Are you *drunk?*"

Wait, I know this one. Style it out. This is definitely one of those times when you do not tell the truth. No, Peter. Just tell her no.

"Yes."

Bugger.

"What"—and every word was distinct and cold—"did you drink?"

"Dry martini," I said. "Lemon peel. Only without the vermouth, and . . . we didn't have any lemon."

"So . . . neat gin."

"It's Agent Blankman's drink. He's a spy," I added helpfully. "Spies are cool."

"And how much of this *sophisticated* cocktail did Agent Blankman imbibe?" In terms of deadliness, Mum's voice was now somewhere between anthrax and the electric chair.

"Only about this much." But it was tough to hold my finger and thumb a reassuring distance apart when they were blurring in front of me.

In retrospect, I might have overdone the gin. In my defence, it was my first experiment with alcohol. You might have thought that a tot of the rot was just the thing for a young man with a tendency to jump at shadows, but I didn't generally drink for two very good reasons: (1) Judging by my . . . enthusiastic relationship with food, if I started relying on liquor to get me through panic attacks, I would be reduced to a dribbling wreck in a skip by midmorning of every day with a vowel in it, but more important, (2) . . .

"Your father drank," Mum said.

The bite had gone out of her voice. Now she just sounded immeasurably tired, which was worse. I'd once asked her why she'd kept his name, why Bel and I both bore it. She'd grunted and said, *I got it from him, he got it from his dad. It's not his name any more than it is mine. Besides, the alternative is* my *father's name, and he was a prick too.*

She looked at me and sighed. "Alcohol, pyromania, this isn't you, Pete. What's going on?"

I eyed the burnt-out wastepaper basket.

"It was meant to be a sort of . . . Viking funeral."

"A Viking funeral," Mum echoed. "A Viking spy funeral."

"Double cool."

"If this was a funeral, may I ask who the guest of honour was?"

"Me," I reassured her. "Although, I'm not dead."

"That"—Mum eyed me steadily—"remains to be seen."

She gingerly picked through the bin, but finding only ash and blackened card inside, turned to the *ARIA* notebooks queued up for immolation on the corner of the desk. I swallowed, my throat raw from the booze and smoke. I wanted to get up, to wrestle them away from her, but my leg, the fug of alcohol, and a growing awareness of the truly mythic scale of the trouble I was in kept me pinned to the carpet.

She read without speaking for more than fifteen minutes, the only sound the scratch of pages turning. I watched her eyes scan the aborted blueprint of my personality, and felt very small, and very cold.

"How long have you been doing this?" she asked at last.

"I can't remember a time when I wasn't," I replied truthfully.

"So you thought that you, a fifteen-year-old schoolboy, could mathematically map the evolution of your consciousness—a problem which has baffled the greatest minds in the world—in your spare time with a paper and *pen*?"

"Well, in my defence I would have asked a computer," I replied, "if I could phrase the question in a language a computer could understand."

She closed the notebook and laid it on her lap, took off her glasses, and looked at me gravely.

"Why?"

I stared at her. Why? Why did she think? She'd just seen me splayed out across the page in my own handwriting. Wasn't it obvious?

"Because I couldn't bear not knowing," I said.

"Not knowing what?"

"If it would always be like . . . *this* . . ." I said hopelessly. "This"—I pointed at the cast, and the red welt scarifying on my brow—"and this. I wanted to know if I'd ever be able to walk into a roomful of strangers without feeling like my chest was being crushed, or sit in a cinema without being scared of the dark. I just . . ." I spread my hands helplessly. "I just wanted to stop being afraid. I thought if I could pin myself down in an equation, I might get a bit closer to fixing myself."

"And today you put a match to it." Mum's tone stayed as neutral as distilled water from Switzerland. "Why?"

I remembered Gödel's shriven face, staring at me from the book.

"Because it's a pipe dream. There's no way of even knowing if there *is* an answer, let alone finding it. The whole thing was a mistake."

There was a long silence, broken only by dripping from the extinguished ceiling.

"Yes," Mum said softly. "It was. Come with me."

Notebook still in one hand, she grabbed my wrist with the other, pulled me up, and dragged me downstairs. "Ow, ow, ow!" I protested. "Slow down, my leg!" But irritation turned to disbelief as we ploughed through the doorway under the staircase. The *thump-thump-thump* of my cast turned hollow on the basement's bare wooden steps.

She can't. She can't be taking me to . . .

She was.

In front of us, dark and weathered, lock secured by a combination keypad, stood the door to Mum's study.

Mum was forever threatening to extract our brains through our nostrils using Egyptian mummification hooks if we skipped school, or paint us with honey and feed us to hungry chinchillas if we left messy saucepans in the kitchen. The penalty for breaking into her study, though, was much simpler, and much starker:

Try to get in here, she'd said, standing us in front of this very same door the day after our seventh birthday, *and we're done. You leave this house. You never, ever come back. Understand?*

We did. She'd never had to repeat it.

The warning was so dire that now my muscles stalled when she tried to lead me across the threshold.

"It's okay, Peter." She held out her hand. "Come on, look."

After all the fevered imaginings of my seven-year-old self, the four-by-five-metre room was more than a little disappointing. No mutant experiments, no reanimated corpses, not even a tangle of glass pipework bubbling over with noxious chemicals; just a desk, a laptop, and row after row of white shelves. The desk was old, one leg so worm-eaten it looked like a good shove would break it. The shelves were filled with identical black notebooks.

"What am I looking at?" I asked.

"Mistakes."

She pulled down a book, flicked to the middle, and showed me: it was a beautifully detailed sketch of an octopus, springing from undersea rocks. It was surrounded by Mum's tiny, cramped handwriting.

"This is the blue-ringed octopus. Mistakes copying its genetic code from generation to generation not only gave it the only octopus venom that's potent enough to kill a human, but also the ability to camouflage itself perfectly against its surroundings."

"This"—another shelf, another book, a sketch of an insect embedded in a fossil—"is *Rhyniognatha hirsti*. Mistakes made it the first creature on Earth to be capable of flight. This—"

"So," I interrupted. It was rude, but I could feel this conversation rattling away down the tracks, and I couldn't bear the inevitable platitude coming at the end of the line. "The octopus gets to change colour, the bug gets wings. I get dubious bowel control around spiders and loud noises. I won't lie to you, Ma. It's tough not to feel a little shortchanged."

She didn't even blink.

"What's 187 squared?" she asked.

I rolled my eyes.

"Well?"

"34,969," I replied. "But . . ."

"Camouflage and flight are adaptations to a threat environment, Peter. So is that." She slapped my notebook, the ARIA notebook, into my chest. "There's some incredible work here. I am *stupendously* proud of you. Do you think you would have been able to do that if you hadn't been exactly who and what you are?"

I didn't answer.

"Want to know what my biggest mistake was?" she asked.

"What?"

"You."

I gaped at her.

"I was twenty-four, all career all the time, single and living off baked beans, spite, and ambition on a graduate-student income. You think if God had invited me to choose from the menu I would have picked twins?"

I could only stare at her as she smiled.

"You think the fact that I didn't intend you means I *regret* you?" she asked. "You think I love you any less because you weren't in the plan? We have to love our mistakes, Peter. They're all we have." She laid a hand gently on my cheek. "Don't feel like you need to burn yours behind you, and don't ever, ever, feel like you need fixing."

"So, what? I'm perfect, just as I am?" Train pulling into platitude central; please mind the gap to the real world as you disembark.

"Perfect?" Mum laughed. "Evolutionarily speaking, perfection's just the art of embodying as many fuck-ups as possible while staying alive," she said. "Perfection's a process, Peter, not a state. No one's perfect. What you are is *extraordinary*. Exactly as I would have you."

She pulled me into a hug, and I clung to her.

"It's like the fear's stalking me," I whispered. "I can feel it in the back of my mind all the time, just waiting. I just . . . I don't want to be afraid anymore."

"I know, honey," she said, and clung to me fiercely, like she'd never let me go. "I know. I've got you."

She said it over and over, murmuring into my hair. It took eleven times for my sobs to quiet. "I've got you."

NOW

I doubt the catering's up to much, but let me tell you, if you're a fan of plastic, an Edinburgh psychiatric ward is the place to be.

Eight and a quarter metres away from me, on the other side of what only Caledonian optimism has allowed to be called the "Sunroom," a man and a woman sit side by side with plastic knives and plastic forks, shovelling plastic-looking food into their mouths from unbreakable plastic trays, all the while sitting on a sofa covered in vinyl, which is, lest we forget, a kind of plastic. Three yellow plastic geraniums sit in a plastic vase on a plastic table under a plastic-framed window. The window itself, alas, isn't plastic, but the glass *is* shot through with steel wires, so that none of the residents can shatter it and use a shard to open up their own or each other's throats. They've gone for a scab-brown carpet, though, so I guess you can't be too prepared.

"Do you have any idea," Ingrid whispers, leaning towards me, "how stupid this is?"

She'd asked me the same question at 4 this morning in the car park, bundled up against a hacksaw wind, laptop open on the bonnet of a car to catch the hospital's Wi-Fi: the digital surgeon, up to her elbows in the intestines of the National Health Service's record system.

"I know exactly how stupid this is," I'd told her then, but she'd pressed on regardless.

"LeClare has already been to see Rigby, remember? She's watching him. When she gets word his dead son's been visiting him . . ." She shook her head in disgust. "She's not going to jump to *haunting* as an explanation. If she doesn't already know we're in Edinburgh, she will by tomorrow. Petey, we have to go, now."

"Then go. I'm staying."

"Why?"

I don't answer, but in my mind Bel squeezes my hand while I lie in a hospital bed. *Who did this to you, Pete?*

Ingrid's expression, etched by the laptop light, was helpless. But she understood, and she made no move to go.

"Thank you," I said, and I meant it. "Now, hand me the laptop." She passed it over and I backdated the record seventy-two hours, the minimum notice period for doing anything in the psychiatric arm of our great medical bureaucracy.

"Pete," she huffed, but her tone was conciliatory. "How come you know all this stuff about mental hospitals, anyway?"

I didn't need to reply. She could read it off my face. *Because if I'm an expert in two things, Ingrid, it's numbers and being scared. And the numbers around mental hospitals are particularly scary.*

Around thirty thousand people are detained against their will under the Mental Health Act every year. Then comes the ambulance, the hospital, and the key turning in the lock. From that point on, the state takes control: decides when you eat, when you sleep, when you wash. And if you resist—out come the rubber restraints, the knee in the spine, the haloperidol dripping into your strapped-down arm, spinning your stomach, and dampening your world to fuzzy apathy.

Thirty thousand: in the grand scheme of things it's not so many. Less than one two-thousandth of the population of the country. But it adds up. Over my lifetime it'll be more than two million. Do I think there are two million people in Britain who are a bigger danger to themselves than I am?

—Pitching, heels over shoulders. Wind rushing. Red brick blurring. Heads or tails, heads or tails—

I do not.

For at least half a decade I've accepted my path will one day lead to an asylum. So I've taken precautions. I grasped my gargantuan powers of obsessive nerdism and trained them on the Mental Health Act 1983. I memorised everything the law permitted, and everything it forbade. Every trick, every loophole, every drop of bureaucratic oil that might one day grease my passage between the toothy cogs of the psych ward machine is stored safely in my brain for the day I hear the ambulance outside my door.

I just never, ever thought I'd go *looking* for it.

At a chipped Formica table, a grizzled man is crying. It started out as a low murmur, but now he's wailing, unselfconscious as a baby, and just as inconsolable; not that that matters, as nobody is trying to console him. No one's even looking at him. I wince at one especially loud shriek and dig my nails into my palms. I feel the familiar pressure building in my chest, the room starting to tunnel. In my head I can hear the click of doors locking, of tumblers turning. I'm starting to sweat. The hiss of a leaking radiator is playing out the voice in my head:

. . . *get out get out get out . . .*

Focus, Pete. Concentrate. *Breathe.* Do not panic. There's no time to panic. A door swings open at the corner of my peripheral vision and I stand, and try to smile, even though this will be the cruellest thing I've ever done.

I turn, my stomach churning like a washing machine, and there she stands, a pitifully small suitcase at her side.

She's changed from the photo Ingrid dredged up. Her hair's almost completely grey, even though she's only been inside for eighteen months. She looks nervous and birdlike, with a turkey wattle of skin at the neck where her flesh has ebbed away. Her fingers, stained yellow with nicotine, peck restlessly at the front of her jumper.

Even so, I was always going to recognise Rachel Rigby instantly. The face of the son who so took after her is acid-etched on my brain.

I just about manage to pry my mouth open and say, "Mum."

It's up to her now. She stares at me for a second and I see it, fleeing her face like a shadow in front of a torch beam: hope.

Dear Christ, she was still *hoping*.

Eighteen months she's spent buried on this ward, seventy-eight weeks, five hundred and forty-six slow days and nights, pleading and protesting, over and over: *My son's been murdered, please believe me, I shouldn't be here, help me*, please *help me*. Hushed and ignored and, for all I know, strapped down and sedated, she was told she was disturbed, told that Ben was fine, that he'd be in to see her soon. *You're out of sorts, you're not well, rest, calm down, just a little longer and you'll see.*

And now on day five hundred and forty-seven, they walk in and tell her that the son she was so insistent was a rotting corpse is waiting in the sunroom, come to take her home.

You wouldn't be human, would you, if in the minutes it took you to walk from your cell, you didn't begin to doubt yourself? If you didn't begin to think that the doctors with all the impressive letters after their names were right; that this had all been a bad dream, and when you push open the door, your son will be there to wake you up and guide you finally back to your old life?

And instead all you're faced with—staring at you with the same eyes as the woman who put you here and pleading with you to play along—is me.

Shit, lady. I am so sorry.

I see micro details in slow motion: the muscles in her jaw, her chapped lips parting. She's going to scream, I'm sure of it. She's going to shriek *Liar, impostor,* and blow the whole game. My legs tense to run but I know that the second she cries out, burly nurses will burst through that door, pin Ingrid and me down, and drip benzodiazepines into our veins until the cavalry from 57 arrives.

Ingrid's staring at me, aghast. I've fucked us.

"Ben," Rachel Rigby says.

I blink. She crosses the carpet towards me in four steps and falls into my stranger's embrace. Her arms clamp around me;

they're thin, but they grip like steel bands. She pulls away and looks at my face intently. Then she closes her eyes and leans into my shoulder. She's the consummate actress, I'll give her that. There's no sign in her voice or expression of the lie. Only I, with her sparrow's body pressed against me, can feel the tremor running through her.

"Bring me the forms," I say over her shoulder to the chief administrator, who, having escorted her in, is still hovering by the door.

"This is . . . rather irregular, Mr. Rigby." He walked towards us. "We need seventy-two hours' notice to release a patient."

"You've had them. Check your records."

"And a patient's release has to be on the instruction of his or her *nearest* relative, who we have on file as your father, Dominic."

"Dad's in a coma up the road at the Royal Infirmary."

Rachel Rigby stiffens in my arms but doesn't let go.

"Feel free to call them. I'm her nearest responsible relative now, and I'm discharging her as is her right, under Section Three of the Mental Health Act."

He wavers for a second. He looks uneasy and I'm instantly alert.

You know, I realise. *Someone's told you this one's special. Someone's told you not to release her. They haven't told you why, but you know your job's on the line if you let her go.*

And suddenly I'm sure of it; he won't let us go. He doesn't have an excuse to keep her; he doesn't need one. In his eyes I'm still a kid. I can feel the plan unravelling around me like toilet paper in the jaws of a puppy.

Desperately, I grope for some way to tip him, and that's when I recall a name I saw over Ingrid's shoulder on the screen last night.

"Sir John Ferguson. You know who he is?"

He blinks at me. "Of course; he's the chief inspector of hospitals."

"He's also a close family friend. Bring me the forms or

don't bring me the forms, but in ten minutes' time, we're walking out of here, and if you stop us, he's the first person I'll be calling. Your reasons for ignoring the law will have to be pretty convincing if you want to avoid a full-on, messy spot audit. You know, the sort that turns up the kind of gory breaches of procedure that play so well on the front page of the *Mail*."

At the table, the grizzled guy is still crying.

On the steps outside, Ingrid whispers, "The chief inspector of hospitals? A family friend?"

"You know what they say, Ingrid: blind panic is the mother of invention."

"Literally no one says that."

"That's because they haven't met me."

Rachel Rigby doesn't speak until we're well clear of the hospital. As soon as its Georgian crags are out of sight, she makes a beeline for the nearest corner shop.

"Money," she says shortly. I pull a tenner out of my pocket and hand it to her. She hesitates, composes herself, then vanishes inside. She reemerges with a carton of Marlboros and four packets of Maltesers. She sits down on a bollard and, ignoring the cars blaring past, systematically opens each pack, popping the chocolate-covered spheres into her mouth one by one and sucking them clean before crunching down on them.

Finally, she crumples the last bright red packet in her palm, stares out at the traffic, sighs, and lights a cigarette.

"You look like her," she says without turning her head. I don't need to ask which *her* she means.

"She's my mum."

She smiles. In the sunshine, her narrowed eyes are like liquid lead.

"So it's a family business, is it? Fucking up lives? Am I to take it that your . . . intervention just now is because your mum's reconsidered, and chosen to take her thousand-pound designer heel off my throat?"

I swallow.

"No."

She peers at me through the smoke.

"No?"

"We're on our own. And so are you. If you want to stay free, you're going to have to run. It'll be hard, but not impossible."

I look to Ingrid, who's leaning against a lamppost, arms folded, with this "*oh, we're having this conversation out here on the street, are we? Well, fuck everything I learned at spy school, then*" expression on her face.

"I have some experience with the organisation Louise Blankman works for," she says reluctantly. "I can tell you the kinds of trail they'll look for and how to avoid leaving them."

"Your timing's good," I add. "Mum's firm has got its hands kind of full at the moment."

"With what?"

Ingrid and I look at each other. *With the girl who slashed your son's throat and got me to cling-film his body inside a mouldy carpet and stage a gas explosion to get rid of it*—is what we emphatically do *not* say aloud.

"What you said in there," Rachel Rigby asks, "about Dom. Is it true?"

"Near enough." It's blunt, but I figure she's had enough of being treated fragile to last a lifetime.

"He gonna make it?"

"I don't know. The doctors aren't optimistic."

She blows out a long stream of smoke and her lips are trembling.

"Good," she says. "I don't know if I could stand being out here knowing he was too."

Cars whine past the roundabout, their horns filling the silence as they swing up towards the hill and Edinburgh Castle sitting dark and craggy on top of it. Ingrid kicks herself off her lamppost.

"We need to get on with this, Pete."

"Mrs. Rigby—" I begin.

"Rachel." The correction's not a friendly gesture.

"Rachel, it's kind of noisy here, and there's a lot you need to hear. Can we go somewhere quieter?"

Without a word, Rachel stands and starts walking, her suitcase wheels burring behind her over the pavement. We follow her in silence to a muddy meadow hemmed in by the talons of winter trees. Now we walk on either side of her: seven circuits, eight, while I tell her what I know about Mum's work, and Ingrid quietly relays the tedious, crucial details that must form the spine of her life from now on: what bank accounts she should access in the next two hours, the black databases on the Internet where she can safely stash the money until she can open clean ones in a new identity, what she can get away with in the first 12 hours, then 24, then 48; the address of a man in Glasgow who can arrange a fake passport and the countries that have weak enough surveillance setups that she can settle in them long term. Listening to her I feel a chill that's nothing to do with the autumn wind—it could be *my* future she's describing. My life.

At the end of circuit nine, we're done. Ingrid hesitates and reaches out and touches Rachel's shoulder. "Good luck," she says. Rachel hasn't made a sound this whole time. She keeps her eyes fixed on the ground as she says, "I'm not going to run."

She lights another cigarette, the last in the pack. She looks up at me.

"Your mother told me I had thirty years left to live and that I shouldn't waste them. Well, I don't intend to. I'm going to dedicate every minute of them to getting the opportunity, and then, when I have it, I'm going to kill her."

She says it clearly and simply, as if she's predicting the afternoon's weather.

"I'm going to kill your mother. I think you should know that."

Her certainty leaves an icy footprint on my heart, but what can I say? I nod once, and she turns and walks away.

It's only when we're back amidst the bustle and bagpipe whine of the Royal Mile that I notice Ingrid's shaking.

"What is it?" I ask urgently. She's rubbing her hands and plucking at her gloves. Her fingers curl and she starts to dig her nails in. Her eyes are open but unseeing. I have to yank her back when she almost steps into the road as a black cab blares past. I recognise the symptoms; she's having an attack—a six-pointer on the ballsuck at the very least.

I hesitate for a second, but there's nothing for it.

I pull her sideways into an alley between two close-leaning medieval buildings and into the open door of a pub.

Thank the saltire for Scottish drinking culture, because even though it's barely 11:30 in the morning, there are seven punters to distract the barmaid as I barrel Ingrid into the ladies'. The bottles of hand wash and iodine she keeps in her jacket clatter into the sink. The tap roars and she gets her hands under the flow. Her movements are sharp, frantic, but the rest of her seems to calm. That's the thing about crutches—sometimes you need them to hold you up.

"Ingrid," I say gently. "What is it?"

"Rachel," she gasps through a thin film of saliva that stretches between her lips. Her eyes are unfocussed, still staring blindly at her hands. "She's just . . . she's so *lonely*. I got swamped by it. I tried not to but . . ." She exhaled hard. "She has *no one*. You understand? Her son's dead. Her husband's soon to be, and she hates him anyway, and who could blame her?"

"You think I should have told her?" I ask.

"Told her what?"

"What he told us. The reason he did it. That he loved her. That he was trying to protect her."

She turns slowly and the look in her eye chills me.

"Don't do that, Pete."

"What?"

"Make excuses for him. Every prick who does this has a reason, and it's never, ever good enough. Dominic Rigby had exactly the same reason as every other man who's ever put their knuckles to their wife. I—" She hisses in frustration and corrects herself. There's something birdlike in the way she's holding her head. "*She* made a choice he didn't like, and he used his fists to take that choice away from her. And when she was too strong for that to work, he called in the rest of the fucking state to finish the job."

"Your old firm would have killed her—you know that."

"Then she would have *died*," she says flatly. There's blood in the sink now. "But that was her decision to make, not his."

The door creaks open and I look round. A woman in a biker jacket enters, takes one look at us, and walks out. Behind me, Ingrid says softly, "Pete, how many times have I washed my hands?"

"Seventeen."

"You're sure?"

"If you can't trust yourself . . ."

She snorts, but a few seconds later the tap squeaks shut. She bends over the sink and just breathes, long and slow.

"Now," she says at last, dabbing iodine against the back of her hands and tearing off a plaster with her teeth. "Can we get out of this bloody city before my firm shows up? I don't much fancy an extended holiday in Diego Garcia."

"Absolutely . . ."

"Thank you." She begins to gather her things.

"But you won't like where we're going."

She stops, throwing another anxious glance at the sink.

"Where?" She reads my face and goes very white.

"No," she says firmly.

"We have to."

"It's the first place 57 will look!"

"I know."

"Pete, I worked for these people for a decade, so trust me. When they're hunting you, you run and you hide; you do *not* get up all in their face like this. There's only one way that ends."

"Even so."

"Pete—" She's pleading with me.

"We have to find out why Bel flipped on Mum," I insist. "Mum was covering up a murder *she* committed. There must be a reason Bel attacked her."

Ingrid starts to protest. "Pete—"

"You saw what she did to him." I cut her off. "And yeah maybe he deserved it, but she was *enraged*. This was personal. Please, Ingrid. You don't have to come, but *I* have to know. I have to keep following her footsteps."

"But we followed her footsteps; they led us *here*. The trail's dead."

"It's not. There's the notebook; Rigby said Bel had a black notebook."

In my mind's eye I see my mother: in our devastated kitchen in her dressing gown, in a dark blue cocktail dress waiting to receive her award, rushing after me to meet her daughter's knife. And in every one of those images, she's carrying her slim black hardback notebook.

"Bel's been reading Mum's notes. There's something in her work that set her off—there *must* be."

"Pete—"

"Think about it." I'm pleading now. This has to be it. "Who are the only two people to survive Bel's attacks? Rigby and Mum. Both times she was enraged. She wasn't as clinical as usual. With Rigby she'd been reading Mum's work notes, and then at the museum . . ."

"She was about to watch her get an award for that work." Ingrid finished the sentence, sounding troubled.

"It's Mum's work. Something in those notes that turned Bel against her. Something bad enough that she couldn't stand watching her glory in it."

"You can't be *sure*." Ingrid's protest has the tone of a last-ditch effort. "Your sister's crazy. What if she doesn't need reasons? You already asked her *why* once, remember? She said your mum made her mad. What if that's all there is to it? After all"—she shrugs sullenly—"nothing 'turned her' on her first victim. Nothing sent her gunning for Ben Rigby."

I feel the base of my throat close up.

I see Bel sitting on my hospital bed. She's holding my hand, avoiding the needle lodged in my skin. Her voice is gentle, but her eyes are hard. "Who did this to you, Pete?"

"Sure something did," I say.

Ingrid looks at me quizzically. "What?"

"Me."

RECURSION: 2 YEARS, 9 MONTHS AGO

The first thing I noticed when I woke up was something hard and sharp lodged in the skin on the back of my hand. The second was my incredible thirst. I opened my eyes and the world blurred for a moment before resolving into a beige wall with seven red-jacketed clockwork soldiers painted on it. My tongue was Velcroed to the roof of my mouth and I croaked for water. My brain felt like a rock in my head.

I tasted fear on the back of my tongue. I didn't recognise the soldiers. I didn't recognise the wall. I didn't recognise the lumpy mechanised bed I found myself in, or the mouthwash-green smock draped over me. My left leg felt *huge*. I sat up, tried to move it, and screamed.

It felt as if the bone was pulling itself apart from the tendons. I collapsed back on the bed, gasping and sobbing. Hospital. I was in hospital. What had *happened* to me? The door to the little room opened and a familiar figure hurtled in, looking back over her shoulder to snap, "Of course I've sterilised, you cretin. My dandruff has a better working knowledge of microbiology than you do."

Way to charm the people responsible for my pain relief, Mum.

"Peter." She hovered over me. "How are you feeling?"

"My leg . . ."

"You broke it. You fell off a roof."

"My head . . ."

"You broke that too, and you should be grateful."

"Grate . . . ?" I watched Mum break about sixty medical practice guidelines by plugging a syringe into her own son's IV. Instantly my thoughts slowed. My head started to feel like a snow globe, a storm of random ideas drifting through a liquid suspension. I looked down at my hand; it was swollen and scraped raw, the other end of the plastic tube feeding out of it. Ah. Morphine. Good. As the proud owner of the world's most habit-forming personality, it would be just like me to come to hospital with a broken femur and leave with an opiate addiction.

"You cracked your skull," Mum said. "But not on the pavement, thank god. There were bits of bark in your scalp. Best guess, you clobbered your head on a tree branch on the way down and it spun you around. If it hadn't, you'd have taken the full force of the impact on your neck. You're going to have one hell of a scar."

Lightly, she brushed the bandage wrapped around my forehead. I could feel blood soaking through; head wounds bleed like a bitch.

"But you're incredibly lucky, Peter."

"Yeah." My stomach curdled with disappointment as I remembered the wet car park rushing up towards me. "Lucky me."

"What were you even doing on that roof?" Mum worried at her thumb cuticle with her teeth. I'd never seen her do that before.

"Exploring," I lied automatically. "I didn't know where the door led to. The slates were slick and I slipped."

"Really?"

"Yeah. Come on, Mum. You know what I'm like with heights. You don't think I'd have gone up there on purpose, do you?"

Her face became a little less grey.

"Well, then I suppose we just have to be grateful it wasn't—"

"Mum?" Bel's voice interrupted her and I started. My sister must have been sitting quietly in the corner of the room this whole time. Watching me wake, hearing me scream, not saying a word.

"Can I talk to Pete alone?"

Mum hesitated, shrugged, smiled, and withdrew. Only when

the door clunked shut did Bel approach the bed. She perched by my feet, her face hidden by a curtain of red curls, and she didn't meet my eye as she spoke.

"How did you fall off the roof, Pete?"

I felt myself go still.

"You were here just now. You heard . . ."

"I heard what you're going to tell everyone else." She stared into her cupped hands. "What are you going to tell me?"

I swallowed and made a decision.

"I jumped."

I was expecting Bel to swear, to yell, to hug me or hit me, but she just nodded and asked, "Why?"

"I panicked."

"Why?

"I found out there are unsolvable problems in mathematics."

It hung there in the air between us, for six full seconds, and then Bel started, helplessly, to laugh.

"Bel!"

"I'm sorry, Pete, but that is just . . . so fucking *you*. The only kid in the world who nearly died from *maths*."

I had no right to be surprised, but somehow I was disappointed anyway.

"You don't understand."

"No shit."

"Okay, look. There are seventeen—"

"Oh Christ, Pete, no. Please, not more numbers."

"There are *seventeen*," I insisted, and she must have seen the tears in my eyes because she shut up. "Seventeen elementary particles. They make up everything in the universe from black holes to brain cells. When you get right down it, *everything's* made of the same building blocks. What makes the difference is how many, the pattern of how they're arranged; what makes the difference, *always*, is numbers."

I twisted the bedsheet, deliberately hurting my grazed hands as I spoke.

"The difference between 495 and 620 micrometres on the length of a light wave is the difference between red and blue. The difference between 54 and 56 kilos of uranium is the difference between a very toxic paperweight and a nuclear explosion. You think I would have been the first kid to die of maths, Bel? Everyone who's *ever* died, died of maths."

She stared at me. I'd never felt so far away from her. It was as though we no longer shared the same language, but I had no choice but to keep jabbering on in my own, trying to make her understand.

"*'Why are you so scared, Pete?'* All my life people have been asking me that. So I went looking for an answer. I went looking for the number that's the difference between a normal, healthy, brave brain and mine."

Bel nodded; that at least made sense to her.

"I believed there was no question maths couldn't answer, if only I understood it well enough." I breathed out hard. "But I was *wrong*. Maths is incomplete. There are questions, questions *about numbers*, even, that it can't answer, equations that it can't decide are true or false. So I'm fucked. Gödel proved it in the thirties. It just took me this long to find out."

Bel was slowly working the knuckle of her left hand into the palm of her right. Now she looked up, and asked quietly, "How?"

"What?"

"How did he prove it?"

"You really want to know?" I was taken aback.

"Do I want to understand how a German geek who's been dead fifty years managed to get my little brother who's petrified of heights to jump off a fifty-foot building?" Her tone was kindling-dry. "You could say I was curious."

"Eight minutes older," I grumbled. "And he was Austrian."

"Whatever. Spill it." Her gaze was intent. "Make me understand."

"*Okay*," I said, and took a deep, painful breath. "Okay, I'll try."

"The first thing you have to get," I said, "is that to know that anything in maths is true, you have to prove it, and not with the kind of proof you can get looking through a microscope. You need *certainty*, not just evidence."

"But how can you prove anything without evidence?"

"With logic," I told her. "There are foundational beliefs that we just *accept* without proof because it . . . *hurts* to doubt them. Stuff like one equals one." I smile at her, and it feels good. "In maths we call them axioms."

She smiled back. She liked that.

"To prove a theorem, you have to find the chain of bullet-proof logic that shows that it follows from those axioms," I went on. "That chain of logic? *That's* your proof.

"For two thousand years of blissful ignorance, we thought that every equation had one. The true theorems had proofs vindicating them, and the false ones had proofs demonstrating their falsehood. We believed in *completeness*. That any question you could ask in maths could be answered with it too.

"But there was a flaw. It was absolute, and being absolute it took only one counter example—one equation maths couldn't decide—to shatter that belief.

"And Gödel"—yesterday I'd only vaguely heard of him; today his name was like bleach in my mouth—"he had a candidate in mind."

I groped around until I found the pen by my medical chart. With it, on the pale blue sheet of my hospital bed I wrote:

This statement is a lie.

And then crossed out the last two words and added:

This statement is ~~a lie~~ unprovable.

"*That*," I spat, slumping back against the pillows. "You can't prove it, because proving it true proves it false. So it must *be* true, even though you can never prove it. It's undecidable, forever poised, like a coin that only ever lands on the edge. If Gödel could find an equation that said *that*, then maths itself would be fundamentally limited."

"And did he?" Bel's gaze was intent.

I nodded.

"He did it in three steps.

"Step one: Encrypt. He created a code that changed equations—theorems and the proofs that proved them—into numbers, and so turned *proof*—the relationship between theorems and proofs, into an *arithmetic* relationship between numbers.

"Step two: Invert. He defined the *opposite* of that relationship. The relation of 'not being proven by.' He hypothesised an equation that, when encoded, had that relationship with *all* numbers: an equation for which a proof was impossible.

"Step three: Recursion, *Recoil*. He *defined* the unprovable equation *as the equation that stated that the unprovable equation had no proof.* It calls on itself. Eats its own tail. And it's so simple, so elegant."

On the sheet, underneath *This statement is* ~~*a lie*~~ *unprovable,* I wrote:

$$F \vdash G_F \leftrightarrow \neg Prov_F(\ulcorner G_F \urcorner)$$

"That's it," I said. "The unprovable equation. And *that* is a total fucking disaster, because if it's *possible* for one equation to be unprovable, then *any* equation could be. Any sum you try to solve could stall you for the rest of your life. Maths can't justify itself. It doesn't always work, and there's nothing outside of it that can tell you when it will."

I tailed off, gulping at air. Speaking this aloud made me nauseated.

Three steps, I thought: *Encrypt, Invert, Recoil, and just like that you've destroyed the world.*

Bel hadn't said a word the whole time, but finally she seemed to feel the need to clarify.

"And *that's* why you jumped off a building?"

"Yes."

There was another long silence in which all I could hear was my own laboured breath.

"You *dickhead!*"

I hadn't even realised there were flowers in the room until a vase came sailing over my head and shattered against the wall. Soil and pottery fragments showered down the back of my neck.

"You massive, weeping, septic *penis!*"

I began to laugh; I couldn't help it. The jerking sent little spikes of pain down my collarbones. But then she was standing right beside me and my laughter dried up. She wasn't joking around; her eyes were red and streaming.

"You tried to leave," she said. "You tried to abandon us."

At that word *abandon*, it felt like someone had jumped on my chest.

"I—I—I—" I stammered and pawed at the ink on the sheet, smearing it, desperate to say something, anything to erase that look of betrayal on her face. "I was just so tired, tired of being scared, tired of running, I . . ."

Her demeanour changed abruptly. She went very still and her eyes locked on mine.

"Running from who, Pete?"

I swallowed.

"No, it's not like that."

"Running from who?"

"Bel, I—"

"Were you alone up on that roof?"

"No, but . . ."

"Who was it? Who was up there with you?"

I stared at her, feeling the warmth of connection, of being *understood*, fading like a dying fire.

"Who?" she insisted. And I got it; she wanted a culprit, someone to blame, someone to hate for me. Flesh and blood, that's what she understood, not symbols on a hospital sheet. She sat on the edge of the bed, took my hand, careful to avoid the needle lodged in my skin, and asked, "Who did this to you, Pete?"

And in that instant, it was so easy to give one to her, even though I knew *who* was irrelevant; if it hadn't been Ben Rigby, it would have been someone else: Gödel had proved that. But it was so easy to interlace fingers with my sister against the old enemy, to take all my frustration and fear and loneliness and crush it into a bullet and fire it at him.

"Ben Rigby," I said, and then added quietly, "I wish he was dead."

NOW

Winchester Rise is deserted. From the corner of the street I can see my house, the shiny paint of the front door peeking above the holly bush. We crouch with our backs pressed against a low garden wall and watch through billows of our own breath, steaming white under the moon.

Twenty-four windows, I think, *twenty-four windows overlook the pavement between here and my front door.* I shrink back from the watchers who I've imagined behind every pane of glass. A breeze picks up, and for an instant, I think I hear radio static in the rattle of brittle branches. Then the wind dies and the street is silent again, still as a trap before it's sprung.

"That one." Ingrid points at a beaten-up hatchback parked directly across the road from my house, its dirty white paint job turned a sour yellow by the streetlights.

"How can you tell?" I whisper. "Special aerial for the radio? Artificially lowered suspension belying its piece-of-crap appearance?"

"No."

"Then how?"

Ingrid looks at me. "Peter, how long have you lived on this street?"

"Fourteen years, since we were three."

"And how many times have you walked up and down this street?"

"Thousands."

"And have you ever, ever, in all your trips down the length and breadth of this pavement, seen that car before?"

There's a long silence.

"Oh," I say, crestfallen. "Being a spy's just common sense, isn't it?"

The glare intensifies.

"No, it's very specific, well-trained sense."

I scan the other cars, trying to remember which I've seen before.

"Just that one?" I ask hopefully.

"Just that one," Ingrid confirms.

"So . . . it worked."

It was a shot-to-nothing from yesterday afternoon. Using a phone and a credit card we pinched from a bagpiper's ruck-sack on the Royal Mile, I'd booked two plane tickets leaving Edinburgh for Marrakesh that same night, in the names of Maggie Case and Benjamin Rigby. "You're right," I'd told her. "57 must know I'm using Ben's name by now. And after Bel's"—I'd faltered, remembering the blood droplets clinging to my sister's hair like leftover dye—"efforts back at school, we know they're stretched. With a bit of luck, they'll take the bait and pull some folks off watching my house to come and shove black bags over our faces at the departure gate."

As an afterthought, I'd added a third alias, *Beth Bradley*, to the booking.

"Why the third name?" Ingrid had asked, peering over my shoulder.

"For Bel," I'd replied. *I'm betting on you, Sis.* "If they haven't captured her, they might think she's with us. Then they'll *have* to send their best."

"*Shit.*" Ingrid's mutter drags me back to the present. She's staring intently at the car.

"What?"

"Only one seat in that car is occupied."

"Isn't that a good thing?"

"It is hugely not. We use teams of two for watching, no

exceptions. There must be someone else. And if he's not in the car, then he's inside the house."

"Can we take them separately?"

Ingrid's expression turns incredulous.

"I'm sorry," she hisses. "I've been a bit short on sleep recently, so I must have drifted off for a couple of years there while *you trained as a ninja*."

There is a hurt silence.

"No need to be snide about it."

"They'll have an open radio link. Whoever we try to hit second will be screaming for reinforcements the minute we so much as tickle his partner." She exhales noisily in frustration and closes her eyes, tilting her head this way and that as she considers scenarios. Judging by her pallor, none of them are good.

"We need to leave," she says at last. "This is seventeen kinds of suicidal. We could go anywhere: Tokyo, Mumbai, Mombasa. We're still twenty-four hours ahead of them—one full day's lead that I could make last a lifetime—but not if we do this." She opens her eyes, and in the darkness they're very pale. "Please, Pete. Don't. If we do this, we throw everything away."

I leave the plea hanging in the air and turn back to the car.

"If I deal with *him*," I ask, "can you handle the one in the house at the same time?"

"*Pete?*"

"Can you? Just answer."

She shrugs helplessly.

"Depends on who they've got in there. I had two months at knuckle school, same as any other field agent, but my grades"—she rubs her throat as if she's soothing a remembered injury—"were middling."

I consider my options.

I could walk away now: *Tokyo, Mumbai, Mombasa*, car horns, exhaust fumes, the anonymity of teeming people in a new city; new name, new life, new language, get a job, start a family, always with the past I've tried to forget splintering my sleep, jumping at the sound of every footstep on the stair. And worst of all, never knowing.

Never knowing why.

They called Gödel "Mr. Why," and look what happened to him.

Sometimes courage is just knowing what you're more afraid of.

"Do it," I tell her.

"But, Pete." Ingrid sounds utterly lost. "How will you even . . . *Pete!*"

But I'm already up, walking, rounding the corner. I stifle a ridiculous urge to whistle.

Just doing what I always do: walking up my street like I always do, passing the naked birch tree like I always have, hopping between the cracks in the pavement—I might fall through!

Already the white car seems to have doubled in size; soon it's going to swallow me, swallow the world. Dark windows glower and I can feel the whole street bearing down on me, its pressure, its weight. *Stop, Pete!* My home might be hostile territory now, but I still know it well. As I pass the driveway of number sixteen, I gather the loose brick from the gatepost, crouching without breaking my stride. *Christ,* it's cold. I toss the brick in my hand like a ball, as if I've come out to play in the street like all the kids I ever watched from my bedroom window but didn't dare to approach.

The car is enormous now. Fear packs in around my heart and *squeezes.* Only twenty strides to go, twenty chances to change my mind. I can hear the crunch of my feet on the frosty pavement, crushing those chances away.

Nineteen, eighteen, seventeen . . .

Panic pinches my throat, forcing out breaths in little steam-engine puffs. Ingrid's question echoes in my skull: *Pete, how will you . . . ?*

I think of Seamus, eyeball-to-eyeball with me, the terror on his face in the instant before Bel's bullet exploded his head. I think of Dominic Rigby; he was tortured by Bel, but that look he gave me from that hospital bed, that look of abject fear; it was almost as if it were *me* who'd done that to him; *my* gaze he was desperate to break.

Fourteen, thirteen.

Bel hurt them; Bel killed them, but I *scared* them. I don't know how, but I did. The fear came from me.

I step off the curb, and it feels like stepping off a platform in front of an oncoming train.

Ten, nine, eight, seven. I'm level with the back of the car. He must have seen me in his mirrors by now. Maybe he's talking to snipers in the windows, maybe crosshairs are zeroing in on the nape of my neck. *This is seventeen kinds of suicidal.*

Every nerve ending inside me is screaming, *Wolf! Wolf! Wolf!*

Three . . . two . . .

"But the wolf is my sister," I whisper aloud as I draw level with the driver's door. "And the fear is my friend."

One.

I swing the brick.

The window dissolves into glittering rain, shattering the silence. I glimpse a pair of startled eyes and plunge my arms through the gap, ripping my sleeves on the glass teeth that cling to the frame. My eyes are screwed up in fright, but I can just make out a man shape, grappling with his jacket, fumbling for something under his armpit. *He's got a gun.* My blindly questing hands touch his hair, soaked with sweat. They slip off and I grab his ears, wrenching his skull round to face me.

Strong hands clamp onto my wrists. Acid boils up in my throat. *Shit! He's going to pull me off him; he's going to shoot me. Bang bang, Petey. You're dead. YOU'RE DEAD!* He's yanking down on my wrists so hard I think they're going to break. I picture the bones splintering, severing arteries, my arms turning purple-black as I bleed out internally. *He's been to knuckle school, I'm a scrawny wimp, I'm not strong enough to hold on . . .*

But you don't need to be strong, Petey, you just need to make him weak.

I force my eyes open, force myself to look into his face. Heartbeats pass. The pressure on my arms slackens.

He's staring back at me through the shattered window, his face bloodless. He tries to pull my arms down, but he's as weak as a toddler, and it's easy to resist. He's trembling, his mouth opening and closing silently around stillborn protestations.

And there it is. I can feel it in him.

Panic. *My* panic.

I feel it in the way his scalp shivers in my palms, I can smell it in the sour sweat that soaks his hair, I hear it in his trembling breath. I have no idea how much time passes. It could be hours, it could be microseconds.

I feel a pang of sympathy. I know exactly where he is; I've been stranded in that mine shaft more times than I can count. I belt him across the back of the head with the brick. He slumps forward, his eyes glazed.

"Pete." I turn, and Ingrid's standing in the open doorway to the house, her eyes wide.

"What did you do to him?"

"I don't know," I reply. But I *do* know. I gave him my panic; I infected him with it, and it dawns on me slowly . . . *like I always do.*

I feel sick and guilty, but a part of me is giddy with the *power* of it, and an even deeper part is eyeing my bleeding forearms and wondering how I can do better next time.

You practice, Bel's voice whispers to me.

Shut up.

Quickly Ingrid steps forward and opens the car door. She gropes under the slumped man's armpits for his phone and his gun and checks his pulse.

"Hmm," she muses. "He *might* wake up while we're here. There's some towrope in the boot. Grab it and tie him up, eh?"

While I obey, she slinks off and returns with a handful of

dark cloth she shoves into the spy's unresisting mouth. I bind it in with more rope. He stirs groggily. She hesitates, shaping to whack him with her forearm, but then thinks better of it, checking his breathing through his nose instead.

"Ingrid?" I feel I have to ask.

"Yes?"

"Are those my *socks* you've stuck in his mouth?"

"They were the first thing that came to hand," she answers defensively.

"But . . . my feet sweat *a lot*."

She shrugs and heads back up into the house.

"*Sorry*," I whisper to the unconscious spy, "*about the socks.*" Dark blood glitters in his hair and on his neck. "*And . . . everything.*" I turn and scamper after Ingrid.

I catch up to her standing at the bottom of the stairs, her back to me. Long shadows cast by the streetlight stretch over the parquet floor towards her. My hand flicks automatically towards the light switch, and I jerk it back. All the doors off the hall are open, except for the one to the living room. There are dark fingerprints on the handle.

"Was there another agent?" I ask.

"Yes."

"In the living room?"

"Yes."

"Did you . . ." I take a step towards the door.

"Pete!" She still has her back to me. Her voice is harp-wire taut. "Don't. Please. He's . . . I had to . . ." She gulps air and then steadies herself. "I don't want you to see him. I don't want you to think of me like that."

My fingers fall away from the doorknob. Instead I dive left into the laundry room, and root around under the washing machine until my fingers close on the ancient toolbox I know is there, and yank it out. Ingrid hovers beside me, silent as a moth.

"Basement," I say. We clatter down the bare wooden steps to the door of Mum's study, secured by its keypad lock.

"Do you know the combination?" Ingrid whispers.

"Nope."

"Do you at least know how many digits it is?"

"Six, I think."

"Christ, Pete!" she hisses. "That's a million permutations!"

My old firm will be sending a lead-pipe team down here as soon as the watchers we just mugged don't report in, so correct me if I'm wrong, but I don't think we have time to brute-force it."

"You're wrong." I root in the toolbox for a screwdriver and the lump hammer. I jam the screwdriver in between the door and the jamb about six inches down, then swing as hard as I can. The impact judders through my hands, and I almost drop the damn thing, but I swing again, and again. At the fourth impact the wood splinters. At the fifth, the hinge rips itself free of the doorway; another half-dozen swings take care of the second hinge. My forearms feel like I've spent an hour clinging to a washing machine on a fast spin cycle, but a couple of kicks later and there's a gap between the door and the jamb big enough to squeeze through.

"*Jesus.*" Ingrid's staring wide-eyed.

"I mean there's brute force and there's brute *force.*"

It's a pretty crap joke, but she starts to laugh anyway, and that sets me off, and our laughter fills up the narrow concrete cellar, chasing away my fear. It doesn't last, though, and when the sound of it has faded, there's nothing else for it.

Try to get in here, we're done. You leave this house and you never, ever come back.

Even now that injunction weighs heavily. I creep forward with half steps.

Why, Mum? What didn't you want me to see?

One by one, we squeeze through the gap.

The study's exactly as I remember it: the rickety desk with the one wormy leg, nothing on it but a lamp and laptop; the white shelves, with their black notebooks packed in tightly, twenty to a shelf: rank after rank, like bats in a cave. Ingrid eyes them in dismay.

"We'll never have time to search them all," she says.

"We won't have to."

I feel the ghosts of my mother's hands on my shoulders, yanking me around towards the desk, just when I was about to look . . . *where?*

Behind the door.

I turn to face back the way we came. More black notebooks sit snug to the doorframe, lobes of my mother's outboard brain. Ingrid grabs one. I open another: a detailed sketch of an axon, scribbled notes on neurotransmitters; crossings-out and reiterations, an argument in the margins, in different-coloured inks but all in her cramped, scratchy hand. I replace the notebook and pull out another. A photo of some kind of sea worm is pasted onto the front cover, then on following pages, an MRI of its brain. Mum's ringed various bits of the cortex. I see the words *Distributed or local?* and *Prey response* scrawled next to one, and an unexpected chill runs through me.

I put it back and take another; Ingrid's already on her fifth. I look at her, and she shakes her head.

A choking feeling is settling in my chest and I don't know if it's disappointment or relief. I check my watch. We've been down here four and a quarter minutes already. How long before 57 reinforcements come charging down those steps?

"Not long enough," Ingrid says, reading my thoughts. "If we want to run for it, we need to do it now, while there's still time to put some space between us and this place."

But if you do that, Pete, you won't find out what set me off, will you?

Shut up, Bel. I need to think.

I squeeze the notebook back into place and stand back to look at the shelves again. There's something *off* about them. Something my symmetry-seeking brain's latched onto but that I can't quite define. It's like when you walk into an old house and it takes you a while to realise that all the wood and plaster has warped and there are no right angles left in the place.

"Pete?" Ingrid says again, the note of urgency in her voice stronger now. "We really need to—"

"Wait." I stare at the perfectly straight volumes, all crammed in tight on their shelves, top to bottom, twenty to a . . .

Oh.

That's it.

The books are jammed in tight, not a playing card's width between them. And there are twenty on every row, except the bottom one. That shelf is no less tightly packed, but only sixteen spines face out.

I all but throw myself to the floor and claw the books away from the wall, and there, yes, *there*. It's been cut on a curve from the top so it's hard to see, but the left-hand wall of the bookshelf is considerably thicker than its twin on the right.

It takes me a fraction of a second with the Stanley knife from the toolbox to find the crack and lever the false side away.

Three notebooks sit flush against the brick wall. I remove them carefully, almost tenderly, like a priest with a sacred text, or a virologist with a deadly sample, and carry them to the desk. Their pages are yellow with age and stiff at the edges. Whatever's in them was put there a long time ago.

We each take one. My fingers hesitate, just for a fraction of a second, on the cover of mine, and Ingrid says, "Pete."

The catch in her voice stops me cold. I turn back to her. She's holding up the notebook she took. Scrawled on the inside cover are two words.

Red Wolf.

I hold my breath, half afraid that if I exhale on the paper, all my answers will disintegrate into dust.

She turns the book back to face her and, as gently as if she were peeling a dressing back from a wound, she turns the page. She stares at it, but she doesn't speak.

"Ingrid?" My throat tightens. "What does it say?"

"I don't . . ." She shakes her head. "It just jumps in—I don't understand it. It's like it's missing a chunk."

Missing a chunk, I think. Like another, earlier notebook? Is that the one that Bel found?

"Read it to me."

She licks her lips, hesitates, then obeys: "As noted earlier—see entry 31/1/95—preliminary data suggest that the rage response can be compounded via synaptic loop . . ."

Loop. A chill grips me.

"'Increased adrenaline *may* yield enhancements in speed and strength—evidence is inconclusive—but the principle advantage is in the long-term commitment to violence.'"

In the back of my head, I hear Bel's voice, the panting breath as she stood over Seamus's blown-apart skull with the calm, focussed excitement of someone doing exactly what they were put on this earth for.

I practised. It's all I've ever really wanted to do.

Ingrid turns a page. She hesitates.

"Pete, are you—?"

"Keep. Reading." I bite the words off. She blanches and obeys.

"'There are significant defence applications, obviously, military intelligence swarming like piranhas. I could finally buy that new washing machine!'"

For a second I feel utterly lost, swimming in darkness miles below the light. Mum made Bel.

Mum *made* Bel.

Bel's voice whispers in my mind; the answer she gave when I asked her *why*.

She made me mad.

I can be pretty literal when I'm scared, but apparently not literal enough.

Why didn't you tell me, Bel? But I already know the answer.

You wouldn't have believed me, Pete.

I would. She's my axiom. But would *she* have believed that I would have believed? Loops on loops. Even five days ago, before

Ingrid dropped her own bombshell, I would have thought the idea insane. Not now. Now—overlaying her voice as she continues to read from the notebook—Ingrid's advice from days ago, echoes back to me: *You're a mathematician Pete, a scientist. This is the scientific method; adjust your theory to fit the evidence. I'm here. I'm evidence. So adjust.*

Bel was *engineered* this way.

A cold current of shock goes through me, but it's fringed with something else, something warm, even comforting:

Relief.

It's not her fault. After the hideous, lurching uncertainty of the past six days, the realisation is like solid ground under my feet again. *Bel was engineered this way; it's not her fault.* Her brain chemistry was torqued so hard to feel rage that she couldn't help herself.

I feel numb, distant. In front of me, Ingrid's still reading, but I can barely hear her:

"'. . . the most powerful primer for the kind of fury we're looking for is *fear*, but requiring a super-soldier to be petrified the whole time is a bit of a design flaw. The fear would need to be introduced from *outside*, transmitted by a counterpart who could be removed before deployment . . .'"

Jesus. I feel overwhelming pity for my sister. *Bel, I mean, Christ. I can't imagine how that would feel, to find out your own mother deliberately designed you with a neurological disord . . .*

"Oh."

Ingrid's stopped reading. She sags, looking heartbroken for me, like she's been let in on a cruel joke at my expense, and is waiting for me to catch up. Her gaze falls from my face to rest on the second notebook, the one still gripped in my hand.

It takes a second, but my brain catches up with my ears.

. . . counterpart . . .

Slowly, I lift the second book and open the cover. Two words are neatly inscribed on the first page:

White Rabbit.

Over the years, I've become a connoisseur of fear, but what I feel now is very different from the familiar frantic pawing of anxiety at my heart. Now I feel *dread;* cold and heavy and coffin-lid certain.

My fingers are numb, clumsy. They shake like they're freezing. I try and try to turn the page, but the harder I try the harder they shake. I get paper cuts but keep fumbling. My muscles conspire against me. It's like Bel's wall. I can't move; *I can't* make myself look.

Ingrid eases the book from my grasp. I lift my eyes to hers, pleading.

"It's okay, Pete," she says. "I've got you."

I press my back to the wall and close my eyes. I know she's using the gentlest voice she can muster as she begins to read:

"'In order for the subject to most effectively promote RW's violent tendencies, WR must be able to both sustain and *transmit* significant quanta of fear. Maybe I can leverage the existing empathic machinery of the human body. We know that sweat excreted under stress contains pheromones that stimulate a fear response in mammals of the same species, and that anxious facial expressions elicit anxiety from those looking at them. If WR's pheromones can be *refined* so that they "prime" surrounding subjects to respond more intensely to its *expressions . . .*'"

Facial expressions, I think.

The spy in the car, Seamus, Dominic Rigby, even Tanya Berkeley in the girls' bathroom three years ago; I remember the terror on their faces when they looked me in the eye, even though it was me who was beyond scared and fighting for control.

Staring me in the face. Panicking when *I* panicked.

I remember Seamus's voice as I knelt in the mud behind our school: *If you even think about turning to face me, I will blow your head clean off your shoulders and all the way to Ballymena. Clear?*

Is that why you didn't want me to turn, Seamus? Because if you looked me in the eye, my fear would become yours?

His expression was such a perfect mirror to my own, an instant before my sister's bullet exploded his skull.

In front of me, here and now, Ingrid's face is wretched with pity. She desperately wants to stop reading.

She's a good friend; she doesn't.

"'. . . Obviously, RW and WR's relationship must be handled carefully. It would be all too easy for RW's fury to scare WR off. On the other hand, if they can be close—and the closer the better, friends is too contingent, family is better—WR could find RW's assertiveness attractive, seeing RW as a protector, creating a dependence and an incentive for WR to stay close to RW to fulfill its role.'"

My *role*. I am a cog in the machinery of my sister.

"'As for the generation of the fear itself, once I've isolated the circuit in the brain that produces the fear, it should be as simple as building in a loop. WR will find its own fear terrifying, looping back on and refining itself, like a centrifuge. This is just a beginning—a subject capable of spreading unreasoning panic in a population has its own military applications, potentially huge ones. Memo: Examine further at the office. Meantime, this will require continuous observation in a variety of contexts. We're all working without a net here—'"

"Stop." I hold up a hand, and she breaks off.

. . . as for the generation of the fear . . .

. . . the fear itself . . .

I start to laugh, quiet at first, and then louder and shriller, looping back on itself; laughing because I'm laughing, hysterical fucking turtles all the way down. I think of all the people I've ever met, all the friends I couldn't make, their faces as they looked at me, uncertain, evasive, as if they couldn't wait to get away.

Afraid.

"What was Mum working on?" I'd asked Rita.

Her eyes looking at me over the top of a surgical mask. Frankie saying.
"You have to expect us to have a few secrets."
Well, now I know.
Mum's words, spoken in this very room, seem to leach out of the walls.
What you are is exactly as I would have you.
I scream suddenly and sweep an arm across the desk. The lamp bulb shatters on the floor; the laptop bounces and skitters. My legs give way, and I slide down the wall. Startled, Ingrid drops the notebook, and the way its pages flap and flutter reminds me of something.
[This sentence is a lie.]
I love you, Petey.
[A lie that undermines everything.]
I can't believe it, and yet I *know* it's true. Even now my arms are half curled in expectation of the hug from Mum that will make it all better, my ear cocked for her whispered reassurance. Discovering a betrayal isn't like flicking a switch; it's more like poisoning a water table. It takes time to seep into all the parts of you.
I don't even realise I've closed my eyes until I'm opening them again. A pale, rectangular shape coalesces on the floor in front of me.
The third notebook.
I must have swept it off the desk with everything else. The front cover's fallen open.
Black Butterfly, it says on the title page. Underneath, Mum's taken the time to sketch the insect, intricately detailed in black ink.
We've had me, I think desperately, *we've had my sister—who the fuck's left?*
I reach across the floorboards for the notebook, but Ingrid steps in front of it. She puts a hand on my shoulder.
"Pete, the lead-pipe team. 57 are on their way by now. We have to go."

"But . . . but the third notebook."

"It's nothing."

"N-nothing?" I say weakly. I feel dazed.

"It's not relevant. I looked while you were having your . . . moment then."

"But—" Shakily, I get to my feet. I pull free of her hand and try to go around her, but she sidesteps, staying between me and the third book. I try again and she sidesteps again, like some absurd little dance. She's turned 180 degrees now; her back's to the desk, but she's still between me and the book.

"Ingrid, don't be stupid, that book was hidden away with the other two. It's *obviously* important."

"What's stupid, Pete, is us sticking around to get our heads stoved-in when we've got what we came for. Let's *go*."

She reaches out again, but I shove her hand away. Her eyes are twitching eagerly across my face, drinking in the thoughts there. She looks scared.

Of course, she does, you idiot. She feels what you feel, and right now you feel like your intestines are about to drop in a neat little package out from between your legs.

Yeah, except: I'm a connoisseur of fear, and what I'm seeing on Agent Blonde Calculating Machine's face isn't the same as the bewildered horror that's clutching at me.

She looks *nervous*.

"Why don't you want me to see that book, Ingrid?"

I take a step towards her and she steps back, planting a foot on the book.

"I don't . . . It's not . . . We just have to go."

"Then why don't we take it with us?"

"There's nothing in it."

"Nothing?" I take another step, and she's backed right up against the desk now. "What do you mean, nothing?"

"Fine. Let's take the fucking thing with us, but we have to leave *now*."

She spits it angrily, trying to seize the initiative back, but it's too late because I've taken another step and she's backed into the table. She reaches behind her to steady herself, and she glances back, and—just for a fraction of a second—her hand hesitates in the air above the worm-eaten right leg that would cave if she put her weight on it.

She's been in here before.

She frowns, studying my features. *Shit, look away*, but it's too late.

"Well," she sighs. "That's that, then."

She reaches into her jacket and pulls out the gun she took from the spy upstairs. I hear the snap as she flicks the safety off.

"You told me"—I lick parched lips—"you told me you'd never met my mother before I invited you round for dinner."

"I did," she admits.

"I guess that whole reading-my-mind thing makes it embarrassingly easy to lie to me, huh?"

She cocks her head to one side, considering it.

"I was never embarrassed by it."

"Well, aren't you a model of self-possession!"

The barb gets nothing from her, but perhaps there's nothing to get. Her eyes are narrow, and I know she sees past my poorly erected bravado. She's pained by my pain maybe, but her grip on the gun is strong.

Why risk it? I wonder fleetingly. *Why let me come down here if you knew this was here?* But then, did I give her any choice? I remember her pleading, tearful face under the streetlight; *Please, Pete, don't.* And then later, when we got into the house: *I don't want you to think of me like that.*

"Was there ever a second agent in the house?" I ask.

She shrugs.

"Lies and betrayal, fourteen hours a day, huh?"

"I've been pulling a lot of overtime recently."

I bet you have. Day in, day out. Tears on demand. Kisses in the dark. Every word out of your mouth moulding the thoughts you read off my face; that's got to take it out of you. And all to find my sister. You had her once, but she slipped away. So you doubled down, stuck to your cover, because you knew I was your best route back to her.

"What's in that third book?"

"Me," she says simply.

I nod. *Black Butterfly*. I stare down at the perfectly symmetrical wings of the ink-drawn butterfly on the front page. Each the mirror image of the other. Ingrid's a mirror. I see my own fear and confusion reflected in her features, but the gun barrel is as steady as a promontory of rock.

"What did she do to you?" My voice rasps in my ears.

"It doesn't matter."

"My best friend's pointing a gun at me. I think I have a right to know why." They called Gödel Mr. Why, and I think I know how he felt.

At first, I don't think she's going to answer; after all, it's not like I'm in any position to make demands, but then she gets this *look*. It's an expression I remember down-lit from the bare bulb in 57's paint cupboard, when, tearfully she'd told me:

"You don't know how lucky you are to have someone who knows you that well."

There's a faint bitter cast to her voice as she says, "Shall we hear it from the woman herself?"

She stoops, careful to keep the gun on me, and gathers the notebook. She lifts it so she can eye me over the top while she reads.

"'If the empathic bond between RW and WR can be generalised, it might be possible to create an all-purpose empath: obvious investigative and intelligence applications. Henry Black is expecting baby, and keen. We'll begin preliminary tests on Wednesday—*exciting*!'"

Ingrid's mouth puckers, as if Mum's enthusiasm is acidic. She flicks forward a few pages.

"'It's becoming clear that the toughest challenge with BB is to "clear" her, make room for others' emotions. She spent the whole of last session unable to feel anything other than how excited she is about a stray kitten she's adopted. Honestly, more affection than a domesticated predator really warrants, I feel.'"

She smiles, but it looks painful. Her jaw's set hard enough I can see the muscle twitch. She turns a page.

"'BB inconsolable today, spent whole day screaming and crying, presumably because Henry shot her cat. Can't be helped, but we can't keep her indoors forever. We must teach her to police her own interactions. *No close relationships*, not even with animals.'"

"Jesus Christ," I mutter, but Ingrid presses relentlessly on.

"'Test results improving. The strategy of keeping BB isolated from others her own age is working, but her attachment to her *parents* remains an issue. Her isolation is increasing her dependency on those who are left in her life.

"'It seems that while BB adopts her immediate emotional state from whoever she's with, her decision matrix, her *will*, is governed by a deeper set of desires, as all of ours are. The difference is that BB derives those desires, not from within, but wholesale from someone else, the person she spends the most time with. Their loyalties and passions become *her* loyalties and passions. They will be embedded deep, like a tattoo, while her other emotions are a surface phenomenon sloughed off like layers of skin.' Huh," Ingrid adds, almost to herself. "I never had your mum pegged as the poetic type."

She turns another page. She stares at the book as though stricken by an awful memory. The gun flickers and for a fraction of a second I think I might have an opening, but then she steadies.

"'Success! Fantastic day at the office. Need a drink, though. Was *very* nervous. Gave BB a rabbit to look after several months ago. High risk, could have undone years of work, but had to be done. When I asked how she felt about rabbit, BB said, "I love it," but nervously—she knows this is not allowed. Still, she's only seven. When I asked how rabbit feels about her, she said, "He loves me," which made me even more nervous. No need to be, though! When I gave her the wire, and made her understand that it was what I really wanted, she strangled the rabbit there and then.'"

She says it flatly, like she's announcing train times. I gape at her.

"'Ancillary reactions; lacrimation and erratic breathing while the poor thing struggled and squealed, indicate she suffered *no loss of empathy* for the rabbit during its execution. Incredible! Twenty minutes later she displayed no signs of discomfort, quote. "It was what you wanted, so it was what I wanted, Dr. B." What a darling!' Aw, wasn't I cute?"

Ingrid closes the book and drops it back onto the floor with a smack.

"Get the point, Pete?"

It was what you wanted, so it was what I wanted, Dr. B.

Mum's desires are tattooed on her. My feelings are only scrawled on her surface. I think of her strangling her pet rabbit. She might cry when she pulls the trigger, but her tears won't cloud her aim.

"There," she says. "You've had your answers. Now it's my turn. You know your sister better than anyone, and this is where the trail led you. Did anything, *anything* in those notebooks give you any fucking idea where she is now?"

"No." I can feel my neck heating up. My throat's closing, and the room's starting to spin.

"No?"

No.

Except . . .

Swimming treacherously to the surface of my brain despite my attempts to drown it is a phrase from the second notebook, the one about me.

Continuous observation in a variety of contexts . . . Ingrid's eyes narrow, flickering back and forth as she reads my face. Shit. Don't think about that. Think about *anything* else.

"Pete, what was that?"

Fuck. Um. What do I do, what do I do, what do I do?

There's nothing you can do. She can read your mind.

She can read your mind.

She feels what you feel. So think about the gun pointing at your head. Think about the bullet travelling at 365 metres a second and flattening to the size of a ten pence piece as it shatters your skull. Think about the equation for trying to reconstruct the geometry of that skull, then laugh despairingly at its complexity. Think about how much it's going to *hurt.* Think about the sound of the *bang.* Think about the surging in your chest and the sweat in your eyes and the sudden hot, bubbling pressure of the shit in your colon. Now *panic.* You hear me, Peter Blankman? Don't count, don't talk.

Just panic.

I take a step towards her, never taking my eyes off hers. Sweat glimmers on her brow and she twitches. I know she's feeling everything I am, and if she wants it to stop, she's going to have to look away.

But she won't she won't she'll shoot me it's over I'm dead I'm dead I'm dead . . .

She flinches, but the gun doesn't move.

"I know what you're trying to d-do," she says. She has to force the words out. I sympathise. If I even open my mouth, I think I'll puke.

I take another step.

"I-i-t won't w-work," she stammers "I—I've had t-t-too much practice w-with your bullshit f-f-fear. *S-s-stop!*"

One more step and the ring of the pistol barrel is blissfully cool against my forehead. I feel it shudder. Is that me trembling? Or her?

"S-stop!" she cries.

If you think I can just stop, *Ana,* you should have been paying more attention.

"I—I'll *shoot!*"

No, you won't. After all, I may just be a cog in my sister's mechanism, but I'm a pretty vital one. I don't think my—*our*—dear mother would take it too kindly if you broke me.

The gun's definitely trembling now. Ana Black's eyes shift right and left and right again in endless reflexive indecision.

"Goodbye, Ana," I say quietly. The gun slides slickly off my sweaty forehead as I turn, squeeze around the door, and mount the stairs. My legs give way under me on the second step, and I crawl the rest of the way, splinters from the bare boards burrowing into my palms.

I just about make it outside, get back to my feet, and stagger sideways into a hedge. I slump over it, wheezing. If Ana was telling the truth for once and 57 reinforcements *are* on their way, well, they can have me. I sprawl on my back on the freezing grass and stare at the moon.

Gradually, my chest stops feeling like I have a routed cavalry charge running round it, and, as my panic eases, the thought I so frantically buried under it reemerges. A phrase innocently slipped into the White Rabbit notebook. A phrase about me.

. . . *will require continuous observation.*

After several unsuccessful attempts to get enough purchase on the bush to stand upright, I decide to just roll *through* it. I lurch to my feet on the pavement, bleeding and stuck with thorns, but I don't stop to pull them out.

Finally, I know where Bel is. And I know what she's trying to do.

Continuous observation in a variety of contexts.

Ana Black wasn't the only one watching me.

I stagger into a run.

3:
RECOIL

RECURSION: 5 DAYS AGO

Just before she left, Mum took one last look at the kitchen I'd devastated. Her brow furrowed, and she bent and retrieved a framed photo from amidst the eggshells and flour dust and broken glass. She wiped the muck from it and set it back on top of the fridge, where it belonged. She gave me a gentle smile. A "we can beat this" smile; an "I believe in you" smile. Then she disappeared through the door.

For a few moments, I leaned on my broom, shivering and aching in the wake of my adrenaline. I stared at that picture. It was a black-and-white shot of Franklin Delano Roosevelt giving his first inaugural address. Printed across the bottom of it was that speech's most famous maxim:

THE ONLY THING WE HAVE TO FEAR IS FEAR ITSELF.

As the memory fades, I hear Ana Black's voice, quoting from the notebook that contains my life. "As for the generation of the fear itself . . ."

Mum always said she found that quote inspiring.

I rub my eyes and lift my finger . . .

NOW

. . . to the doorbell, but something makes me hesitate. There are no lights on in the front of the house, but given the time, that's hardly surprising. Even so . . .

I crouch beside the brick-edged flower bed. The soil's still damp from the rain and a rich, loamy scent wafts when I turn over the fourth brick. I breathe a little easier. A lot can change in two years, but the key's there, pressed into the earth. A worm burrows its way into hiding; *Lucky git*, I think.

Because the voice I can never quiet is whispering to me.

What if I freeze? What if I panic and get us both killed?

Fear mounting on fear mounting on fear: like an ocean wave rearing over me, waiting to crash down. I have no choice but to walk in its shadow.

Just walk.

I let myself in as quietly as possible, but the key in the lock still sounds like a bone splintering. I pause for my eyes to adjust to the gloom. There's a semicircular table by the door. On it is an open Tupperware box, with one set of keys inside it, and beside it, another, different set, outside on the wood. Otherwise, the hall is completely empty, just walls, ceiling, and carpet. No pictures. I slip through a door to the right and find myself in the kitchen.

A tank battalion of Tupperware is drawn up on the countertop, 14 boxes in all. Underneath the Braille labels, I can still make out marker pen, old labels he'd had to abandon as the disease chewed up more and more of his retinas: *SALT*,

BASIL, TURMERIC. Dr. A likes to cook. Bottles of oil and vinegar stand against a wall, spirit shot-pourers screwed into their
necks, their stations marked by dots of dried superglue on the
tiles. A fully stocked cutlery canteen sits out on the surface. I
imagine him navigating this place by touch and memory, fas-
tidiously tidying after himself, so everything will be where he
needs it for next time. Everything with a place, and everything
in its place.

The carving knife missing from the fancy Japanese rack all
but screams its absence.

Beyond the kitchen is the living room. The furniture is
pressed up against the walls. Cables are tied down. Every table
has more Tupperware boxes, containing everything from neatly
stacked denominations of change to remote controls. Oddly,
the books in the case against the back wall are jammed in any
old how, flopping and falling like a house of cards. I wonder if
that's because Dean reads to Dr. A. I hope it is.

I retreat to the hallway. The front door beckons, its inset glass
gold with streetlamp light. I could just leave. But that empty slot
in the knife rack won't let me. I turn and mount the stairs.

There's barely any light on the landing, and in another house
the shape I see as I reach the top step could have been anything:
a tangle of sloughed-off clothes, a jumble of bags, haphazardly
arranged to trick my eye into seeing knees, elbows, a spine. In
any other house, but not in this compulsively, *necessarily* tidy
one. It's all I can do not to cross the landing at a run.

It's only when I'm close to that I recognise him, and my
breath catches with guilty relief. It's not Dr. A; it's Dean. I put
my fingers on his neck. He's warm, but for a miserable, heart-
hitch of a second I feel no pulse. Then—thank god, there it is;
a solid, strong 52 beats a minute.

"Dean?" Dr. A's voice is strangled, tremulous. "Please, Dean,
answer me."

It's coming from the room on my right. I stand, place my
fingertips on the door, and push.

The bedroom's as neat as the rest of the house, except for two things: the bedsheets, sloughed and rucked like an arctic waste seen from a plane window, and Dr. A.

The muscles in my chest lock hard at the sight of him, and for a moment I can't breathe. He's in a half crouch in the far corner, the front of his pyjama shirt dark with blood from what looks like a broken nose. His beard is matted with it. His hands curl and uncurl uselessly, bleeding from slashes across palms raised against the black-clad assailant he can't see.

I watch as, despairingly, he tries to run out of his corner, crying "Dean!" but Bel shoves him down with one gloved hand to the chest. Her other hand holds the knife.

"Dean's going to be fine, Dr. A," I say quietly. Bel turns to look at me but doesn't speak. "She didn't come here for him."

"Peter?" Dr. A cries. "Peter, what are you doing here? RUN!"

"That's what *she* told me to do." But looking at her, I feel my pulse ease and the tide of nausea recede from my throat. Even like this, poised for murder over a man I'd considered a friend, she calms me.

"She told me to run," I continue, "and I thought she was trying to protect me, like she's always done. Turns out, she was just trying to get me out of the way, so she could do this."

Bel takes three quick steps back into the corner of the room so she can watch us both at once.

"I *was* protecting you," she says quietly. "He manipulated you, Pete. He betrayed you." There's a pleading tone in her voice, and despite myself, I feel a spike of pride.

Bel, this killing engine, needs me, just *me*, to believe her, side with her, to not blame her.

And I don't blame her. I know it's not her fault.

"Peter," Dr. A is gasping. "Please, I don't understand. What's happening? I don't know what she's talking about. Tell her. She'll listen to you. She'll *listen*." His voice tightens up, and a keening sound escapes his throat. I cross the room to him, casting a wary glance at my sister in the corner.

"Come on, Dr. A. It's all right." I keep my voice as calm as I can. "Sit down. Your legs are shaking."

"But D-Dean."

"Dean will be okay, I just checked on him. He's fine." I take his hands. They're an old man's hands, meaty and white-haired. His palms are slippery with blood. I ease him down onto the carpet until he's sitting with his back against the wall, bare feet splayed out. I settle myself cross-legged in front of him.

"How long have you been my maths teacher, Dr. A?" I ask gently.

He gapes, uncomprehending.

"How long?" I press.

"F-four, or five years?"

"Five," I confirm. "And do you remember our first lesson together, five years ago?"

"N-no?"

"It was probability. My first time with it, and I loved it: 'The odds of any two independent events occurring purely by chance is the probability of one times the probability of the other, so that the odds of *both together* are lower than the odds of either one alone.' Remember that?"

He nods, perplexed. "Peter, what are you—?"

"There are fewer than a hundred legally blind teachers in the country," I say. "That makes the odds of any given teacher being blind about one in six thousand. Now, what do you think the odds are of *me*, a giant maths nerd, purely by chance, getting a blind maths teacher, for five years running, especially when . . ."

But I don't need to finish the sentence; I can see on his face that he already knows what I'm going to say.

When blindness is the only thing that can protect you from me.

I've been watching his eyes the whole time, but of course they've never focussed on me. He trembles, plucks at his beard, makes small noises that might be abortive attempts to speak.

He's afraid—but his fear is all his own.

"You're part of it," I say softly. "You're one of them."

And then Bel's there, crouching beside us, so soundless that Dr. A doesn't react when she holds the knife over his shoulder, just where his pyjama shirt flaps open, and draws a thin shadow across the liver-spotted skin over his collarbone. Her knuckles pale as they tense around the handle. I study Arthurson's face. *He betrayed you.* Bel's not wrong. Mum did too, and Ingrid. Everyone has, except Bel. Bel's doing this for me. What right do I have to question her?

"*Don't,*" I breathe, so quietly that for a moment I'm scared she didn't hear it, but the knife doesn't move. "Leave him," I tell her.

"Why?"

My eyes find hers in the dark.

"So you know you can."

She looks away.

Don't, I think. *Don't be what she made you. You don't have to be. Think again.* I try to pour it into her, all my doubt, my hesitancy. It's exactly seventeen seconds, but it feels like an eternity until she speaks.

"So . . . what do we do with him?"

We. I breathe a fraction easier.

"How much longer will Dean be unconscious for?" I ask.

"The guy on the landing?" She shrugs. "Some." I am momentarily scandalised by her lack of precision.

"Tie him up," I say, looking down at Dr. A. "Dean can find him when he wakes. Drop every phone and computer in the house in the toilet; that should buy us enough time."

It's both a relief and a little sickening that she doesn't ask *Time for what?* We were always of one mind.

I head for the door without looking to see if she'll follow.

Outside on the street, it's like it never happened. The moon is full and bright, the pavement speckled with frost. A sound like damned souls being torn apart in some subdimension of hell comes from one of the gardens behind the terrace; so presumably some foxes are having sex. Bel no longer has the knife. I washed it up and put it back in the rack while she was gathering up the phones. A kind of apology, I suppose.

She's twitchy. She's up on her toes ahead of me as we walk, talking a lot about nothing.

"How did you know?" I ask. "About Arthurson?" Somehow I doubt she'd worked it out based on probabilities.

She shrugs. "They had a teacher watching me too: Ferris. He gave Arthurson up."

After you did what to persuade him? I wonder, but I don't ask.

Instead, I say, "I don't blame you, Bel. I know it's not your fault."

She stops walking, turns her head.

"Fault?" She speaks slowly, carefully. "You think I'm *ashamed* of what I've done?"

"Bel, sixteen people are *de*—" But she cuts me off with a hand gesture. I shrink back. I've misread her. And I can see it now, in her face: anger feeding off anger feeding off anger. I can hear it in the way her sentences almost overlap.

"Those men terrified their wives," she says. "They did it for years so they could control them. They inflicted years of fear, and doubt and pain—*years*—and they made those women believe they deserved it. All I did was kill them. They got off light."

"What?" she demands as I stare at her. "You going to try to tell me it wasn't right? That what I gave them is worse than what they did? Really? You?"

I don't speak. I can't.

"No," she says at last, and in my mind I hear her accusation from the hospital bed, all those years ago: *You tried to leave.* "You know better."

She shakes her head and keeps walking. "I let your maths teacher go because you asked me to, but don't expect me to change, Pete. I *like* me."

I do too, I think. She's done terrible things, things that will stalk my nightmares for years, but the fact is, I can't stop loving her. And I don't want to.

And she's not the only one, which is what makes it necessary to say, "I don't expect you to change, sis. In fact, you can't. Not yet. There's still something we need to do."

She pauses midstep. She doesn't look round. She knows what I mean. Of course she does.

"We can't just leave her there, not with them."

I hear the bloody-minded determination in my voice. I inherited that from her. We have to give her a chance. Maybe she can explain, maybe there's a side I'm not seeing. We can't just leave her behind. *I* can't. She's my mum.

"Can't get to her," Bel says shortly. "I don't know where they're keeping her."

"No, but I do."

RECURSION: 5 DAYS AGO

My sister stomped into the kitchen, scratching sleepily at her head, took in the devastation, shrugged like it was no big deal, and dropped to her knees in the middle of it. I rushed to her side, and we worked together, sorting and tidying, rebuilding and making right. We're quite the team.

"... *In order for the subject to most effectively promote RW's violent tendencies* ..."

A red-pelted wolf bounding through a forest of numerals. She's my inverse, my opposite. Without her, I'm incomplete.

Quite. The. Team.

NOW

Ding-dong!

The bell is offensively cheery for five in the morning, but the door opens before I've counted to three, and the eyes in the wizened face that appears around the edge of it have no hint of sleep clinging to their corners.

"Mrs. Greave!" I cry, throwing back the hood of my anorak. "Good to see you! Pete, Pete Blankman. I was here five days ago with my mum. You might remember her—she was . . ."

But the words *gushing blood from an abdominal wound* never make it past my lips, because 57's ancient doorkeeper has thrown her door wide open, her face set and grim. She stares over my left shoulder and nods.

"Who are you nodding to, Mrs. G?" I look theatrically back over my shoulder and follow her gaze to the dormer windows of the house opposite, their panes aglow with the blue dawn light.

"Oh right! The *boys*. Your snipers. Well, they want me alive, at least I hope they want me alive, so a head shot's out. Leg, then? Ankle? Knee? Oh lord, *spine?* Would they try to paralyse me? Too much to hope they have tranquilisers, I suppose; I could use the sleep . . ."

My gabbling makes no discernible impact on Mrs. Greave's oaky features, but it buys me a few extra seconds.

"They are taking their time, aren't they? Do you suppose their guns have jammed? Could they be on a tea break? Hell of a time for it, not that I don't get the appeal of a nice slice of Battenberg, but still . . . Anyway, I'm sure they'll be right back."

A ratcheting crack splits the air and the muscles around my spine seize, then relax. It was only the latch on the front door to the house opposite, shockingly loud in the early morning hush. Mrs. Greave and I watch as the door swings inwards.

When the figure steps from the doorway onto the street, my prattling bravado shrivels inside me.

Bel is barely recognisable. Her hair and clothes are streaked with blood, dark and clotting. She's drenched in it, not like a killer, more like an abattoir labourer, stretching sore muscles after working all day at the slaughterhouse. Her eyes, white amidst all that red, are unblinking as she crosses the street.

Demon.

That's what our headmistress once called her, and now she really looks the part. Behind her the door she's emerged from hangs open like a portal to hell. I can't help but imagine the tableau she must have left behind to look like this, marksmen dismembered, or impaled on the blunt barrels of their own rifles. Even her gait seems unnatural, stately and yet impossibly *quick*. In an instant she's standing in front of us; the metal stink of her surges into my nostrils. Mrs. Greave looks stricken. Her eyes flicker from one to the other of us, and a tight breath wheezes from her throat.

"Maze. Keys," my sister says softly. *"Now."*

Mrs. Greave doesn't give us any trouble. She's still trembling when we lock her in the upstairs linen cupboard. Bel looks pleased with herself, trotting blithely back down the stairs, trailing bloody fingertips across the portrait of the tartan-clad terrier. She roots around in the backpack she's left by the door and pulls out a black box about the size of a deck of cards.

"Wi-Fi jammer," she says, mistaking my stare for a question. "Same one I used to block the signal from the cameras at the museum. You said they've got CCTV down there."

I keep staring at her.

"Of course, being a pro security service, it would be just plain *embarrassing* if they used wireless cameras, which is where these"—she pulls a couple of harnesses out of the bag, studded with small LEDs—"and *this*"—she tugs out a nine-pound club hammer—"come in. Not exactly subtle, but . . ."

I'm still staring.

"What?" she asks. "Listen, right now the top brass are most likely bickering over whether they can deal with me by themselves, or if they need the cops, and if they do call the cops, how are they going to keep the location of this place secret? My bet is they'll try to take us alone, so we *probably* have a bit of time, but not for certain, and not forever. So please, can we get going?"

She turns to the hall cupboard door, pulls it shut, and puts in the key. I'm on the third step, staring.

"We had a deal," I say. My voice is small, betrayed. "You promised."

She shrugs. "And?"

"You said you wouldn't kill anyone."

"*Unless* it was in my unavoidable self-defence," she corrects me, holding up a lawyerly finger.

"*That*"—I point at her slowly stiffening shirt—"as a fashion statement is less 'unavoidable self-defence' and more 'ecstatic bloodbath.'"

She shrugs but smiles. "Yeah, but it's a *fashion* statement; those are almost never true. Don't stress, Pete. The snipers over the way are out for the count, but otherwise right as rain."

"What's that all over you, then?" I demand. "*Ketchup?*"

She shakes her head. "Ketchup doesn't dry right. This is mostly just water, syrup, and food colouring, but still . . ." She grins wickedly. She pulls the collar of her shirt aside to reveal an immaculately bandaged cut stretching along the length of her collarbone.

"Gotta have *some* of the real stuff, for the smell. Come here."

She holds out her arms to me, and I go obediently. Of course I do. The blood smell punches me in the stomach, but the rest of her—her strength, her warmth, her solid self—are so familiar and so right that I collapse into the hug, and she has to hold me up.

"I'm sorry," she whispers. "I should have told you. But you were perfect and we had to move fast, which means we needed to *intimidate* her fast, and I think your face scared her even more than mine did."

My face, I think. *My fear.* I feel my heart slamming in my chest where it's pressed to Bel's. If all we need in order to frighten 57 into submission is for *me* to be terrified, we're all set.

Bel eases me from her shoulder and looks me in the eyes, her fingers tacky in my hair.

"I can keep my end of the bargain, little bro."

"You're only eight minutes older," I say. But I can't help but think of the self-inflicted gash on her shoulder. Sometimes it seems like she must have learned so much in those 480 seconds that I'll never catch up. I'll never be able to predict or understand her. All I can do is trust her. She's my axiom.

Bel drapes first me and then herself in LED bandoliers. Nothing visible changes when we flick the switches, but I know I'm now a walking cloud of UV light, baffling to cameras.

"Ready?" she asks.

"No."

"Okay, then."

She turns the key in the closet door, and it's so silent that for a moment I think it hasn't worked. But then the cupboard collapses inwards, and the wedge of darkness opens up, the steel staircase spiralling up to meet us. I think about what Bel said, about 57 not wanting to call the cops. They could have locked us out, I'm sure of it. They didn't, because they want us here. They're inviting us in. I swallow back the acid taste that's starting to flood my mouth.

Stop it. You're being paranoid.

Am I? Well, of course I am. This is me, but am I being unreasonably *paranoid?*

I guess in the final analysis it doesn't matter. Whether they want us there or not, down there's where we have to go. My sister's feet clank on the metal steps like war drums.

She holds out a bloody hand and I take it, and after that the next step is easier, and somehow I match her rhythm as we descend into the dark.

RECURSION: 5 DAYS AGO

"Loyalty and payback are all very well, Peter." Rita's tone was as gentle and brittle as a snowflake. "But they're personal motives, not institutional ones, and our firm usually wouldn't indulge them." But then, only a handful of seconds later, talking about my father, she said:

"He scares us too."

And she might have been lying, she might have faked the fervour in her eyes, modulated the tremble in her voice, but I didn't think so. And deep down some part of me I was barely conscious of took note.

A spy agency doesn't seek revenge, doesn't get jealous . . .

. . . but it can be frightened, and that's something.

NOW

"This way," I tell Bel as I study the scrap of bandage in my hand. The blue Biro sequence of *Ls* and *Rs* is still just about legible against the blood-stiffened fabric.

We hurry through the tunnels, marvelling at each second we go un-captured, un-shot, un-killed. Each breath gives us the courage to believe in just one more.

The maze is as unpleasant as it was five days ago, the light from the fluorescent tubes bolted to the ceiling as harsh as bleach against my eyes, the choking dust rising off the bricks, the ceiling that feels like it's poised to collapse on my head out of sheer spite, but at least *now* I'm not stumbling. Now, afraid as I am, I move with purpose.

Between brief whispers of reassurance to each other, the only sounds are our hurried footsteps, the pant of our breath, and the occasional crunch as Bel swings her twelve-pound hammer into another security camera.

"Little casual, aren't they?" Bel's tone is impatient. *She can't wait*, I think, awed. Her skin is so like mine, the same freckle-spattered shade, but underneath it she's so different. Every particle of her is seething for a fight.

"Why haven't they come for us yet?" she demands.

"I think they're afraid." Maybe I'm imagining it, but I can *feel* the fear of this place, chiming with mine. Is that another side effect of Mum's tampering? My bones hum: forks tuned to the key of *absolutely bricking it.*

"Of what? There are only two of us."

"Yeah, that's what's scaring them."

She looks at me questioningly, but it seems obvious to me. 57's instincts for paranoia and second-guessing are all too familiar to me, like a cul-de-sac-riddled neighbourhood that would be disorienting if you hadn't grown up walking its streets.

"They're spies, not soldiers. For them, there's always a conspiracy, always another bluff to call. I don't think it would occur to them that two seventeen-year-old kids would even consider attacking the UK's most secret spy agency head-on."

And when I put it like that, who could blame them?

"Besides," I add, skipping out of the way of the glittering shower as Bel crushes another camera, "they're watchers by profession and you're busy putting their eyes out. There's a blind spot in the middle of their maze now. They don't know what might be lurking in it, and they don't want to get murdered rushing in to find out. They're stalling, waiting for us to tip our hand."

Bel turns to look at me, impressed, and I glow.

"Check you out," she says. "Doctor of *Fear*."

"I like the way you say that."

"Oh?"

"Like it's a superpower, rather than the product of living seventeen years with various nervous bowel conditions."

She shrugs. "Any reason it can't be both?"

I smile shyly, but all I say is, "Left here."

This time Bel shoots an uncertain look at the directions scrawled on the bandage. By now she's noticed we aren't following them.

And this is the way it has to be. If we charge straight at them, they'll massacre us. We have a tiny window, a handful of minutes' grace as they hesitate, trying to work out what we're up to. They'll be understandably wary of the redheaded hurricane of bloodlust merrily jogging beside me. That's our opening, and we have to use it.

Crunch . . .

One last camera. One last *crunch* and snow of pulverised glass.

"That's enough," I say. It had better be. The four minutes we've been down here feel like months. The eighty or so millilitres of sweat I've squeezed out feel like an ocean. My shirt feels laminated to my back.

"*Finally*," Bel breathes out hard.

"Remember the deal," I say.

"I'll keep up my end, if you keep yours." She looks at me as if appraising me for the first time.

"You know, Pete, you might have that doctorate in fear, but I'm learning fast."

"Yeah?"

"Yeah."

"Why?"

"Because—and this isn't something people notice about you right away—you're pretty scary."

Her palms are still red, her sweat keeping it from drying. Slowly, deliberately, she smears it over my forehead and my cheeks. My gorge rises. It smells like real blood to me.

"Ready?" she asks.

"Still not in any way, no."

"Then go."

Away from Bel, I'm suddenly awash with fear. I feel crippled, like someone's slashed my hamstring with a razor. I mutter directions to myself like prayers, trying to invert the code, to retrace my steps, pawing my way along the wall. "*We went right so go left*," and . . . "*We went left so go . . . Shit, I can't.*"

What if I forget a turn? They all look the same. If I go wrong just once, how will I ever get back?

"OW!" I forget myself and my voice echoes loudly. I look down. There's blood on my hand; a needle-thin shard glitters in my palm, picked up from a ledge on the bricks. I squint upwards at a demolished camera, and my pulse eases.

Well, duh, Pete. That's how.

I follow the trail of shattered glass back to our starting point, and from there the instructions on the bandage lead me to the huge metal door. In front of it, a single camera peers down from the ceiling. I stand, blinking in its gaze.

"*Please,*" I mouth exaggeratedly to the camera. "*Help me.*"

Nothing happens. The seconds stretch out like a water drop. I remind myself of what they know, what *they've actually seen.* Today: an undifferentiated ball of light from the LEDs, meaningless static; over the past week: a trail of corpses left by my sister. They know she's unstable and dangerous. They know what she *was* to me, but they can't be sure what she is to me now.

"*Please,*" I mouth. "*She's coming back.*"

Come on, boys, come out and save me.

With a grinding whir, the door starts to move.

They emerge with weapons lowered, calming hand gestures, soothing words, trusting expressions: traps I'm learning to recognise.

I hope they can't say the same.

I spin on my heel. Their shouts don't quite drown out the sound of safety switches clicking off.

RECURSION: 5 DAYS AGO

I followed Rita's green silk-clad back through the tunnels, squinting in the glare of the strip lights. *Left, right, right, left again.* I was trying to scrawl the turnings on my bandaged hand, but I was falling behind. I had visions of her vanishing into a side tunnel, her laughter echoing behind her, leaving me to trace frantic circles on my own, until I dashed my head off the walls in frustration.

A maze, I remember thinking. *There's a theorem about mazes. Dr. A taught it to me. "Learn this," he'd said, "and you'll never be lost."* But no matter how I'd grasped after the details, they'd slipped away from me like snowflakes on the breeze. I couldn't remember them then,

    . . . but I can remember them now.
    It's Euler, I recall from somewhere buried deep. It's Euler.

NOW

Reassuring words become orders to stop, become threats to shoot, become gunshots.

BANG!

The sound alone, confined in the tunnel, almost knocks me down. The wall snorts out splinters and dust millimetres from my calf. I stagger and catch myself, my palms grazed hot and puffy against the bricks. I lurch around the corner.

"*Cease fire!*" I hear barked, and "*Alive!*" And now the only sounds are my ragged breath and the syncopated thump of the boots pursuing me.

Screaming inwardly, I flee, hurling myself blindly through junctions almost at random, barely seeing the trail of crushed camera lenses. My mouth tastes like puke and metal. The tunnels warp the echoes and I have no idea how close behind my pursuers are. Each time I slow to take a corner, I feel them almost grab me, but somehow I stay ahead.

It's a harum-scarum flight, ricocheting off the walls. My breath is corrosive in my lungs and my legs have turned to lead, yet somehow they keep pumping and somehow the ground keeps flowing away under my feet.

Catch me if you can, boys! I'm more afraid than anyone you've ever chased! That's gotta be worth at least a couple of miles per hour.

But wait, was that . . . ? *Listen*, I try to order myself. *Listen!* But the drumming of my feet and the blood in my veins is too loud. I wrestle with the lizard that's taken up the driver's seat in

my brain, try to ease his clawed foot off the accelerator so I can
hear . . .

Yes. I'm sure of it. The boots behind me are slowing. Not
much, but I can just hear their rhythm falter, the uncertainty in
their steps.

A vicious glee swells in my chest.

You're lost! I exult. *You know the safe paths through your maze, the
right ways in and out, but you never bothered to learn all the wrong
ones. You're off the map.*

In the long run it wouldn't matter, of course. No doubt
they're geared up with GPS trackers and are maintaining open
radio links to base. No doubt that even without their precious
cameras, HQ is watching them as a cluster of glowing green dots
on an electronic map and could talk them home again—

—given enough time.

I hear shouts, then screams, then gunfire drowning the
voices out. I lurch, feeling every shot like a heart attack, and
I fight not to whirl around and run back and help Bel, but I
don't. I have to trust her. She's my axiom.

The cry boils up from the tunnel in a series of echoes: *"Where
did she come from?"*

Where monsters always come from, I think, and, chest heaving, I
retch noisily onto the floor. I wipe my face and stagger on. *Out
of a maze.*

I picture her, slipping out of a passageway, striking so quickly
the enemy doesn't even know they've been hit before she disappears. I picture them whirling in circles, yelling into their radios
for help. I picture their controller sitting before screens full of
static, headphones full of screams, blind and helpless and mute,
watching his green dots, one by one, go still.

The boots begin running again. Some of them recede,
growing fainter and fainter in headlong flight, but two, no,
three sets of them are closing on me. *Fast.* I hear instructions,
bitten off whispers between rasping breaths: *"Rabbit"* and a word
that chills me: *"Hostage."*

So I run again, leading them away, and they chase me like the rabbit they named me for; but I'm not a rabbit, not any longer . . .

A brief cry, and three sets of boots become two. I don't want it to, but this feels good, it feels *right*. I never knew how I'd ached for this until I felt it. Every shadow is sharp, every echo crisp. I can't keep a vicious grin off my face.

. . . Wolves hunt in packs.

When I stop running, I collapse immediately.

The muscles in my legs and arms feel pulped. My lungs heave in my chest, almost too exhausted to draw in air. If any agents managed to slip past Bel, I'm done for. It feels like an unknowable age since I last heard pursuing feet, but it's probably only been two minutes.

The bricks against which I slump are remarkably comfortable. Honestly, I'm sure it's fine. I'm sure she got them all. If I could just have a little nap right . . . *Keep your fucking eyes open, Blankman!* Yes, Sarge!

Stupefied, I stare at the ceiling for four, five, six seconds before dragging myself upright. I look around me. I'm in a square brick chamber. Four brick exits; all pristine, untouched by hammer or bullets or blood; all identical. I have no idea which is north, south, east or west. I've run myself ragged and directionless.

I'm lost in the maze.

I feel the first stirrings of panic and try to tamp it down.

It's okay, I tell myself, willing myself to believe. *It's Euler.*

I grope in my pocket and for one cataclysmic moment I think I've dropped the bloody things. But then a fold in the fabric of my trousers gives way and I pull the slim box out. Ten slender white cylinders glow in the dim light. My fingers shake as I take one out and roll it around in my hand. The crayon leaves a waxy residue on my skin.

Euler, I repeat to myself, willing my stampeding heart to slow. *Euler.*

Euler, shockingly, *didn't* conceive his theorem to help neurologically engineered teenagers crack mazes protecting top secret government facilities. He was studying networks: webs of connected points. Lucky for me, any maze can be reduced to a network. All that matters are the places where you choose, left or right. Onwards or back. The length of the pathways between those junctures, their twists and turns and switchbacks, are irrelevant. A maze is just a series of choices, like a life.

Euler's theorem proves that any point in the maze can be reached, from any other point, without a map, in a finite time as long as you never, ever repeat a path.

I set the point of my crayon against the wall, take a deep, jagged breath, and start walking.

The maze *feels* infinite, but that's what mazes are for: they play upon your ape's intuition of distance, fool you with folding, until your despair overcomes you. Mazes are designed to make you panic. All I have to do is not give in.

I know, right? Ha.

I rehearse Euler's arguments to myself aloud, keeping myself company while I walk. My voice sounds tinny and unconvincing in the tunnel, the panicky bit of me scoffs at it: *You're lost, you're fucked. Accept it and you can rest. Don't you want to rest? Aren't you tired?*

I lick sweat off my top lip, make small bargains with myself, and break them: Ten more steps, then you can stop. Okay, twenty. Okay, thirty.

The voice turns nasty: *You're wrong, you've miscalculated, you've abandoned Bel, you left her there to die. Her corpse is all that's waiting for you.* The walls are closing in, squeezing my vision, squeezing my heart. Swearing and sweating, I mutter to myself, "One: get moving."

And keep moving.

Defeating my own nature is a strategy of millimetres—ten to a centimetre; seven hundred and sixty to a stride; one million, six hundred and four thousand, three hundred and forty-four to a mile. Keep walking and don't stop. Whatever you do, don't stop.

To begin with I take random turnings, then rarely at first, but then more and more often, I run across loops: turnings where a virgin wall gives way to a shaky line of gleaming white wax. A sign I've been here before. I recognise these traps and am heartened by them. *All you have to do is make sure you never, ever repeat a path.* I am exhausting the maze. I am brute-forcing it. The maze is recycling itself because it is *not* infinite. Its power has limits and I am reaching them. The crayon in a death grip in my fist. I steer towards new, unmarked paths.

Keep walking.

She's dead.

Just keep walking.

"Pete!"

"Bel!" I look sharply to my right, and there she is, at the far end of a tunnel. Relief threatens to burst my heart. I break into a run towards her, but I stumble over something soft and look down. There are three of them, unmoving. Two have necks at unnatural angles. The third is oozing slowly out onto the floor.

"Pete?"

I look back up at her. Her eyes are very wide. "I tried. I really did. The others, I . . . I only broke bones. I put them under quick, but these three came up so fast and I just, it was instinct . . . I know we had a deal, but . . . Please don't hate me."

She tails off. The body at my feet stares up at me, a dull sheen on his eyeballs. I'm shaking, but I hug her. She's utterly still in my arms.

"It's all right. It was self-defence. You did good, sis, you did good."

I become aware of the quiet of the tunnel and I ease her back off my shoulder. We smile at each other through our tears.

"Show me the others."

She leads me around through a series of sharp turnings. In

each passage we pass a single black-clad figure, groaning or slumped silently in the dust. A lot of limbs are bent in too many places, but the rise and fall of their chests eases the pressure in mine.

"You used the maze to isolate them."

She shrugs as if this was merely competent.

"That was the deal," she says. "You said alive, and alive is tricky." She wobbles a hand to and fro like a plumber describing an expensive repair. "Could only manage it one on one."

There are eleven in total including the dead, a number that bothers me, but I can't put my finger on why. We come to one who seems less damaged than the others, a shaven-headed young man huddled into a corner, chin on his chest. Aside from a bloody scrape down one cheek, he could just have fallen asleep.

"Let's use him," Bel says. "He's not even concussed. I've been choking him out again every couple of minutes. His retina ought to get us through that door."

We drag him upright by his armpits and his head lolls alarmingly. *Eleven*, I think. *What's wrong with that number?* And then I have it—I see a flash of red leaves and green paramedic uniforms. Eleven isn't divisible by four, and the 57 agents I've seen on operations have always worked in teams of four.

"Bel, do you think we got all of—?"

BANG!

I'm falling before I hear the shot. I feel hot liquid seeping through my shirt, but there's no pain. My first reaction is relief— I blink, and behind my eyelids I see the school roof. *Got there in the end*, I think.

But *I'm* not bleeding.

It's Bel. Oh Christ, it's Bel. She's falling and pulling me down with her. She's glassy-eyed, breath catching with the pain, but still she shoves me into the wall. She drags the shaven-headed man up onto his shoulder, between us and the gunfire. He shudders in time to three more shots.

BANG. BANG. BANG.

His eyes don't open again, but the tang of blood in the air thickens. Breathing is like drinking it, and I almost puke. Above our human barricade, I see a figure duck back into a side tunnel. I only glimpse her for a second, but it's enough. Rita.

26, 17, 448, 0.3337, 9 billion, pi, triangles, cosines, integrals. My head is full of mathematical shrapnel, my thoughts shattered by the shots. My heart feels like it's ripping its way out of my chest. I barely hear Bel's shriek.

"PETEY!"

Squirming from behind the bulk of the shaven-headed man, I stagger to my feet, thinking only one thing: to pour all the sheer, crippling fear I feel into my face, my hands, my voice, and *hurl* it at my enemy; enough to burst a heart, enough to kill. I am a weapon. They made me one, and now they can repent.

I scream, shrill and teeth-shaking. It fills the tunnel and I imagine my fear following it, invisible and toxic, like a nerve gas. Rita sidesteps out of cover, and our eyes meet along the barrel of her pistol.

Fucking have that, you manipulative shit, I think.

She doesn't even blink before she fires.

Again I'm falling, but this time I *am* shot. Right shoulder, a tearing, burning sensation like someone's pressed a car cigarette lighter to my clavicle. My scream shakes my teeth to their roots. My back hits the floor. Bel's looking down at me, and it's only when my tears clear that I see her incredulous relief.

"You're fine!" she yells. "It barely grazed you. Now *run!*"

More shots, more shattering concussions. Bel has a gun. She's firing from the cover of the dead guy, her eyes alight.

"*Run!*" she yells again, jerking her head behind her.

A doorway yawns open only two metres behind us. She's covering me, wasting her bullets so I can escape. I hesitate. *You can't leave her. Not again. Jesus,* my shoulder hurts.

I roll onto my belly and elbow-drag my way past the cooling form of the shaven-headed man. There's a pistol strapped to his hip and I grab it. It's heavy and alien in my hand. I struggle onto my knees, glimpse Rita through stinging, tear-filled eyes, and jerk the trigger back.

Fuck! The recoil hurls me backwards. The bullet ploughs into the ceiling, and masonry fragments shower down. My shoulder feels like it's been ripped off. I blink, flat on my back, the dust from my misfire stinging my eyes.

A hand grabs my collar and hauls me to my feet.

"Peter William Fucking Blankman," Bel yells. I can barely see her through the brick dust. "If you die here, I swear I will hate you forever. Now *run.*"

She shoves me hard, off-balance, my gun dragging like an anchor on my punctured arm. The last thing I see before I stagger through the doorway is my sister's silhouette, slipping away through the dust.

Hunting.

RECURSION: 5 DAYS AGO

Rita folded her arms. Her brown eyes watched me patiently. In her bloodstained dress she exuded a surgeon's unnerving pragmatism. Behind her, the huge metal door hung open, ready to swallow me whole.

"You're the boy who's afraid of everything," she said. "And I am tremendously scary."

I think of those brown eyes sighting steadily down a gun barrel levelled at my sister's skull . . .

Yes, *I thought then, and I think it again now,* you really are.

NOW

57's front door gapes open, heavy as a mausoleum gateway. This time, instead of Rita standing before it, arms folded and pugnacious, men and women stream out of it.

They hurry, head down and silent, scattering down the tunnels, their shadows flitting over the bricks. There are dozens of them. I vaguely recognise one or two of them, analysts from my first time here. Their hands are empty, not a file or laptop anywhere.

My breath stalls, jagged and painful in my chest. I huddle into my brick crevice, certain that one of them will spot me and cry out in vengeful recognition. The gun is a dead weight in my hand. I shiver and try to imagine myself pulling the trigger again, but I can't.

But as the seconds tick by, no one comes near me. Slowly, my terror-fogged brain sieves the pattern from their flight.

Random doorways; they must each be heading for an exit, taking the shortest path to open air. They're not hunting me. They're fleeing. *What are you running from?* I wonder stupidly. And suddenly it's obvious: *You're running from us.*

They're spies, not soldiers. Of course. They will have been primed for this, ready on a hair trigger to flee at all times. No panic, an orderly evacuation. Why would they bother defending this place? It's just a shell, a disguise; once discovered, it's no longer useful. All they care about is the intelligence they guard. The moment their kill team started screaming for help into their headsets, they would have been shovelling documents into furnaces and hammering *delete* commands into computers. The data, the precious pattern, would be backed up safe and sound at some other secret location.

But ones and zeroes on a hard disk aren't the only way to store secrets. The last store is the spies *themselves*, the secrets inscribed in the architecture of their brains, and so they flee, saving themselves, scattering like deer to confuse the predator stalking them. A predator that wears my sister's face . . .

. . . and mine.

"You're pretty scary."

Thanks, Bel, I'll try to live up to that. Coming from you, it means a lot.

I wait for the last—a burly, broken-nosed man—to slip away. My fingers tighten their grip on the gun and I walk towards the open door, the empty husk that was 57.

The office is a graveyard of blank computer screens, wires splaying from their backs like nerve clusters where the processors have been ripped away and carted to the incinerator.

It is twelve strides to the lift. Twelve chances for my nerve to fail me. I look back at the exit. I know I shouldn't but I do. *You can still run away, Pete. You're so* good *at running away. You're a real world-beater at it.*

The exit is a black hole behind me, exerting its gravity. It tempts me with the same violent pull I get from a cheesecake when my stomach's already bursting.

Give in, it says. *Run. Get it over with. If you don't, you'll only face the same choice in the next second and the next and the next after that. How many times do you think you can hold out?*

"Eleven . . . *twelve*." I let out an explosive breath. I hadn't realised I was counting, let alone aloud. I punch a sweaty thumb onto the button and am grateful that the doors hiss open immediately. I step in, holding myself rigid as a corpse, and don't look around until I've heard them hiss closed again.

Part of me hopes that the doorway to the little repurposed office will be locked. It's not. The handle turns easily.

The same part of me hopes that the bed will be empty. It's not. Indeed almost nothing about the makeshift hospital ward has changed: the black scuffs made by the wheels of the bed on the threshold; the strip lighting glaring off the white lino floor; the window looking out onto the flat-roofed London terrace, under the same bright autumn sky.

The sole difference is that the room's only occupant is sitting up in bed, hands folded in the lap of her mint-green hospital gown. Her eyes are very calm.

"Hello, Peter," she says.

Relief breaks over me like a wave. I run to her. The gun clatters to the floor as I hug her tight. I laugh and cry into her shoulder. *You're all right,* I whisper, my tears blotting her gown. *You're all right. I was so scared.*

Except I don't. I want to, but I don't. Instead, I lock the door behind me, and then one painful inch at a time, I raise the gun until it's pointed at her forehead.

"Hello, Mum," I say.

RECURSION: 5 DAYS AGO

We stood in the car park, huddling tighter into our coats as the wind picked up. The huge edifice of the museum blotted out what sunlight there was. Bel sauntered ahead, but Mum stopped me with a touch on the arm.

She held my face in her hands. Pride glowed in her eyes, and like fire giving off a drifting ember, it kindled in me and I glowed too.

"Peter, today is *because* of you and your sister. My work, my life, I wouldn't have any of it without you, you know?"

Yes, Mum, now I know.

NOW

Improbable things happen every day. You shouldn't be surprised when they happen to you.

I stand in the headquarters of the UK's most secret intelligence service, crying and bursting with the need to pee. I'm holding a gun on my own mother, and when she speaks, her voice is as calm as a lake on a windless day.

"What has she told you?"

She. There's only one person Mum speaks of with that tone of voice.

"Nothing. Bel told me nothing. I found out myself."

"Found out what?"

I stare at her, denying the question. The throbbing in my head surges, as if the blood vessels in my temples are trying to squeeze marbles through them. Black spots dance in front of my eyes.

"Peter—"

"You couldn't resist, could you?" My vision clears and I see she's wearing Look No. 49: *Perplexed Maternal Concern.* "Or maybe you didn't even try. Twins—two minds, two lives to control, right from conception. You'd had the idea and here was your opportunity to put it into practice. It must have seemed like providence. What scientist could resist?"

"Peter, I—"

"'You'll get better, Petey!'" I croak through my tear-hoarse throat. "'We'll beat this together, Petey,' you said. You *lied.* For all that time, all our *lives*, you lied and I stayed scared and Bel stayed angry, because that's how *you* designed us. To read each other's moods and write each other's minds. Write read, read write. *White Rabbit, Red Wolf!*"

I scream the code names at her. The pain in my shoulder makes the gun shake in my grip, and she flinches. I wonder, does she even think of us as Peter and Anabel, or do we go by our code names in her head?

Her concerned look is gone: tried, failed, and cast aside. Now her face is fixed in shock—a mask of innocence.

"Peter, I don't know what you're talking about." She shakes her head slowly but doesn't break eye contact. "Yes, I lied. I admit that. The work I do—for the government—it means I have to lie sometimes, even to you. But I would never, ever, do anything to hurt you. I know you get scared. I know you do, honey. But the way you *deal* with that, for what you've achieved in the face of it, I'm so proud of you."

And this at least is true. She *is* proud of me. Her word for me echoes in my head and I mutter it aloud.

"*Extraordinary.*"

"That's right," she says with conviction. "You are."

And it's only then I really get it. For her, *that's* what makes this all all right. For Mum, there could be nothing worse than being ordinary.

I remember standing in her study two years ago, drunk for the first and only time in my life, her showing me her notes on the capabilities of exotic animals: the octopus with its poison, the prehistoric fly with its wings, while I did party-trick sums for her.

Camouflage and flight are adaptations to a threat environment, Peter. So is that.

In every atom of her being, she believes she's given me a gift.

"I don't want to be extraordinary. I just want to stop being scared all the time."

She shrugs. "None of us gets to choose that, Pete."

I can't swallow. I can't breathe, I'm so angry.

"It *hurts*—do you get that?" I howl it at her. "Do you get that the way you made me fucking *hurts* every day?"

She looks aghast. "I don't know what you're saying. I would never hurt you. I love you—you're my son."

"You love me," I echo woodenly. "I'm your work."

The corner of her mouth twitches, a crack in her mask, but I can't interpret it. I can't read her. I guess I never could.

"Peter," she says. "Please. Just calm down and talk to me. If you're saying what I think you're saying it . . . it isn't possible."

"*Don't.*" My voice is hard and flat, and she falls silent, eyes on the gun. "I've been into your study. I found your notebooks, the hidden ones. I know."

"My . . . notebooks?" Now she looks puzzled, afraid, stricken, hurt. "Peter, those are complex ideas, written in shorthand. I don't know what you think you read or how you deciphered them, but—"

"Ingrid read them. She confirmed it." I'm pleading with her to stop, just stop *lying*. I'm holding the gun and I'm pleading. "Okay? Ingrid—*Ana* confessed. So stop pretending. I *know.*"

Her face finally stills, and I see an expression I've never seen before. Better give it a new number, then:

Look No. 277: *Pity. Hopeless, anguished, pity.*

And before she opens her mouth, I know what she's going to say.

"Peter." Her voice is dreadfully gentle. "Ingrid's not real."

RECURSION: 5 DAYS AGO

The three of us crouched in the woods behind the school, the trees around us on fire with autumn. We heard shouts, running footsteps, and the sounds of breaking undergrowth, coming closer every second. I was sweating, shaking, somehow functioning, in a state the other side of panic.

Bel flicked the safety off her gun, seemed to consider giving it to me, and then, thank Christ, thought better of it. Instead, she swung it almost idly past me and—oh shit oh shit oh shit oh shit—she aimed it at Ingrid's forehead.

She knows about Ingrid, I thought.

But did she? Remembering it now, the sound of 57 agents crashing towards us through the woods, coming from the trees *directly* behind Ingrid's head.

I turn the memory over and over in my mind, like checking a proof, looking for the one, oh-so-natural, unjustified leap in logic.

Was Bel aiming her gun *at* Ingrid? Or was she aiming *through* her?

Did she even see her at all? Had she *ever*?

Had *anyone*?

Yes! There was . . .

RECURSION: 1 DAY AGO

. . . Rachel Rigby! Smoking and pacing the rutted tracks of the Edinburgh meadow, while Ingrid explained the intricacies of a life on the run.

Relief unwinds in my chest, but it's short-lived, because my anxious, sceptical speculations are already crawling over the memory like mortuary beetles, and now that I think on it, I can't remember a single time Rachel spoke directly to Ingrid, or acknowledged her at all. Her words were addressed only to *me*.

I'm going to kill your mother, I think you should know that.

And now I'm trying to remember the sound of Ingrid's voice, and it sounds too much like mine. I can't . . . I can't tell the difference between the two. The harder I focus the more it sounds just like my own inside-the-head voice, the one I hear when I'm reading.

The memories are coming thick and fast. I shuffle through and discard them like cards, looking for any other human acknowledgment of Ingrid's existence, but they whirl past me in a blur, too fast to focus on.

And then, like a soloist in a choir, something rises above the clamour . . .

RECURSION: 5 DAYS AGO

"So why not read her mind?" I asked. I was talking about Rita. We stood under the bare bulb in the maintenance cupboard that served 57 as a prison cell. "That's what you do, isn't it? Why not make sure?"

"I can't read minds, Peter." She eyed me sullenly. "I can only read yours."

Recursion . . .

Recursion . . .

Recursion . . .

NOW

There's a long silence.

"You gave her chicken Kiev." It's all I can think of to say. The gun's hanging by my side now. I'm wrung out, and it's all I can do to stand.

"And pasta, and apple pie and sausage and mash and stir-fry." Mum sighs. "I always made extra when you said she was coming round. Food going cold in front of an empty chair." Her blue eyes crinkle, and her voice aches with sympathy. "Perhaps I should have tried harder to tell you. *Made* you understand. But she seemed to make you so much happier. You were so lonely. So I figured, what's the harm?"

She actually laughs then, staring down the gun, but the laughter quickly dries.

"Besides, any friend, even an imaginary one, had to be a good thing if it made you less dependent on your sister."

I shake my head weakly. "It doesn't make sense."

It makes perfect sense.

"If Ingrid's a delusion, my defence mechanism against loneliness, if I imagined her, then why would I *imagine* her betraying me? Why would I hurt myself like that?"

Because that's what always happens. The medicine always gets taken to overdose.

Get counting.

. . . and counting becomes a prison.

Get eating.

. . . until your stomach's fit to burst.

Get moving.

. . . and hurl yourself from a rooftop.

Get talking.

. . . that's what we've been doing, and tell me, Pete, isn't it just the worst?

"My sister's a g-good person," I stammer stubbornly.

"Your sister's a killer. A thug. She killed a fifteen-year-old boy. A child. I had to cover it up."

Me too, a treacherous voice in me whispers, but instead I yell at her.

"You had to cover it up because it was *your* fault! *You* made her that way!"

She looks sad then, sadder than I've ever seen her. Two new faces in as many minutes. Look No. 278: *Heartbroken.*

"Of course you'd think that. You could never bear to blame her for anything."

I fall silent because how can I refute it? *She's my axiom*, the basic founding assumption. The one you don't need to prove. The one all your understanding is built on. The one person without whom everything comes crashing down.

"So you blamed me instead." Mum nods slowly, like she's putting it together. "Poor Pete; so good at connecting the dots, at finding the pattern, even when there isn't one. Only you could dream up this insane conspiracy, so nothing would be her fault." She looks up sharply. "When did you find out? That she'd killed that boy?"

Two years ago, I almost say, but I don't, because maybe *five days ago* would be more accurate. Five days ago, when I remembered.

And now the panic's really mounting. The strip lights are suddenly too bright and my blood's searing in my temples and my heart's jackhammering in my chest and the gun's like an anvil in my hands and I can't think can't think *can't think.*

I picture an ankle, sticking out pale and stiff from a roll of carpet in an alleyway behind my house; I picture a note, decoded and crumpled on my duvet saying: *I killed someone*, and I picture me, two years on, sitting in Anita Vadi's kitchen, slumped and exhausted, not even remembering that night until I'd found out that my neuroscientist mother did secret work for the government, until I had fragments of a pattern I could clutch at, a story I could tell myself that brought Bel out clean.

Memory. ARIA. What an incredible thing.

"It's okay, Pete," Mum says soothingly. "It's all going to be okay. I'll help you, like I've always helped you. That's why I stayed. It's just us. I'm here for you; just give me the gun."

"A . . . and Bel?"

Mum slumps a little in her bed. She looks, suddenly, very old.

"I don't think there's anything I can do for her. And believe me, I've tried."

I stare at her. I don't know what to believe.

"Give me the gun, Pete, please."

Now I have a problem. *Only one?* sneers the part of me that counts everything. But yes, there is only one that matters right now, maybe the only one that's ever mattered.

Ingrid isn't real.

Mum knows me better than anyone, maybe even better than Bel. If she was going to lie to me, this is *exactly* the lie she would tell. To make me doubt myself, my eyes, my mind.

My treacherous brain dredges up the first time I remember seeing Ingrid: in maths class, all those years ago—not on the first day of school, not walking in midterm to stand awkwardly in front of the class while Arthurson introduced her, but just *there*, all of a sudden, when I was at my loneliest. Like an answer to a prayer.

Could she be a useful fiction? Like the imaginary number that scientists use to make planes fly and bridges stand? The square root of minus one . . .

. . . the number mathematicians call *i*.

Images flicker in my mind as once again I ransack my memory, searching for a moment when the existence of Agent Blonde Calculating Machine was acknowledged by anyone other than me.

. . . Girls clustered in the bathroom, watching Ingrid while she scraped at her knuckles. Phone screens glimmering as they filmed her, but had they been filming or just texting? Were they laughing at Ingrid or just laughing? Tanya Berkeley's voice rose clear in my ears, "Oh my god, get out!"

. . . Me, strapped to a bed in the basement of this very building as they interrogated me. They'd tied me up, but I lashed out first, flailing, jaws snapping. Had they hooded me because they were frightened of contracting the fear on my face? Or just because I'd tried to bite?

Ingrid had asked the questions, but were there even any questions? Was I being interrogated? Or just restrained?

But they'd burned me, electrocuted me, wires plastered to my temples, my chest . . .

My chest!

Slowly, I take my right hand from the gunstock and probe under my shirt. My questing fingers find a burn scar, but it feels old and smooth, not fresh and flaking. I remember a steaming kettle, hot water bottle overflowing, scalding water splashing on me, and I can't tell if it's remembered or imagined.

I never can. I never could.

I return my shaking hand to the gun. The pain throbs from the shot in my shoulder and I can barely hold its weight. Whatever I remember, or think I remember, it doesn't matter. It's all tainted, ruined.

Memory is who we are.

Memory is flawed.

You can't use one memory to corroborate another if you know your memories can lie to you. But memories are all we have.

Memory can't prove itself, but there's nothing outside of it I can rely on to do the job.

"Encrypt." My lips slowly shape the words. *"Invert, Recoil."*

Just like maths.

I picture Gödel lying wasted in his hospital bed, croaking: *There's no way to be sure.*

Mum smiles at me. "It's okay, Pete. It's over. Take all the time you need. We'll get through this. We'll beat this, together, just like always. Just give me the gun."

True or false.

Heads or tails.

Mum or Bel.

There's no way to know the right choice. I just have to choose.

"Give me the gun, Pete." Her hands are outstretched.

The gun is so ugly and awkward in my hands. Suddenly I can't bear to touch it any longer. I try to imagine myself using it, and I just . . . can't.

"Give me the gun."

The pistol muzzle twitches as I start to lower it. It's the only choice I can make.

I don't even think I hear the shot, just *feel* it. It sucks the air out of the room, so close it's like being punched. Mum's head snaps back hard on her neck. Red slashes the wall behind her.

I gape. My finger is on the trigger, but . . . I didn't. I couldn't. My brain is a mess of static. No signal. No resolution. Just chaos.

There's no smoke rising from the barrel of the gun in my hand. I press it to my palm, but I'm so feverish I can't tell if the metal is hot or not. As it clatters to the floor I realise. The shot came from *behind* me.

Ears ringing, I turn.

Hands, wrapped in fingerless gloves, clutch a pistol that's identical to mine. I blink furiously, and my vision clears, and I see a messy thatch of short blonde hair framing a face that looks far, far too much like Ada Lovelace's.

"Imagine that," she says softly.

Her eyes are wide, grey and empty as the winter sky. I rush to her and catch her as she falls, ease her down into the corner.

"Are you—" I begin.

"What do you think?" she whispers. She looks as lost as it is possible to be. Bereft and vacant; it's like looking in a mirror.

Mirror. I think. *Black Butterfly.* She reflects emotions, desires, but her *own* desires are deeper. Drawn from only one person, the one she spent the most time with. The one she's just shot in the head.

She looks up at me. She always knew what I was thinking. So the silent *Why?* I form with my lips is redundant.

"After three years, if you can't trust yourself, trust me," she says.

"But back at the house . . ." I protest. She shrugs and smiles, but it looks forced.

"Bit of a crisis of loyalty," she says.

"I can relate."

"I know."

Running feet drum up the corridor towards us. Shouts of alarm.

"She said we were alone," I say.

"She lied," Ingrid answers faintly. "She did that a lot."

Whatever Mum did or didn't do, hearing that past tense is like a knife in the gut.

"Dr. Blankman!" a male voice yells. "Dr. Blankman, are you all right?"

The door shudders and rattles, but it doesn't open. Ingrid must have relocked it after she came in.

I flinch as two shots splinter the lock. A boot thuds into wood. My stomach leaps into my throat as I hurl myself to the ground, groping for the gun, but my fingertips only push it farther away; the wound in my shoulder shrieks as I stretch for it. On some half-baked instinct, I lurch upright to get between Ingrid and the first shot.

But there is no first shot. There's only a body, burly, male and crew-cut, lying in the corridor, and my sister stepping delicately over it like a drunk in the street.

"Jesus," she mutters. She takes one look at the bed and pulls me into a fierce hug. The strength in her arms feels like the foundation of everything. "You okay, Pete?"

I almost laugh at the question. But it's not quite laughter, more like a brief bout of whooping cough.

"You did the right thing," Bel whispers.

I didn't. I didn't do anything. But I don't say that. Because I'm trying too hard not to look at the angle of Mum's head and the gore clinging to the wall behind her. Trying not to imagine the trajectory of the shot that killed her. Trying not to feel the ache in my right wrist that the recoil of a pistol might cause. Trying not to look at Ingrid in her corner, far too pale, far too much like a ghost.

Something tickles the back of my throat, then scratches, then claws. I start to cough, eyes watering. Sweat pricks my scalp and shoulders.

"I set a fire," Bel says, eyes streaming. She lets out her own hacking cough, but smiles. Bel always liked a good fire.

"Why?"

"Cops. Once 57 had cleaned all the intel out of the place, they finally called them. They're swarming out the front, so we need to exit round the back. The fire should slow them down a bit, but we have to move. Come on."

She pulls me to the window, yanks it open. Cold, fresh air and the scream of sirens rush at me.

"Wait," I gasp.

"Pete—"

I squirm out of her grip and run to Ingrid. She's still sitting where I left her. The smoke's thick enough now that it's dragging nails over my larynx and I'm choking, but Ingrid isn't coughing, just staring. I grab her arm and pull, but she's waxy, unresponsive. For a split second I picture her in the fire, not burning but melting, pooling on the floor like a candle.

"Come on!" I yell at her.

She doesn't move.

"I need you! 23-17-11-54!"

At that, at last, she yields. I throw her arm across my shoulders and drag her; her toes skid along the floor, then she skips, then stumbles into a regular gait.

"Pete, *come on!*" Bel yells. She's sitting on the windowsill, her legs hanging over the edge. She beckons once, and then pushes herself off, dropping in a heart-stopping instant below view.

I heave Ingrid over to the window and look down. Bel's looking up from the flat roof less than three metres down. Raked gables fall away on either side, their tiles as red as autumn leaves.

Ingrid goes first, kissing me gently on the cheek before clambering onto the sill and dropping to the glittering tarred surface. Showing me the way.

Bel never takes her eyes off my face. I swing my legs over the sill, hesitate.

"Pete, it's okay, it's easy, like falling off a log."

"Or a roof," Ingrid adds. I guess she can be pretty literal when she's scared.

Leap of faith, Petey, sometimes that's all you've got.

I jump.

The impact hammers up through my knees and I buckle sideways, but Bel's arm, warm, strong, confident, pulls me into an embrace.

"I've got you," she whispers. And she's right.

The air is a chaos of wind and flames and sirens. Bel laughs, a sound of genuine delight. She twines her fingers with mine and I let her, even as I twine mine with Ingrid's. The three of us stand on the roof. White Rabbit. Red Wolf. Black Butterfly. All three of Mum's children.

Three.

Bel tries to pull me away, but I resist.

"Pete?" she says uncertainly. "What's wrong? We don't have time to hang around."

I look at Ingrid, whose hand I'm still holding.

"Bel?" I say. "Can you see—"

But the question stalls in my throat, forever incomplete.

ACKNOWLEDGEMENTS

It's a strange paradox that the more personal a book is, the more I seem to need to rely on other people to help make it a real thing. And this is a very personal book. So I owe a lot of people a lot of thanks.

First up, my heroic agent, Nancy Miles, without whom this book would have been half-baked at best, and not in the delicious ice-cream way. Thank you for not only selling it, but for insisting on it being the best book we could make it beforehand. Huge thanks also to Barry Goldblatt, Caroline Hill-Trevor and Emily Hayward-Whitlock for your tireless (and continuing) efforts at getting this story to as many brains in as many places and in as many forms as superhumanly possible.

To the teams at Walker and Soho: Frances Taffinder, Gill Evans, Rosi Crawley, Maria Soler Cantón, Anna Robinette, Emma Draude, Annabelle Wright, Kirsten Cozens and John Moore; Dan Ehrenhaft, Rachel Kowal, Monica White, Abby Koski, Rudy Martinez and Paul Oliver. It's a thrill working with such talented, passionate people, and I'm honoured to call you colleagues.

I always lean pretty heavily on my friends, and they never complain. They're good like that. Emma Trevayne, James Smythe, Gillian Redfearn, Laura Lam, Emily Richards and Will Hill not only gave feedback on early drafts that made this book a lot, lot better, but also provided the psychological cake that got me through my various long dark tea times of the soul.

My family have to take the credit/blame for making me who I am. So Sarah, Matt and Jasper, Mum, Dad, Sally, Livs, Chris, Aislinn, Hugo, Toby, Arianna, Barbara, Robin, Moira, James and Rachel this is for you all.

Finally, and most of all, Lizzie, the one to whom I am devoted, thank you for continuing to put up with this, and me.